Praise for Elizabeth

ALMO

"Essex will have readers longing to set sail alongside her daring heroine and dashing hero. This wild ride of a high seas adventure/desire-in-disguise romance has it all: nonstop action, witty repartee, and deft plotting. From the bow to the mast, from battles to ballrooms, Essex delivers another reckless bride and another read to remember."

—*RT Book Reviews*

"Elizabeth Essex will dazzle you with her sophisticated blend of vivid historical detail, exquisite characterization, and delicious sexual tension. *Almost a Scandal* is a breathtaking tale of rapturous romance and awe-inspiring adventure!"

—*USA Today* bestselling author Julianne MacLean

"Elizabeth Essex writes the perfect blend of fast-paced adventure and deliciously sexy romance. I couldn't put this book down! *Almost a Scandal* gets a place on my keeper shelf—I will read anything Elizabeth Essex writes!"

—*New York Times* bestselling author Celeste Bradley

"The first book in the Reckless Brides Trilogy is a seafarer's delight. Col and Sally's high-stakes adventure is fast-paced and fraught with peril. Well-timed humor punctuates the action and the use of frigate-speak adds authenticity to the shipboard dialogue. The love story teases the reader at first, as Col and Sally struggle to conceal their attraction on board the *Audacious*. Then things turn desperate when the circumstances of war seem intent on driving them apart. A smartly written, emotional tempest."

—*Reader to Reader Reviews*

MORE . . .

ALSO BY ELIZABETH ESSEX

Almost a Scandal
A Breath of Scandal

in the Night

ELIZABETH ESSEX

St. Martin's Paperbacks

This is a work of fiction. All of the characters, organizations, and events portrayed in this novel are either products of the author's imagination or are used fictitiously.

SCANDAL IN THE NIGHT

Copyright © 2013 by Elizabeth Essex.

For information address St. Martin's Press, 175 Fifth Avenue, New York, NY 10010.

ISBN: 978-1-250-00381-2

Printed in the United States of America

St. Martin's Paperbacks edition / July 2013

St. Martin's Paperbacks are published by St. Martin's Press, 175 Fifth Avenue, New York, NY 10010.

10 9 8 7 6 5 4 3 2 1

To my New York girls:
Barbara Poelle and Holly Blanck.
For believing in this story long before I did.

Chapter One

Wimbourne Chase, Hampshire
Early summer, 1830

In India, there was an ancient proverb: Pilgrims seldom come home saints.

Thomas Jellicoe stood as the proof. He had been a pilgrim in the wide, wicked world for so many years he had long ago lost his faith—misplaced on some dusty, less-traveled roadside—and he had all but forgotten how to find his wandering way home.

He could only stand before the ancient lodge gate like a supplicant, and hope he had finally come to the place where—no matter how long he had been gone, or what he had done—they would finally let him in.

"My God, Thomas! Is that you?"

Thomas shaded his eyes against the unfamiliar, dazzlingly clear English sunshine and hoped the man hailing him across the lawn of the walled courtyard was his older brother, James, Viscount Jeffrey, the owner of this ancient estate. The years had wrought so many changes, Thomas couldn't be sure.

Nothing was familiar. Not the lush, verdant English countryside. Not the large, ancient manor house beyond the lodge gate. Not the tight, constricting English clothes he wore, not even the language he was trying to force out of his mouth.

"James." His voice sounded rough and frayed, tattered around the edges, and he knew he must appear as disreputable and worn as he felt. What if his brother, his own flesh and blood, didn't recognize him? It had been so long, he'd forgotten himself.

He could only stand on the locked side of the gate and hope that despite his rough demeanor, his brother would recognize him enough to gain him admission.

His brother the viscount did peer hard through the barred barrier of the gate before his face finally lightened in recognition. "Thomas. It is you. It's been too long." His brother's voice was thick with emotion, and in another moment, the gates were unlocked and flung open, and Thomas found himself enveloped in a crushing, bruisingly heartfelt embrace. "You ought to have sent word you were coming. You ought— But no matter. Everyone is here." James clapped him on the shoulder, and then drew back to survey him head to toe. "Look at you. God, but it's good to have you back. Welcome home, Thomas. Welcome home."

Was it home?

It ought to be good to be back in England. It *had* been too long. In India, the monsoon season would have started, bringing endless curtains of lukewarm, swampy rain and steaming brown mud. In Hampshire, the sun was shining in the glittering, cool air and every color was shocking in its sharp, crystalline brilliance. The English trees were a thousand different shades of deep, leafy green, and the sky shone a diamond bright blue.

But how could it be home when everything was so foreign and new?

"Good Lord." James gestured to the crumpled saddlebag the gate porter passed to one of the footmen, while a stable hand led Thomas's mount away toward the stable block. "Is that all your baggage? After all these years, you return with less than you took? I expected chests of rubies at the very least."

"The rubies are to follow." Thomas tried to answer with something approximating his usual wry humor. "I rode. From Liverpool. I was on my way to Downpark, but I stopped at an inn at Sixpenny Handley and heard your name mentioned."

"Not in vain, I hope?" James joked. "Liverpool? What on earth were you doing there? I thought you were meant to be in India all these years? Never mind—what matters is you're here, at last. Come in, come in."

"Thank you."

James kept a loose hold of Thomas's arm as he pulled him across the lawn of the forecourt, as though, after so long an absence, he wasn't prepared to let go. As if he wanted to make sure Thomas didn't disappear for another fifteen-odd years before he made it into the safe confines of the house.

It was touching to find he had been missed. The tight weariness loosened its grip on his chest.

"We'll go straight out." Instead of ushering him into the house, James was leading him through an arched passage-way in the wall that led to the open park beyond. "The whole family is out on the west lawn—all of them but William and his family—so it's a good thing you didn't go home to Downpark, for they're all here, Father and Mother, and the others. We're having a bit of a garden party. Strawberries and cream with the children. You've come just in time for Annabel's christening."

Thomas slowed before the archway. "Annabel?"

"My youngest, born while you were in transit, no doubt." James smiled, his tone full of the patient warmth of a man happy in fatherhood. "There are rather a lot of them, my children. But you'll know everyone else here."

A group of people were gathering around a table set up on the lawn. Strangers still from this distance. Thomas put his hand against the warm brick of the wall, to steady himself and gain another small moment of preparation after so long. "But my dirt. From the road."

"No matter." James pulled him along anyway. "They'll

be ecstatic to see you, though we'll have to make sure Mama is sitting down. It has been a long time."

"Yes," Thomas echoed, still not fathoming the passage of so much time. "I suppose it has."

It hadn't felt like fifteen years until he'd left Scotland and set foot upon English soil two days ago to find everything so unfamiliar and changed. Fifteen years of nomadic travel. Fifteen years of living as a man apart. Fifteen undeniably long, unforgettable years.

"God, you were a twig when you left, and look at you now. You're taller than I. Come." James smiled and threw an arm around his shoulders to steer him across the parterre, toward the group of people on the lawn. His family.

"Everyone, look who's here," James called out to the rest of the party. "The prodigal returns. Our Thomas has finally come home."

Faces turned in surprise. Or perhaps shock. Voices raised in greeting, some familiar, some not. There was his father, an older, grayer version of the man who had sent Thomas off to seek his fortune with the East India Company, striding toward him. Others rose from chairs, astonishment written across their faces. His mother, with her hand pressed against her mouth, looking older than he would have thought. And his sister, impossibly grown-up.

Thomas tried to step forward to greet them. And staggered.

As though he had not yet had time to become accustomed to solid ground beneath his feet. As though he had debarked from the ship hours instead of days ago. His family would think him ill with some sort of jungle fever.

"Steady on, old man," James murmured at his side.

Perhaps, after all those healthy years traversing the Hindu Kush, he *had* finally contracted a fever, if not in Calcutta or on the ship, then in Glasgow or Liverpool.

Because he could have sworn the young woman he saw at the far edge of the sweeping lawn was Catriona Rowan.

Catriona Rowan. Here, in Hampshire, England, at his older brother's estate, when he had looked everywhere else in the world. In every village from Saharanpur to Delhi. And farther south in Agra, and a thousand villages along the Jumma and Ganges rivers to Calcutta. Then in Glasgow and Liverpool and another hundred villages and towns in between.

Perhaps she was a fever dream. Perhaps his weary mind was playing tricks on him now that he had finally resigned himself to the fruitlessness of his obsession. Now that he had grudgingly accepted his failure to find her. Now that he had at last given up and come home.

Thomas narrowed his eyes against the sharp northern sun, raised his hand to block the light glaring off the ornamental fountain, and looked again, determined to rid his brain of this useless, tormenting vision—her long, lithe body clad in gray, the pale, freckled skin, the sweep of fine hair escaping the confines of restrictive pins and bonnet to fly away in the sunlit breeze.

But his heart and mind slammed against each other, like storm waves crashing, until the roar of her name in his head was deafening. Catriona. Catriona. Catriona.

My God. Either he had finally gone mad, or it was she.

How fitting. How bloody ironic. He had searched the world over, when all he had needed to do was to come home. To a place he had never been before.

He told himself to move—to go to her, to haul her into his arms, to make sure she was not a hallucination, to touch her and hold on to her in reality, the way James was holding on to him now. But his body would not obey his mind. He was paralyzed.

He was bloody *staggered.*

Right there on the lush, green lawn of his brother's exquisitely manicured estate, in the middle of a bloody summer garden party—so improbably, quintessentially English—cool, green, and orderly, all graciousness and peaceful ease. Nothing like the seemingly barren, dangerous mountain passes north of the Punjab. Nothing like the crowded, intrigue-riddled bazaars of Lahore. Nothing in these surroundings should make him feel such a disorderly, contradictory rush of numbness and pain—as though he were crawling out of his own grave.

"Thomas? I say, old man, are you all right?" James took a firmer grip of his arm.

He was not all right. He felt as if one of his high-bred mountain horses had kicked him hard in the chest, knocking him stupid.

His Cat. Alive and here, all along. Walking toward him, with children hanging from her arms. Waiting for him.

How could she have found him? It ought to have been impossible. He had told no one he was coming. He hadn't even known it himself, until he had abandoned his search in Liverpool, and gotten on his horse and ridden south. He would have gone to the family seat at Downpark, but for the fact he'd chanced to overhear an ostler at a nearby inn mention his brother's name.

Another staggering thought had him reaching for the stranglehold of his brutally tight English collar and cravat—*children*. Were they hers?

No. The children clutching her hands could not be her own. They were too old—the one on the right was at least four years of age. And there were too many. There had not been time enough for her to hatch such a brood. Please, God, they were only his own romping collection of nieces and nephews, his brother's or sister's children, whom he knew of only through his family's constant letters. Their missals had been sent faithfully at regular intervals, though he had received them in great bunches but once or twice each year, and read them slowly, committing their words to memory before he had fed them one by one into the fire.

The children were shrieking their merry way into the arms of tolerant parents, amused aunties, and indulgent grandparents—his parents, his family—the ones he had traveled all these thousands of miles to see. The ones who were waiting patiently to greet him as he stood like a crazed man, staring at a ghost.

Because he was afraid to take his eyes off her, lest she waver and disappear like a mirage in the dusty glare of the high desert. But she did not dissolve into the crystalline air. She came on, walking steadily along the level grass, her head bent low to murmur encouragement to the awkward child clinging to her hand.

Impatient bodies interposed themselves between them, blocking his line of sight. He shifted to the right.

"Jack, lad! Come and meet your uncle Thomas." James was still at his elbow, trying to subtly recall him to his duty, to the attention he owed his family. "I've told them what little we've known about you, gallivanting about far-off, exotic India."

Small voices rose around him, clamoring for his attention, until he found himself being bowled into and patted on the back by grubby, admiring hands.

"Uncle Thomas? Is India as hot as they say?"

"You're awfully brown, like a pirate," complained a voice. "But you haven't got a ring in your ear."

"I don't like him," was the final decree from one suspicious moppet. "He doesn't look like he has any presents."

But Thomas ignored the voices. He had eyes only for Cat.

She still had not noticed him.

She stopped just beyond the gathered circle of people, waiting with polite disinterest from a distance as his family stirred and swarmed around him. Her eyes followed the children, keeping track as they congregated around him and then broke apart.

My God. Did she not recognize him?

He told himself it was only natural. Six months ago, before he left India, his own family would not have recognized him. "How long has she been here?"

"Beg your pardon?" James did not take his meaning. "I imagine everyone will stay at least a fortnight or so, though Father may have to return to London. We've plenty of room. No need to hurry away—"

"No. Her." Thomas let James follow his gaze. He had lost her before. He would not take his eyes off her now.

"Oh, Miss Cates? I forgot, she will be a stranger to you.

Steady on there, Thomas." James's voice held the first faint beginnings of a warning. "Miss Cates is our governess. She's absolutely marvelous with the children. A wonder. They adore her."

Of course they did. Children, and most people, not to mention any number of species of animals, could not help but adore her. They had an instinct for the truth—something he had lost first, before he had lost her.

But Miss Cates, James had said, not Rowan. That was less than the truth. It meant she was hiding. Clever, clever girl. Right here all along. He couldn't have thought of any place better himself. Something that he would only allow to be relief welled inside his chest. "Did she ask for me?"

"Miss Cates?" James's laugh was uneasy, and a little placating. He put a steadying hand to Thomas's shoulder. "No, Thomas. Why on earth would she?"

A thousand and one reasons, but mostly just one. She was *his*.

"How long has she been here?"

James was frowning with more than concern now. "Not above a six-month, though Cassandra has been working for well over a year to steal her from Lady Grimoy, over at Oakley. Vanessa Grimoy was loath to give her up, though her youngest was already out. Why do you ask? Thomas?"

So she was a real, proper governess, not just pretending at it to find a place with his brother's family. How had she managed to find him when he, a man long experienced in finding out secrets, had spent the better part of the past two years searching fruitlessly for her?

In his frozen state, he could not puzzle it out. But he could not stand there, rooted to the ground like a fakir in his roadside shrine, if he wanted the answer. "Introduce me."

"To Miss Cates? Thomas, are you quite all right? Come, man, the family is waiting—"

"Introduce me." His raw voice was nothing short of unconditional. Unmovable as the granite hills.

"All right, if you insist," James muttered in a frustrated tone that said he didn't know what else to do with his clearly lunatic brother. "Miss Cates," he called to her, "may I introduce you to my brother, the Honorable Thomas Jellicoe? My brother is only just lately returned from abroad, from India. Just this moment, in fact. Thomas, Miss Cates."

She looked up at James, the pale oval of her face showing nothing more than polite interest. But Thomas was sure. His body stirred painfully back to life. He had been half dead with grief, searching for her in vain. But if she were alive—so, too, must he be.

He closed the distance remaining between them as fast as his unsteady legs would allow, and stepped close, so he could satisfy himself it truly was his Cat, and then closer still, so he could smell the mingled scent of lavender and starch rising from her skin. So close, she was forced to change her focus from James and notice him.

At first, she only looked at the hand he extended, roughened by weather and work with horses, and still far too brown for an Englishman. And then her gaze slid to his wrist, to the single, beaten silver bracelet he still wore.

Yes. Her disbelieving gaze ricocheted up to his face, and her eyes darkened in shock. Remembrance and confusion raced across her skin like a hot shadow, and then fled, leaving her drained of color. Even her freckles blanched. She pulled away abruptly, and pressed her hand to her throat, stumbling a little sideways, as if her world were tilting off its upright, starched axis.

He reached out to right her. In India, she had smelled of jasmine and lemons, not lavender and starch. He would remind her of the jasmine.

"Miss Cates and I are acquainted."

Chapter Two

Catriona should have had some warning. Some suitably dramatic cataclysm of nature—a fire or a flood—to warn her hell was about to open up and spit out this particularly unexpected devil.

"You are mistaken, sir." She tried to say the words clearly, but they fell from her numb lips in a whispered rush, drained of all her hard-won confidence.

And he was *mistaken*. Because she had never seen the man standing before her, looking so impossibly handsome in his rumpled yet beautifully tailored English clothes, and so out of place, so exceptionally wrong, standing in front of her in the rolling, green English countryside.

Oh, but she did recognize him. She would know those incandescent green eyes anywhere, even if little else about him—or her—remained the same.

Yet, that was only part of the truth. Miss Anne Cates—as her employers, Viscount Jeffrey and his wife, Lady Cassandra Jeffrey, knew her—was *not* acquainted with the Honorable Thomas Jellicoe. They had *not* been introduced. In fact, *they* had never even met.

Because Catriona Rowan had known him, and he had known her in the fullest sense of the word, as an altogether different man. A man as forbidden to her as the fruit of knowledge was in the Garden of Eden.

Her fall from grace had begun in the bazaar in Saharanpur, the volatile outpost cantonment far north of Delhi, on the edge of the frontier, over two years ago.

If she closed her eyes, Catriona could conjure up the pungent scents of jasmine and marigold that had hung heavy in the still morning air. Flower sellers had spread their garlands of petals in mounding piles over every available inch of space of the Rani Bazaar, in readiness for some Hindu festival she could no longer remember, perfuming the air with a riot of scent to match the riot of hazy, saturated color.

The children in her care, her young cousins, had been delighted by the outing despite the heat. Let loose from the strictures of the English cantonment, they were excited to have the run of the bazaar—Arthur and Alice had wandered ahead, while Charlotte and young George made discoveries closer to their nursemaid.

Catriona had loved it all—the heat and the color. The searing spring sun had felt good on her skin, its warming rays welcome after the cold, raw winds of her recent journey from Scotland.

"Cat, look!" Her cousin Alice held up a garland of bright pink rosebuds, and then darted ahead to a stall filled with vividly colored sari silks.

Catriona had smiled, happy to share the girl's simple joy. She had come to India to do just that—find some portion of joy. To forgo the crushing bleakness that would have been her life had she stayed in Scotland, and find solace in the only family she had left. To ease the ache that had only just begun to subside. To escape her inescapable grief.

To forget.

She had sailed for India and her aunt, Lady Summers, and her family without asking permission, without even writing to warn them she was coming. There had been no time. She couldn't afford to wait, and couldn't risk having them reject her—she had only enough money for the passage, and only enough time for this one, nerve-rattling throw of the dice. Her father had said that Lord Summers was the son of a duke, and that his family had everything Catriona had not—wealth, power, and influence. It had been a terrible gamble, to pitch herself upon their mercy, but Catriona had had nowhere else to go. She had no other escape.

But it wasn't just escape she had wanted. It was the chance to start anew. The chance to be part of a family. The chance to enjoy these rambunctious, affectionate children.

And as she had stood in the middle of the bazaar watching those rambunctious children, *he* had appeared. Riding at the head of a caravan of horses clattering over the hard-packed roadway, like a vision from a storybook, a secret prince full of magic and mischief—all swirling turban, flowing robes, and plush, full *salwar* riding trousers spilling over the tops of his wine-red, soft leather boots.

An Afghani or Pathan, she guessed, thinking of her reading on the fierce tribes to the north, with his waistband bristling with ancient-looking guns and knives. Certainly the man was striking. His piercing, almost glowing green eyes were a startling contrast to the dark caramel of his skin. But it was his smile, a blinding slash of white teeth across the darkness of his beard, that snared her as easily as a fishnet. A roguish, knowing smile. A ready smile—as if he held himself ready to be pleased with life, ready to snatch up any and all pleasures that wandered too close to his tenacious grasp. Such a smile that everyone who saw it was included in its laughter, and Catriona had found her mouth curving as well, hopelessly drawn into the circle of his infectious enthusiasm.

"Who is that man?"

The *ayah,* Namita, who had been assigned to be her constant shadow ever since the day Catriona had arrived unescorted and unexpected at her aunt and uncle's doorstep, did not need any further direction. "Oho, mem! That man is *Huzoor* Tanvir Singh, the great horse trader of the Punjab." Namita's eyes were bright with admiration—an admiration reflected in the eyes and smiles of nearly every other female in the bazaar between the ages of eight and eighty. "He is a wealthy and influential trader. His caravans are said to travel to the back of beyond, far into the mountains and countries to the north."

Of course he was a horseman. Catriona looked with better informed eyes and saw he could be nothing else, even with the bright warrior's dagger thrust into his belt. The Punjabi was both relaxed and instinctively in tune with his animal, his hands light and quiet on the reins, his knee glued to the horse's side, as if the two were but one being, even though he had slung his other leg casually across the pommel of his saddle. The trader walked the horse easily through the throng, presenting a picture of innate horsemanship as he laughed out loud in answer to the raucous, high-spirited cries of the people who called out to him along the whole length of the bazaar while he tossed mangoes from his copious pockets to the children gathered by the sides of the stalls.

His passage, Catriona realized, was meant to be noted by one and all. So that within minutes, word might pass from tongue to ear, and ear to tongue, from the bazaar throughout all Saharanpur, that Tanvir Singh had brought his caravan of fine, northern-blood horses down from the mountains to sell.

Cat knew his horse-trading kind of old, for hadn't she taken the measure of his like along the meandering banks of the Clyde, and a hundred small towns and villages between there and Glasgow when she was a girl? And she knew a rogue when she saw one. But he knew his business, this rogue, this storybook prince of a horseman. Despite the heat and dust, despite what must have been long weeks of marches down through the mountains at the back of beyond, as the *ayah* called the *Himalaya*, the horses were fit and fine—strong boned and well muscled, sleek and well fed. Her grandfather would have loved to have seen such well-bred animals, and to have mentally compared their lines to his own tall Clyde-bred draft horses.

But her grandfather was cold in his grave, Scotland was thousands of miles away, across the dark, brooding sea, and all the horses were sold and led away.

The sharp stab of pain and longing, at the thought of all she had lost, was as familiar as it was quick, yet under the wide umbrella of the Punjabi's dazzling smile, she was able to deflect it to the side, an ache to nurse later. She would not brood now. Not when there were such horses as Tanvir Singh's to be seen.

Without another thought, her feet carried her forward.

"Aie," the *ayah* cried in fear, pulling at Catriona's arm. "Thou wilt be crushed by the beasts!"

But Catriona had no fear of such high-bred horses. They were brother and sister to her. She could divine their hearts and minds as easily as she could divine her own. Even as she went forward—instinctively crooning soft words of praise in Scots Gaelic, though she knew the horse would not understand her—a haughty, curious black mare with high, white stockings turned her long, noble head and stepped carefully forward the few feet her lead rope would allow to twitch her ears and whuff at the air by way of greeting.

As the mare came near enough to lower her head to have her ears scratched, Catriona closed her eyes and inhaled deeply. The achingly familiar, soft, earthy scent of the animal was like a balm to her soul.

"Puithar," she whispered into the mare's long, elegant ear. "My sister, have you come as far as I? Was the way over the mountains as hard as the way over the sea? Was it all as strange and wondrous for you?" Her fingers instinctively rummaged through her pockets to find the half-eaten remains of the Kashmiri apple she had bought from a stall for one of the children. But one did not give an animal not one's own a treat without permission. She knew it as well as she knew her own name.

Catriona turned her eyes to find the Punjabi horseman, Tanvir Singh, regarding her with those jewel-bright, amused eyes. So she held up the apple and raised her brows in wordless universal pantomime, for after only a few weeks on the subcontinent, she knew little Hindi or Urdu as yet, and absolutely no Punjabi.

Without a word, and without leaving his lofty perch atop his horse, the prince of rogues smiled at her. A smile so blindingly brilliant it could melt the snowcaps high on the mountains beyond the Doab Valley's hills. A smile that felt as if it were for her alone, and no one else in the world. He smiled and salaamed her with an elegant flourish, a deep bow and sweep of arm worthy of a pasha dispensing life-changing favors.

And it had changed her life. The little stone that was all that was left of her heart, hardened by death and exile, stirred—just a little—like the pitted seed of a peach learning to take root in rocky ground.

Foolish, treacherous heart.

"Have you forgotten?"

The warm memories washing over Catriona were as welcome as a cold wave from the Firth of Clyde, sweeping away every last trace of her composure, leaving her numb and all but shaking. She had been living at Wimbourne Manor as Miss Anne Cates if not in a state of constant fear, then in unhappy awareness that her past might very well catch up with her one day. Her guilt had been a stone lodged fast within her heart—a constant, uncomfortable reminder of sins left unabsolved.

But she had not expected *him,* of all people, to be the law's mortal messenger. Why should Tanvir Singh—the man who had once been her friend, her only lover—have come looking for her? Why would he have left his Punjab to travel across thousands of miles of sea, to do the East India Company's bidding, and bring her to their particular version of justice?

He had betrayed *her,* not the other way around.

Yet, here he was. In the flesh. Standing so close she had to tip her head back to convince herself this strangely familiar Englishman was in fact Tanvir Singh. She had forgotten how impossibly tall he was. She had made herself forget.

As if he could decipher her thoughts, the man who was

not Tanvir Singh, but Thomas Jellicoe, asked, "Do you need me to remind you?" His voice was low and raw with accusation, and his eyes—his fierce green eyes—weighed her out as relentlessly as an executioner.

She needed no reminder. She had not forgotten as well as she had thought—in fact, she remembered every small thing. The bright, translucent green glow of his eyes regarding her through the dark veil of his lashes. The feel of his warm skin beneath her hands. The taste of his mouth upon hers. The precise power of his body. The crippling pain of his ultimate betrayal. His callous indifference.

Catriona pulled sharply against the hand that still held her. "You will excuse me," was all she could manage, as she disentangled little Mariah's hand from her own, and handed the child off to her older sister—Mariah could do without her, with so many adult relations near. Catriona had to get away from him. From the past that had finally caught up with her.

But how on earth could he have found her, when she had taken such great pains not to be found? Because all along he was not just Tanvir Singh, but Thomas Jellicoe, Lord Jeffrey's brother? Had Lord Jeffrey written to him about her? And how much had this Thomas Jellicoe already told Lord Jeffrey?

God help her. The numbness began to be replaced by a hard knot of dread.

Her gaze shot to her employer, who was looking back and forth between her and his brother. Whatever it was Lord Jeffrey saw in her face—guilt, or at the very least, amazed horror—galvanized him into action. He stepped between them, and laid a restraining hand on his brother's arm.

"Thomas." He spoke quietly, but firmly. "That's quite enough."

Thomas Jellicoe ignored his brother, shaking him off with a ripple of his blade-lean shoulder. He reached for her again, even as she edged back, following her step by step, crowding against her skirts until she nearly tripped on her hems.

She had to draw her arms back, so he could not touch her. "Sir. Please!"

"For God's sake, Thomas," Lord Jeffrey hissed. "What is wrong with you? Kindly leave off and let my governess be. Your family is waiting. And watching, for Christ's sake."

Thomas Jellicoe—the name rang in her head like an echo from a hilltop—finally turned those fierce green eyes of his away, and his hold on her was broken. As if her bonds had snapped, she was free of him.

Catriona immediately put her head down and hurried away from the group, all but running across the lawn, moving instinctively toward the gap in the hulking shelter of the nearest yew hedge.

What must Lord and Lady Jeffrey think of her? Even though her employers seemed as shocked at his behavior as she, this Honorable Thomas Jellicoe was Lord Jeffrey's brother, and blood was bound to be thicker than even the deepest gratitude. No matter how fond of her as a governess they may have grown, Lord and Lady Jeffrey would never take her part over his. And Catriona didn't think she could face the look on Lady Cassandra Jeffrey's lovely face when her mistress learned what the Honorable Thomas Jellicoe was sure to tell her—that Catriona Rowan was wanted for murder.

The metallic tang of fear slowly suffused her mouth. It would be as it was before. Powerful voices would speak against her, and there would be nothing she could do to prevent it.

No. She would prevent it. She would run.

She would be gone as soon as she could throw her possessions and the monies she had saved into a bag, and walk away across the fields, just as she had before, in India, and before that, in Scotland. She would not wait for the inexorable process of the law to slowly grind her up. She would be gone before he had a chance to spread his accusation like deadly poison.

Catriona gathered up her skirts in unmannerly fists to run down the short set of stone steps leading off the lawn, cursing the particularly cruel twist of fate that had brought the man who had been Tanvir Singh back into her life. Of all the places to hide in plain sight, she had somehow, blindly, unwittingly, chosen his brother's house.

A sharp, sulfuric crack of lightning landed nearby, and rolled across the lawn just as a clump of grass in front of Catriona sprayed up with a dense hiss of green blades and brown soil. She stopped short as the concussion of thunder rolled through her chest.

But it was all wrong.

She glanced up to confirm the sky was still clear and cloudless. Yet a storm must be brewing. If so, they ought to take the children in. Little Mariah, especially, would be afraid of the clashing thunder.

She was about to turn, to look back over her shoulder, to perhaps speak to Lady Jeffrey about Mariah, when another loud crack echoed from somewhere to her left. A branch dropped off the yew hedge in front of her. And her shock-addled brain could no longer deny the evidence of her eyes. They were gunshots.

Thomas Jellicoe was too impatient to wait for the inexorable process of law to drag her back to India. He would not let her escape. He was shooting her now. In front of his family. In front of the children. Sweet Saint Margaret.

The air turned thick, slowing her motions. She heard the panicked cries of alarm behind her, and felt the heavy pounding of footsteps across the lawn as everyone began to run for cover, but when she finally managed to turn, screaming for them to shield the children, all she could see was the strange English version of Tanvir Singh bearing down on her with such a look of death and destruction, there was no room for anything else.

It was too late for her to escape. His hard, uncompromising body slammed into hers, carrying her to the ground beneath him, knocking the wind from her lungs.

"For pity's sake," he growled into her ear when she tried to fight her way out from under him. His large brown hand covered the back of her head, and shoved her face unceremoniously into the grass. His voice was like gravel grinding into her. "Stay down!"

He lay directly on top of her, all fifteen-odd stone of him, squashing her into the earth. Her chest began to ache with the struggle to draw breath. She squirmed against him, desperate to ease the air back into her lungs.

He bit off an exceedingly blunt Anglo-Saxon oath and shifted sideways. "Stop that. For God's sake, don't move like that."

They were all tangled together—his leg had insinuated itself between her petticoats, and the hard ridge of his knee pushed against the inside of her thigh. His arms surrounded her, both pinning her against the ground and pulling her into him. He curved his long body around her, caging her with his strength.

Another shot whistled close by and his hands dug into her. "Now!" he ordered as he sprang to his feet and practically dragged her by the fabric of her gown, pulling and pushing, shoving her through a small gap at the base of the tall hedge of evergreens, and through them, into a veritable cave of dark quiet up against the low stone wall behind. He threw his back against the stone and pulled her roughly down next to him, wedging her hard into the corner where the wall and stone stairway separating the lawn from the maze came together. "Are you all right? Are you hit?"

She wasn't hit, but she could not possibly be all right. Her bonnet was crushed and hanging limply askew, its ribbons sawing into her neck. She could taste dirt in her mouth, and she still had not been able to draw breath. One of the whalebone stays of her corset must have cracked under his onslaught. It bit into her like the blade of a knife. But mostly, she was decidedly *not* all right because the man who used to be Tanvir Singh was crouched next to her, his body still shielding hers. Protecting her. Damn him to hell and back.

Damn them both. Because if Thomas Jellicoe thought he was protecting her, then someone else entirely was shooting at her.

Catriona fought to control the searing panic spreading through her chest, and pull air into her lungs. To stay calm in the midst of such ungovernable chaos. "The children? Was anybody hit?"

In the dim, filtered light, Catriona felt, rather than saw, his head swivel toward her. "Taken out of range. The lawn is empty." While he answered, his hands were busy taking inventory of her body, running along her limbs with the same sort of practiced, professional expertise and care he had used to examine his horses. There had been a time, once, when he had looked at her, and run his hands down her person in much the same way, yet there had been nothing practical or impersonal about his focused attention and open admiration.

The unwelcome thought was a painful reminder of what she no longer was to him.

"Stop that." She wrenched his hands away. "I am quite all right. Apart from you nearly pummeling me to death."

His hands withdrew, and there was a long moment of potent quiet and stillness while her blood pounded in her ears, and her eyes adjusted to the low gray-green light. But when he spoke, she could *feel* the wry humor in Tanvir Singh's voice, as if his amused laughter were touching her where his hands were not.

"You're welcome, mem. I'll try to remember not to pummel you the next time I save your life."

Chapter Three

"Save my life?" Catriona retreated into Miss Anne Cate's starched primness to ward off the power of his roguish charm. She busied herself untangling the bonnet strings that were choking her in an effort to distract him from her lies. "Don't be ridiculous."

Had he really come to save her? Or had he come to bring her to justice despite the gunshots being fired in her general direction? It just might suit this newly English Tanvir Singh's flexible moral scruples and ironic sense of justice, to save her from a stray bullet only so she might be properly dispatched by the noose.

But he was smiling. The incongruous slash of his white teeth gleamed across the dark shadow of his face. "Did it somehow escape your notice—Miss *Cates,* was it?—that you were being shot at?"

Nothing about this ridiculous situation had escaped her notice, especially not the unnerving fact that she had been shot at by someone so ruthlessly underhanded and cowardly, he would hide behind a wall and try to dispatch her from a reckless, unreliable distance, when all he had to do was walk up to the front gate and declare Miss Anne Cates to be a fraud, as well as a fugitive from the law—wanted by magisterial authorities in no fewer than two, and quite possibly three, countries.

It was ridiculous that she seemed to have rivals for her demise. It was ridiculous that after so long, any of them should have taken the trouble to track her down. She had done nothing to provoke such interest. She hadn't spilled so much as one bloody secret. She had kept her word.

But ridiculous seemed to be the way of her world. "What do you mean to do?"

The man who had become the Honorable Thomas Jellicoe misunderstood her. He looked out through the hedge. "At the moment, nothing. You're safe enough here. The shots came from over the wall to the north, outside the estate, I should think. I imagine my brother is mustering his people in defense. At least I hope so."

His voice was the same, low and textured, just rough enough for the sound to hum and vibrate through her. But the English diction and the enunciation sounded entirely alien, lacking all the formal, melodic undertones of the subcontinent. He no longer sounded like the voice in her dreams, her painful reminder through the sleepless nights of continuous exile, the murmuring ghost of sins past.

But it did not matter what he sounded like. He was not there to whisper love words into her ears. The thought compelled her to move. She started up, determined to crawl through the vicious bramble of branches at the base of the wall if it meant escape.

A large hand closed around her ankle like a shackle, and hauled her back. "Don't be daft, Cat. You're not going anywhere before that gunman is stopped. Sit down." He all but pulled her into his lap. "And don't argue," he added before she could protest. "You'll give away our position."

As his hands had finally ceased their minute topographical exploration of her person, she did not argue. She had much better save her breath to cool her overheated brain, and think—to find a way out of her latest desperate situation. The children were safe. One blessing, then, in this small ocean of misfortune. And she was still alive. Another blessing from a fickle, disinterested God.

Air crept warily back into her lungs. Catriona subsided

into her corner, working hard to regain some composure, to stay calm and think.

It would have to be America for her. Lord and Lady Jeffrey had been generous in her salary, and she had saved almost everything she had earned from her previous employer, Lady Grimoy, as well as most of the money Lord Summers's mother, the dowager duchess, had settled on her to make her disappear.

She should have known. She should have gone sooner. She had waited too long. She had let herself be lulled into thinking she was safe. She had let herself become accustomed to Lord and Lady Jeffrey's regard, and let herself become attached to their children despite her best efforts not to—the children who had once again become her family, her only remaining solace.

But the problem still remained. How did she get away from this Thomas Jellicoe?

His left arm was still wrapped around her middle, and his large hand was moving minutely, stroking along her ribs almost idly, as if he were unaware he did it. But she was more than aware. Each one of his small, idle movements sent a shaft of heat tingling under her skin until she began to grow fidgety with sensation. The steady warmth of his body at her side was a marked contrast to the cool damp of the earth beneath her hands, and she dug her fingers into the soil to hold herself still. And to keep from touching him.

All squashed up next to him, feeling the tensile strength of his long, lithe body folded up next to hers, she was overcome with the rush of remembrance. Of wanting him, wanting to rely upon him, his heat and his strength, even as she knew she should not. She could not.

Oh, but she was weak, for she could not help but look at him and marvel at the changes two years had wrought. His smooth chin was tipped skyward, as he listened to whatever clues there were to what was happening beyond the small cocoon of their safe shelter. She had never seen him clean shaven, without the long, carefully groomed beard that was the hallmark of the monotheistic Sikhs of the

Punjab. Without it, he looked strangely bare, almost naked, the strong, chiseled plains of his cheekbones and jaw intimately exposed, slightly paler than the rest of his face. And his hair, which had once been long and flowing when he had released it from its winding turban, had been ruthlessly cropped in the English style. Her fingers itched and twitched in the dirt, with the sudden urge to run her fingers through the short, uneven strands.

Too late, Catriona became aware that he was watching her catalogue the altered landscape of his face in amused silence, one corner of his mouth sliding upward to smile in that nearly irresistible way of his. "Well, how do you do, Miss Cates. Here we are. Getting shot at during a garden party, in merry old England. If I had known Hampshire would prove to be so full of such interesting intrigue, I'd have come home much sooner."

It was so like him, like Tanvir Singh, to find the humor in the ridiculousness of the situation. It was so like him to try to amuse her while her world was falling down around her. She had once found it charming. Now she found it heartbreaking.

Especially when he continued. "Or is it perhaps just *you*," he said, "and not England, who is full of interesting intrigue. It seems people are always getting shot at when you are involved."

There it was, finally—the mention of murder.

He had not come to charm and amuse her. He had surely come to accuse her.

But his low voice was full of a strange sort of gentle, exasperated wonder, and he was regarding her through those dangerous, soot-dipped lashes, with such minute attention, as if she looked as strange and foreign as he. As if she were the map of a place he had forgotten he had visited.

No matter how hard her heart, or how turbulent her mind, what remained of her vanity could not withstand the onslaught. She put a hand up to push the messy wisps of her flyaway hair out of her face.

He shook his head silently, a slow negation, before he

reached across the gulf between them and ran his thumb along the line of her cheekbone.

"You've dirt," he murmured, as he smudged something off her skin, "on your face. And you've done something to your hair to make it darker and duller. Such a crime. And you are still attiring yourself in that horrid gray. Always gray. But somehow, despite all that, you look so lovely, I have the strongest urge to kiss you."

That way lay madness. Or at the very least, bad, bad, regrettable decisions. He was no longer Tanvir Singh. He was no longer her friend.

She squelched it all down—the vanity and whatever unmet longing was attempting to stir itself back to life. "I beg you would suppress it."

"No." He shook his head again even as the corner of his mouth hitched into a single lovely, bittersweet dimple. "I think not. I think I've come a deuced long way to find you, and I'm done with polite, English caution."

Yet, he took her face in his hands cautiously, slowly and carefully, in the way a man raised a too full glass to his lips, bringing his mouth to hers. Even as she told herself she should not—she should push him away, and run as fast as she could in the opposite direction and not stop until she had reached the ocean—she let him come nearer and nearer. She watched, her eyes open wide, searching his face, helpless with the need to reconcile this handsome Englishman with her memories of Tanvir Singh.

The first touch of his lips was soft, almost tentative, as if he, too, were tasting and comparing. As if he, too, were feeling his way across the passage of time and miles. She prayed fervently for a moment that she might be spared, that she might feel nothing for him, that her well of frustrated longing for him might have finally run dry.

But his lips were still the texture of ripe fruit, smooth and taut, and tasting of plums. He pulled back for a moment, his eyes closed, and took in a deep breath, as if he could take her in. As if she were as necessary to him as air.

In response, her own mouth dropped open, parched and

thirsty, longing foolishly—so foolishly—for another taste of him. And like a dying woman in a desert who will drink even the deadliest brine, she took another sip, pressing her lips to his.

He slanted his mouth across hers and kissed her more deeply, searching her out, pushing his hands into the tight constriction she had made of her hair, pulling apart the low fist of the bun, scattering pins into the ground. And she was falling or melting, or going somewhere far, far away, dissolving into nothingness, and everything-ness, all at the same time. With his thumbs fanned along her cheeks and his big hands wrapped around the back of her head, drawing her into him, he kissed her with heat and abandon, drawing her out with lips and tongue, and with the very breath from his body, as if she were his air and his water.

A part of her mind told her she must think, she must use his lust and desire to her own ends, but she could not sustain the thought. Everything else faded, until there was nothing but the longing for the feel of his mouth on hers, and the pleasure so sharp she could not tell it from pain. Catriona was enveloped in the heat and scent of him. The heat, radiating out of him in leaping bonfires, was familiar, though the scent, a uniquely English combination of horse, leather, and privilege, was entirely foreign, and she realized she had been seeking it out—nosing along the slide of his neck below his ear, tasting his skin with little open-mouthed kisses—seeking the faint hint of the patchouli that had once perfumed his long, long, beautiful dark hair.

A low growl of appreciation and encouragement wound out of his chest and she lost herself to him. Every pulse in her body beat with him. Every breath was mingled with his. She was weightless, floating higher and higher on the rising tide of her need.

They were no longer tentative. They had nothing left of what he had called English caution. They kissed with the knowledge that they were hidden from anyone else's eyes and that they wanted this joining—had longed for this fervent press of flesh and pleasure. Indeed, her hands were wrapped around his strong wrists and she was all but pulling him closer, holding him near so she could lose herself in the awful, dangerous pleasure. In the promise of his passion.

The rough texture of his skin, shaved free of his beard, but with the beginning of whiskers, rasped against hers as he arched her head back to kiss down the curve of her throat. His teeth slid down her neck to worry and nip at the hollow at the base of her throat.

"God, yes, Cat. My Cat."

Her eyes fell shut, and she was nodding in agreement, and waiting for more of the bliss that spread under her skin like honey, hearing nothing but the roaring of her pulse in her ears and the harsh cadence of his breath above her. Her breath was just as unruly. She was all but panting for him. Wanting him. Needing nothing but the feel of his hands on her body and his lips against hers.

"Let me touch you," he rasped. "Let me have you."

His fingers were plucking at the lacing of her gray gown, and a feeling of such abiding sweetness and relief blossomed within her, she felt almost faint. "Tanvir," she whispered.

"Yes, my *kaur,* yes. I've found you. I've got you."

She opened her eyes to see him, to find the promise of his dark green eyes. But he was not Tanvir Singh. He was not her lover. He was an Englishman named Thomas. A man who had shared his body, but never his truth.

She was not his *kaur,* because he was no longer her Tanvir. And even if he were, all Tanvir Singh had apparently ever wanted from her was what she was currently so foolishly giving him.

The realization stopped her cold.

She brought her elbows between them and levered herself away. "Oh, God. What am I doing? I don't *know* you."

He let her go, and blew out a low gust of frustrated laughter, though his breath was sawing in and out of his chest as if he had run a race. And his eyes, those laughing, mocking eyes, regarded her steadily through a fall of dark hair, like a jackal staring down a hare.

"You don't know me? Well, let me enlighten you, *kaur*. I'm the man you once fucked as ruthlessly as any courtesan."

Catriona flinched. She should have known some accusation, heavy as a blow, was coming. She should have been prepared. She should have understood that despite his kisses, he thought the very worst of her.

Fine. If he had not forgiven her mistakes, she would not forgive his deceit. "Don't call me that. I am not your princess, nor was I ever. You *left* me. You left me there to die. Or had *you* forgotten?" She shoved at his chest. "Get away from me. Don't touch me."

This time, it was *his* head that reeled back as if she had hit him. The tight set of his jaw told her the truth of her accusation had found its mark.

"Perhaps," he said when he had recovered, "I should have just let whoever the bastard is who wants to kill you put a bullet between your eyes. Then you wouldn't give a damn who touched you. Because you'd already be dead." He leaned forward, his fire-green eyes lancing into her. "But I'll be damned if I've come all this way to find you, just to let that happen. So you'd better get bloody used to me, *kaur*."

Whoever the bastard is.

He didn't know who wanted to kill her?

She ought to feel some relief. But the tight, caged feeling in her lungs was still too close to panic for anything approaching relief. And the intense heat in his eyes, scant inches from hers, pouring his angry distrust over her, was enough to make her want to weep.

How could he *not* know—he who had seen everything? How had they come to this—this intensely hard feeling that was perilously close to hate? How had something so sweet and fine become so twisted and mean? But she would not cry. She would not. She was done with spilling useless tears for him. "Leave me alone."

"Sir?" The tentative call came from the lawn beyond

their dark shelter. "Mr. Jellicoe? Can you hear me? Lord Jeffrey sent me to give you the all clear."

Thomas Jellicoe looked for a moment as if he would not reveal their place, as if he would keep her there by force and be-damned to the consequences. But finally he rose, and pushed his way through the dense branches, holding them back and extending his hand to assist her.

But she would not willingly touch him again. Catriona turned her shoulder and edged around him, heedless of the clawing branches scratching at her skin and gown.

He ignored her snub and snared her elbow in his implacable grip. "Thank you," he addressed Michael, the groundskeeper's son, who knuckled his forehead in response. "Has the bastard been caught?"

"Was anybody hit?" Catriona interrupted with her own pressing question instead. "The children?"

"No, miss. Nary a one. We seem to have come through this all to rights."

"Thank God." Now she did feel at least some relief. She drew a shaky breath into her cold lungs.

"And the gunman?" Thomas Jellicoe repeated his question.

"No. If it please you, sir," Michael answered, "my father tracked fresh hoofprints south back down the road from Sixpenny Handley. And his lordship's set him to take riders to follow and track the assassin down."

Thomas Jellicoe nodded, and narrowed his eyes to scan the tree line beyond the manor walls. In that moment, she could see the canny Punjabi, the wily and brilliant *sawar* Tanvir Singh inside the trappings of this English gentleman. But when he spoke, his voice was again that of Lord Jeffrey's brother, son of the Earl Sanderson, all assumed, imperious command. "Good man. Where are Lord Jeffrey and the earl, now?"

How blind had she been, never to have seen it—that his sense of command came from an innate sense of privilege? How stupidly infatuated had she been that she had never seen the obvious truth of the man standing so close to her?

Too close. Again, she tried to wrest her elbow from his grasp.

He tugged her closer.

"Gun room, sir." Michael was saying. "My Lord Jeffrey says I'm to take you there now, if our Miss Cates isn't hurt."

It gave her strength, that "our Miss Cates," that feeling of belonging. She found her voice somewhere in the back of her aching throat. "No. I'm not hurt."

Michael chanced returning a small smile. "I'm glad, miss. Then you're to go to Lady Jeffrey and the children."

"Yes, of course. Thank you." She tugged against Thomas Jellicoe's grip again, harder. "I'll go directly."

But Thomas Jellicoe wouldn't let her go. He continued to ignore Michael's, or more properly, Lord Jeffrey's request—continued to do just as he pleased, just as he always had. "I'll escort *your* Miss Cates."

"I am not *your* Miss Cates, either. I am not your anything."

He loomed over her, intimidating her with his height and breadth, and his dark English coat. "We are not done, Cat," he promised her. "Not by a long measure."

She looked up at him, and it was as if she were seeing him clearly for the first time—the hard, implacable English bedrock beneath the honeyed skin and dazzling smile. And despite the fact that she wanted to think she might see the last of him, Catriona didn't doubt him in the least.

Chapter Four

The moment he was forced by the demands of good breeding and his obligation to his family to let Catriona go, Thomas's fingers ached for the loss. And without her to hold, to actively keep safe, he immediately felt the enormous lack of a weapon in his hands. Nearly fifteen years in hostile, dangerous lands and he had not spent a moment without a knife and a gun tucked into his waistband. Two days back in peaceful England and he was unarmed, and unable to prevent a shooting at a garden party.

Bloody, bloody hell. Thomas watched Catriona hurry into the house and away behind the baize door to the servants' corridors with a feeling close to panic. Every instinct told him not to let her out of his sight, to keep her safe by his side, not to let another moment go by without prying the truth out of her. There was still too much to say, too much that needed explaining.

But there was also much to do. The estate had to be made secure, and Thomas doubted James, for all his typical efficiency and legions of staff, could be as experienced in such nefarious matters as he. If his bloody double life had cost such a high price, Thomas wanted to at least know he'd gotten value for his ill-spent money.

The gun room, located within the northeast portion of the house, its windowless walls furnished with dark oak cabinets, was a hive of activity. Shuttered safety lamps revealed James and their father, the Earl Sanderson, together at a central table, poring over a map with a man who was either the steward, the gamekeeper, or possibly the grounds-keeper—Thomas's recollection of the hierarchy of English outdoor servants was sketchy. Nearly fifteen years of being thought little better than a servant himself by his fellow Englishmen had left him with a skewed perception of both his betters and his equals.

They stopped speaking as he entered.

Thomas asserted himself into the silence. "Have you secured the perimeter of the estate from the walls outward? The shots came from over the manor wall to the west and—"

The look James gave him was nearly a glare, so sharp and probing it could have cut glass, though his voice was brittle with calm. "Thank you, Thomas. I've already sent my men out. Thank you, Peters," he said to his steward. "You'll see to it? Have Foster from the home farm come up to see me as well. You may go, all of you, while I have a word with my brother."

James saw his steward out of the room, and returned to his maps with impeccable self-discipline. But Thomas could see his brother's knuckles were white where his hands clenched the edge of the table in an effort to remain calm and in control.

For the first time in a very, very long time, Thomas felt the need to explain himself. "James, I have experience—"

"No doubt." His brother's tone grew sharper as his fright for his family overtook his good manners. "I could see that by the *experienced* way you tossed poor Miss Cates about like a sack of grain. Tell me what the hell is going on, Thomas. Tell me your *experience* hasn't followed you here, to *my home,* to threaten my *children* and family." James's voice rose, raw with suppressed fear. "Tell me."

It hadn't gone unnoticed by Thomas that in the course of fifteen years of clandestine service, he might have acquired an enemy or two. He had spent years in careful consideration of such a possibility, always on the watch for trouble. But he hadn't expected such trouble to follow him home, to soft, sweet England, to his brother's manor of all places, a house he had never set eyes upon until a scant half hour ago.

No. The gunshots had not been fired at him. Nor, as far as he could tell, at the rest of the party. "My apologies, James. I assure you I am very conscious of the safety of your family. But the shots were not for me. There was a single gunman. He fired, from my recollection, three shots, in succession at timed intervals, which suggests some army training. And every single one of them was fired at your Miss Cates. Thank God I got here when I did."

"Miss Cates? That's ridiculous." James echoed Cat's sentiments. "Who would want to shoot a poor governess?"

The list, by Thomas's calculation, was not extensive. Just brutally efficient. "I think you should know, there is more to your Miss Cates than meets the eye."

James crossed his arms over his chest and took a more careful, measured look at his younger brother. "I could say as much about you, Thomas. Miss Cates has been living amongst us in the neighborhood quite peacefully until you showed up. And you're the one who scared her half to death. You frightened her even before the shooting. Why?"

Thomas weighed his truths out as carefully as possible. "I knew her in India."

"So I gathered. She did not seem pleased to renew the acquaintance."

"No, she didn't." Thomas had imagined their reunion many, many times in the past two years. In each imagining Catriona had been glad—more than glad. She had been deliriously happy to see him. She had thrown her arms around his neck and kissed him passionately. She had not pulled away in disgust and said, "Leave me alone."

"Did you manhandle her there as well? I hope I don't need tell you, Thomas, as pleased as I am to see you, I won't stand for anyone, even my long-lost brother, bullying or mistreating my servants. Miss Cates is greatly valued by Lady Jeffrey. Greatly."

Thomas looked at his brother and his father—whom he hadn't even greeted properly—and felt the weight of his own shortcomings, his own failures. Cat had been right. She was not ecstatic to see him because he had failed her. Miserably.

"I understand completely. Again, my apologies. Hello, Father."

His father, the Earl Sanderson, extended his hand and gave his youngest son a deep, slow smile. "It is, of course, a pleasure—more than a pleasure—to see you after all these years, Thomas, but . . . It has not been the most auspicious of homecomings."

"No. I am sorry."

James was only partially mollified. "Sorry doesn't explain why someone shot at my family. Or, as you insist, at my governess."

Thomas's natural inclination was to keep the few of Cat's secrets that he did know to himself, for they were rightly hers to tell. But James was right—his family had been exposed to gunfire. Thomas owed them a larger measure of the truth. "How much of what I did in India do you know?"

James looked to their father.

"A little." The earl settled into a leather armchair. "A very little. I could find only that you were asked by the company to assume another identity, though even I couldn't learn anything beyond that. I assume you were a spy."

"That's as neat a description as any." It gave Thomas little pleasure to have his work described thusly. However good he had been at gathering intelligence, spying was hardly an honorable profession for a gentleman. He had hoped never to mention his erstwhile career to his family—only to tell them he had made his fortune in horse trading and breeding.

But his father, it seemed, had intelligence sources of his own. "It was not, perhaps, a career I would have chosen for you," his father admitted. "Indeed, I had hoped your service in India would lead eventually to a political career."

His *career,* such as it was, was over. Finished.

"I didn't choose it, either. It seemed to have chosen me." Not for the first time in the past year, Thomas wished for a drink. After years of honoring the vow of abstinence he had taken in his identity as Tanvir Singh, this was what his tangled obsession with Catriona Rowan had reduced him to. Even this early in the afternoon, he felt the need for the fortification only strong spirits could afford. But he must begin as he meant to go on—honestly.

"You see, in India there was a northern proverb: 'Let thy hair grow long and talk Punjabi, and thou shalt make a Sikh.'"

Thomas had first heard it spoken by his superior, Colonel Augustus Balfour, on the day almost fourteen years before, when Thomas had ridden back from his first assignment for the East India Company. Alone.

"Almost as soon as I had arrived in India, I was sent upon a particularly mortal expedition to buy horses for breeding stock in Baluchistan. Of all the Englishmen sent out by the company on that expedition—twenty-three men—only I lived."

Even after the passage of so many intervening years, the loss still ached like a bruise that should have long since healed.

Only he had survived the rigors of a year of caravan travel, the exposure to disease, the ravages of climate, and the predations of bandits and tribesmen, to return a different man than the boy who had left. When he had finally made it back to Delhi, he had looked and spoken more like a native than any son of pale Albion.

"A Colonel Balfour was the resident commissioner of the northwest provinces back then, and when I had told him all the things I had seen and heard in the course of the long journey, and what I had learned to make of them, well, that cagey gentleman concocted a devious but simple plan. It was decided that I would go with him to Saharanpur, and Tanvir Singh, Sikh, trader of horses, finder of information, giver and keeper of secrets, I would become. I wrapped my hair that had grown overlong and unruly in a turban, and donned the *kirpan* and *kara,* the ceremonial dagger and silver bracelet, as the outward signs of the Sikh religion."

James leaned forward in morbid curiosity. "Just like that? You take up a pagan religion?"

"It's not pagan, it's monotheistic." But he did not have the leisure to debate theology with his brother. "I was a spy, James. That's how it's done. You can dissect my moral compromises at some later date."

He had become the company's most secret weapon, passing across borders with impunity. He had learned to cull the meaningful facts out of his observations, while at the same time keeping himself invisible, hidden in plain sight amongst the teeming masses. "I took up a lot of things for expediency's sake."

"Including Miss Cates?" his father probed.

"No." Thomas's tone was every bit as steely and uncom-promising as his sire's, hard and tempered by experience, full of the man he had become. "Do *not* make unfounded assumptions. There was nothing expedient about my asso-ciation with your Miss Cates."

Yet, how could he explain what Cat had been to him? It would do him little credit in his family's eyes to know he *had* abandoned the English way of life without looking back, and never thought another thing about it, through all the years he had roamed back and forth across kingdoms, deserts, and frontiers, until that late spring morning two years ago, when an *angrezi* woman in Rani Bazaar had looked at him, and made him feel something keen and bit-tersweet about the life he had so easily left behind.

It had been altogether unwelcome, that pang. He had loved his role as a clandestine agent in the Great Game of espionage between all the many powers in the shadows of the Hindu Kush. He had loved the horses, loved their beauty and their heart, and he loved most of all the freedom to go where he liked, and the intrigue of finding what went on everywhere he looked.

"It suited me—Balfour's version of spying. I was free to travel, and trade and breed horses. I earned an independent fortune doing so. I was beholden to no one, so long as I brought secrets, along with my horses, down from the Maharajah Ranjiit Singh's powerful kingdom of the Punjab and offered them to the company."

And they had taken him and his intelligence for granted, the company, like a plate of sweetmeats left outside a door by an obedient, invisible servant.

Yet, that morning, in the Rani Bazaar, the girl had appeared to him like the insistent vision of a remorseful angel, come to remind him of what he was, and who he had once been below the surface of his darkened skin. She drew his eye like a bright flame, a cold-burning torch amid the heat and profusion of the bazaar. An *angrezi* woman so very white, she was exotic.

She hadn't looked like all the typical memsahibs, full of starched righteousness and stewed faces, with wilted, disapproving lips. Yet she was most assuredly European, with her vividly pale, freckled skin, strawberry-ginger hair, and tall stature, despite the fact she was dressed unconventionally for either bazaar or bungalow. She wore a pale gray muslin *angrezi* frock, but her head and shoulders were swathed in a bright orange silk veil that matched her hair and formed an arching halo about her head as the hot breeze lifted the translucent material, giving her the appearance of an otherworldly, Hindu-influenced, Renaissance madonna. Half-forgotten tales from schoolbooks flooded his mind—of Boadicea, the pagan Celtic queen, or the warrior goddess Freya, with her red-gold tears.

"*Huzoor,* what is thy pleasure?" A confused *sa'is,* one of the many Afghani and Balti grooms in his employ, had called to him, for Thomas had turned his mount toward the girl instinctively, moving away from his caravan without sparing a thought for the consequences.

She had looked up at him then, with her pale, clear gray eyes so composed and solemn, and something within him— the part of his soul that had unbeknownst to him grown weary of deception and restlessness—stilled and came to rest. Something within him whispered *home.*

He had tried to dismiss such a cock-brained notion. Home was wherever a man was content to lay his head, for however long that might be. It was wherever he could laugh with friends and be happy. And he was happy as Tanvir Singh, a creature of the road, a denizen of every town and village from the back of beyond to the front, and friend to everyone he met. He was no longer the Honorable Thomas Jellicoe to be staring at pretty English girls. He was a fierce, respected *sawar.* He ought to be mocking himself for even noticing such a pale *angrezi* woman.

Yet, how could he not? Tanvir Singh was a man, and any man—nay, every man in Rani Bazaar that day—had followed her pale, exotic beauty with his eyes. Memsahibs rarely found their way to the bazaars in the city, well outside the protected confines of the English cantonment, and certainly did not come alone, without a carriage or train of protective manservants to buffer them from contact with the teeming populace.

But that girl—for all her solemnity she could not have seen more than twenty summers—had seemed to have passed through the throng unmolested by the demands of merchants and beggars alike. As if they, too, could see she was a goddess from some cold, far-off northern place, come to vanquish the gods of the sweltering plains, and left her unprovoked.

He should have turned, or looked away, but he had held fast, transfixed by his vision and his inexplicable longing for something he had never experienced—the regard of an English girl. Because of her, for the first time in years, he felt *apart.* He felt all the weight of the double life, the work he had chosen of his own free will, settle heavily upon his shoulders.

And so he looked. At her solemn smile as she gazed in open admiration at his horses, at the pale, subtle apricot of her lips, at the bold shower of freckles across her face and nose from the sun. And at the promise of the endlessly long, white limbs hidden by the flowing folds of her skirts.

Limbs he thought about twining around his waist like a vine and . . .

Oh, yes. He didn't even know her name, yet he had been ridiculously, unaccountably, irreversibly smitten. And so he had contrived to give her the mare.

"I gave her a horse."

It was as good a place to start as any, but Thomas looked up to find his family regarding him as they had upon his arrival—as if he had contracted a rare and debilitating brain fever.

"Actually, or more correctly, I sold the animal, one of my prize Marwari mares, to her uncle, the resident commissioner, Lord Summers."

"Ah." His father narrowed his eyes and nodded. "I begin to see."

"See what?" James frowned and straightened up. "What do you see?"

"Lord Summers is, or was, the third son of the late Duke of Westing. Lord Summers was also—correct me if I am wrong—" he said aside to Thomas, "killed in India. A tragic fire, some two years ago, was it? There were some rumors of a tawdry love triangle, but it was all hushed up. He was Miss Cates's uncle?"

"It was Lady Summers who was Miss Cates's"—the name still felt awkward on his tongue—"mother's younger sister. And Lord and Lady Summers were both killed in the fire. Their home, Miss Cates's home, the residency of Saharanpur, was entirely consumed."

"How ghastly." James's face was tight with concern. "I had no idea. She never mentioned a word."

"I imagine she was too terrified. Both then and now." Thomas had been terrified as well, torn to shreds by the seething frustration of knowing she was alive, but not knowing where she was. Throughout the past two years, he had been unable to stop himself from imagining what it must have been like for her in the confused aftermath. He was still haunted by dark dream images playing out across his brain, over and over again, from when he had thought her dead. And he was still ripped up to find she no longer trusted him. So ripped up he had just accused her of inexcusable things. *As ruthless as a courtesan.* He was the one who ought to be shot. "Especially after she was accused."

"Miss Cates?" James foundered, caught between his clear fondness for his employee and the enormity of the accusation. "Of setting the fire that killed them? How could that be?"

"She was easy to accuse. There was no one to . . . speak on her behalf." Even now, even as he chose the careful words, his excuses sounded trite and unworthy. "She was accused and would have been charged. But by then, she had disappeared. And I've been looking for her ever since."

"Good Lord."

"Thomas." The immutable strength in the Earl Sanderson's voice brought them back to the inescapable issue at hand. "Did you believe her guilty?" he asked from his place in his chair. "*Do* you believe her guilty?"

Thomas shook his head. He had been told by the English authorities she was guilty—told the evidence was incontrovertible—until he *had* half believed some part of it might be true. And she had disappeared, another proof, it was said, of her guilt.

"No. She was not guilty." She could not have started the fire that the company men claimed she had set in order to cover up the murders of Lord and Lady Summers, for one simple reason. Because she had been with him—with Tanvir Singh—at the time.

But by the time Thomas had understood that he alone held the power of her deliverance, it was too late. She was gone without a trace.

"What I don't understand," James interjected into the silence, "is what all this has to do with your supposition that Miss Cates was being shot at. You are the missing penny here, Thomas. Nobody was being shot at until *you* turned up. From Liverpool, of all places. What else haven't you told us?"

"Everything." Thomas might have laughed, if he hadn't been so goddamned weary. So tired of carrying the incessant worry. Tired of the burden of his guilt. Tired of trying to figure it all out. And now that he'd found her, it seemed that instead of being resolved, the situation had become even more complicated. And dangerous. "There's simply too much to tell."

"Well, then, Thomas," his father prompted in his calm, unruffled voice. "Why don't you begin with the horse."

Chapter Five

The mare in question had been a three-year-old of his own breeding, in whom Rajput Marwari bloodlines were most prominent. She was a strong, high-spirited filly, but she had taken to the girl in the bazaar easily enough, eating an apple from her hand as familiarly as if she did so every morning, though the beastie had regularly torn strips out of the less nimble of the *sa'is*.

Thomas had been rather fond of her—the mare. She was beautiful, tall black with white socks, a delicate face that showed traces of Arabian blood, and the characteristic sweet, inward-pointing ears of the native Rajput Marwari breed. She was young and had not yet been bred—he would be sorry not to have the chance to breed her. But he came and went between Hindustan and the Punjab freely in his role as a Sikh horse trader—it was therefore necessary he actually *trade* in horses. And if he sold the mare to the girl of flame, he would be able to see her. And her mistress.

If he were honest—and he was not, he was a spy—the mare was merely an excuse, the means by which he had decided to satisfy his absurd curiosity without anyone being the wiser. Beautiful young women who appealed to him were thin on the ground in company cantonments on the edge of the frontier, and though the English kept quite largely to themselves, they would be astonished to know much of their daily lives was the fodder of open conversation throughout the bazaar and the whole of the city, and how many of their servants were happy to share the details of their lives for the cost of a bowl of rice. Tanvir Singh had only to keep his ears and his purse open to learn the bright young woman with the hair like flame and an incomprehensible, unpronounceable *angrezi* name was the niece of Lord Summers Sahib, the new resident commissioner of Saharanpur.

That news of a *new* resident commissioner had stung, like the venom from the bees high in the Himalayan caves—a small but burning hurt. It had surprised and wounded him to learn that Colonel Balfour had so summarily been replaced. That the only man Thomas had entrusted with his true identity had been so swiftly pushed aside. It stung Thomas's pride and offended his sense of loyalty.

And he had made up his mind, right there in the Rani Bazaar, to play a game with this new man. To toy with the man who was ostensibly Thomas's superior, by keeping him ignorant of Thomas's true identity. To Lord Summers, Tanvir Singh would be nothing more than he appeared to be—a nomadic native horse trader who kept his ear to the ground in exchange for steady remuneration.

If Thomas had been a prudent man, or if he had actually been the man he was supposed to be, he would have turned away there and then. Tanvir Singh would have closed his mind to all thoughts of a girl who was clearly forbidden to him. But he was also Thomas Jellicoe, the son of an English peer, and he liked a challenge. He was an independent, clandestine agent of the Great Game, who thrived on risk. What better, harmless game was there than to challenge the narrow conventions, and disrupt the false serenity of the company's grandees? He had laughed aloud at just the thought.

And the game had proved to be almost laughably easy. Lord Summers was rumored to be a man who liked his horses—one of his great pleasures in his assignment in

India was his polo. All Tanvir Singh had had to do was suggest, while mingling among the ranks of East India Company officers and sepoys who came to his encampment to bargain for horses, that he considered his prized mare, bred from an Arabian stallion and a Marwari dam, too fine for any of the Englishmen in Saharanpur. He would be taking her south to Delhi, or perhaps east to Ranpur, he said, to sell to a more discerning clientele.

Within a few short hours, the talk had made its rounds from the camp to the bazaar, and from the bazaar to the cantonment, whence Tanvir Singh was duly summoned by the express request of the resident commissioner himself, Lord Summers.

A request Thomas had blithely ignored.

Lord Summers, in the way of a great functionary, then sent his minions—his secretaries and undercommissioners of one sort and another—to try and treat with Tanvir Singh. But the wily *sawar* had serenely resisted their overtures, steadfastly refusing to let the emissaries so much as see his beautiful mare.

It was all a part of the greater game, this little game he played with the new resident commissioner, who came himself, of course, and at last.

Lord Summers, the third son of the Duke of Westing, brought himself to visit in the cool of the morning two days after Thomas and his caravan had arrived in Saharanpur, tooling across the bumpy ground of Tanvir Singh's encampment along the small tributary river to the north of the town in an open, unshaded carriage driven by a tightly liveried *sa'is*.

Lord Summers's appearance did little to dispel Thomas's first impression of him as altogether too much of the new style of company man to be entirely trusted. The old-style men, like his mentor, Colonel Balfour, who had cultivated a deep understanding and appreciation of Hindustan and her ways and customs, had been pushed aside for the likes of Summers, who was said to stride about speaking only English, and seemed indifferent, or even happy to give offense so long as he made money exploiting the native population and treating them like ignorant children, or worse, like savages who were unfit to rule their own country.

"And so you are Tanvir Singh, about whom I have heard so much," was Lord Summers's greeting, when the resident commissioner strode into Tanvir Singh's tent.

Thomas awaited them on his own terms, reclining on deep, pristinely white cushions beneath the shade of an open-air tent set in front a wide grassy area from whence he could observe his animals being brought forward for buyers' perusal. He did not rise, though he brought his palm up and made a shallow, courtly salaam. "As thou may see, Excellency."

The resident's layers of tight-fitting English clothing—high-collared shirt and cravat under a waistcoat and jacket, so unsuitable to the climate even in the easy heat of the morning—made him look uncomfortably pop-eyed and waspish. The impression of a fussy autocrat wasn't aided by the fact that the resident was accompanied by a scarlet-clad officer of the company's Saharanpur regiment, the deputy assistant commissary, Lieutenant Birkstead.

Thomas inclined his head slightly to the officer. "Lieutenant sahib."

Neither the lieutenant, whom Thomas had met once or twice before, when he had last made his way to Saharanpur with important intelligence for the company, nor the resident commissioner returned the civility. Instead the lieutenant gave Tanvir Singh a contemptuous look meant to show his superiority, but which revealed his discomfort in this situation over which he had so little control.

Thomas was too used to such impotent snubs to give them any attention. Despite the fact that he had once been very much like Birkstead—young and wanting to make his mark—he couldn't like the junior officer. He was far too insinuating, too much the bullyboy for Thomas's tastes, and he was spoken ill of in the bazaar. And from what Thomas had heard, he thought it singularly unwise of Lord Summers to trust Birkstead.

Lord Summers wasted no time on what he clearly saw as peculiar, time-wasting, Oriental preliminaries. "I understand you have a very fine mare for sale."

"I have many fine war mares, Excellency." Thomas swept his arm to encompass the large encampment. "And I have sold many to thy regiment. But please, I invite thee to come and sit, and take thy leisure so we might talk of business."

Lord Summers was happy to walk under the shade of the colorful canvas awning, but he was ill at home on the low cushions. He settled precariously on the edge of a large tufted pillow. "This mare, I have heard, is special."

"Ah." Thomas gave Lord Summers a quiet smile but said nothing more while he occupied himself in pouring small glasses of thick, aromatic Arabic coffee. Birkstead chose not to sit, but to remain standing behind Lord Summers, in what the young officer no doubt thought was a manly, intimidating fashion.

Lord Summers smiled back at Thomas, content in thinking Tanvir Singh surprised. "I have my sources, you see. I hear everything."

Everything Thomas had intended for him to hear, at least. He inclined his head in a small nod of acknowledgment to Summers. "I have heard some things also. It is said in the marketplace that the lord sahib is a great admirer of a fine horse. Wilt thou take some refreshment?"

"Is it said? I thank you." Summers was polite, or politic enough to take the small glass and sip at it, even though it was clearly not to his taste. Yet Lord Summers could not hide the small flush of pride that rose from under his chin, though he waved the purported compliment aside. "Well, I daresay bazaar gossip is cheaply come by."

"As thou sayest," Thomas continued in his unruffled, easy way. "But no one in the bazaar, nor even in all the district of Saharanpur, has such an animal as I, Excellency."

"You think so, do you?" When Thomas again made no answer but a small inclination of his head, Summers politely changed tack. "I suppose I'd be very much obliged if you would let me have a look at her."

Thomas had to give the man credit. While the new resident wasn't a Colonel Balfour, and had none of that man's knowledge and affinity of Hindustan, Lord Summers was perhaps not solely the pompous, belligerent caricature Thomas would have made him out to be. The lieutenant, on the other hand, looked decidedly perturbed by the resident commissioner's deigning to use his good manners on a native.

Thomas decided to be tolerant. The honeybee came only to the sweet flowers, and Thomas wanted honey. "As thou wishes, sahib." He motioned to the *sa'is* to bring the mare forward.

Like a princess who knows exactly what to do with the weight of curious eyes upon her, the animal pricked up her ears and picked her regal way across the grass, seeming to look down her long, elegant nose directly at Lord Summers with her large, intelligent eyes.

Thomas said no more, and simply let Summers look. Tanvir Singh had long ago learned better than to bait his trap too heavily.

"Mmm. Very nice." Lord Summers made a low murmur of admiration as the *sa'is* set the mare working on a long lunge line. "Is she broken?"

"Trained for the saddle with excellent gaits for riding. Very, very fine. I fear she is much too fine for regimental use, Excellency. I have an esteemed client in Gwalior who will find such a mare to be a fitting gift for his favorite wife."

The resident watched silently for a long time while the groom slowly worked the mare through her paces, before he commented. "I see what you mean by her fineness. Which is ideal. I've an idea of her being for a young lady—my Lady Summers's niece."

Thomas felt both elation and a perverse disappointment at so easily steering the powerful Englishman to his purpose. To this easily manipulated man, he was to entrust his intelligence of what he was sure was a coming war in the Punjab? The thought did not comfort.

"Your niece?" Behind the new resident commissioner's shoulder, Lieutenant Birkstead was frowning in a way that told Thomas the lieutenant thought he had missed something—some chance to profit by this new information.

"Oh, didn't you know?" the resident answered casually. "We've a new addition to the household, Birkstead. Lady Summers's late sister's girl. Scots-Irish, you know, but surprisingly lovely and very, very obliging. Been with us a few weeks or so now. Been a godsend—she's wonderful with the children, and I admit to being quite taken with her, as well. Manages everything just so, to spare her aunt the difficulty and trouble. The climate, you understand, does not agree with Lady Summers."

Thomas's well-trained ear was trying to parse the exact amount of affection the resident commissioner had conceived for his new niece-in-law, while his inquisitive eye caught something more than a smirk in the expression on the lieutenant's face, revealed only to him behind the commissioner's back. Something sharp and cold, and much more calculating.

Although Thomas had never been introduced to Lady Summers, he had seen and taken note of her. Much was said of her in the bazaar, most of it unflattering. Lady Summers, it was said, was typical of that breed of *angrezi* memsahib laid low, or at least given excuse for her indolence, by the extremes of the climate. It was said, as freely in the cantonment as in the bazaar, that she didn't give a farthing for the upbringing of her children, as she made sure her life intersected but rarely with theirs. It was said she saved all of her inconsiderable energies for pursuing her social life, with or without the company of her husband. It was also said the lieutenant sahib figured prominently in that social life.

Lord Summers appeared to be oblivious to such rumors. Perhaps he was more interested in "being taken" with the more subtle charms of his niece-in-law?

A haze of red heat spread upward from Thomas's lungs until it filled his body with an unfamiliar rage—frustrated ire at the thought of that beautiful, pale, flaming goddess of a girl with such an unworthy man, an obtuse functionary who was old enough to be her father, and who ought to have been acting like one, instead of like a dirty old gaffer.

It was all Thomas could do to force his mind and his unwilling body into obedience, and back to the task at hand. "A *young* English lady? Excellency, surely thou canst see that this mare is too spirited an animal for a young person."

"She is a very good rider, you may be assured. Very used to horses. Has a way about her. You needn't be concerned. I'm thinking she will do well by your mare." Lord Summers turned back to speak confidentially to Birkstead, though he did not lower his voice appreciably. "Now, you'll tell me whatever price is correct for a transaction of this nature so this mountain devil doesn't take advantage of me, won't you, Lieutenant?"

"My dear sir," the lieutenant promised. "I will most assuredly see to it that he gives you better than a fair price. But frankly, I don't see why we should have to deal for these native *ponies* at all." He said the word dismissively, as if the bloodlines of Tanvir Singh's fine horses were not apparent to one and all. "We can very well send for animals with better bloodlines from the company stud at Ghazipur."

Idiots, both of them. How could the lieutenant not know that it was Tanvir Singh who supplied breeding stock for the company stud as well? Like an unfortunate number of his countrymen, the lieutenant spoke as if he, Tanvir Singh, were not right there, no more than three feet away, sitting at his ease, sharing his hospitality with them. As if he were deaf, or just plain stupid, or incapable of understanding their language even as he spoke it. Such willful arrogance would one day very soon bring the Lieutenant Birksteads of the world, and their beloved East India Company, low. And they would deserve the end they got.

He could almost feel sorry for them. Almost.

"For a *fair price,*" Thomas used the same low, confidential tone, "I have also in my caravan twenty-three more horses, well trained, strong, and full of heart. All very fit for troop work in the mountains. Horses bred of the plains will not do well in the mountains. Their lungs are not accustomed to the air."

"Twenty-three only? The regiment has many sepoys to mount." Lord Summers looked up at Lieutenant Birkstead, as if he were seeking confirmation. As if he really did not know the exact number and strength and state of training of all the men under his ultimate command. Foolish man not to know such things. Foolish man to trust such things to the lieutenant.

And Thomas would show him why. "Alas, Excellency, I could not bring to Saharanpur any more. I found the majority of my war mares were needed in Lahore." He paused to give weight to the place-name, to see if the new resident commissioner would understand the implications before they were explained to him. "The stables of His Majesty the Maharajah Ranjiit Singh needs must be filled first. And as the maharajah seems to have a very great need for strong mountain-bred horses at present, he is perhaps not as careful with his coin, in the way of the lord sahibs of the English cantonment."

Lord Summers began to pleat his florid face into a frown. "Is he, now?"

"These fellows are all alike, my lord," Birkstead warned. "They think they can squeeze a bit more from John Company's fist."

Thomas felt a curl of pleasure at the thought of illustrating for the lieutenant just what sort of fellow he really was beneath his suntanned skin. Rank always held an inordinate sway for men like Birkstead. But even without rank, Thomas had his ways. "The Lord Summers Sahib must know there are many other buyers for my excellent horses. Why should I want to travel all the way here, when there are buyers aplenty just now in the Kingdom of the Punjab? The word in the streets and stables of Lahore is that His Majesty the Maharajah Ranjiit Singh is gathering his armies against his upstart enemies in the north and east, and he and his generals will have need of many, many mountain-bred horses."

"Does he?" Lord Summers's eyes flicked sharply to Thomas, narrowed with shrewd attention. Finally. "You begin to intrigue me, Tanvir Singh. And what else do you hear in the stables of the maharajah?"

"As thou begins to understand me, Excellency. Perhaps the lieutenant sahib would like to make a more careful inspection of the mare to assure himself that she is not a *pony*"—Thomas gave his pronunciation of the word an amused, foreign emphasis—"but every bit as fine as promised, while Excellency and I talk of warhorses and of information."

A quiet quarter hour spent enjoying a plate of ripe fruit of the Doab while giving the commissioner detailed information about which of the maharajah's generals were leading which troops of exactly what strength made Tanvir Singh a very tidy profit. And without the lieutenant's sneering presence, Thomas could begin to appreciate some of the new resident commissioner's finer points—his keen intelligence and ability to understand the meaning of the information brought to him, without Thomas having to explain it. And yet he had still found it prudent not to tell Lord Summers everything about Tanvir Singh. Not yet.

It was pride, he supposed, goading him on. Pride and something far more insecure, which had him wanting to find out more about the resident's flame-gold niece from the safety of his disguised identity.

And then, having wrung more rupees from John Company's coffers than the resident commissioner had originally been prepared to give, Thomas indulged himself for such excellent work with the reward of delivering the mare himself.

The residency stood at the western side of the cantonment, itself a large district laid out on the other side of the thin ribbon of river that meandered like a loose seam along the frayed edge of the town. The residency was a newish, large red-brick mansion surrounded by deep, arched verandas, built in the boxy Birmingham-looking style favored by the English company men, and furnished exclusively with furniture and appointments brought from England, so its inhabitants might attempt to re-create their leafy English way of life as closely as possible without any reference to the world beyond their gates.

Thomas judged that a visit to the rigidly precise avenues of the cantonment called for a much higher level of sartorial display than even the boisterous trip through the bazaar, and so he took the time to change into a clean set of clothes—a richly woven, immaculate white tunic, and a turban of two entwined silk fabrics more suited to the supposedly elevated station of those he visited. And a waist sash of the same silk; to show off his gleaming *kirpan,* the ceremonial dagger he was never without.

No matter his attention to the proprieties, he and his *sa'is* were left to cool their heels outside the gate of the residency by the *darwan,* while that wide-eyed porter fetched the haughty *sircar* who had charge of the house, and who in turn finally admitted them to the stable yard of Lord Summers.

But once Tanvir Singh was admitted to the premises, Lord Summers did him the courtesy of coming out to greet him personally as Thomas rode into the wide yard astride his own tall mare. "Tanvir Singh, you have come yourself, have you?"

"Lord Summers Sahib." Thomas dismounted and gave him a salaam. "I worry that thou wilt find the mare too strong for thy young English lady, and ask me to take her back."

"Ha, ha. We shall see. We shall see." Lord Summers turned to the *sircar* hovering in the background. "Fetch memsab's niece, Miss Rowan, down."

The low heat of anticipation fired deep in his gut, and Thomas had to steel himself not to react when she came out not a moment later, blowing onto the veranda like a fresh breeze from the cool northern mountains.

"There you are, my dear." Lord Summers was holding his hands out in greeting.

She flew down the wide steps toward them, moving

swiftly from the darker shade of the veranda out into the dappled light of the yard with a falconlike directness and grace, a blur of bright, white movement.

Thomas made a small gesture of a salaam, his cupped hand rising to his chin, but he stilled at the sound of her long, liquid intake of breath. Even the mare turned her head toward the source, as transfixed as Thomas by the appearance of his flame-girl.

She was an even stranger creature close up—full of contradictions. She was full inches above Lord Summers, long and towering over him like an Amazon warrior—though she did not top Thomas's shoulder—but with a delicate, oval face. The shape brought to mind the exquisite faces of the Tibetans, with their beautiful wide eyes. But the color was completely wrong—pale white and flaming orange, and gray-blue ocean, as if someone had set England, pale Albion, on fire. She was an elvish warrior princess, a long-limbed dream of the Tuatha De Danann, some goddesslike pairing of the old Norse gods and a swan.

Damn him for a jackal. He was acting as if he had inhaled too much of the heady hashish smoke that wafted from the tombs near where his caravan had camped on the outskirts of the town. He must be hallucinating to turn a simple girl into a swan goddess. And a man like Tanvir Singh wasn't supposed to even know about Norse or Celtic gods.

Lord Summer took her outstretched hand. "Catriona, my dear."

Catriona. Thomas repeated the name in the quiet of his mind, swirling the taste of it around in his mouth like a tart pomegranate seed.

"I have a surprise for you." Lord Summers gestured to the mare like a magician, as if he, and not Thomas, had conjured the animal out of desert heat and mountain mist for her pleasure alone. "What do you think of her?"

Catriona Rowan went quietly to the mare's head with the same graceful directness with which she had come down the stairs, but less of the speed. She alighted like a hawk in front of the mare, quiet and watchful, offering herself to the animal for inspection while she whispered calm nothings in her ears. Next to the glossy dark of the mare, this Catriona appeared even more colorful, more bright and vivid, more alive in the dappled shade of her uncle's courtyard than she had in the pressing heat of the bazaar. And like any fire, he could feel her heat the closer she got.

"Oh, but she is not a surprise, my lord. For we already know each other, don't we, my beauty?" She spoke to the animal, as much as to answer Lord Summers. "We met in the bazaar."

There was a faint, musical lilt to her voice that matched the symphony of color created by her hair and eyes. Scots-Irish, her uncle had said. The source of her translucent flame.

She was gazing at the mare in a direct, almost reverent way, and did not see the tinge of surprise creep its way across her uncle-in-law's full cheeks.

"Do you mean to say you were in the cantonment bazaar, or out in the city? My dear, I should caution you to be careful of going adventuring about the city. Your aunt should have warned you against that, for your safety." Lord Summers shook his head in admonishment. "Not at all the thing to wander the native bazaar alone. There is no reason for you to go amongst them. If there is anything you require, you have merely to send a servant to do your bidding in your stead."

Thomas turned aside his own reaction to the implied insult, and let it slide off his back like so much dirty water, because he happened to agree with Lord Summers. Unescorted young women of any creed or race should not be going adventuring without an able escort. The kind of escort he would be more than happy to provide.

But Miss Catriona Rowan, she of the flaming hair and perhaps equally colorful temper, was not so easy with her uncle's gentle command. Her cheeks flushed the color of a sweet blood orange at the rebuke, however mild it had been, and her solemn mouth narrowed ever so slightly. And instead of casting her eyes down and demurring to her uncle's advice like any good, obedient English girl, she astonished Thomas by an almost imperceptible straightening of her spine before she turned to regard him directly, her gray eyes as keen and true as a knife blade, even as she spoke to Lord Summers, behind her.

"I beg your pardon, Uncle. But I'm afraid it's too late to avoid the acquaintance, as I have already met both the *sawar* Tanvir Singh and his horse. How do you do today, *huzoor*?" She copied his gesture of salaam, and then she put out her hand for him to shake.

For all the world as if he were an Englishman. As if they were two gentlemen together, bargaining over a horse at Tattersall's, and not a fey swan of a girl and a browned Sikh horse trader who ought to be nothing but a servant to her. And why was he thinking of something so ridiculous and far off as Tattersall's? It was entirely out of character, not to mention dangerous. Tanvir Singh should not know, or even care, that Tattersall's existed.

Yet, despite his years of training, and despite Lord Summers's astonishment, Thomas's hand seemed to swing toward her of its own volition, without consulting his head as to the propriety of shaking the hand of an unmarried *angrezi* girl, or the advisability of antagonizing the new resident commissioner with such familiarity. If he chose, Lord Summers could have even as useful a man as Tanvir Singh shot, or at the very least horsewhipped within an inch of his life, for daring to so much as look at his niece, before Thomas might have a chance to prove his true identity.

But all his mind and body wanted was to indulge in the pleasure that would come from touching her, however briefly. Just a touch. Just once.

And he was not disappointed. She shook his hand with a single, firm grip that was far, far removed from the soft, boneless fish of a handshake most women offered up to a man. Within his own large, callused hand, hers was small but strong, her grip sure.

One firm shake, and then it was done. She let go.

But it was as if he had touched icy fire. His hand was the opposite of numb—it was nothing but feeling, as if every sensation in his body had migrated to his palm and left it vibrating.

Oh, yes. He was smitten.

As intoxicated by her regard as if he *had* smoked hashish. But to save them both a horsewhipping, he bowed respectfully, pressing his hands together in front of his chest in *namaste*. "Thou hast done me a great honor, Memsahib Rowan."

"As do you, *huzoor*." She nodded solemnly and copied his gesture before she turned back to the mare, who pivoted and swished her tail daintily, preening for Catriona Rowan. "You know very well what a treasure you've brought to my Lord Summers."

The mare's flirtatious caprices had them turning, shielding them from Lord Summers's direct view, and Thomas could not keep himself from confiding in a low voice meant only for Catriona Rowan's ears, "I did not bring her for my Lord Summers, memsahib. In fact, I did not bring her at all—*she* hast brought me to find thee for her mistress. She has chosen *thee*."

For the briefest moment, her serious, composed face was surprised into astonishment. A deep flood of color stained her cheeks—clearly, she was not used to even so mild a flirtation. But she rallied, rising to the challenge. Thomas thought he could see the beginnings of pleasure warm the corners of her gray eyes, and she was almost smiling when she turned back to the mare, an almost imperceptible, secret curving of marmalade lips.

"Oh, you are *very* good, *huzoor*. And does she do all your bargaining for you as well, clever girl that she is?"

He wanted to throw back his head and laugh, until she laughed as well. He wanted to charm the smile full across her face, until her lips parted with mirth and—

"My dear?" Lord Summers interjected himself back into the conversation before Thomas could do any of the unpardonable things he was thinking of doing with Catriona Rowan's mouth. "What do you think, my dear? Will she do for you?"

"She's absolutely marvelous, and she knows her own worth. Don't you, you gorgeous, proud creature?"

The mare rubbed her nose agreeably against the girl's hand, as if in confirmation of this obvious fact.

"What do you say to giving her a trial? If you don't find her gaits to your liking," the lord commissioner mused aloud, "then perhaps I might see if Lady Summers would like the animal for a carriage—if she's docile enough. Or perhaps we could sell her on to one of the Fielding chits. What are their names?"

"Oh, no, no." Catriona Rowan protested before her uncle could find his answer. "No. She shan't be put to a carriage. She is very much to my liking. Now that I've been lucky enough to be offered such an animal as this, I shall never consent to be parted from her."

It was strangely dramatic—the heartfelt insistence of her oath—but it was exactly what Thomas wanted to hear. And her uncle as well.

"Well, then, my dear." Lord Summers was all beaming indulgence, pleased that his gift had met with such approval. "You shall have her."

Thomas was rewarded by the sight of her smile, as small as it was genuine, like a single shaft of light, illuminating her gravity with quiet joy—an arrow silently piercing the armor of his assumed identity.

Yet, Catriona Rowan was serenely oblivious to the havoc she was creating within him. "Thank you, Uncle. You are most kind. I will treasure her."

But then she astonished them all again by turning back to Tanvir Singh, spitting in her palm, and holding it out to him. Just as if they were two men, not at Tattersall's but in a Scottish village square, confirming their deal in time-honored, masculine fashion.

Oh, but there was nothing, nothing masculine about her. They were more than a world away from Scotland, and she was everything fey and delicate and female, and everything forbidden to Tanvir Singh.

But he could no more resist the chance to touch her again than he could carry her away across the wide desert, or ride with her into the cool mountains, or dance with her at a London ball. So he did her the honor of spitting into his own hand, and once more grasping hers in his own, sealing their pact.

And with it, sealing his fate.

Chapter Six

Catriona took the narrow, twisting steps of Wimbourne Manor's servants' stair two at a time. She had to make haste. She had to move now, while the household was still at sixes and sevens. While she was alone and free to go. Before anyone could stop her. Or kill her.

If Lord Jeffrey's groundsmen were chasing tracks to the south, she would go north. There was a mail coach that came through the village at two o'clock every afternoon that would take her north to Windsor and from there east toward London and the docks. There was time enough to catch that.

Or if she missed it, she would simply find a farm cart going east toward the forest. Anywhere but south. If asked along the road, she would concoct some likely story about going on to London after leaving an imaginary sailor husband at Portsmouth.

It ought to shame her, the ease and willingness with which she thought up such lies. It really ought. But honesty was a luxury she could no longer afford. Not now, not really in India, and certainly not before that, in Scotland. Oh, no. Every year it had become even harder and more expensive to cleave to the truth.

Despite her normal state of fitness, bolstered by long walks and plenty of exuberant play with the children,

Catriona was winded by the time she reached the sanctuary of the lovely, light-filled suite of rooms Lady Jeffrey had created for her charges at the top of the house. Or perhaps it was just the shock of seeing Tanvir Singh—who was really Thomas Jellicoe—that had her pausing to catch her breath in the doorway of the schoolroom.

The room was quiet now that it was empty of the children, almost serene. Oh, but she liked it better when it wasn't serene, when they were having loud discussions, when the room hummed with young energy. Catriona was bitterly proud of all she had accomplished there. Of the work that covered the walls—the botanical specimens, the time line of English kings, and the map of the county hung with the flagged pins of all the places she and the children had visited and explored together—but most especially of the bonds she had created with the children. It was a terrible, bitter wrench to have to leave it. To have to leave them.

To leave another family.

Catriona had to dash some reprehensible wetness from her eyes—she refused to call it tears. Refused. Sentiment was another luxury she could ill afford.

"Miss?" Annie Farrier, one of the upstairs maids, hurried down the corridor. "Lady Jeffrey sent me to bring you to her rooms."

Catriona turned away from the schoolroom and took a deep, steadying breath. And with it she drew on Miss Anne Cates's cheerful composure as if it were a sensible, well-made cloak. "Of course, Annie. Thank you. Will you be so kind as to let her ladyship know I'll be down to see her as soon as I have put myself to rights? I'm sure my face is smirched with dirt, and as for my hat—" She plucked at the knotted and mangled ribbons hanging from her throat. "I very much fear it's ruined beyond all hope of restoration."

"Oh, no, miss. Surely not." Annie reached out and carefully dusted something off the brim. "Just a good brushing, a bit of steam, and new ribbon, and it'll be right as rain. You'll recover it yet."

"Thank you. I hope you're right. It would be a shocking

waste, would it not, to lose a hat so fine?" It was not in actuality a fine hat. It was a merely ordinary hat. But it was her *only* hat. A hat she had purchased in Paris with the hush money the dowager Duchess Westing had left for her—just left it, the heavy purse, with the same casual accident with which the shrewd old woman had also left behind an expensive pair of gloves. Gloves which Catriona had also kept to cover her browned and blistered hands. She could ill afford not to. Pride was another luxury, as expensive as the truth.

And there was still enough of the thrifty, sharp-eyed Scotswoman Catriona Rowan under Miss Anne Cates's erudite English accent to want to preserve the investment she had made in the tattered hat. And if she were going to buy passage on a ship to the Americas, she couldn't be splashing her hard-earned wages about on anything so frivolous as a new hat.

But the hat was not her problem, really. Whether or not to obey Lady Jeffrey's summons was. As was deciding what she might possibly say to her mistress. Which convenient half-truth she should select, like an arrow from her quiver of lies.

Every instinct Catriona possessed was jumping up and down for attention like one of her overexcited charges, clamoring for her to leave immediately. And over the past few years, she had learned to her detriment never to ignore her instincts. They had been all that had kept her alive. But there were things she must do first. Responsibilities to complete. Debts to repay.

"Thank you, Annie. Please tell her ladyship I'll be along as soon as may be." Her fingers worked at the tangled ribbons, but her hands had begun to shake so that she only tightened the knots.

"Are you all right, miss?" Annie was wide-eyed with a sort of terrified wonder that calm, collected Miss Cates should exhibit such human frailty. "It must have given you an awful fright, out there on the lawn. We could hear the shots from all the way back in the kitchens."

"Yes. I'm fine," Catriona lied again, and then amended her statement in the face of her patent tremors. "Rather, I will be fine in a moment. If you'll just tell her ladyship to give me a few minutes?"

"Yes, miss." Annie bobbed another curtsy, and with a kind, pitying smile, took herself back down the stairs.

Disdain she might endure, but never pity. Catriona crossed the sitting room, past the deep-cushioned window seats which were so perfect for reading, and past the cheerful, thoughtfully low furniture suitable for children, to enter her own bright, comfortable bedchamber. As with the other rooms in the nursery wing, Lady Jeffrey had seen to the fitting out of the room herself, insisting that Miss Cates should have everything she needed to be comfortable—a wide, soft bed thick with eiderdowns, an elegant writing desk in front of the tall dormer window, and bookcases filled with as many books as she could read. Generous to a fault was Lady Jeffrey.

And Catriona had answered that generosity with gratitude and determined hard work. And her earnestness had been rewarded by her ladyship's trust, and the enthusiastic devotion of her charges. But now she had stayed too long. She had put these generous, giving people and their children into danger by getting herself found.

Regret and apprehension needled at her more painfully than the broken stay digging into her side. And forced her to move. Catriona shook off the hat, and addressed her reflection in the small looking glass. She looked as if she had been dragged through a hedge backward. Which she had been.

But both vanity and sentimentality would have to wait. She was far better off thinking only of practical realities. Of how she was going to elude Thomas Jellicoe, and whoever else had found her, and get out of the house without being shot like a summer goose.

Catriona pushed the rising cloud of fear from her mind and crossed to her wardrobe. She canvassed the small collection of clothing stored within—three dresses, a cloak, one pair of well-mended half-boots. Not much for twenty-two years on earth. Not much to show for her life.

But it was enough.

She was only feeling alone and vulnerable. And quite literally bowled over by her encounter with the Honorable Thomas Jellicoe.

It would not do. Only decisive action would. Catriona pulled out the small traveling case tucked away at the bottom of the wardrobe—the cheap traveling case she had also purchased in Paris with the dowager duchess's funds, along with the trunk that sat at the end of her bed like an anchor, tying her to the past. But she could take only the small traveling case—the trunk would have to be left behind. She would take only the clothes she could carry, the money she had laboriously saved for just such an emergency, and her father's gun.

It had come a long way with her, that gun, her only possession to have survived both Scotland and India. She hadn't touched the piece lying at the bottom of the trunk since she had arrived at Wimbourne, and only then to move it when she had unpacked.

She took it up now, and set herself to loading it, but as she tried to make herself remember the once familiar task—she had checked the firing mechanism every day on the long journey from Saharanpur, and every day for the first year she had been back in England—her hands shook so much, she spilled some of the combustible black powder on the lid of the trunk.

And not only her hands were shaking. Her whole body had begun to tremble. Shock was lurching its clumsy way through her body, like an obnoxious drunk, knocking her knees out from under her and crashing into her middle, until she dropped the gun to the lid of the chest, and curled into herself, hugging herself tight.

She couldn't fall apart now. Not now. She would do so later, when everyone was safe. When *she* was safe. When she was aboard some ship, and battened down behind a sturdy door, and no one could see. When it didn't matter.

Catriona took a deep breath, and willed the chaotic tension to subside—an ache to nurse later, when the stakes were not as mortally high.

She chose her sturdiest clothes—even in summer, the rain could be drenching. Not that she had anything else but sturdy clothing—a sturdy, tightly woven wool cloak, sturdy, thick-soled boots, and sturdy, practical, unremarkable gowns in the dullest and plainest colors possible. Colors suitable for blending in with the walls or the ground or the rain. No wide, elegant gigot sleeves or lace for her. Nothing that would make her stand out, nothing to cause anyone to remark upon her in any way.

Anyone except the Honorable Thomas Jellicoe. "That horrid gray," he had said. "Always gray." She had not known wearing the dull hue had become such a habit. She had thought herself careful and vigilant and immune to foolish consistencies.

But never mind. She would be neither foolish nor consistent from now on. She would be inventive and clever. But above all, she would be fast. Fast enough to get away from both Thomas Jellicoe and her shooter.

"Miss Cates?"

Not fast enough. The knock at the door startled her into a hot, guilty flush of heat. It was the quiet voice of Lady Jeffrey, who had grown tired of waiting for her employee to obey her summons.

Catriona hastily shoved the traveling case back into the depths of the wardrobe, and went to the door. "My lady." She stepped out of the room to find her elegant employer pacing anxiously in the little sitting room of the nursery suite, though Lady Jeffrey looked as beautiful and flawlessly dressed as ever in a fresh walking dress of rich blue silk that deepened the lavender of her eyes. In the face of such solicitous perfection, Catriona's flimsy vanity reasserted itself. She curtsied politely to her mistress, but her hands had gone instinctively to her hair, pushing the wispy, flyaway bits that had come loose behind her ear in an attempt to reestablish Miss Anne Cates's unruffled, calm demeanor. "My apologies, Lady Jeffrey. I thought to collect myself and wash before—"

"No matter, my dear Miss Cates." Lady Jeffrey's words came out in a quiet rush as she reached out to clasp Catriona's hands. "I only wanted to assure myself you were unharmed. I have been so worried."

"As have I, my lady. The children—they are all unharmed as well? All to rights?"

"As well as can be expected. I stayed with them until we were all calmer, but they were worried about you. I assured them as best I could, and sent them all up for warm baths"—she gestured to the rising background noise of water and the murmurs of the nursery maids as tubs were being filled in the bathing chamber at the far end of the passageway—"to distract them so I could see you for myself, and assure myself *you* were quite all right."

"I am, my lady, I thank you. But you must not concern yourself with me."

A shaky sigh eased out over Lady Jeffrey's smile. "Of course I must. I am so very relieved. I must tell you, I feared the worst. Please, let us be more comfortable." She gestured to the chairs in the nursery sitting room. "I have asked for some tea to be sent up for you—and here is Moore with it now. Thank you, Moore—and ordered the fire lit. A shock can take people cold, so I'm told by my sister, and sweet, hot tea, so I'm also told by her, is the best remedy. A great one for always knowing just what to do in a crisis, my sister, Antigone." Lady Jeffrey linked her arm with Catriona's to draw her across the nursery sitting room toward the warmth of the fire and the comfort of the softly upholstered chairs.

Catriona could not but be grateful for such solicitous care. For the lady to concern herself so deeply with a mere employee was touching. "You are too kind, my lady. Truly."

And such kindness could not be repaid by excuses or evasion. Whatever her affinity and fondness for lies, Catriona could not evade such openness and generosity. Now was the time to speak, while they were alone, and her disgrace could be kept private.

Catriona swallowed over the pulse thumping in her throat. "My lady, in light of today's events, I feel it only right that I should offer you my resignation, and leave you."

Lady Jeffrey's answer was as immediate as it was sure. "I won't hear of it. What would we do without you? What will Mariah—" The lady's voice became hot and high, heated by the rising swell of her own emotions, and Lady Jeffrey reached over to clasp Catriona's hand tight. "I beg you would reconsider, Miss Cates, please. If it is Lord Jeffrey's brother that concerns you, put him from your mind. I will not let his unruly behavior discommode you. I will *not*. The children are too important."

"But he is your husband's family, my lady," Catriona reminded her gently. "He is your brother."

Lady Jeffrey shook her head vehemently, her normally serene face tight with disagreement. "And as such, he is an esteemed visitor here. But a visitor still. This is *your* home, not his. I hope you do feel it is your home, that you are welcome here always?"

It was as hard to swallow over the hot tightness in her own throat as it was to persist in the face of such sweet determination. "You are very kind, my lady. And I thank you, from the bottom of my heart. Please don't think that I *want* to leave you. This *has* been my home. But the danger—"

"Put it from your mind. We will keep you safe. I have every confidence Lord Jeffrey will keep us *all* safe. You need not have any fear, my dear Miss Cates, that we would not protect you. You must know you are too valuable to Wimbourne. You have restored our daughter to us."

She meant little Mariah, of course. "Restore" was a generous, though perhaps incorrect, word when applied to dear Mariah. There was no avoiding the fact that the poor child had some great debility of mind. She would never be as the other children were, but she was perhaps less locked into the tower of her own mind than she had been when

Catriona had arrived. She no longer pulled her hair out, or howled inconsolably, or smeared herself with her food, but she still walked only on her tiptoes, her gaze often unfocused and vague, and her body swaying rhythmically from side to side, as if she danced to some enchanted music only she could hear.

But then again, Catriona had seen to it that the poor mite was no longer forced to endure the punishing regime of cold baths some benighted idiot of a doctor had prescribed, and she was no longer shut off from her brothers and sisters, or tied to her cot like an animal on a leash. There was nothing extraordinary, nor particularly insightful, about Catriona's work with the little girl, but under compassionate, sensible care, it was no wonder the sweet child had made improvements. And it was no wonder Lady Jeffrey was deeply, deeply grateful.

It wrenched Catriona's heart to think of leaving Mariah, of leaving them all—Jack, and the twins, Pippa and Gemma, young Christopher, stalwart Amelia, all the way to darling baby Annabel—but staying at Wimbourne would put Mariah and all of them in danger. Especially Mariah. She was more vulnerable than the others, more sensitive to anything amiss or upsetting in her world.

God knew, gunshots in one's garden were more than upsetting to even the most normal of persons—if ever there was an excuse for all-out hysteria, getting shot at during a garden party was one of them.

"As much as it pains me to leave, my lady, I cannot allow any of the children to be put into danger. I will leave detailed instruction for Mariah's care and tuition—as I will for all the children. I've made a very thorough plan of education for each child, as well as notes on each child's progress and ability. You need have no fear that any future governess will not be readily able to follow my instruct—"

"Miss Cates, did my brother-in-law importune you?"

The bald question surprised her. Catriona took a long moment to consider how best to answer—there was no sense in lying, not when Thomas Jellicoe was downstairs this very moment, ready to contradict her—when Lady Jeffrey answered for her.

"Of course he did. Speaking to you like that, mistaking you for another. And then the whole distressing scene on the lawn." Her ladyship closed her eyes as if she could blot out the memory. "I fear his presence here is very upsetting to you. I will admit it is to me. Here is a man whom I have not seen since my wedding some fifteen years ago—fifteen years. How can it be so long? But now Thomas comes home and immediately bullets start flying. It is most unsettling and importuning."

Thomas Jellicoe had done more than merely unsettle or importune her. He had kissed her so thoroughly she had all but forgotten her own name. And she had kissed him back. She had closed her eyes and fallen headfirst into the bittersweet pain of her infatuation for him. It was as if she had learned nothing at all. As if she were still the same hopeful girl she had been that night in the garden at Colonel Balfour's walled palace.

She could not think about that time without pain. Her memories of the place were so caught up with her tangled emotions that she often felt that she must have dreamt it all. Dreamt the color and the perfume, the heat and dust. Dreamt the love and joyful affection. Dreamt of being so happy.

It had even felt like a dream that night in Saharanpur, when she had been invited to her first grown-up party.

Oh, she had been so terribly excited. Catriona had never been invited to a party of any kind before—there had been no thought, no time or money for such things in Scotland. But Lord and Lady Summers socialized regularly—nearly every night there was some kind of function or another, often in the cool, high-ceilinged rooms of the residency itself. But until that night, Catriona had been content to remain an observer only to the parties and soirees, peeking over the railing at the top of the great house where the nursery was located, down the two floors to the spacious, candlelit hall below. She and her cousins had watched the elegant men and refined women, the lords and ladies in their beautiful gowns and sparkling jewels as they gathered and mingled and chatted. From so high above, their voices had risen up as one excited murmur, a cushion of sound that filled up the echoing space with its energy and glamour.

And it had been more than enough just to watch and listen. It had made her happy to look without ever once thinking to partake. Her life in Saharanpur had already seemed too enchanted, too full of ease and the loving companionship of her young cousins to wish for anything more.

But that night, her thoughtful new uncle decided that she was to be included in the invitation to an event—an evening dinner party at the home of the mysterious Colonel Balfour, the preceding resident commissioner, to welcome and fete the new resident. Lord Summers had insisted, and Aunt Lettice had bestirred herself enough to see to it that Catriona was properly fitted out. She was in a new dress made by a British seamstress, Mrs. MacElroy, a sergeant major's clever wife who kept a store of the latest fashion plates—"latest" being a relative term in the hinterlands of the frontier—in her small bungalow, and a small group of Indian seamstresses in her even smaller back room to carry out the work.

Catriona remembered that exquisite dress as if she had just folded it carefully into her traveling case—embroidered gauze with a tiny, satin-sashed waist, and elaborate, wide sleeves decorated in delicate hand embroidery and cutwork in demure, dewy debutante's white that Mrs. MacElroy had tea-stained, "To look just so with your fair, fair skin."

And, oh, how it had suited her. Catriona had felt like a fairy princess with such sleeves as wide as angel's wings.

And she remembered being filled with a sort of optimism that she hadn't felt in years, since her mother had died and all the warmth and easy comfort had disappeared from her life. Her excitement—the giddy combination of anticipation and expectation fluttering around in her stomach like butterflies drunk on nectar—had carried her up to the strange, dark, battered door of Colonel Balfour's home.

It hadn't looked like much from the outside, that crumbling wall and creaking wooden gate that the English children whispered hid a house as haunted as any Gothic castle, but behind the massive portal was a scene straight out of Scheherazade's tales. Once through the outer gate, Catriona had been enchanted to find they were within the walls of an ancient Mughal palace so beautiful, she was sure she had taken a wrong turn and walked uninvited into the very garden of paradise.

The first courtyard led on to another, and every courtyard was filled with sinuous palms and lemon trees laden with bright fruit. Everywhere she looked a thousand and one blazing torches illuminated walkways and bubbling fountains. And across the central garden courtyard, across the twinkling pools and night-blooming flower beds, was a tiered pavilion—floor upon floor stacked up like a wedding cake upon pillars. There were no walls to speak of— the spaces between the carved stone pillars were hung with jewel-toned curtains in shimmering silks and transparent gauze that fluttered in the evening breeze. Some of those curtained spaces were set with wide, white cotton mattresses, and colorful bolster cushions and pillows in the Oriental fashion, while others contained furniture that could have graced a duke's drawing room.

Above on a gallery sat a group of musicians playing a low, vibrating, insistent music that danced along with the beat of her pulse. And in the center of the pavilion the curtains had been hung to create an airy central dining room, complete with a mahogany table so long Catriona was sure the King of England himself did not have one so large at Windsor Palace.

Everywhere around her was color and music and movement. Catriona had never seen anything so beautiful and so intrinsically, alluringly exotic.

She had stood stock-still in breathless awe, bewitched by the flowing, liquid beauty of the night.

"Well, look at you." Her uncle had smiled indulgently at

her. "If you aren't the prettiest young lady at the dinner party, I shall eat my hat instead of whatever strange curry old Colonel Balfour will feed us. I daresay it will taste about the same!"

Catriona had laughed and blushed, and said something thankful and demure, and let her uncle take her arm on one side, and his wife's on the other, to escort them toward the pavilion. "With you looking like that," Lord Summers said with an indulgent smile, "we shall have to beat off all the young men vying for your hand. But we shall be very choosy."

"My dear Lord Summers." Her aunt had loosened a languid little laugh. "There is no need for such great haste. I, for one, am in no hurry to see dear Catriona leave us so soon—she has only just arrived." Her aunt turned to Catriona in kind, if condescending, explanation. "The children already love you so, I do not know how they ever did without you. Indeed, I shouldn't like to do without you ever again. You do remind me of my own dear sister so."

The night had been so full of magic that Catriona had chosen not to take umbrage at her aunt's subtly patronizing tone, or think about Aunt Lettice's motives in making such a speech. She had chosen instead to be charmed and grateful for their very real generosity. "You have been so very kind to me."

"And what do you think, Lettice, about Henry Carruthers?" Lord Summers dealt out potential bridegrooms like cards from a deck. "Or my secretary, Mr. George Lamont?"

"My dear sir." Aunt Lettice had laughed again, a little huff of amused dismissal. "Such a pea goose of a man."

"Not dashing enough for our pretty niece? Ah, I know just the man. How about Lieutenant Birkstead for her? Eh?" He nudged Catriona affectionately. "That would be the catch of the country, would it not? And a very good match for him as well, for I mean to see that our pretty niece has a fortune to go with her lovely face."

"Sir!" Catriona had been astonished at this unlooked-for good fortune. "You are too kind."

"Well." Aunt Lettice's laugh was less amused than it was dismissive. "Oh, he has dash, the lieutenant, to be sure. But I hardly think such a man will do for our sweet little niece. Nor she for him."

Catriona had not heeded the undercurrent of scorn in her aunt's jaded tones. She was too grateful her relations were thinking of her at all in such a way, too happy in the thought that her new uncle would be so exceptionally generous, too pleased with the marvelously heady possibility she might find a husband to marry.

It was all part of the enchantment, the wondrous, giddy charm of that special evening.

Colonel Balfour had enhanced that charm by greeting them himself upon the steps of the pavilion, wearing a shining silk robe and plumed turban fit for a Mughal emperor. He looked everything kind and gracious and learned, and he bowed low over her hand like the most courteous of gentlemen, a cavalier of the old school.

And when she looked up from Colonel Balfour, there *he* was. The tall Sikh *sawar,* Tanvir Singh. Her secret storybook prince.

There had been nothing of the rogue in him that night. Nothing of sly amusement turning up the corners of his eyes or widening his bright slashing smile. But there was everything of the noble *huzoor.* Tanvir Singh stood upon the steps of the pavilion attired almost entirely in crimson. There was no other word that better described the shining, deep, deep red silk tunic belted at the waist with a sash of white shot through with gold threads. Above his dark hair he wore a turban of the same white silk, a bright contrast to the glowing tan of his skin.

He bowed his head to her in a gorgeous, courtly salaam, and she felt a sort of giddy triumph at having merited so much of his attention. He was so unlike all the others there. He looked relaxed and composed and graceful all at the same time. He moved in a way that she had never noticed in a man before—folding himself down with effortless elegance to sit comfortably on the cushions, while the Englishmen around him in their starched, formal evening dress crouched down awkwardly.

She had laughed to herself in wonder that no one else seemed able to see that he was so obviously a long-lost prince.

But she had not had time to do anything more than smile her pleasure back at him, because her uncle led her by, determined to see her amongst the company set—carrying her away into the whirl of officers and company officials. Into the closed circle of pleasant, clubby chitchat.

And she had not objected when her uncle introduced her to gentlemen, nor when her aunt had introduced her to the ladies. She was grateful and unfailingly polite to the Mrs. Carstairs and the Miss Fieldings and the Mrs. Cowpers of their world. She set herself diligently to remembering their husband's names and ranks and positions, determined to be accommodating, and useful and gracious.

She would have been better served to step back, and open her eyes and unstop her ears. She would have been better off to take heed of the treacherous undercurrents flowing around her. She would have better prepared to utilize her well-honed Scots skepticism to take a more critical, sharp-eyed look at those around her. If she had, she might have better recognized the malice that hung like incense in the sultry, perfumed air.

It had not been her first encounter with perfidy, that night in Saharanpur. But it certainly had proved the most instructive. And the most lasting.

But what was done, was done. There could be no turning back, no chance of reliving the moment, of making different choices. No chance of redemption.

Catriona recalled herself to the present, to the inconvenient task that awaited her at Wimbourne and steeled herself to speak to Lady Jeffrey one more time. "My lady, please understand. It is impossible. You see, Mr. Thomas Jellicoe did not mistake me for another."

"No," her inconvenient prince said from the doorway. "I never have."

Chapter Seven

And he wasn't mistaking her now. He could feel the tense readiness, the watchful thinking, emanating from Cat in waves. She meant to leave. Without him.

He could see her knowledge in her eyes—see the determination, that absolute conviction he had once admired. The steely purpose beneath the prim, starched exterior.

It had always been there, that well-honed sense of surety. Miss Anne Cates's face might look as impassive and stoic as the *Himalaya*, frozen and unmoving as she sat so calmly by the unnecessary fire, but he did not for one moment think she was unfeeling. No. She felt. But like the remote, timeless mountains, Catriona Rowan was alive beneath the heavy covering of snow, shifting slowly, merely biding her time. She could not hide herself so thoroughly from him, though she gazed at him with all the calm certainty of a queen—in the world, but not of it.

And he, who knew everything of masks and keeping his thoughts from his face, was impressed by her resolve and her control. He had seen it before.

He had first seen it that night in Saharanpur, at the party Colonel Balfour had carefully orchestrated to try and bring the new resident commissioner into some greater knowledge and appreciation of Hind and its richly varied peoples and cultures.

That night Thomas had scrubbed all traces of the horseman from his hands, and dressed himself in silks and satins, and wrapped his long hair in a fine white turban. All the while thinking only of her. Keeping his mind conveniently blank as to his true motives. Telling himself he was only playing a little game.

But it had not been a game, the way he had watched her, his northern flame-gold goddess.

Watching was what Tanvir Singh was good at—observing people, noticing the little things they did not know they did, finding the ways their hands or their eyes gave the lie to the words they spoke.

And that was what had made Miss Catriona Rowan so very interesting, and so very, very different. In the veritable viper's nest of petty deceptions on display—the sweating upper-level company clerk, Mr. Pillock, in charge of the warehousing of export trade goods, who was standing in the corner sporting a diamond pin that was surely too expensive for such a minor functionary, had most assuredly been skimming profits from the company's coffers; the young subaltern chatting with the matron and her daughter had eyes only for his regiment's master sergeant; and the fat cotton merchant Rama Kumar was augmenting his profits by dabbling in smuggled opium—where nearly every person alternated between platitudes and outright lies, Miss Catriona Rowan all but radiated pure truth and conviction.

Her every action, from her clear open gaze to her quick agile fingers as she shook hands with everyone she met, spoke of a forthright character, and an intelligence that never strayed to cunning. She did not say one thing and mean another. She spoke the uncomfortable truth.

The Lady Summers had steered her niece to the little cluster of English ladies, and was introducing her around. "You remember my niece, Miss Rowan? Mrs. Foster. Mrs. Foster is Mrs. Fielding's sister, you know."

"Yes, of course. We met after church services last Sunday. How nice to see you again, ma'am."

From as far away as he could bear to stand and observe her, Tanvir Singh saw her smile and nod politely, and then step back, just as she ought, so that her aunt could take the place of precedence in her little pride of lionesses.

Only the English ladies were on hand for the evening. While Colonel Balfour was a friend to all and a confidant to many besides Tanvir Singh and Thomas Jellicoe, the rich cotton merchants like Rama Kumar and Sanjay Lupalti, who had fattened their purses to bursting trading with the East India Company under the aegis of the colonel, kept their women safe at home, and did not mix business and family. Only the English brought their tight-corseted, fainting wives and daughters. And nieces.

Miss Catriona Rowan was not the only younger, unmarried woman to walk under the high archway of the palace gate, but she was clearly the most beautiful. At least to Thomas. Because she was the only one who was alive to the beauty around her.

She was the only one who looked around her in open, happy amazement. She was the only one unafraid to cast admiring eyes on the beauty and splendor of the old Mughal fort Balfour had long ago made his own when he had married an almond-eyed local beauty. The Begum, as the colonel called his wife, was by her religion a Mohammedan, and as such, not at home to strangers. But the dear kind lady, who had done so much to help young Thomas Jellicoe when he first came to India, was no doubt keeping her eye on the proceedings from one of the screened windows high above, and her ladies would have their ears attuned to every conversation that carried upward from the courtyard or the spacious, tiered colonnades surrounding the hall where the European-style dinner table had been set.

Those ladies of the *zenana* were most assuredly listening to Lady Summers talking amongst her *angrezi* coterie. "Doing it a bit brown, the colonel," the lady said in reference to the opulent decor. "He's a bit of a relic—a holdover from a past age. He's the only one who doesn't know it yet."

"Yes." One of the pursed-lipped matrons was quick to

wave her wrist in offhand dismissal of the billowing silk curtains surrounding them. "It *is* all a bit much, don't you think, the whole effect?"

"Hmm," agreed Lady Summers, with a considerable jaded rolling of her eye. "Not at all the thing."

"I think it's magnificent." Miss Catriona Rowan was bold enough to quietly disagree with the popular opinion. She looked about with a generous gaze. "Colorful and enchanting. This is a beautiful home. I admire it greatly."

"Oh, my dear." Lady Summers turned her condescension upon her niece. "We'll have to see what we can do to rid you of all that blushing naïveté."

His northern goddess was undaunted. "I'm hardly naïve, Aunt Lettice."

Clearly Lady Summers was not used to being contradicted. One arched eyebrow rose high. "My darling child. One journey out of Scotland—such a savage place"—Lady Summer shuddered delicately—"hardly qualifies you as having a knowledge of the world. But it's not your fault that your upbringing was so hopelessly provincial."

Miss Rowan—she of the burning hair and just as cold-burning temper—stilled, pausing while the other ladies smiled and made patronizing murmurs of agreement. When she spoke, her voice was calm and deceptively soft. "My dear aunt Lettice, I hardly think the years I spent at school in Paris would qualify me as *provincial*."

"Paris?" Lady Summers's voice could not hope to regain its aggrandized heights.

Oh, it had pleased him so, to see his goddess thus. Catriona Rowan had calmly done what none of the other women of the clubby, cliquish expatriate set had ever done. She had easily given Lettice Summers as good as she got. Catriona Rowan might have looked ethereal, a spun-sugar confection of a girl in that gown the color of a virginal blush, but underneath was a spine as strong and unyielding as tempered steel. She had looked her silly, vain aunt calmly in the eye, and all but dared her to call Paris a provincial backwater. Not even Lettice Summers had that much self-delusion.

But perhaps Thomas Jellicoe had. He had been self-deluded enough that he was not prepared to hear Lord Summers introduce his Catriona Rowan to a new arrival.

"Birkstead. There you are. Been looking for you. Come, I have someone I want to introduce you to."

A rime of frost chilled Thomas's veins. No. Lord Summers could not possibly be so obtuse, or so . . . so destructive. Had the man not eyes and ears? Did he not understand how deeply, deeply ill-advised such a scheme was?

Evidently not. The new resident commissioner was most definitely pushing the scarlet-coated officer toward his niece. "Catriona, my dear, I give you Lieutenant Jonathan Birkstead. Lieutenant, her ladyship's niece, Miss Rowan." The resident commissioner continued with his introduction. "Let me recommend Lieutenant Birkstead to you as an excellent dinner partner, my dear."

Thomas waited, watching for some sign that his all-knowing, all-seeing goddess would instantly see through the lieutenant, that her instinct for truth would show on her open face. But Miss Rowan hid all of her steel, and had retreated into tea-blush solemnity while giving the handsome lieutenant a long look from under her ginger lashes.

And something unruly and feral had rattled itself awake behind the cage of Thomas's chest.

Not Birkstead. Anyone but Birkstead.

Thomas told himself the ferocity was logic—his objection stemmed from the fact that he had heard too much of Lieutenant Birkstead's character to think *any* decent girl a fit companion for him. A girl as lovely and true as Catriona Rowan would be chewed up and spat out in no time by such a bounder as Birkstead.

But it was not logic. The feeling growling in his chest was an emotion he had forgotten he possessed—rank jealousy, unsheathing itself and sliding into his veins like a cold, insidious blade. A blade he wanted to bury to the hilt, deep in Birkstead's rotten gut, when the man obediently took Miss Rowan's arm and led her in to dinner.

This, then, ought to have been the end of his foolish infatuation. He ought to have forced himself to forget Thomas Jellicoe's dangerous yearnings, and become Tanvir Singh once more, a man of self-discipline and keen understanding. A man who was too smart, too canny to give in to unbidden, dangerous desires.

But fate was a cruel, cruel, demanding mistress, and she was not done playing dice with him. As a single man, Tanvir Singh was seated near the officers, and at an unfortunately convenient distance to watch Birkstead, out of eyeshot of Lord Summers, ignore Miss Rowan at dinner. To the lieutenant, she was a discard, a cipher so far beneath his notice and that of his clubby, closed-minded mates that they talked around her—sitting right next to them at the table—as if she were deaf and dumb, and not a beautiful, sentient, thinking human being.

"I understand Miss Rowan is from Scotland? No wonder she came out to India," the lieutenant joked, nodding in apparent great humor to the man on his right. "India is bad enough, but Scotland? Lord save us from that posting."

Thomas was incensed for her, even though he had suffered much the same treatment at many of the same hands. But he had been disregarded because his skin was browned and his hair was wrapped in a turban. She was one of *them*. They should be cleaving to her and making her one of their own.

But perhaps, his traitorous mind whispered, just perhaps the pale Miss Rowan had no more wish to be one of them than Thomas had. Perhaps. Because she withdrew from the lieutenant even more, and ate very little, holding herself back behind the fortress of her self-control.

Her quiet, self-possessed distress was all the fuel Thomas needed to fan the fire of his growing obsession with this *angrezi* girl, whom he imagined saw the world much as he did. But as Tanvir Singh, he had to wait and bide his time, pretending to pay attention to self-important men and their self-aggrandizing prating, when all he was really doing was keeping track of Miss Rowan.

At nine thirty-five, when the ladies excused themselves from the dinner table, she stood quietly and let the whole of the company women pass before she followed, walking behind two aging matrons who were too engrossed in their gossip to include her in the conversation. At ten-fifteen, she walked to the other side of the pavilion slowly, with a sort of fey, unhurried grace that would drive the brittle harpies amongst them to make up stories about her. At ten thirty-four she spoke briefly to Lord Summer, who smiled and patted her on the head fondly as if she were a spaniel dog. And at eleven forty-seven, after gentlemen joined the ladies on their side of the pavilion for polite, stilted chit-chat where the English ladies hardly knew how to speak to a native man like Tanvir Singh and so kept mum, leaving him to silence, she excused herself. She squared her shoulders, and shook out her skirts, and headed determinedly outside, slipping away into the garden.

But unlike him, poor Miss Rowan was not as adept at watching and reading people. And although she may have seen the handsome Lieutenant Birkstead wander off into the gardens, she clearly had not seen her aunt slip out first into the covering seclusion of the dark.

And so Thomas followed Miss Rowan.

He shouldn't have done it. He shouldn't have disregarded all instinct, practical experience, and professional acumen to spend an evening satisfying his curiosity about a girl—an English girl, who was off-limits for more reasons that he cared to contemplate, but who drew him the way some ancient memory drew migrating swallows south to warmer climes for the winter.

And that was the measure of how stupid he had become—he was thinking of swallows, English swallows, swooping and diving swiftly over English fields. He hadn't thought of them in years. By disciplined necessity, his mind had remained completely occupied with the here and now, by grand strategies and minute, telling details alike, by reading the truth in men's faces and not in their words. In deciding how to preserve his identity while uncovering the identities of other players in the Great Game.

But that night Thomas had closed his mind to the game. He had not reminded himself that it was no business of Tanvir Singh's if bright young things got themselves harsh lessons in reality, or if pompous idiots like her uncle, Lord Summers, got themselves cuckolded at dinner parties. No.

Instead, he had followed her. He followed her through the lantern-lit courtyard and toward the seclusion of the gazebo in the dark, walled, private garden. He followed her simply because he wanted to. He wanted to see more of her. He wanted to prove to himself that his pale goddess could not possibly be attracted to that oily scoundrel Birkstead—the lieutenant was spoken of in the bazaar as *Badmash* Sahib, Sir Scoundrel.

He wanted to believe she was different.

So he followed Catriona Rowan's swift, graceful flight through the dark meanders of the garden, led along by the pale shimmer of her dress billowing out like wings. But at the heart of the garden she stopped. Abruptly. And took two small steps back, as still as a hovering falcon, listening to the voices coming from the little gazebo.

"You far outshine all the other ladies, Lettice. You know that." The voice was Birkstead at his most ingratiatingly false.

"Even my pale little niece?"

Thomas could picture Lettice Summers's sinuous simper. But in the shadow outside the gazebo, all he could see was Catriona Rowan's pale, frowning face at the mention of her own name. She stepped fractionally closer, listening with even more attention. Thomas leaned his head back against the wall and closed his eyes. He could not bear to see her so abruptly disillusioned.

"Who?" Birkstead murmured.

Lettice's musical little laugh wafted out over the gardenias. "My Scots-Irish little niece, with whom you had dinner. You know he brought her here for you, dear

Lieutenant—Summers did. I think he thinks to make a match for you with the little midge of a girl."

The handsome lieutenant was as shallow as he was indiscreet. "Scots-Irish? Savages the lot. Whey-faced Scottish chits don't interest me, Lettice darling. You do."

Lettice Summers let out a breathless, throaty laugh of encouragement. "Well, then, you'll have to *pretend* to keep Summers happy."

"*Have* to? I'm to let myself be seen courting a Scots-Irish girl with a brogue as thick as oatmeal? Good God, Lettice, have you no pride for me?"

"You have enough pride for both of us, darling. But Jonathan, you don't have to marry her, you just have to court her. Don't you see—she presents the perfect excuse for you to visit the residency, and come to *me*."

"Ah. Now that *is* almost an interesting proposition. Why don't you see if you can get your husband to dower the little red chit, and then I won't have to pretend."

"Jonathan. You're *too* bad." Lady Summers's laugh was encouraging.

"And that's why you come to me, Lettice darling. To be very bad with me."

Catriona Rowan finally turned away. The pale slice of the moon washed her face in cool silver, and all traces of the glowing, flame-bright goddess had vanished. Her lovely, open face had closed like a fist to absorb the blow, trying desperately to find somewhere safe to hide the inescapable pain and mortification deep within herself.

And he, Thomas Jellicoe, who never felt anything when he watched people lie and steal and hope and die, felt . . . responsible somehow. Because he had known this was going to happen, and he had done nothing to prevent her being hurt. Because he had wanted her to be disillusioned by the lieutenant. Even if it meant discovering her aunt was an adulterer.

And as Tanvir Singh, he knew what it meant to be judged on one's race and ancestry, to be an outsider. To never feel at ease, to remain always at least one step apart. If he were honest, it was the metaphorical lash across his back—the impetus that drove him toward her.

But he wasn't strictly honest. He was smitten.

Thomas toed a pebble loose and sent it skittering toward her, to warn her that she was not alone. To give her time to recover herself before he spoke. "Miss Rowan." He whispered low, and bowed to her, courteously, correctly. "Come away."

She shook her head, as if she would insist on staying—on punishing herself by listening to the unmistakable sound of rushing breath, and lips meeting flesh in the prelude to carnal knowledge. But then she changed her mind.

He was about to say, "Let me show you the way," when she spoke.

"Please, don't. Don't say a word," she said as she rushed past, away from the gazebo and the palace house and their inhabitants, into the deeper darkness so that she could hide the livid flush of humiliation that stained her otherwise pale cheeks.

But she had not his intimate knowledge of the deep garden, and in another moment she would run herself down the high-hedged path into a locked gate, with nowhere to turn but back toward him.

He had trailed after her, he told himself, only to show her the way back. To ease her way, and make her dignified return as painless as possible. He owed her that much by playing with her for his own selfish purposes.

But Miss Catriona Rowan was not taking her disappointment like the elegant, self-controlled lady he thought her. She was determined and angry, and when he came into sight of the gate, she was hiking up her voluminous skirts and giving him an astonishingly good view of her slender, stockinged legs as she hitched her petticoats into the top of her garters.

The sight of her long white legs made him stupid. "What are you doing?" So bloody stupid he sounded like Thomas Jellicoe, and not Tanvir Singh.

But she was too angry to notice his lapse out of the vernacular. "Climbing over," was all she said, before she balanced one slippered foot on the iron hinge in preparation to throw her other leg over the top, and climb into the begum's private garden.

"Hold," he said, even as his hands were closing about her waist to lift her safely down. And he was not thinking of how light and nimble she was, weighing next to nothing in his arms, an enchanting combination of grit and gossamer. He was not thinking that his rough horseman's hands could nearly span her sashed, soft, muslin-clad waist. And he most definitely was not thinking about the fact that his fingers had detected the somehow erotic restraint of boned stays under Miss Rowan's trim little waistline.

Because all the thinking in the world could not contain the heat that whipped across his body like a lash, stinging him with its intensity the moment he had touched her. He had wanted nothing more than to pull her long, lithe back against his front, and whisper all the ways *he* would never disappoint her. And show her all the clever ways he could please her.

But when he had taken a deep breath and could think again, he realized that despite all obvious temptations not to, he was going to have to do a *much* better job of maintaining Tanvir Singh's character.

So he did what a roguish, nomadic horse trader would do. He smiled and picked the lock.

"Allow me, mem." He made very short work of opening the gate, partially because the mechanism was old and well-known to him—he had practiced on this very lock when he had first learned the art—and partially because his skills with the steel tools he kept hidden discreetly in the folds of his turban had grown considerably over the intervening years.

A sort of surprise, more curious than shocked, lit her peach-white face as he stepped back and gestured for her to pass through.

"Did you just pick that lock?"

He bowed in acknowledgment. "I assisted it in opening,

as thou seemed to want it opened. Was I wrong to do so, mem?"

"Oh, no." But she was looking at him with new eyes. Perhaps even admiring eyes. "Thank you."

A low excitement began to throb through him, like the slow beating of a drum. "Thou art most welcome. The begum's garden is most beautiful in the evenings."

He thought now she might be done with him, and simply brush by, anxious to be alone in the comfort of the dark to cry the tears of humiliation glinting in her eyes. But she didn't rush by this time. She walked cautiously around him, before she turned to look back to level him with those solemn, but now ever so slightly defiant, gray eyes.

"Are you coming?"

The heat of the lash faded into the steady roar of fire warming his gut. Oh, yes, he was coming with her. Most certainly. "I would be honored."

Mere curiosity, he lied to himself, and politeness. She really oughtn't to be left alone in the dark garden. Who knew if she was perhaps despondent enough to cast herself into the dark, slowly swirling depths of the river on the other side of the wall? Who knew what such a quixotic girl was capable of?

That was what he told himself, rehearsing excuses and apologies should anyone find them together. Because it was wrong for him to be alone with her. And he knew it.

And still he stayed.

Because she wasn't despondent. The glimmer of sorrow he thought he had seen in her eyes had ebbed, transforming itself, until she had worked herself into being marvelously, gloriously angry. It animated her in an entirely different way than her calm surety, and lit her northern flame from within, as she strode along the length of the reflecting pool, a bright flicker reflected in the cool dark surface of the water.

"Damnation." She let out a long, gusty breath. "I heartily dislike being made a fool of."

Her voice had regained the full, rolling cadence of her

Scottish lilt, and Thomas was even more smitten. She was rather magnificent in her ire. "Thou art right to be angry, mem." He used the familiar, diminutive address even though he knew he shouldn't dare such intimacy. Even though she should not permit it.

But she made no objection at all to his familiarity. She was focused almost entirely on what she clearly saw as more important issues. "I *am* angry," she said with a sort of fresh wonder, as if the emotion were something of a revelation to her. "Because the lieutenant is a right proper bastard. And my aunt is not any better."

He was shocked by her strong language. And pleased. He gave her a smile of deep appreciation for her mettle. "Very good, mem. This is an English word I do know— 'bastard.' The officers are very fond of this word. But I think you should not know it."

She heard the wry amusement in his tone and smiled, her indignation falling away before her own good humor. "Well, *huzoor,* the cold fact of the matter is that the world is full of bastards—quite as many in India as there ever were in Scotland. And I am of the mind that it behooves a lady to be able to spot them."

So incongruously, deliciously militant in her soft confection of a gown. She looked for all the world like a soft, spun-sugar meringue of a girl, but he was happy to see there was something of Scottish granite beneath the airy layers. "I am of the same mind, mem, though I am sorry that there should be a need for you to know of such men."

"Oh, so am I. I am heartily sick of them." She meandered to a stop next to the cool gurgle of the fountain, and drew in a deep, audible breath. "How much did you hear?"

He tipped his head to the side, a small gesture of mitigation. "Enough."

"Enough to understand they—my aunt and Lieutenant Birkstead—are having an affair?" She looked at him directly. "My aunt is having an affair with the man my uncle-in-law was only this evening recommending *I* take for a husband." She took another deep breath, and exhaled into the night as if she could blow the memory of what she had heard away. "Well. At least now I have the answer as to why my aunt lavishes me with her contempt. I thought it was all for my mother, for the embarrassment of who my mother had chosen to become by marrying my imprudent, impoverished father—a nobody. But it turns out she hates me for my own self."

He tried not to react to the ache hidden under the brisk self-awareness in her voice. To do so seemed indiscreet, an intrusion upon her. Yet it was impossible for him not to have sympathy for her. If he could, he would take her pain away.

And she felt it, too, the strange sympathetic intimacy between them. "I am very sorry, *huzoor*. I have no idea why I'm telling you all this. I'm sure it's rather rude to be spilling one's troubles out like marbles from one's pocket, loose and skittering about underfoot."

What a marvelous image. "Thou mayest spill thy marbles as thou likest, mem. But first thou must tell me, what are 'marbles'?"

"Oh." Her face had lightened momentarily, just as he had hoped. "It is a game one plays with little round pieces of polished glass. One shoots the marble from outside a circle—"

"Ah, yes. We have this game for children here, too—but the pieces are made out of clay."

She smiled, and blew out a sigh of laughter, as if she had been holding too much inside for too long. As if she were becoming comfortable with their rapport. "It is rather mortifying to learn truths about people, isn't it? And especially mortifying to hear unflattering truths about oneself. And it's certainly more than mortifying to hear oneself spoken about with such contempt."

"They have wounded thee."

"Perhaps." She shrugged up one delicate shoulder, to show him she was determined not to let the lieutenant or her aunt's shallow desires bother her anymore. "I'll live. The truth is, I've heard worse."

He felt his smile widen and tip up one side of his face. This was the rapport he felt, the deep sense of understanding. "So have I."

In response, she gifted him with a small, bittersweet smile of camaraderie. "I imagine you have."

He spread his hands in the air before him—his gesture to show *he* didn't care. "The lieutenant sahib excels at this contempt for all of Hindustan, not just me."

A small dimple arose from the far corner of her mouth and pressed itself into her gingersnap cheek. "It's nice to know I'm in such good company. And now that I have recovered some of my equanimity, I note that you, *huzoor,* did not seem surprised at all by this revelation of my aunt and the lieutenant's perfidy."

He would have shrugged in dismissal, or made any of the many other gestures he had perfected to say the lieutenant's behavior was of no import to him, but his red-gold goddess, Miss Catriona Rowan, was looking at him with such steady, uncompromising expectation—an air of almost savage serenity—that made him understand she was brave enough for the fullness of the vicious, ugly truth.

"All the world and his wife, as they say in Hindustan, from the meanest beggar to the wealthiest merchant in the bazaar, knows that the lieutenant sahib is a lying jackal of a man, lower in honor than the lowest beetle upon a dung heap."

Oh, she liked that. Her smile broke across her face as brilliant and colorful as a pink-gold sunrise. "And does all the world and every wife in Saharanpur know with whom the jackal lies?"

Thomas spread his hands again. "The world, and especially his wife, has eyes and ears and mouths. And relatives."

"Talkative relatives in the bazaar?"

"And the cantonment. Sooner or later, everyone in Saharanapur, and most especially his wife, comes to the bazaar." It was a wonderful, well-timed game, this little match of word play.

"Except the Englishmen? But clearly they"—she gestured back down the path the way they had come to indicate her aunt and the lieutenant—"are not very discreet, if they are having assignations at dinner parties. Surely I cannot be the only person to find them out?"

"There are many things that many people may know, that they choose not to understand, or to speak of." The subtle politics of life for a subjected, subservient people were complicated. As were the less subtle politics of the ambitious people of the cantonment. "Many fear the lieutenant, even if they cannot respect him."

"Oh. Oh, I see." But then she shook her head. "Well, I shan't fear him, or respect him, either. Oh, Lord." A new thought blanked her pale face. "What about my uncle, Lord Summers, the resident commissioner? Do you think he knows? Please tell me I am not a pawn in some awful game he is playing with my aunt?" She shook her head again, and threw up her hand as if she could ward off that particular evil. "Please tell me he wasn't pushing me at the lieutenant just to try and spite her?"

This was a possibility that Thomas had not thought of himself. She was clever, this girl, this ruthlessly insightful gossamer confection. "What sort of man would willingly let his wife make love to another man, if he knew of it? Lord Summers does not strike me as such a man, mem. I do not think he knows."

She contemplated his answer for a moment, before she looked to him again. "Well, then, before I'm tempted or flattered into making a complete ass of myself over a man again, are there any more dung beetles masquerading as gentlemen, whom I should avoid? My relations seem anxious to marry me off, but I think it prudent from this point on to be a trifle less trusting of their judgment. Wouldn't you agree?"

Despite her forthright words, she could not hope to keep her true feelings from him, who had trained himself to watch and understand. There was still hurt pooling in the corner of her eyes, and held in the tight set of her jaw and in the way she pleated her lips between her teeth. And especially in the way she rearranged the folds of her gown just so, trying to impose some small measure of order on an unruly, disorderly world.

"Thou hast had a great shock."

She accepted his sympathy philosophically. "Yes, I suppose I have. It *was* quite shocking to find that my aunt is cuckolding my uncle. And with one of his subordinate officers, to boot. Well, I'm glad I shall no longer have to find a reason to like him—the lieutenant—or her, for that matter. It brings me to mind of a line from my favorite book. *'She was returned to all the pleasure of her former dislike.'* That's me."

Oh, she had a sly sense of humor, his red-gold goddess. "I am glad you are able to smile. I feared the lieutenant sahib had upset you with his thoughtless words."

"He did. And so did my aunt—I'm not forgetting her share in this tawdry affair. But I'm striving to get over it, to overcome the blow to my pride, which must be more considerable than I had previously imagined."

She was funny as well as sweet. He could not remember the last time he had even wanted to talk to any girl like this, let alone an English girl. But he *did* want to talk to her, because when she looked at him, she seemed to see *him,* Thomas, and not the man he had so carefully constructed out of whole turban cloth. She did not see just another native, an exhibit in a menagerie, a dumb animal who did not understand her language, or empathize with her thoughts.

It was enchanting. And deeply seductive.

He was enchanted and seduced by this fey, ginger, spun-sugar confection of a girl in the dress that made her look like she was about to fly away and mingle with the mischievous northern fairies.

"If I may be so bold, Memsahib Rowan, the lieutenant is a fool. Thou art clearly the most beautiful woman in attendance here this evening. Thou lookest both enchanted and enchanting."

"Thank you. You are very kind." Her head tucked down

before she looked up at him from under her gold-tipped lashes. A blush the color of pale apricots was blossoming across her cheek. She really was not used to even so mild a flirtation. "The dress is very pretty isn't it? A very prettily made piece of irony. I hope you can appreciate that these are called *imbécile* sleeves." She fluffed up the wide puff of one sleeve as she pronounced the French word. "And I fear they made me very silly and imbecilic indeed, thinking I could be like *them*."

She gave the word a particular emphasis, as if in obvious evidence that she never had been like them—like all the clubby little misses gathered in closed-shouldered clumps in the pavilion.

"A very pretty irony, indeed." Thomas could not find it in him to care that Tanvir Singh ought not to understand such a subtle linguistic joke, and he laughed for her, if for no other reason than to see her smile again. And to encourage her to continue to confide in him.

Which she did. "I don't mean to be ungrateful. I know I am supposed to be happy that they have given me a home, and taken an interest in me—that someone as important as Lord Summers should bother himself with something so unimportant as getting an impoverished niece a husband. I *am* grateful for the attention, and the intended kindness. I only wish I did not feel as if I were one of your mares, traded away and given to the highest bidder."

"That is unfair to horse traders, mem. I am very particular to whom I sell my mares."

She laughed, a sweet, easy, unforced expression of quick-witted humor, just as he had hoped she would. "I hope I may take that as a compliment. Thank you. It is very kind of you to try and cheer me up."

"Kind" was not an adjective that was often applied to Thomas Jellicoe, and never to Tanvir Singh. Kind was soft and warm and good-hearted. Kind was dangerous.

Because her gentle praise made him want to be a better version of his English self. To be the kind of man her uncle would want for her husband. And for the first time in over a decade, he was tempted to become that kind of man. So he might spend more time with her. So he might truly have her.

Why? Why could he not stop thinking about her? What was it about her that was so different? So different he was tempted to abandon everything he had worked years and years to accomplish? It wasn't as if she were the kind of jolly girl who would toss up her skirts, and give him the kind of uncomplicated, thorough rogering that might put paid to his absurd obsession. She was a lady, with powerful relations, who wanted her to marry well, and not dally in gardens with people who were pretending to be people they were not.

But Catriona Rowan was different, in a way that he could not fully articulate, but in a way that called to him. That called forth a yearning he could not control.

And she was looking around her now, with that appreciative curiosity he had seen in the Rani Bazaar, moving slowly, touching the plants with a sort of reverent wonder. "This is an astonishingly beautiful garden. Such a collection of exotic plants I've never seen before, but so very beautiful." She tipped her long, elegant nose into the air. "I can't quite place that lovely, warm scent."

"Night-blooming jasmine, mem. It is a favorite of the begum."

"Oh, it is sublime. The Begum? Who is the Begum?"

"Mrs. Balfour, as thou wouldst have it. The colonel's wife."

"Oh!" The pale, shining moon of her face swung back to his. "I had assumed he was a widower, since his wife was not at the party. How very ignorant of me. Is she ill, or frail then, that she would not attend?"

"She is not frail. She is not at the colonel's party because she is a Mohammedan, and by tradition, she keeps herself secluded from strange men. This garden is attached to her *zenana,* the women's part of the house."

"Oh, I had no idea I was intruding upon her privacy. There is so much I don't know!" In the midst of her very real distress at the thought of her trespass, she tried to level a sweet little scowl at him. "You should have told me."

He could not stop smiling for her. "I am telling thee now."

She smiled back, an open expression of almost impudent delight. "You should have told me before you picked the lock."

"Ah." He dismissed her worry with a wave of his hand. "That lock and I are old friends. But do not make thyself uneasy. The Begum will not mind us walking and talking in her garden." Indeed the begum might even welcome this little intrusion into her world for the charming drama, for she was the one other person in the world besides her husband who knew Thomas's secret. He could not have become Tanvir Singh without her help. "I daresay she and her ladies are listening right now."

He pointed to the upper stories of the latticed buildings that surrounded the garden on three sides, and the answering acknowledgment of a gently chiding chuckle fell down on them from the screened balcony above.

"There. The begum and her ladies are our honored chaperones. We will make our salaam. Come." Thomas indulged himself by putting his hand to the flare of her back and urging her around next to him, where he made a courtly, elegant salaam to the night air.

Catriona Rowan copied his gesture, but then looked up at the walls, and added an elegant, melting European curtsy, as deep and respectful as if she were meeting the queen. And she was in a way.

This was what was so different about her. She was wide awake to the world around her, alive to the possibilities that came with a different place, a different culture than her own. She had not yet been lulled by the company and its cloistered expatriate community into their indifferent slumber.

That was the answer to his question. Catriona Rowan called forth his admiration as well as his infatuation. And something more. Something dangerously close to obsession. Because his time in the garden with Miss Catriona

Rowan had only fueled the fires banked deep within. And blinded him to things he should have seen.

Yes, she had looked so much like a confection of spun sugar, but there had been granite beneath. And he had been impressed by her. So impressed, he had never thought to wonder how she had come to be that way.

Chapter Eight

There had been days when Catriona felt she must have dreamt it all—the warmth and the colors and the heady excitement of falling in love. But she had fallen slowly, inexorably, irreversibly in love. She had not dreamt it. Nor had she dreamt the malice that had followed her all the way to Wimbourne Manor. That was all too real. And too lasting. She had not dreamt the bullets that had embedded themselves in the lawn. And she had not in a thousand and one years dreamt up the tall Englishman filling the doorway.

There was no other choice. Catriona rooted herself more firmly in the unpleasant present, and faced Lady Jeffrey. "I thank you for your kind concern, my lady, but as you can see, I'm quite fine. So if you'll excuse me, I'll go see to the children now." And take herself as far as possible from Mr. Thomas Jellicoe's vigilant presence.

"My dear Miss Cates." Lady Jeffrey reached over to clasp Catriona's hand once more. "What would we do without you? You are our rock. You're quite the bravest girl. I should still be shaking in my boots, but you think nothing of your own safety, and only of the children. I daresay you were not even afraid."

Safety was a relative, mutable thing—another luxury she could not afford. If she were to ensure the safety of the viscountess's children she could not stay—to do so would be to invite the danger within the manor walls. And if she were to survive her present trial, and elude her determined pursuers, including Mr. Thomas Jellicoe, she would have to use her very real fear to compel her to leave the relative safety of Wimbourne. Quietly. Stealthily.

But the truth was that she was not in the least bit brave. She was deeply, deeply afraid. If she had had any courage, any bravery at all, she never would have left India—she never would have left Scotland. She would have faced her fears, and faced her accusers. But she had not. And so the fear had grown inside her until it was a weight pressing relentlessly against her soul. An ache she could never manage to put aside.

She was deeply afraid of being taken up by the Honorable Thomas Jellicoe, and sent back to India. Of being tried for a crime she did not commit. Of dying in the most public way, of being demeaned and abased the way her father had been.

She was deeply afraid of the gunman roaming free outside the walls. And deeply, deeply afraid of the malice he held toward her.

She didn't have time to try and explain the complicated tangle of circumstance and unjust accusations to Lady Jeffrey. She couldn't take the chance that her mistress might feel compelled to turn her over to her brother-in-law immediately if she knew Catriona faced a charge of murder. "I must go, my lady."

"And go where?" Thomas Jellicoe had to duck his head to step under the lintel of the nursery sitting room door. "Running away won't help, Miss Anne Cates."

Catriona didn't know if he said her assumed name in an effort to remind himself of who she was supposed to be, or to remind *her* that he was the one who held her secrets and her fate in the palm of his hand.

But it was not she who bristled like an angry hedgehog at his entrance, but his own sister-in-law, Cassandra, the Viscountess Jeffrey. "I am sure politeness dictates that I ought to welcome you back, Thomas, but I do so *only* for the sake of politeness."

The lady surprised Catriona. Perhaps gratitude was at least as thick as blood. Her mistress's tone was stiff and unyielding, and the viscountess rose out of her chair to confront her brother-in-law, as if she might physically bar him from approaching her Miss Cates any nearer.

The thought was laughable. Her ladyship might still think of her brother-in-law as the schoolboy he had been the last time she had seen him, but Thomas Jellicoe was now a towering man in his prime, as tall and capable and hardened by experience as an axe, and the viscountess was a fine china teacup of a woman. Not even the wide, petticoated skirts and full sleeves of her rich blue silk day gown could increase her stature sufficiently to make her seem anything but a beautiful, exquisite doll compared to the rough giant that was Thomas Jellicoe.

But Lady Jeffrey *had* stopped him from coming any nearer. Perhaps it was the force of her character that made Mr. Jellicoe step back, herded into the doorway like some great bull held at bay by a sleek, little collie. Lady Jeffrey might look insignificant, but she had bite.

The poor man had to settle for looming over his sister-in-law and scowling down into her face. "Surely you don't think I'm going to hurt her? I am very sorry for my rough handling of her out on the lawn, but I assure you, I am not going to harm Miss Cates. I did what I did today to *protect* her. Tell her, C—" He recovered himself. "Cassandra, even Miss Cates will tell you that I have always sought to protect her. In India, I even went so far as to make enemies to protect her."

Lady Jeffrey turned her guileless lavender eyes to Catriona. "Is that true?"

Catriona closed her hand around the arm of the chair to keep the room from shifting. She couldn't seem to find her balance. Everything about the man seemed to knock her off her feet. "Yes," she finally admitted. It was undoubtedly true. She had forgotten. He *had* made enemies for her.

He had sought to protect her time after time, from that first evening on.

He had made an enemy out of Lieutenant Birkstead, to spare her the trouble of doing it alone. It had been something they shared, their enmity for the fair-haired boy of the regiment. Something that drew them together. Like their love of horses. Like the superb mare. Her memories of the awful turmoil of her last hours in Saharanpur had made her forgot how much he had once done for her.

What had he said to her that first night at Colonel Balfour's to cheer her up? "I am glad that the lieutenant sahib has disappointed thee. Thou art worthy of a far, far better man. One who appreciates thy finer qualities." But then his gravity had disappeared, and he began again to lavish her with his easy charm. "Now that we have our proper chaperone in the begum and her ladies, we may talk of better, more pleasant and interesting things than the lieutenant, who is not worth our breath. Let us talk of the mare."

Catriona had been more than willing to talk of the marvelous animal that had been the means of introducing her to Tanvir Singh. "I have mounted her only briefly, within the grounds of the residency, as I did not yet have a saddle. But my uncle, Lord Summers, was kind enough to insist that I be measured for my own sidesaddle, which has been delivered to the residency this afternoon. But I still fear we won't be allowed to range any farther afield."

It had pleased her so much, and embarrassed her a little, that generous attention from her new uncle, but mostly pleased. Her uncle-in-law was a kindhearted man, if a little blind when it came to things he would rather not know.

But Tanvir Singh had heard what she had wanted him to hear. "I will also offer my services to thee, if thou shouldst care for accompaniment on thy rides. I confess I cannot rest easy until I am assured that thou art an accomplished horsewoman, and that my mare will not be able to play her tricks upon thee. I cannot have it said that Tanvir Singh sells dangerous horses to his Excellency, Lord Summers."

"Oh, yes, please. I should like that of all things." Catriona had been too happy to stop and examine the swarm of feelings fluttering about her insides. She had rushed headlong toward infatuation. "I have wanted to take my cousins out into the countryside on their ponies in the mornings, but I've been hesitant to let them out of the cantonment alone since I don't know the area well yet."

"I should like nothing more than to accompany you."

Delight had warmed her inside out, chasing away the last of the chill of her aunt's deception. She had absolutely no fears that the mare would prove too much for her, but she grasped on to the excuse to spend more time with her charming Punjabi rogue, her prince among gentlemen, her friend. "Thank you, *huzoor*." She took a moment to school her smile back under more prudence, before she suggested, "I understand there is a fine botanical garden in the town. Perhaps that might be a good place to meet." She had wanted somewhere away from the residency, away from the cantonment lines, and nosy cantonment ears and eyes.

"The Farahat-Baksh is a very fine place to meet, mem." Was it a trick of the moonlight, or were his eyes twinkling with the same pleasure she knew must be warming her own?

"Perfect." She held out her hand. "Until then."

At her easy agreement, he had made her an elegant salaam, and then bowed low over her hand. "Until then, my friend."

But then he had looked up at her from under the dark sweep of his lashes and touched his lips to the heretofore unremarkable skin on the back of her knuckles, and sent sensation sweeping up her arm, like the ripple of a wave crashing against her shore. Tipping her off center.

She hadn't really regained her feet since.

But back then, she hadn't wanted to.

The dawn had come mercifully early that next morning, pale and golden, filling the Doab Valley with warm, flat yellow light. Catriona had arisen early and pushed open the heavy slatted shutters to see a jackal slinking his menacing grace through the cool avenues of the cantonment toward the obscuring haze lying low across the river.

But nothing could mar the infinite possibility of the

morning. Of course there were in reality myriad things—objections from Namita, an out-of-hand request from her aunt to deliver something to one of the families in the cantonment, a slight fever in one of the children—but she would not allow them to interfere with her plans. She was anxious to be up and out of the house, and riding with her friend, the great horseman Tanvir Singh. To show him that she was worthy of his mare. And perhaps to prove to herself that the gently charming friend from last night truly did exist behind the careless smiles of the handsome rogue of a horse trader.

Within the hour, she was leading her cousins across the river toward the large botanical garden in the center of the town, where Mr. John Forbes Royal was in charge of collecting medicinal plants for cataloguing and attempting to grow tea bushes smuggled over the borders from China. Their little party arrived at the garden well ahead of time, as both she and the children had been anxious to get out before the heat of the day sent them napping on their netted beds. Or at least that was the reason she had given them for her haste.

She had taken only Arthur and Alice with her. George had a slight fever from cutting a molar tooth, and Charlotte was still a bit too young for a long ride. Although Charlotte had begged and pleaded and cried to be taken along, Cat had thought it prudent not to take her up in front of her in the saddle on the first day she took the spirited mare out. "Next time," she had promised.

Once within the gates of the garden, Cat had directed them to let their mounts walk along the cool, shaded lanes, while anticipation tumbled happy little somersaults in her belly. What a marvelous feeling—to feel happy and alive and open to all the sights and scenes that the day might bring.

As soon as she heard the steady drum of hoofbeats on the hard-packed earth, she turned to greet Tanvir Singh, but the smile of anticipation froze on her face.

It was not Tanvir Singh who approached, but Lieutenant Birkstead, the blond-haired, blue-eyed devil of the night before. The one man in all the world she had absolutely no desire to meet.

And he was coming at an angle that would surely intersect their path if she did not immediately change direction. Catriona's instinct was as it had always been—to leave at once. To get herself as far away from the lieutenant as possible. To avoid so much as having to make eye contact with the man. To run.

She turned the mare toward another tree-lined lane where they would be out of the lieutenant's direct line of sight. "Let us head this way, Arthur. Shall we have a bit of a race? We'll let the ponies have their heads." And away they clattered at a noisy gallop in the opposite direction from the red-coated intruder.

But Lieutenant Birkstead proved himself to be nothing if not supremely tenacious. And intent upon a meeting. Dangerously so.

While they were enjoying their rather sedate, pony-paced gallop, he chased them down. Catriona was concentrating on keeping her very well behaved but new mare in check so she wouldn't overtake the children's small but sturdy little mountain ponies, when Lieutenant Birkstead's horse charged at her at speed.

Catriona was forced to rein the mare much more abruptly and sharply than she liked, just to avoid a collision, and her intelligent animal quite rightly took exception, rearing back from the intruder.

"Sir!" Catriona's heart was slamming against her chest. But with her fright came something just as strong. Affront. And derision. She could not abide a man who did not know how to control himself on a horse. Such a man was a danger not only to himself, but to others and to his animal. His poor gelding was fretting and foaming, showing her the whites of his eyes and tossing his head fractiously from the constant hard bite of the bit in his mouth.

She had to bring her own mare under control with her legs rather than her hands, because the lieutenant had taken up her reins. "It's quite all right, Miss Rowan. I've got your mount under control now."

"*My* mount?" The bloody, bloody, arrogant, asinine . . . ass. "Sir, clearly you've taken too much sun. Release her immediately." She hated that he had forced such a confrontation upon her. She was shaking, inside and out, but she could not let his behavior pass. "You are interfering with our ride and my supervision of the children. Kindly let go of my rein, sir."

But Lieutenant Birkstead ignored her, and held on to the rein, though the mare tried to back away steadily, and tugged her head away from him, fighting him for control. "I can't imagine what possessed your uncle to purchase this ridiculous animal for you. But I've got you under control now." His tone was strangely pleased and condescending all at the same time, as if he assumed she would be grateful for his notice.

But she wasn't in the last bit grateful. She was bloody annoyed. And growing more so by the minute. She had done everything she could to avoid the man. She would rather have left the garden and missed her appointment with Tanvir Singh than have to speak to Lieutenant Birkstead. But now that her temper had been riled, there was no going back. No retreat from the confrontation that had been forced upon her.

"Sir." Catriona made her tone as flinty as highland granite—anger brought out the Scots in her. "My uncle, Lord Summer, was possessed to buy her because he recognized a superior animal when he saw her, and he understood that she would suit me. Perhaps *you* are not used to ladies who ride well, but I assure you, until your interruption, I was enjoying a very sedate canter with my family, on a very straight and level path. There was no need for such alarm, or interference, or for intruding upon our family group."

But the lieutenant was proving to be as annoyingly persistent as he was impervious. "Oh, come, Miss Rowan. You needn't poker up with me." He smiled at her, all lazy, sure smarm, as if his condescension were a gift. "A man likes nothing so much as a damsel in distress."

Of all the patronizing, stupid, arrogant things—to charge at another animal for nothing more substantial than some misbegotten notion of gallantry, or pride, or whatever it was. For Saint Margaret's sake, the man didn't even like her. What an unmitigated, unbridled ass.

It was on the tip of her tongue to say, "I'm sure my aunt Lettice will be glad to play your damsel," but she didn't. She couldn't. Not with Arthur and Alice listening and watching the interplay between Catriona and the lieutenant with such deeply curious eyes.

So Catriona caught the words before they left her mouth, and forced herself to choose more moderate ones, to put a damper on the hot and scathing tone she wanted to use. "I thank you for your concern, sir, however unnecessary. You may release my rein."

He did not. "Hardly unnecessary," he countered, and brought his mount closer to her, as if she hadn't just dismissed him. As if she had somehow invited him instead. His tone became low and ingratiating. "You haven't been here long enough, I daresay, to understand a white woman doesn't go out riding alone. As an English gentleman it's my duty to protect you." He smiled again, as if he expected his fair-haired good looks would dazzle her, and reached out his hand across the gap between them, as if he would actually pat her hands.

It was utterly infuriating. He was infuriating. She was infuriated. Infuriated that the man had the gall to call himself a gentleman. Catriona touched her heel to the mare's inside flank, and the superbly trained animal instantly made a graceful pivot that removed her as far as she could from the bloody man.

The short distance afforded her some small measure of control. And with control came clarity. Behind the lieutenant, she could see Tanvir Singh with two riders a short distance away, watching and waiting with the stealthy, predatory awareness of a hawk.

A new heat spread into her lungs. She was not alone. The sight of him emboldened her. She was done with subtlety, no matter how damaging blunt speaking might prove. "You need not exercise yourself on my account, Lieutenant. I am not alone. I am with my family, and a very able escort. And I am hardly unprotected."

To illustrate her point, she recklessly drew from the folds of her riding skirt the ancient pistol she had carried with her like a tombstone all the way from Scotland, and laid the worn but lethally efficient mechanism across her pommel in a show of controlled calm, which she did not feel in the least. Her insides were all tumbled up like cats clawing at each other in a fight.

She hated the gun. Hated it. But some instinct for self-preservation had seen her loading and providentially stowing the weapon in her pocket before their ride.

And the feeling of control, however shaky, gave her some semblance of calm. "As you so cogently pointed out to my aunt Lettice last night, Lieutenant, Scotland *is* a savage place, so we whey-faced Scots chits are quite in the habit of arming ourselves against, shall we say, unwanted and *unworthy* attention."

It took a long moment for Lieutenant Birkstead to look beyond the sleek pistol and understand what she had just told him. She saw the moment when the realization struck him like a hammer to his forehead, because he finally had the grace to color. But not, unfortunately, the intelligence to let the matter drop, and take his leave. Indeed, her response seemed to have awakened, rather than dampened, his misplaced enthusiasm. Instead of apologizing, like a *gentleman,* his tone became even more intimate and even insinuating. "Did she tell you I said that, your aunt Lettice? I daresay she's a little jealous at having such a beautiful young rival living in her house."

That wasn't the line he had fed her aunt in the cozy dark of the gazebo, but it was horrible of him to try and lay the entirety of the blame on Lettice's head. Especially in front of Catriona's young cousins. Odious, selfish, self-deceiving man. He actually *liked* the idea of two women fighting over him.

"Sir, you overstep." She spoke for the children's benefit, as well as her own. "I am not her rival in any way."

He smiled, and slouched closer. "She clearly does not see it that way. Let me give you a little piece of advice, dear girl. You will want a friend here to help you find your way amongst the jealous Lettice Summerses of our world. And I can be that friend."

Sweet Saint Margaret. Catriona would have laughed if she hadn't been so deeply disgusted. And deeply afraid. The lieutenant was a practiced, practical liar. Did the women of his normal acquaintance swallow such bouncers? Did Lettice buy his obvious lies? He must think all women the rankest idiots. *Friendship,* indeed—but at what cost? Men like the lieutenant did not offer things so extravagant as friendship if they did not expect something astonishingly compensatory in return.

The man continued to smile at her in a way that was meant to be charming, but to Catriona, Lieutenant Birkstead's version of tawny handsomeness brought to mind nothing so much as the golden jackal she had seen that very morning, hungry and amoral, slinking through the dawn, already having stolen its full. Dangerous and lethal.

Catriona felt her hand tighten around the smooth stock of the gun, and she had to force herself to relax her stiff fingers.

What did the lieutenant think to steal from her—apart from the obvious, which was hardly necessary since he was currently getting it from Lettice? Or had Lord Summers been so imprudent as to share the fullness of his intended generosity—the size of the fortune he meant to settle upon her—with the lieutenant? After Birkstead's pointed dismissal of Lettice's suggestions, nothing else could account for the lieutenant's sudden interest. Nor his dogged determination. His interest in her must have been lit by avarice, and not by anything so unprofitable as love or admiration.

"I hope we can be very good friends, you and I," he lied

pleasantly to her face. He even reached out again, as if he would touch her cheek with the back of his glove, but she drew the mare back abruptly so that his hand only reached her forearm before it fell back to his side. "Very good friends."

She could suffer neither his touch, nor his presence a moment longer. "Perhaps, sir, you don't understand me because of my accent as thick as porridge, so please listen closely." She leaned toward him, and quietly enunciated each word in a flawless imitation of her aunt's cutting, upper-class ennui. "I have no interest in the sort of friendship you pretend to be offering, nor the kind of *friendship* you are currently pursuing with other men's wives in dark gardens and no doubt darker bungalows. No interest whatsoever." She tried to back the mare again. "You will excuse me now. Good day to you, sir."

But Birkstead would not be outmaneuvered. He swung his foaming and fretting mount alongside Catriona to look at her more closely, his face darkened with some emotion other than embarrassment.

And for the first time in her rather eventful life, Catriona felt her flesh crawl, as if a snake had slithered across her skin. She had clearly done the wrong thing with her anger and her brash words. She had awakened rather than averted his interest.

"Oh, no." The lieutenant smiled that all-too-self-possessed smile even as he shook his head. "I will not excuse you, dear Miss Rowan. And here I thought you were a quiet little Scottish mouse—a quiet little nothing. But you're really nothing of the sort. Well, well, well." He let his eyes slide down the length of her body in appreciation of his discovery. "Bringing you to hand is going to be much more fun than I had thought. You're a hot-tempered little thing. You've got spark. And I think I'm going to like letting my fingers get burned."

Chapter Nine

"You were afraid of him—the lieutenant." The thought was something of a revelation to Thomas. He hadn't seen it in India, the way her eyes went dark and her breath shortened almost imperceptibly. Or if he had seen the signs, he had mistaken it for something more flattering to himself. He had seen only what he wanted to see.

In India, she had seemed too filled with surety and moral conviction for anything so pedestrian as fear. She certainly hadn't appeared afraid, especially when she had coolly pulled the gun on the lieutenant like a seasoned veteran.

But clearly she was afraid now. Clever girl, to understand so quickly. But she was trying to mask it, trying to keep her emotions in check behind the cool, collected cloak of Miss Anne Cates's identity. But he could see it all—the subtle flare of her nostrils, the tension along the line of her jaw and neck, and the tight whiteness at the corners of her mouth. If he were closer to her, he would be able to feel the cold heat of fear emanating from her body. But Cassandra was still guarding the way.

"Afraid of whom?" his sister-in-law demanded.

"Lieutenant Jonathan Birkstead."

"And who is Lieutenant Jonathan Birkstead?" The name held no meaning for Cassandra.

But Catriona had closed her eyes at the mere mention of

the man's name, as if she would try to shut out the very thought of the lieutenant. "No one," she answered.

"An officer of the East India Company regiment," Thomas countered. "And her suitor."

"Oh." Cassandra looked at Cat and then back at Thomas. "I had rather assumed *you* were her suitor."

"I was." It was past time he admitted it. Past time she understood. "I am."

His words penetrated the cool veneer of Cat's composure more effectively than the mention of Birkstead. Her mouth dropped open in complete startlement for a moment before she could find enough presence of mind to speak. "You were not," Catriona contradicted, her cheeks white and her eyes blazing with the truth of her conviction. "Or if you were, then you changed your mind rather emphatically."

"*I* changed my mind?" Thomas took another step closer. "I'm not the one—"

"Thomas. Miss Cates. Please." Cassandra stayed calmly but firmly rooted between them. "Can you not explain what happened without raising your voices like ill-behaved schoolchildren?"

Thomas pulled a deep breath into his lungs and let it out slowly. He *was* acting like a lovelorn lad—on a hair trigger of stupidity. "My apologies. By my recollection, the lieutenant was rather single-minded in his pursuit of Miss Cates. And Miss Cates was not at all receptive to his repeated overtures. Or was I wrong about that?"

"No." Catriona shook her head and looked at him with eyes that were a hundred years old. "You were not wrong. He was relentless. I *was* afraid of him. I'd have been a fool not to be. He never gave up. Never."

Thomas had seen her that morning in the Farahat-Baksh. He had held his *sa'is* back, watching and waiting, not wanting to intrude upon her conversation with Birkstead if he were not wanted. But everything about her—her rigid posture, her sharp tone, and her repeated attempts to back away—spoke of opposition. And the moment she had pulled that gun in open hostility, Thomas had had more than enough.

And it had been for the poor fool's protection as much as for Cat's. The lieutenant hadn't seen that Miss Rowan— she of the blazing hair and equally colorful temper—was, if not quite ready to shoot him, then ready enough to bash him over the head with the heavy butt of her ancient pistol. Her hand had already made the necessary adjustment to do just that, if the bastard attempted to touch her again. Thomas had seen her intent—that cold burning surety—in the sharp clear gray of her eyes.

And Thomas had been happy—damn, bloody, fucking happy—of any excuse to put paid to Birkstead's absurd ambitions for Miss Rowan. It was juvenile and purely male, the fierce anticipatory satisfaction speeding through his veins. But undeniably great, great fun. The best game of them all.

Thomas had spurred his tall mount forward, glad that he had taken the precaution of bringing two of his Balti *sa'is* with him. He had thought their dark, hulking presence riding ahead and behind the party at a discreet distance would ensure both the party's privacy and their safety, so he might be able to spend his time more pleasurably in talking to Miss Rowan, but now their imposing presence also served to give greater weight to his.

Birkstead had been so intent upon his own little game of intimidation with Miss Rowan that he did not see the three men until they were nearly upon him.

"Lieutenant Sahib." Thomas had pitched his voice low with all the dark gravity he had learned from Tanvir Singh's years upon the road, and directed his mount so that he drew up beside Miss Rowan, and cut off any of Birkstead's further attempts to come beside her. "The memsahib has spoken her wishes most clearly."

Birkstead had been both completely flummoxed and suddenly furious to find himself outflanked by the dark-eyed warriors. "By God," he fumed, looking first one way and then the other to find the view was much the same— blocked by narrow-eyed Balti warriors who looked as if they would slit his throat as easily as a goat's. "Who the devil do you think you are?"

Thomas had almost smiled at the impotent frustration seething out of the lieutenant, but he kept his countenance grave and sharply inquiring. As if the lieutenant were the greenest recruit. "Thou knowest I am Tanvir Singh, sahib, as thou seest. Thou wast at my tents these few past days buying my horses."

"I don't care who you are. You're not needed here, you *boxwallah*." He tossed the casual insult at Tanvir Singh. "Go."

Though they could not speak much Hindi, his Baltis had known enough bazaar talk to take instant umbrage at the lieutenant's dishonorable slight in calling Tanvir Singh a lowly itinerant peddler, and their answer had been to make aggressively guttural sounds of menacing disdain.

Thomas calmed them with a quiet raised hand, but not until the lieutenant finally had the sense to drop Miss Rowan's rein.

"Lieutenant Sahib." Thomas had made his tone mildly chiding, almost patronizing, and shook his head gently, just once, to tell the scarlet-clad officer his posturing was unnecessary, and entirely ineffective. Then he had simply turned to Miss Rowan, ignoring Birkstead completely. "Memsahib, doest thou wish to proceed?"

"Yes, thank you, *huzoor*." She had kept her eyes on Birkstead as she carefully uncocked her pistol, but then turned away to stow the weapon in the pocket beneath her riding habit. "We'll be on our way."

"Huzoor?" Birkstead's sneer was scathing. "This devil has imposed upon your trust, Miss Rowan, if you think him worthy of such an honorific. He's no prince to be called Highness. He's no more than an itinerant horse trader. And worse." He glared at Tanvir Singh, as if to show his disdain for the very information that the company relied upon to ensure its wealth.

His clever goddess had leveled Birkstead with a look of severe instruction. "You think not? I know very well *sawar* Tanvir Singh's profession—which is the same as that of my esteemed grandfather, the brother of his grace the Duke of

Hamilton—just as I know yours, Lieutenant. But I also know how to be polite."

It no longer shocked Thomas, the fine-tempered steel that ran through such a deceptively soft, feminine package. The lieutenant would have done well to respect the sharp blade of Miss Catriona Rowan's resolve. It might have helped restore his equanimity, for as it was, the man's face had grown nearly as red as his tunic.

"Good day, Lieutenant Sahib." Thomas had inclined his head and wheeled his mount, and naturally, Miss Rowan and her intelligent mare moved with him in smooth unison. "Let us talk more of the mare, memsahib." Thomas kept his ears tuned backward as he and his steely goddess walked their mounts forward. "Thy handling of my little tigress is impressive. A Rajput princess could not have done better. Where didst thou learn the way of horses so well?"

Oh, her smile had been all canny, triumphant delight as she raised her voice just enough to make sure her words carried. "Scotland, *huzoor*. We savages know our horses."

If Birkstead registered her hit, he did not let it stop him. He refused to be warned. "Don't turn your back on me, horse trader," he snarled. "Have a care with this lowborn ruffian, my dear. I've heard it said that he killed a man in Ranpur—slit his throat from side to side just so he might watch him bleed to death."

Miss Catriona Rowan gasped in shock, as much for the children as for herself.

Thomas turned back with one aggressive pivot of the animal beneath him. "Lieutenant Sahib." He employed the calm, low, commanding tone he had learned from his older brother, Captain William Jellicoe, while his *sa'is* closed ranks against the lieutenant. "I am perfectly willing to treat with thee at any time, as a man treats with another man— thou knows the way to my tents—but thou art frightening the Lord Summers sahib's children with thy careless, angry talk. It is to no one's benefit that children should carry tales home to their father, His Excellency, the lord resident commissioner sahib, or to their mother, the lady memsahib."

Thomas had no idea if it was the mention of Lord or Lady Summers that worked upon the lieutenant, but however it was, the red-coated and red-faced young devil finally gave in to the inevitable. Birkstead reined his mount sharply, yanking at the poor animal's mouth, and took his hasty leave like the sulking, resentful schoolyard bully he had no doubt once been.

But Thomas had not made the mistake of thinking Birkstead would learn from his lesson, or be prudent enough to put Tanvir Singh and Miss Catriona Rowan from his mind. By no means. The officer would merely nurse his grievances until his sense of wounded pride goaded him to his next imprudent act.

But when he did, both Tanvir Singh and Thomas Jellicoe would be ready.

And it was worth making such an enemy for the look of relief and gratitude on Miss Catriona Rowan's fair face.

"Thank you very much, Tanvir Singh." She blew out a long breath, as if she were trying to clear all traces of the confrontation with Lieutenant Birkstead from her lungs, before she turned to the children. "Is everyone to rights?" At their nodding and settling back into the business of their ride, she returned her gaze to him. "That was very kind of you."

There was that word again—kind.

Tanvir Singh was not supposed to be kind. He was supposed to be ruthless and cunning and slippery. Perhaps he had been too soft on the lieutenant? Perhaps he should have given himself the infinite pleasure of rearranging the lieutenant's all-too-pretty face? But no, there had been the children present. To discompose them would be to discompose and distress Miss Rowan. He would have to postpone the satisfaction of driving his fist through the lieutenant's nose for a different day.

He let the children move ahead with the *sa'is*, while he fell in with the object of his obsession. "Think no more of it, Miss Rowan, memsahib. I am most glad to be of assistance to thee."

"So am I." She gave him a tight, constrained smile. "I don't know what I might have done if you have not intervened."

"I think thou might have bashed the *Badmash* over his very thick head with your pistol. And I think he would have deserved the blow to both his head and to his very great pride."

"Oh, the gun." A lovely flush stole across her pale cheeks, though she shook her head slightly, as if she might rid herself of the weapon by not thinking about it. "I loathe guns. I loathe this gun. I can't think of why I even had it with me."

She was likely thinking she was in charge of younger children, in a place she did not know very well, and meeting a man she knew even less. And he applauded her for her foresight. The world was not always a benevolent place.

"I fear the lieutenant sahib's conversation was very shocking to you."

She smiled her small composed smile and shook her head, all at the same time. The effect was bittersweet. "No, not at all."

She surprised him. She ought to be shocked. She ought not be sitting so composedly with a man of his rather dubious talents. And it made him want to penetrate that armor of composed self-possession. "It did not shock and repulse you to learn that I have killed a man? I would have thought such a thing must change your good opinion of me."

Her answer was as quiet as it was unexpected. "Did he speak any part of the truth? Did you kill him just to watch him bleed to death? Did you enjoy the killing of another man?" she asked, her solemn gaze level and unflinching.

She could not have surprised him any more if *she* had slit *his* throat. He took a long moment to breathe the fair morning air into his tight lungs. "No. I did not slit his throat. But I did kill a man. It was a necessity, to stay alive myself. It gave me no pleasure."

She nodded and looked away. "I understand."

"Do you? Truly?" She was his remorseful angel, forgiving even as she reminded him of something better, something cleaner and free of deceit.

"We all have our darker shadows, Mr. Singh."

Impossible. He could not imagine her, his angel, his goddess, burning with anything but bright, untarnished light. But he thought less of himself for testing her so. "Let us talk and think of other, more pleasant things. Thou art all very good riders"—he raised his voice to include the two children in his compliment—"to keep control of your mounts while the lieutenant's horse was charging about so."

"Thank you, *huzoor*." Young Arthur was polite enough, and smart enough, to copy his older cousin's manners.

As they moved down the lane, Thomas took special care to keep a respectful, careful, and courteous distance between himself and Miss Rowan. If the dung beetle of a lieutenant thought to make trouble for Miss Rowan, any casual observer, and indeed, even those with sharper eyes, would see only that the *sawar* Tanvir Singh was making sure the red-gold goddess of the north knew her business with his extraordinary mare.

"The compliment is all to you, *huzoor*. The mare has beautiful manners. Indeed, she is quite perfect." She leaned forward to stroke the glossy beast's neck. "More beautiful than the spring rains, more beautiful than a sunset, more beautiful than a snowflake, because like a sunset or a snowflake, she is absolutely and perfectly unique."

She was smiling and talking in this exaggerated fashion for the entertainment of the children, but he was entertained as well. And he was a rogue, so he played his role to perfection, clapping his hand over his heart in a theatrical fashion. "This is praise, indeed."

"Indeed it is. She is very fine, but you knew that."

"As thou says. I had the raising of her up from a foal."

"It shows that she has been so very well trained and looked after. We are getting to know each other quite well, indeed, she and I. She shows great steadiness of character. She hardly batted an eye at the lieutenant's ham-fisted charge. Amidst all that to-do, she was as calm as Saint Margaret." Catriona had stroked her hand down the glossy black animal's neck in admiration.

"I am glad thou art pleased with her. And what name shalt thou give to this perfect, well-behaved snowflake of a mare?"

"Oh, do call her Snowflake, Cat," Alice pleaded. "Do!"

"But she's black, Alice," Arthur pointed out. "That will never do. She needs a fierce, noble name, like Queen Bess or . . . I know—Boadicea. She was a fierce queen, too."

Thomas had been amused and pleased that another should mirror his thoughts of Miss Rowan so exactly.

"Very good suggestions." Catriona awarded her cousins with a warm smile. "But I think I shall call her Puithar." She was still stroking the lucky animal's neck, and smiling her small, secret smile that pressed dimples into the apricots of her cheeks.

"Peth-ar?" Alice tried the word out. "What does *that* mean?"

Catriona Rowan's smile turned up at the corner of her soft, plush mouth. "It means she is special to me."

But Thomas needed no further explanation. He had heard her say the word the first day, in her murmured seduction of the horse, and he knew from his years of linguistic study under the careful instruction of his father, the Earl Sanderson, that she had chosen the Scots Gaelic word for "sister." "It sounds a most noble name, Memsahib Rowan. A noble name, indeed."

They turned out of the manicured lanes of the botanical garden and onto the dirt street of the city, and she asked, "I'm glad you think so. Have you a destination in mind for us, *huzoor*? Or are we to wear out the paths of the Fara-hat Baksheesh?"

"*Farahat-Baksh*. Baksh." He repeated the correct pronunciation for her, enchanted by the shape of her lips as she worked to get the pronunciation right. Ripe fruit waiting to be plucked. Enchanting.

But he must not ogle her like the callowest youth—like Birkstead.

Thankfully, she noticed no ogling. "Thank you. I have asked my lord Summers if he would find someone to instruct me in the languages, but he only looks at me, and asks why on earth I should want to do that, as if I had asked him if I may join a circus. And when I tell him, so I may speak and learn and understand the world, he laughs, and tells me that to do so is his job and not mine. But I cannot help but wonder if he is wrong. Because he doesn't seem to speak any of the languages, either. There are languages, in the plural, are there not? Some people speak Hindi and others Urdu, and you, *huzoor,* I think, speak both and Punjabi as well. But I understand none of it."

Thomas was losing himself in the lovely lyrical cadence of her Scots-accented words, and had to recall himself to attentiveness. "Art thou serious about undertaking a course of study?"

"Yes. Very."

His satisfaction was a physical thing—a warm feeling that bound his ribs and held his desires tight. Yet he made himself speak cautiously. Circumspectly. "If thou wishes it, I will make inquiries on thy behalf."

"Thank you, I would be most appreciative. I think speaking the language—or at least trying to speak the language, for I have no idea how I'll get on—will greatly enhance my experience of India."

"So how doest thou find India so far?"

"I find it with a map." And now the smile was no longer a secret, but spread across the ripe fruit of her lips like jam. "I know that was a terrible joke, *huzoor.* I find India . . . extraordinary. I find it extravagant and miserly. I find it colorful and dull." She laughed out loud, a merry, bright sound. "Actually, I find it a lot like Scotland."

How extraordinary. And how interesting of her to try to find similarities inherent in contradiction. "But Scotland is the other end of the wide world, mem. How can that be?"

"There are obvious differences between the two countries." Her brow pleated with seriousness even as she smiled. "But a city smells like a city, no matter which side of the world it falls upon—of masses of sweating, laboring, unwashed bodies, of gutters running with refuse, of the air full of smoke, and of streets full of animal waste. In Glasgow the air was filled with the pungent, earthy smoke of peat fires. The only difference is that in Saharanpur the fires are fueled by dried dung. India *is* remarkably similar to Scotland, if one only substitutes an overlay of overwhelming dust and heat in place of cold and raw damp."

"Thou art missing thy homeland." This he knew without a doubt. Because he suddenly recognized the same wistful emptiness in himself.

"Ah." She made a little moue of acknowledgement. "Perhaps a little. A very little. And you are very perceptive, Tanvir Singh. But I love being with my cousins, and I am enjoying India in general, and Saharanpur in particular, more and more. Do you visit the city often?"

"Several times a year, as the trade takes me. When the sahibs of the East India Company are buying horses, then I like to be the one selling the horses."

"But the company is not your only customer?"

"Alas, no, mem. But now that Saharanpur has added greater attraction for me, perhaps I will visit more often."

She turned aside his implied compliment without any hint of consciousness. She truly wasn't used to flirting. "You seem on very friendly terms with Colonel Balfour?"

"He and I are very old friends. Indeed, he is much like a father to me. I hold him in as much honor as my own esteemed father."

"And where is your esteemed father?"

"Far, far away to the north is my family." He didn't want to lie to her. He wanted to be able to tell her the truth, or at least as much of the truth as was possible. "And thy family? Why have they sent thee to Hind? To marry a rich man of the company—a nabob as the English call them?"

"No. They did not send me. I came alone." She looked

away, out across the fields and orchards as the city gave way to farmland. "They have all passed away, my family. That is why I came to India, to my aunt. Because I had nowhere else to go."

Thomas was surprised. He had thought her solemn when he first saw her, but he had never suspected her to be burdened with grief. "I am very sorry for thy loss, mem. I collect it has been some time?"

"No. Not really. But I thank you." She took another deep breath, and again he had the impression that she was consciously making a decision to put the thought behind her. "You are very kind."

Oh, he really was going to have to work on giving her another adjective for him. Interesting. Compelling. Attractive. Anything but kind. She was killing him with her own sweet kindness. "I am not known in Saharanpur for my kindness, mem."

"Why not? Oh. I hope I have given no offense, *huzoor*. I meant my words only as a compliment. You certainly have been very kind to me. You could have sold my lovely mare to any number of other people, but I am very, very glad you sold her to me."

"Thou hast given no offense. And if I have been kind to thee, it is because it is easy to be kind to those who treat others with respect and kindness themselves."

"Oh. I suppose it is." Her smile was a little bittersweet— just a softening of the corners of her mouth and eyes. "On this we are very much in accord." She paused for a moment, and then turned to him fully. "There doesn't seem to be much of what you call mutual respect between the cantonment and the city. Or the country as a whole, for that matter."

"Ah. Thou hast the tact of a great vizier, mem. Or a maharajah's wife"—he tried teasing her—"if thou wert ambitious."

Again she let his compliment slide like a bead of water off a green leaf. "Now that is too kind of you. I would have thought a maharajah would marry much like an

English prince, to cement alliances and amalgamate power. But unlike our English princes, who are held to just one wife, I understand a maharajah may take as many wives as he pleases, as often as he needs to shore up his allies."

"This is true."

"And what of you? Do you have any wives, *huzoor*?"

Was there something more than simple curiosity in her voice? "Alas, I keep no wives, for where would I put them when I am upon the road with my caravans. But I am not like the maharajahs or the nawabs, mem. I am neither a Mohammedan nor a Hindu. I am a Sikh." He held out his wrist to show her his ceremonial bracelet, one of the visible emblems of his accustomed faith. "Our scriptures teach that women have the same souls as men, and have the same right to spiritual teaching and experience. And when we take a wife, we take only one, and we take her forever."

Thomas could hear the gravity, the quiet conviction in his own voice, and for the first time, he understood that he had completely accepted and assimilated this tenet of faith. That he had changed more than the length of his hair and the color of his skin in the long years since he had first come to India.

And Catriona Rowan heard his gravity, too. "Oh." Her response was very quiet, and she looked away from him, so he could not read the look on her face. "I see. I am sorry. You must think me very ignorant."

"Thou art not ignorant, mem," he disagreed gently. "Thou art only unlearned. But who amongst the people of Lord Summers sahib's house would teach thee the many and different ways of this world?"

"No one. But I should very much like to learn the ways of all this world."

He was warmed that she had unconsciously echoed his words, but the feeling of pleasure deep in his gut was also a warning—a reminder that he could not be the one to teach her the ways of his world. A reminder that his world and hers were not meant to cross.

But it also reminded him that his world—the life he lived and the role he played—were not even his own.

"The lieutenant sahib was wrong about a great many things, but he was right about one thing in particular."

"Was he?" She retreated back into wariness. She did not want the lieutenant to be right about anything.

"Thou art in want of a friend."

"Perhaps I was." She turned to look at him, leveling him with the hopeful gravity in her gray eyes. "But not anymore."

He made himself shake his head. He made himself say the required words, even though elation was sliding like a thief into his veins—like opium, heady, intoxicating, and deeply, dangerously addictive. "I am not a suitable person to be thy friend, mem. But I should like to introduce thee to another, better suited to the role. Colonel Balfour's daughter Mina Begum has arrived at his home to visit her father and mother from her husband's home in Ranpur. She is a very cultured lady who has only lately left her parents' home to marry the heir of the Nawab of Ranpur. I know she will be delighted to make a new friend."

Catriona's full smile blossomed across her rosy apricot-smeared lips. "Married to the heir of the nawab? Then she is a princess. She is to be congratulated for having achieved the ambition of nearly every little girl the world over."

"But not thee?"

"Oh, no. I was no different. I was as ambitious to be a princess as any little girl born into genteel poverty can be."

"Surely not, mem. Thou art as different from the other memsahibs as—to use thy English expression—chalk is from cheese."

"Pray, do not put me upon a pedestal, *huzoor*. I am as human and flawed and ambitious as any other girl under the sun, princess or no." The clear light in her gray eyes darkened to steel. "Do not think me otherwise."

Chapter Ten

It was an admonition Thomas should have heeded. A warning he should have understood. But he had not.

It was a measure of just how far gone he already was that he had put her upon that lofty pedestal, and then had not understood why she had climbed down.

He had invented her—his red-gold fantasy of a girl—as an answer to a question he had not even known he had asked. With her solemn smiles and her quiet steel, with her riding before the wind on the mare he had meant only for her, and her open, vivid face flushed with heat and pleasure, she had answered the longing he had buried deep in his most private heart.

He had wanted her to be a part of his life. No matter the cost.

Now, with the benefit of years of hindsight, he could see that he had been profoundly lonely. So lonely, he had been prepared to put aside his years of training and risk his career to indulge his newly acquired taste for one particular Scots-Irish girl. Many men came to the east and acquired a taste for opium or hashish the way he developed his addiction to her. He wanted to be with her so badly, he had damned the consequences. What had started out as a game had become a necessary obsession, as important to his existence as the air he breathed.

In the days that followed that first ride, he found excuses to stay in Saharanpur when he should have headed north into Kashmir to see which way the wind was blowing in the long valleys where Gulab Singh held the power for his maharajah in Lahore. On the strength of nothing more than a casual invitation—"Perhaps we might do this again, sometime?"—he rearranged his days to spend every available spare moment with Catriona Rowan and the Summers children, riding down the long length of the Doab Valley, or trekking higher into the hills. Riding and talking and laughing.

And watching her. Always watching. And admiring the way she had with the children—her easy camaraderie and diligent care, her readiness to sacrifice her own wants and needs for theirs. She was devoted to them. Perhaps too much so.

So he conspired to find some acceptable way to get her alone.

Colonel Balfour was not enthusiastic. "You mean to bring the new resident commissioner's niece here to meet Mina? To visit the *harim*?" he had asked. "What game do you think to play here?"

That afternoon they had been speaking in Arabic—the harsh, throaty inflections of the language itself another reminder to Thomas that he had other, more important responsibilities, that as Tanvir Singh, he ought to be playing a greater and more important game than chasing an *angrezi* girl. And that he needed to be aware that the words they spoke were meant not to be heard or understood by others. It was an old conceit—the colonel had long ago gotten Thomas into the habit of speaking a changing assortment of languages during their private meetings, which they most often undertook while sitting on comfortable cushions in the shade of the courtyard near to the fountain, where the babble of the water would fill the ears of anyone impertinent enough to try and listen to the colonel and his great friend Tanvir Singh.

Thomas met the colonel's mild reproof with questions

of his own. "You can have no objection to the girl herself. You saw her here at your party. She was everything beautiful and charming. And the begum approved of her."

"Not exactly approved, Tanvir, but yes, the begum spoke of your visit to the garden that night. I must also ask if you think it wise, Tanvir, to be disappearing into gardens with young English girls?"

It was the farthest thing from wise, but he wasn't prepared to let it stop him. "She's not English, she's Scots. And she's not like them—the other English girls. She's . . ."

Perhaps his old friend had recognized the futility of trying to appeal to Thomas's better senses because the colonel tried a different approach. "And what does the resident commissioner, Lord Summers, have to say about you escorting his niece through dark gardens? And out riding every morning? And inviting her here to visit the *harim*?"

It should have given him pause, that second warning that his comings and goings with Catriona Rowan had already been remarked upon, and reported to the colonel. That Miss Rowan and he had already become the subject of notice and scrutiny. He should have appreciated the irony of the fact that Tanvir Singh, who had built his career on knowing exactly what to make of seemingly idle rumors, was now the subject of such speculative chitchat.

But Thomas did not stop. He did not pause. He did not listen.

Instead he carried on, justifying his risky pursuit of the girl with a careless wave of his hand. "I did not invite the resident commissioner. I invited Miss Rowan. It is for her to convince her uncle, or not." And he had shrugged to show the colonel that the result was of no difference to him.

"And what does Mina have to say about this invitation? No, don't answer that. I know my daughter—she will be delighted. But what about the begum? Have you asked *her* if you may invite this English girl into her home? Into her private retreat?"

"I have, Excellency. Of course I have." He had chosen not to comprehend Balfour's reticence. "Miss Rowan is not like the other memsabs, whose nostrils pinch up at the thought of spending time amongst the *natives*. She does not want to spend her time shut up in the halls of the residency, or taking sedate rides along the cantonment's manicured avenues. She wants to see Hind and understand it the way you and I do."

"Tanvir, listen to yourself, my son. You and I are a dying breed. In this day and age, in this political climate, she is to become like us? You ask the impossible."

Thomas had known Colonel Balfour was right. But still he had pushed on, twisting his wishes into justification. "I know I may not spend that kind of time with her. That is why I wish to introduce her to the begum and Mina. So she will have friends, and I may wash my hands of her." Thomas changed the subject quite purposely to one that was sure to engage the colonel's attention and approval. "I cannot linger here much longer. Tensions in the court of the Lion of the Punjab, the maharajah, are high. The talk is of another war."

Colonel Balfour gave his immediate attention to such serious talk. "Ah. And what of the Maharajah Ranjiit Singh's enemies? What say you of the Khan in Kabul, or his old enemy, the Shah in Peshawar?"

Thomas was glad of the noise of the fountain covering their conversation from curious ears. "Not enough of Kabul, but it is said in Lahore that Shuja Shah Durrani is a puppet who will act only as the Lion of the Punjab bids him." But Thomas could not sustain his own attention. His gaze kept straying to the closed gate to the palace grounds in anticipation. "But let me see Miss Rowan introduced to the ladies of the *harim,* and then we will talk more of Kashmir and Peshawar."

"Will we?" The colonel proved not to be so easily diverted after all. "And when will we talk of Lord Summers? And of the talk *you* keep postponing with him?"

"His Excellency has been fully apprised of the situation in the Punjab, and the ramifications to his company."

"Tanvir." His mentor had fixed a gentle, penetrating eye

upon him to let him know that Thomas was fooling no one with his doublespeak. "And does he understand the *pedigree* of this information you bring him?"

It was so like the colonel to be circumspect even though they were assured of privacy, to leave nothing to chance should a stray word appear on the wrong lips. But Thomas had been diverted himself by the sound of the great carved outer door swinging open. "We will talk more later, for I see our guest at your gates."

"Your guest, not mine. Go, then, for I will get nothing more out of you until you've satisfied yourself with her. I will go inform my ladies of their guest. But heed me well, Tanvir. Leave her to the women and concern yourself no more with the resident commissioner's household. It is nothing but a dangerous game you play."

But Thomas had not heeded well. He had barely listened. He had hastened—no, he hadn't hastened. He had *wanted* to hasten. He had wanted to rush across the space between them until he was with her. But he had disciplined himself—or so he thought—and had risen slowly, and with grace, and bowed to his host graciously before he strolled to meet Miss Catriona Rowan in the middle of the courtyard. It was she, he had noted with some pleasure, who had hastened toward him.

"Tanvir Singh." Her eyes were shining in the pale oval of her face. "Thank you for arranging for my visit here today."

"Memsahib." He took her hand in greeting. "Thou art most welcome here." And before he could think better of the impulse, he gave way to the force of his attraction to her. He lowered his head to press a kiss upon her hand—a simple touch of his lips to the soft, silken skin at the turn of her wrist, no more. But her flesh was subtly perfumed with the delicate scent of lemons, and his eyes slid shut while he inhaled her essence. His head swam as if he had drunk forbidden alcoholic spirits. Smitten.

Foolishly, dangerously, increasingly smitten. So smitten he wanted to slide his cheek along the lemony appeal of her soft skin. He wanted to turn her wrist and do away with the buttons guarding the tight barrier of her sleeve. He wanted to touch his tongue and his teeth to the sensitive tendons there. He wanted to fall into the soft surety of her, this flame-bright warrior goddess of his dreams.

But he did not. He was a gentleman. He straightened up.

Her freckled cheeks flushed with high color. "Thank you, *huzoor*. I'm rather excited myself." Her voice had been soft and breathless with the first awakening of pleasure, and she had looked at him with fresh regard, her eyes searching his face, before she turned away to look around the nearly empty courtyard while she regained her composure. "Is no one else here? I thought I was to meet the ladies of the house? The place seems rather deserted."

He had rather it were deserted so he might keep her to himself. But they were undoubtedly already under the watchful eyes of the curious *zenana*. "Thy Scots hardiness lets thee travel out in the heat of the afternoon when others nod comfortably on their divans."

"Oh, no. Have I come at the wrong time, when everyone is resting? I could not come any sooner, until I could leave the children safely occupied or taking their naps."

"It is no matter." He smiled over her worries. "It is always rest time in the *zenana*, and Mina has been looking forward to meeting thee. As has the begum."

"Mina? That is her name? How enchanting. But what is her title that I may address her correctly?"

"Mina will do, whilst she is here among her family. I have known the colonel since the day in my youth when I rode into Saharanpur with a few horses to sell. He took me under his wing. He has been like a father to me, and his family, his children, are like brothers and sisters to me as well. I could not enter the *zenana* otherwise. But now that Mina is married to the son of the Nawab of Ranpur, I see but very little of her."

"But she must be very fine, then, the princess? I've never been introduced to one before—a princess. Will I do?"

Thomas allowed himself the pleasure of pretending to judge the suitability of her slate-blue riding habit—a color he disapproved of as being too like gray for his tastes—while he more particularly admired the cut of the bodice and the way the jacket fit so snugly, accentuating her small waist and her firm upturning . . .

Damn him for a jackal.

"Do not be uneasy, mem. Mina may be a princess, but she is still just a woman like you."

"Hardly." Her answering smile was accompanied by a wry tone. "I think you may be too often in the sole company of your men to understand. My aunt is only married to the third son of a duke, and she depreciates my ancestry to a considerable extent—my father's ancestry in particular, since I share her ancestral relation to the Duke of Hamilton on the other side of the family. But if even Lady Summers is so nice about caste, I can only imagine what the wife of a prince will think of my lowly antecedents."

He tried to smile kindly to reassure her—to try and repair such a hurt as the Lettice Summerses of this world could inflict with their carefully cutting words. "A prince is still a man. In the Sikh way of thinking, all men are equal in the eyes of God. As are all women—in my religion, both men and woman are equal in the eyes of God."

If he had hoped to astonish or impress her, he fell short. She thought about his revolutionary pronouncement for a long moment, before she answered, her eyes twinkling with sharp intelligence. "An admirably enlightened philosophy, *huzoor,* to be sure. An *ideal* philosophy. Which I share. I, too, think all men and women must be equal in the eyes of God, but I also think that they can never be equal in the eyes of other men, and certainly not in the eyes of other women. Nor do I think all women are equal in the eyes of most men." She turned that deliciously sparkling gaze upon him. "Do you not make a distinction between people based upon their beauty? You are a handsome man. Do you not use this to your advantage? Do you not aspire to take an equally handsome wife?"

"You flatter me, mem." And he was flattered. Deeply so.

Her regard was like a sharp inhalation of hashish, sending him into raptures, encouraging him to return her regard even more openly. At last she was seeing him as a man.

"Is that wrong?" she asked quietly. "And I hope I don't give offense. I realize I don't know much about your philosophy, or your religion. I don't mean to make fun of you, but as my mother always said, 'handsome is as handsome does.' Which I took to mean that handsome people will always look for other handsome people to have and hold. Not to do so would go against all human nature."

His own mother, the Countess Sanderson, herself an extraordinarily handsome woman, had always said much the same thing, but with different intent. "Ah. Perhaps I mistake thy English idiom, but I would think thy honored mother's adage means that a person is only as handsome on the surface as they are prepared to act. If their actions and especially their thoughts are not as handsome as their face, then they are ugly in the eyes of God."

She drew to a stop, and reached toward him, all solemn, grave intent. "No one can be ugly in the eyes of God. Of nothing else am I confident, but of this, I am sure."

Everything about her—her very soul—spoke to him. "Thou couldst give no offense. Never. Because thou speakest the truth."

She did touch him then. She reached for his hand and took it with a gentle squeeze, as if she did not trust her feelings to words. The warm pressure of her touch was as fleeting as his kiss had been, and yet he felt it just as strongly, like warm honey poured over his skin.

He took hold of her hand before she could withdraw it. "Thou art as intelligent as a princess. And beautiful."

"Now you *are* flattering me. I think we shall dance on in this fashion—back and forth, and forth and back—without answers, until we are all out of compliments for each other."

"Impossible." It had taken days, and lashings of charm, but at last she was warming to flirtation, and to the intimate rapport between them. "But perhaps thou wilt be so kind as to defer thy compliments for another day, because I can see from the flutter of silk behind the screened windows above that thy arrival is most eagerly awaited within, and I will be roundly scolded for keeping thee to myself."

She glanced up at the walls without seeing beyond the surface. "I cannot imagine anyone scolding you, Tanvir Singh. Nor you accepting a scolding like a schoolboy."

Thomas laughed. "You have not yet met the begum, Miss Rowan. Just as the colonel has been like a father to me, so too the begum has been a most honored mother. So pray, let us not keep the honored lady waiting. Nor her daughter, who will be more voluble with her insults to me if thou art not delivered to her in good time."

He led his red-gold goddess across the wide lawn of the forecourt, and back to the private part of the compound, where the old inner palace and *zenana* were located. She was silent as the Scots mouse Birkstead had called her as Thomas escorted her up the wide steps. But she was all wide-eyed attention as they moved through the imposing front of the palace proper. Her head tipped back so far as she looked up at the intricate filigree of the screened balconies of the upper floors that she had to put a hand to her hat to keep it in place upon her head.

"All those little domes on the roof," she explained when she caught him looking at her. "It makes the building look like it's wearing a hat at each corner. A little domed helmet."

He smiled at her fanciful description. "Those are the *chhattras*—the word means umbella—small, open-air pavilions from which the Begum and the colonel may take in the view of both the city and countryside. The begum especially enjoys being able to see the mosque in the city, the Jama Masjid, and hear the call to prayer from its tall towers."

In another moment they were through the carved wooden door of the private palace and in the inner courtyard, where he led the way to a stair that rose upward to a curtained balcony. Catriona Rowan's clear gray eyes were alight with curiosity and delight as she took in the sight, but her feet slowed as they reached the balcony and approached the low divan where the colonel, his begum, and his youngest daughter, Mina, sat reclining on bolsters and cushions.

Thomas made his salaam and turned to indicate his guest. "Nawab Nashaba Nissa Begum, I give thee Miss Catriona Rowan of Scotland."

The Begum made a kind, nodding acknowledgment of Miss Rowan's less than perfect, nervous salaam, but she was filled with delight when the girl sank into a deep, graceful curtsy worthy of King George of England. "How very pretty," she said with a serene smile.

Catriona rose, and turned as he indicated the Balfours' daughter. "Mina Begum."

Mina smiled in her dazzling way and waved a rather jaunty salaam, and his Miss Rowan curtsied just a degree less low than she had for the begum. Whatever Lady Summers's objections to her niece's antecedents or upbringing, there was clearly nothing wrong with her manners. "I am honored to be asked to meet you."

Mina bounded up with a rustle of silk and a tinkling jangle of her jewelry, which adorned her from the crown of her head down to her hennaed toes. Clearly she had meant to dazzle her visitor. She came and took Catriona's hand. "My brother, what a treasure you have brought us."

"You flatter me, Highness," Catriona said. "But that is exactly what I said when I was introduced to *sawar* Tanvir Singh—that he had brought me a treasure."

Mina waved away Catriona's use of the honorific, just as Thomas had hoped she would. "Come, we are to be friends so let there be no titles between us. And I should very much enjoy saying your name—Catriona. It sounds like bells ringing."

And it tasted like pomegranate.

The thought must have escaped into his expression, for Mina turned her sly smile on Thomas. "Do you not think so, my brother? Is it not most delightful?"

Thomas merely bowed to agree with Mina, and hopefully turn her attention, but she was not yet done with him.

"Catriona looks at us so, wondering why I call you

brother. Tanvir Singh is not my brother in blood, but in spirit. I have known him since I was a girl, living here in the carefree days of my youth."

Mina spoke English almost flawlessly, with only a small melodic intonation. It was the only indication that this beautiful, dark-skinned beauty was half English. More English by some people's standards than Miss Catriona Rowan, with her depreciated Scots-Irish antecedents. And certainly more English than anyone could think Tanvir Singh, though his father was an earl.

"Thy days are carefree now, Mina," he teased.

"This shows that you know nothing of the world of women, nothing of the intrigue of the *zenana*."

"I must confess I know nothing of it myself," Catriona admitted. "This is my first visit to such a place. And it is even more beautiful than I could have imagined."

"Then we must make sure that this is the first of many more visits. For there is much more to see of my mother's house than just this part of the palace. There are gardens and pools and fountains we have not yet explored."

Miss Rowan colored at the mention of the gardens and fountains, and, perhaps remembering her incursion into the lady's private space, she stole a worried glance at the begum. But that lady only smiled and said nothing of the trespass, while Mina chattered on.

"You must come into our world and see it for yourself, as Tanvir Singh cannot."

"Cannot? How can he be here now, if he is not allowed?"

"He may visit at my esteemed mother's invitation, but the *zenana* is a private place for women only, where men cannot come with their loud talk and dirt from the street."

"I know when I am no longer wanted." Thomas pressed his hands together and bowed, but he smiled all the while, a smile that he hoped told Catriona he left only because he had been asked to go, and not because he wanted to. "Thou hast only to send to me when thou art done with thy visit, Miss Rowan, and I will escort thee back to the residency."

A lovely blush warmed her cheeks. "Thank you, *huzoor*."

"In the meantime." The colonel cleared his throat to recapture Thomas's attention. "I hope you will join me in *my* part of the house, Tanvir Singh, where the ladies may make no rules for me." And with a kiss for both the begum and his daughter, his mentor led the way out of the house.

While Thomas's mind was occupied with not thinking about whatever it was that Miss Catriona Rowan was doing with Mina and the begum, he joined the colonel back in his favorite spot, on the shaded divan near the fountain.

This time the colonel spoke in French. "Now that I have your attention again for a time, I will tell you that I had a conversation of great interest with the resident this past night."

"I hope he was listening to your advice?"

"Patience, Tanvir Singh." Colonel Balfour looked up to the pale blue sky through the curtain of the leafy shade trees as though it were an infinite source of unhurried calm. "He was deploring the inefficiency of this station, and more pointedly, my former administration of it."

"The hell you say." Thomas spoke in English, so immediately incensed for his friend was he.

Balfour made a gesture of caution. "He was trying to determine, he told me, which of Saharanpur's administrative functions might be relocated to an even more remote hill station during the hot weather. I hadn't the heart to tell him that this is just the beginning of the hot weather." Balfour chuckled. "But more to the point— 'Here,' he said to me in all seriousness, 'is a man on my books I have never met, and who, it seems, has not done any work for the station in years.'"

"Let me guess."

"'The Honorable Thomas Jellicoe,' says he. 'Drawing pay into an account, and doing absolutely nothing, as far as I can tell. A man I have never even met. The man could be dead for all I know.'"

Thomas laughed, but Colonel Balfour was not so easy. "You will joke, and say the new resident is as great an ass as can be, but you need to speak to him as soon as may be,

or the Honorable Thomas Jellicoe will disappear—struck
off the books. You need to clearly make him understand
the way things are." He leaned in and lowered his voice to
speak. "It may be called the Great Game, my boy, but it is
played in deadly earnest."

"All the more reason to keep my knowledge to myself."

"You owe the resident commissioner—the current resident commissioner, whoever that may be—your allegiance
and your truth."

"There is only one man I trust with the truth, and he is
no longer the resident commissioner."

"And I am honored, Tanvir. But if you won't do it for
yourself, then do it for me. I'm getting to be an old man,
Tanvir Singh. I have already been set aside from the company, and am slowly but very surely losing what little influence I once had. They are different, Tanvir. More like
jackals than men, with their predatory ways. They will not
be satisfied until they have pushed the likes of us out. In
such circumstances, I *cannot* be the only man who knows
Thomas Jellicoe's secret. If you are to secure your future
in the country, you'll have to learn to trust someone else."

Chapter Eleven

But Thomas never told anyone. He had kept his secret close—closer than he had kept Catriona Rowan. He never told her.

It had been a mistake. A grave mistake. Because now she sat not ten feet from him in the nursery at Wimbourne, looking at him as if he were as strange and unwelcome a sight as a leprous fakir begging in her doorway. Resenting his intrusion into her orderly, starched life. Distrusting him—she had learned not to trust anybody. And planning even now to get away.

"I pray you will excuse me, my lady." Catriona rose, and gripped the back of her chair. "It has been a trying morning, your ladyship, and I should like to see the children and then perhaps take a small rest."

But Thomas could not allow her any respite—it already felt too late. Too much useless effort had already been wasted. Too much time had already passed. Outside the windows, the blindingly bright morning had already begun to fade into the long, gray English afternoon he remembered from his boyhood. Darkening clouds had started to pile upon the horizon in a thick line of gray. A storm was moving in.

But a storm could work in his favor. Rain dampened powder and drove hunters—and other bloody miscreants with guns—indoors in search of shelter. And heavy rain might keep her from bolting as well. Might. She was frightened, but determined—a powerful combination.

At the moment she was still, as pale and colorless as the sky—the perfect cipher of a servant. It bothered him, the speed with which she was willing to erase all the force of her character. She was not meant for this menial, self-effacing existence. She was meant for color and vibrancy. She was meant to be full of movement and life. She was not meant to bury herself alive in nothing but English gray.

"Of course." Cassandra was all gracious concern in acceding to Cat's request. "It *has* been a most trying day. We will leave you to take your rest, but I thank you for wanting to see to the children first, before you retire, so they might know for themselves that you are all right."

"Oh, yes, my lady. I'd like to go straightaway."

Her obvious concern for his brother's children was very real and deeply heartfelt. Another family of children substituted for her own.

"Then we will leave you." Cassandra stood, but then impulsively reached for Cat and pressed a hasty kiss on her forehead. "You are very precious to us, Miss Cates. Pray don't forget that."

"Thank you, my lady." Some fragile glint of emotion lit the corners of Cat's eyes, but was quickly hidden by a calm smile.

"Thomas?" Cassandra turned the focus of her attention to him. "Let me show you to your room. I'm sure you need some rest after your travels and the . . . surprises of the day. You'll want to wash and refresh yourself."

It was a reasonable assumption, but Thomas was done with reasonable. He didn't move from the doorway. He kept his eyes on Cat. Trying to see behind the façade. Wanting to understand her fear and desperate, foolish resolution. Looking for . . .

What? Some sign that under all the prim buttons and starched, correct behavior, and unreasoning fear, she still loved him?

He had been so sure of it, her love. He had been so sure that despite everything, despite the loss and the dangers, she had loved him. It had been the thing that kept him going through the years of searching and frustrated, bitter longing. She had loved him, and he had loved her.

But she had refused him once before. He kept managing to forget that inconvenient fact, because forgetfulness was his last bulwark against the doubts that came in the night, and stole around the unguarded corners of his soul. The doubts that whispered his deepest fears into flame— what if he was completely and entirely wrong?

What if she had not chosen him? What if she had been ambitious all along, playing him off against the bastard Birkstead? What if she never meant to come back to him, or let herself be found?

What if she pushed him away, and said, "Don't touch me," and meant it?

"Thomas?" His sister-in-law tried again. "We've all had more than enough turmoil for one day. Let us leave Miss Cates in peace."

But Thomas was not about to make a peaceful, polite, or civilized exit. He was done with civilized. Instead, he took another step into the room. "I should like a quiet word with Miss Cates, if you don't mind."

"But I do mind," Cassandra protested. "And Miss Cates has clearly said that she minds." His surprisingly steely sister-in-law was both incredulous at his cheek, and adamant in her stance, planting herself in front of him as if she could bar his way with the strength of her refined contempt. "Surely you are too old to need lessons on how a gentleman conducts himself with a young lady?"

But Thomas closed his ears to his sister-in-law's pointed set-down. "Cat." He spoke as if they were alone, and he let his low voice fill with all the years of empty regret. "I'd like to speak to you. Please." It was a concession, that little piece of politeness. An indication that he meant to be civil, if not civilized.

Cat looked stubborn and nearly mutinous for a moment,

as if she would rather do *anything* in the world than talk to him, but perhaps she heard the plea, as well as the resolve in his voice, because she finally bowed graciously to the inevitable. "It's all right, my lady. I'll speak to Mr. Jellicoe."

"All right, then." Cassandra resumed her seat, determined to play the careful chaperone.

"Alone." Thomas tried to keep the combativeness from his tone, but it was nearly impossible. He was running dangerously low on patience. The truth was that he meant to have it out with Cat one way or another, and the thought of potential failure frightened the patience out of him.

What in the hell was he going to do with himself if she could not be made to see reason? If he couldn't convince her of his love? The thought left a bleak, gaping hole through his chest.

"Certainly not." Cassandra was just as insistent. "I will not do either of you the discourtesy, nor the disservice, of leaving you alone. The dinner hour can be postponed."

Thomas rubbed his hand across the whiskers already coming in along the steep angles of his cheekbones, and then up into his short, shorn English hair, as if he could chafe some semblance of English civility and patience back into his brain.

But it was impossible. And the situation did not call for English caution and restraint. It called for sly Punjabi wiles. And a subtle display of force.

He turned the force of his gaze on his sister-in-law, looking down at her from under his brows. "Cassandra, I am not above picking you up, and putting you bodily from this room. But I would rather not. I will pledge to you that I will not move from that chair"—he pointed to a straight-backed chair across the room from Cat—"if you will please let me speak to Miss Cates alone, for a few minutes only, about a very private matter."

Cassandra almost gasped in affront—not even his concession could blunt his rather primitive threat.

Across the room, Cat made no sound, but she eyed him warily, measuring him out like a coffin maker. Whatever it was she saw in him, it helped her make up her mind. "I think it best, your ladyship. Perhaps we might leave the door open and Nanny Gaynor can sit with us?"

"Privately, Cat," Thomas reiterated.

Cat made an impatient sound. "Nanny Gaynor is as old as Methuselah's grandmother, and as deaf as an out-of-tune piano, Mr. Jellicoe." She sounded tired, and perhaps a little baffled. As if the constant clash of remembrance and reality had exhausted her as much as it had him.

"An out-of-tune piano?" He had to smile at that. Even closed up here in his brother's walled manor, hiding in her gray, she had a unique way of seeing the world.

"My point, Mr. Jellicoe, is that her presence will serve the proprieties, and preserve my reputation—which is all that I have to myself at present. Will it not, my lady?"

Cassandra conceded with as much ill grace as Thomas had never thought to see in the normally elegant woman. "I suppose so."

He wasn't going to wait for his sister-in-law to change her mind. "Good. Off you go." And if he did not do exactly as he had threatened and put her bodily from the room, then he did something only slightly less physical—he put his hands on his sister-in-law's delicate shoulders, and very firmly *propelled* her from the room. "We'll wait here for your Nanny Gaynor," he said equitably. And then he shut the door firmly in his astonished sister-in-law's face.

"Mr. Jellicoe." Cat's voice told him she was already regretting her accession to his wishes. Or perhaps she was finding the cooled embers of her once redheaded temper again.

Good. She had always been magnificent when she was riled. Thomas held on to the knob as Cassandra rattled it from the other side—there was no lock upon a nursery door—and attempted to rile Cat up a little more. "Don't you think you could manage to call me by my name, now that we're alone?"

"No," Cat insisted in a low voice. "Or did you want me to call you Tanvir Singh, because he was the man I knew—or thought I knew—Mr. Jellicoe? And we're not alone," she added in a furious whisper. "Lady Jeffrey can still hear you."

"I told her—I told them all—we were acquainted."

Cassandra's livid voice came through the panel. "I don't care if you are *engaged,* let alone acquainted, Thomas. A gentleman does not seek to put himself apart with a young lady no matter his degree of acquaintance. This is *not* how a gentleman acts."

Thomas didn't answer. He kept his gaze on Cat, and softened his eyes, letting his smile hitch up one side of his face in the way that had always had power with her. "Do you think we need to tell her that I'm the very farthest thing from a gentleman?"

"I think she already knows." Oh, it was prim and starchy, her pert rejoinder, but there was at least a trace of the tart, pomegranate sweetness sneaking its way through the repressive layers of gray. That glimpse of her wry humor gave him, if not hope, then at least enough encouragement to forge onward.

Out in the corridor, Cassandra was doing her best to be the opposite of encouraging. "If you do not open this door this instant, I'm going to get James," she threatened. "*And* your father, Thomas, if that is what it will take to make you act like a gentleman."

"It's going to take a lot more than that," he answered. But he kept smiling at Cat. Because it was damn fine to look at her, gray dress, dull, dark hair, and all.

She held her tongue and managed to resist his rough attempt at charm, and retreated to the farthest corner of the room, as if she wanted to put as much distance between them—figurative as well as literal—as possible.

Thomas respected that need, and stayed put for the moment, leaning his weight back against the door, listening until he heard Cassandra's angry, rapid little footfalls retreat down the stair. He reckoned he had anywhere between five and twenty minutes alone with Cat at most before his brother came charging back up those stairs and either put paid to this interview, or put him bodily out of the house. "Miss Cates is greatly valued by Lady Jeffrey," James had said. Clearly, Miss Cates was greatly *protected* by Lady Jeffrey, as well.

And since this little tête-à-tête was like to be his only opportunity to see Cat in her natural habitat, as it were, as Miss Anne Cates, he began a slow, circuitous promenade about the nursery, poking his head into the open door of the schoolroom in an effort to divine all of her secrets from the everyday objects with which she surrounded herself.

A glance told him the nursery and schoolroom looked like no other nursery he had ever seen—including his own, growing up the privileged and well-tutored son of an earl. Bookcases had been built along the entire length of one wall, and filled with an amazing variety of books. Thomas noticed that they were placed by topic, with the natural sciences separate from literature, for example, and that a variety of specimens, living and dead, were arranged on wide, open shelves. Drawings, diagrams, and charts filled the rest of the walls, as well as the back of the movable slate board. One large glass bowl was home to a group of floating tadpoles, while another housed some dark, spotted newts. In the sunny window was a birdcage so ornate it looked as if it might have once held a half-dozen lovebirds in some maharajah's *zenana*. At present it housed only a slumberous family of field mice. He'd never seen the like of it in his life.

And all this had been wrought by Miss Anne Cates. How extraordinary. How singular.

Or perhaps not so singular. Perhaps she had done much the same thing in India, with the Summerses' children. She had been forever taking them out for rides and adventures, stopping to collect flowers and all sorts of insects. They could never have spent so much time together, she and he, if they had not been accompanying the children. But he had had only glimpses of what her life might have been like within the walls of the residency. For all he knew, she may have kept ferrets in cages, or charmed snakes from large reed baskets. It bothered him to no end—he who had been trained to see and understand the secrets people preferred to keep hidden—to realize he knew so little about her. To realize that he had invented her—his red-gold warrior goddess—at the expense of the very real woman behind the steely veneer. "You are utterly remarkable, Catriona Rowan."

She made a sound of depreciation very much like a scoff. "'Remarkable for that piece of good breeding peculiar to natural Britons, to wit, defiance'?"

Thomas hadn't expected philosophy. "I don't know if I would say that your most remarkable quality is defiance, but—"

"No. It's a quote from Steele." At his obviously blank look, she clarified. "Richard Steele the writer. In *The Tatler.*" She shut her eyes and made a minute shake of her head in dismissal. "You don't read much."

"I've been out of the country." He'd been out of his mind, but that was another subject entirely, his magnificent obsession—his single-minded pursuit of his invented goddess—she who did not want to be pursued.

His attempt at humor softened the corner of her mouth, but she was still all governess and not goddess. "He wrote at the beginning of the last century. And there were editions of his work in the residency library in Saharanpur, so it has nothing to do with being out of the country."

"It has everything to do with being a nomad. But I'm glad to hear you speak of the residency in Saharanpur." He left the schoolroom doorway and began to move slowly toward her, trying to not appear as if he were stalking her. But he was.

And she knew it. "Mr. Jellicoe. You promised Lady Jeffrey that you would stay put in that chair." She pointed to the piece of furniture in question.

"I lied." He didn't even turn around to look at it.

"Ah, yes." A marmalade eyebrow lifted with precise, elegant disdain. "You're very good at that."

He welcomed the quick pain of her wicked little slice of

truth. At least they were getting to the contested heart of the matter. "Thank you. But you don't mean it as a compliment, whereas I do. You've become quite adept at lying yourself."

She would not admit his point. "No. I'm not like you. I'm not clever the way you are. I can't speak forty languages, or tell if people are lying. I can't pretend to be something I'm not."

"You're pretending to be Miss Anne Cates." He stopped along a shelf to pick up an open book—poetry by Walter Scott—before he let himself glance at her. "Just as I had to create the identity of Tanvir Singh."

"I didn't create a new identity—a new religion and a new life, with new habits and customs. I'm not trying to convince people I'm something I am not. I only took a new name, but I'm still the same beneath it. I still talk the same and think the same and live the same. I'm still only a governess, Mr. Jellicoe."

That time he was sure she said his surname to remind herself, to shore up her defenses against him. But he was a seasoned campaigner. He'd laid siege to taller walls. "I think you've always been much more than just a governess, Cat."

"Don't call me that," she said.

"We're alone now, Cat. You don't have to act like Miss Anne Cates in front of me. Why can you not just be yourself?"

The look she gave him was nearly as blistering as it was bleak. "You of all people, Mr. Jellicoe, ought to know that to be oneself, as one pleases, is a luxury few people can afford. And I am not one of them."

He pounced upon the excuse. "Yes. Yes, you are right. Just as I could not afford the luxury of being myself with you in Saharanpur." But a different spark of instinct flared into flame as she reached out to trace the liquid silver path of a raindrop that had just begun to patter against the windowpanes. "I would take care to stay away from the windows, Cat." He reached for her. "Your shooter may prove to be a sniper."

Cat drew away abruptly. "A sniper?" She frowned at him in confusion.

"Is this a word the well-read governess doesn't know?" He took her lack of response as a yes, and clarified. "A sniper is one who fires from a place of concealment. A sharpshooter."

"I see." She tucked that bit of information away in that blade-sharp brain of hers. "I think not."

Something about her calm rejection of his theory set off more warning flares in the back of his brain. He stepped around a low chair, trying to find a better vantage point from which to see her face, cast in obscurity by the low, flat afternoon light. "You don't think one can shoot from a place of concealment, or you don't think your shooter is a sniper?"

She hesitated, directing a hard, assessing glance at his face—trying to read him—before she answered. "The second."

Clever girl. But did she know? Had she guessed who it was? He wanted to take her in his arms, to hold her and protect her when the realization came, or when he had to tell her. But when he moved toward her, she stepped away again, meandering down the shelves. Keeping her distance. "Why do you think that?"

"If he didn't hit us on the lawn, either his gun is inadequate for the purpose, or he's just a very, very bad shot. Either way, I don't think he's going to be able to shoot me through a third-story dormer window across such an expanse as all that." She gestured out across the empty lawns.

Thomas wasn't conceding an inch of that open space. "So you admit he was shooting at you?"

Her eyes, those clear, pale gray eyes, cut to his sharply— another assessment—as if she were trying to figure out if she could trust him. Looking at him the same exact way he was looking at her. They were circling around each other like two wary elephants, slow and tentative, all but lifting their trunks in the air, searching out a whiff of advantage.

"You were on the lawn alone." He began to lay out his case. "Moving away from the party when the first shot came—well away from the rest of us. I ran to you after that first shot."

She shook her head, and lifted up one shoulder to reject the idea, uncomfortable with even thinking about what might have happened. Of how differently it might have turned out. She blew out a long, ragged breath, and for a moment he thought he had gotten through. For a moment he thought her lofty ramparts were finally beginning to crumble under his careful siege.

But then she retreated behind her walls and said, "I guess we will never know."

"No." He contradicted her immediately. "We will know. I'll know. I'll find out. I've been thinking about nothing else, and narrowing down the possibilities. Easy enough to do, as we had only one real mutual enemy between us. And the others are dead."

She turned toward him at that. "No," was all she said—a sharp, emphatic denial. She stared at him, livid in her perfect, silent stillness.

He had the entirety of her attention now—all that well-used, well-honed intellect focused upon him. He stepped nearer to speak. "It must be the lieutenant, Cat. Birkstead must have followed you here. No one else needs you dead."

She shut her eyes again the moment he pronounced the bastard's name, as if she could shut the memory off as well. But she denied it instantly. "He doesn't need me dead. There's no reason. I've given him no reason."

He came another step closer. "But you do admit that it must be him—Birkstead?"

"No." She turned back toward the windows, shutting out the idea. "I didn't— Why should it matter now? It was years ago."

His gut told him she wasn't lying, but she was leaving something out. "Yes. It was," he acknowledged. "But he has every reason. And you must know that." He was guessing, but it was a guess based on two years of doing nothing but thinking about all the clues, all the possibilities. But he didn't wait for an answer he knew she would not give. "I think you know more than anyone about what really happened, Cat. And the longer you hold on to that knowledge, the more that knowledge is going to hurt you."

She said nothing. She blanked her face, as flat and featureless as the moon, and turned away.

He was relentless. "What happened, Cat? Why did you not tell them what happened? You never defended yourself. You just disappeared without telling anyone what you saw in the residency that night when you went running—oh, my God, I still have nightmares about you plunging into that burning building—looking for the girl. When you went in after Alice and—" He would have shut his eyes if it would have blotted out the image. "You never told anyone the truth."

"No." Oh, her head came around fast at that. The denial leaped from her mouth like a bullet out of a gun, and she spread her hands before her, reaching toward him as if she could ward him away from the idea. "You're wrong. Alice wasn't there. There was no one there. I don't remember anyone. I don't remember. I just don't remember."

Now he was certain she was lying outright. But she had finally come near him. Near enough so that he could see her lovely solemn face again, clear and open and appealing. And very, very afraid—her eyes had gone dark with the fear she could no longer hide behind buttons and starch.

He was again seized by the same irrational compulsion to grab her. To hold her to him and protect her, no matter the cost. To touch her, and slide his hand along the soft line of her jaw and into her hair.

And it seemed he was actually doing it—touching her—because the moment his hand grazed her skin, he was filled with a relief so profound it was a physical thing, a jolt that brought him back to life, as if he were drawing the first breath of air back into his lungs after having been drowned.

"I remember it, Cat. I remember everything about that night." The words spilled out of him like water from an overturned pot. "I've seen it over and over in my mind like a play, time and time again. I remember everything about you. I remember your taste and your smell. I remember the feel of your skin under the pads of my fingers. I remember the way you looked in the moonlight, luminous as the crescent moon, like a pale slice of a star."

She didn't run. She didn't push him away, or say, "Don't touch me." She stayed still and let him touch her, though she trembled under his hands.

He closed his eyes and leaned in, following the homey, starched scent of her, and trailed his mouth along the rigid side of her neck where he could feel the fragile pulsing of her veins beneath his lips. He kissed her there, and slid his lips slowly up the tilted line of her jaw.

"You tasted of almonds," he whispered to the curved arabesque of her ear. "Do you remember? I remember I took down your hair. It had escaped almost all its pins, but there were one or two still holding it up and I let it down. Like silk, but softer, warmer."

She had done the same to him—running her hands through his long, unruly hair. And he could see her remembrance in the way she knotted her fingers into tight, tense fists to stave off the memory.

There were more pins now. Hundreds, it seemed, pulling and scraping her hair into obedient order. But it was too fine, too long and flyaway soft to resist the release of his hands. His fingers stole across her scalp, freeing the pins so the fall of her hair could cascade in a silken curtain across her shoulders.

"Yes, it was like that." The soft strands fell through his fingers, and he held it up to the light to look at the muted, dull colors. Even her hair looked gray. "Such a crime, Cat. What on earth have you done to it?"

"Walnut hulls." Her voice was the barest whisper of apology.

"Please stop it." He had loved the bright flame of her hair. He had not been able to light lanterns in order to see it the only other time he had taken it down. He wanted to gather it up in his hands like sheaves of wheat, and tug her head back so her mouth would fall open. He wanted to bury his face against it, and let it hang down to brush against his chest.

He wanted, he wanted. He wanted more from her than he could explain.

He wanted her love. He wanted her trust. He needed her absolution.

And he could not stop touching her. Lightly, gently, slowly. Waiting for her fear and her distrust to wane. Letting his hands barely skim the surface of her face. Tracing his way back to her, charting the minute changes the years had wrought—the silvery pallor that washed her once glowing skin. The tiny lines of worry that crept toward the corners of her eyes.

Those eyes fell shut as his fingertips grazed across her cheekbones, and caressed down the straight line of her nose, and back around again. His thumbs rose to trace the elegant sweep of her brows.

And lust, pure, undiluted, and primal, roared to life within him, drowning out all thought and sound but the pounding of blood in his ears.

"Ah," he managed to say, though his voice sounded as if it came from far, far away. "You didn't let them grow in."

Her eyes flew open, and for a single, unguarded moment her gray eyes went dark, before she immediately began to back away. But he had seen her knowledge, and he had felt her instinctive response. He had felt the heat ignite under her skin.

"Oh, my God, Cat. What else remains the same?"

Chapter Twelve

Catriona was on fire with mortification. And something much, much more powerful. And more seductive. He pulled her closer and let his eyes roam over her face. And then his hand followed where his eyes had been, tracing along the line of her eyebrows, smoothing the pad of his thumb over her skin.

She turned her head away sharply to dislodge his touch, to keep him from prying any more secrets out of her. He disobliged her by taking her chin in his hand and turning her back to face him. "It's remarkable that you've kept threading your eyebrows."

Awareness blossomed under the newly sensitive surface of her skin. "You are imagining things, Mr. Jellicoe. There is no one with threads in England."

He smiled then, his slow, lazy smile, and his eyes drifted almost closed. "Oh, by all means, yes, I am imagining things. I am imagining exactly what I will find if I raised your very sensible, long skirts, and felt my way over your ankle boots and higher, over the top of your sensible, practical stockings, and felt the bare skin of your legs. Oh, yes, I am imagining things."

Catriona could feel the answering heat spread, stretching and coiling inward, deep into her belly. "Stop it."

"If you wish," he said reasonably, in that low, sooty

whisper. "I will stop imagining things, and I will remember instead." He leaned his mouth closer to her ear so his voice could insinuate itself deep inside her. "I remember the day you did this—the day you let Mira's *ayah* thread your eyebrows and the hair from your skin. I remember what you looked like that day, fresh and startled. And I remember what you looked like later, beneath the prim and proper clothes you wear like armor, when you came to me."

He leaned in to put his mouth so close to her ear that she could feel the warm brush of his breath against her skin. "I remember that even then, under my robes, I was Thomas Jellicoe and not Tanvir Singh. Because I liked it. And I think you liked it, too. And I have been imagining in maddening detail"—his finger glanced over her eyes—"all the other things you may have kept the same. But don't worry. Your secrets are all quite safe with me, Miss Cates. I'll take them to my grave."

There was so much—so many memories and feelings— she had tried to shut away, but he kept unearthing them, one by one. Laying her foibles and failings and petty vanities out in the sun like coffins on the grass.

He would notice her eyebrows. He who saw every little detail and could tease out its meaning without conscious thought. Such a tiny piece of vanity, plucking her brows into a neat curve—something she did now without thinking, without remembering anything at all. She hardly ever thought of Mina and the begum. She had forced herself not to. It was better that way. Safer.

But safety seemed to be as slender as the arch of an eyebrow.

"You are mistaken." Her words sounded feeble to her own ears, but he did not protest her obvious deflection from the truth. In fact, he looked as if he were in pain—his eyes were open and unfocused in the sort of blissful agony of a Renaissance saint in the midst of a vision.

She stepped around him, and quickly reached the sanctuary of her room, sliding behind the barrier of the door before he could recover himself sufficiently to stop her, or say anything else inflammatory. Unlike the nursery-suite door, hers did have a lock—a token effort meant to preserve some semblance of privacy from the omnivorous curiosity of the children. But it was solid and thick, her door, and she put her back to it so she could slide to the floor as her knees gave way beneath her.

The wood flexed beneath her back—Thomas Jellicoe must have leaned against it on the other side. "I'm not giving up, Cat." His voice vibrated through the wood, and hummed its way deep into her bones. "You can't just keep running away. It won't work. I will follow you, Catriona Rowan, day and night, up corridor and down, until you remember the way it was. Until you trust me again."

Oh, but he was wrong. She did remember. And she did want to trust him.

She wanted to trust the anguish she could hear in his voice, and the fierce intelligence behind his penetrating green eyes. She wanted to let him share the burden she had been carrying with her like a tombstone. She wanted to let him hold her, and take the pain and the loneliness away. She wanted him to fight her battles and slay her dragons.

But life wasn't like that. If there were dragons to be slain—and clearly there were—she was going to have to sharpen her own sword, and fend them off herself. Anything else was fantasy.

Because there were some dragons that couldn't be slain with one sharp thrust from a well-honed blade. Some dragons were impervious.

And because she had promised never to tell. She had given her word.

There could be no return to the days of peaceful, carefree sensuality in the begum's *zenana,* or to the serene hours she had spent there. To the colorful garden perfumed by the scent of night jasmine, and to the cool, deep blue of the tiled pool.

It was a gift he had given her, Tanvir Singh, those seemingly endless days, those marvelously selfish hours in the *zenana,* when she hadn't needed to think about anyone or anything else. For the first time in her life, others had taken care of her, instead of the other way round. Not that she had begrudged her young cousins even a second of the hours she spent taking care of them, and reading to them, and playing with them. She did not. She had loved them, and loved every moment of every day they had had together. She loved them still.

And oh, how she missed them. Their absence in her life left a hole in her heart that could never be filled. Never. God and Saint Margaret knew she had tried.

But the *zenana* had been special. It had been the beginning of another entirely new world for Catriona. A world full of exotic, delicious food and clothing in brilliant, saturated colors. A world filled with beautiful, impromptu music and dance, and evocative readings of poetry and literature. A world full of language with subtle meanings that often left her baffled, but always left her wanting to learn more.

And she did learn more. She experienced more.

Mina was a great patron of the arts and always kept a coterie of artists—female poets, musicians, and dancers—who entertained them whenever the mood should strike. She was also attended by many body servants who seemed to exist for no other reason than to pamper and adorn the princess and the begum with oils and perfumes and silks and satins and jewels too costly to enumerate.

Catriona had come to treasure her afternoons in the ancient stone halls of the begum's palace. She had been given an open invitation to visit the ladies of the house any time she might break away from the residency, and she made good use of it. Most days she made herself wait until the children had been seen to, and given their lessons, before she could find the time to indulge herself, but Mina had laughed at her conscientious diligence, and told her to bring the children as well, to play in the cool stone pavilions and frolic in the clear pools, if that would bring Catriona to them sooner and more often. And so she did.

Most days, they went when the full, steaming heat of

the day was upon them, when Aunt Lettice napped and no one in the residency or cantonment would miss them, or remark upon their whereabouts, and when the streets were deserted of almost everyone save the *sa'is*—as she had learned to call the grooms Tanvir Singh sent to accompany her—who rode at a distance behind them as they slipped out of the cantonment lines.

Other days, if it were earlier, or cooler, or for any reason that she could create, Catriona would lead her cousins down the path along the river, because with only a slight divergence from the shortest route to Balfour's palace, they could pass Tanvir Singh's colorful encampment. And often it happened that Tanvir Singh would be making his way to his friend Colonel Balfour's comfortable home at the same time, so they might ride together.

It was always the best part of her day. So good, in fact, that she didn't remark upon Tanvir Singh's almost un-canny ability to anticipate her. She had never thought to question why he was always available to her. Because she didn't want to. She wanted to be with him. With Tanvir Singh, she didn't have to keep to a sedate pace, and she could abandon the parasol meant to shade her fair skin from freckling. She didn't care about freckles—the sun felt good on her face and shoulders. She liked the warmth of the earth seeping into her. She liked the freedom of her mare, and being able to choose her own friends.

"Huzoor." She tried not to smile too widely when she greeted him, this friend of her heart. She tried not to ride or run to him as quickly as she could. She tried not to gravitate to his side as if he were the sun and she a helpless star, revolving around his orbit.

But when she was with him, her heart was happy and content. And she was free.

Free of both the cantonment's and the bazaar's insidious insistence on caste. Free of her aunt's myriad little insults. Free of the chill that had lived in her soul for too long.

India had burned it away.

She had changed.

Tanvir Singh had changed a little, too—at least to her eyes. He appeared less and less the heedless rogue, and more and more the thoughtful, charming prince, with manners as smooth and polished as a maharajah's jewels. He was very much at home in the colonel's palace, where he would leave off his colorful surcoats, and wear only his less formal, though certainly pristine, white cotton tunics and turban. It made him look softer somehow, although the adjective was silly when applied to such a man. More approachable, perhaps. Much less the fierce *sawar* who had stared down Lieutenant Birkstead than the charming, witty friend ready to make her laugh and smile.

And he would walk her slowly across the wide courtyards to the *zenana,* stretching out the time, as if he had nothing better to do in the world than chat idly with her about the day, and what progress she was making with her study of the language, or what she had thought of the poetry that he had given her to read. But eventually he would bow and take his leave, leaving her to the begum and Mina.

God, how she missed Mina. How she wanted her forthright opinions and forceful optimism. How she wanted her advice. But Mina's advice would be the same as it had been in Saharanpur—to trust Tanvir Singh. And to trust herself.

But that was the hardest thing of all. All her confidence, all her surety had been burned away in the fire.

Mina would have chided her for her loss of confidence. Mina had to have been one of the most confident, beautiful, and generous creatures Catriona had ever known. If Tanvir Singh had been a secret, disguised prince, Mina Begum had been every inch the secure, reigning princess. Every day she was sumptuously attired in a close-fitting *salwar kameez* tunic and trousers of shimmering silks and embroidered satins, and richly adorned in magnificent sets of jewels—earrings and hairpieces, bracelets and rings, anklets and necklaces. Confident in her femininity and beauty, for not even the richest jewels were as beautifully alive as she. Her skin was the color of wild honey, and her lightly veiled hair the rich hue of warm, dark chocolate, but her eyes were so light and translucent a green they took Catriona's breath away, and made her want to draw near to assure herself they were real.

And for all of Mina's assurances that Tanvir Singh was only her brother in spirit, to Catriona's eyes Tanvir Singh and Mina looked enough alike in coloring and feature that they might have been related. Perhaps they were—perhaps Tanvir Singh was the natural son of Colonel Balfour. Perhaps he was even his heir—she had never heard of another son. Catriona was still trying to learn about the complicated ties of kinship, religion, and power in India. And she frankly had no idea at all about the different religions to which the family seemed to belong. The begum and especially Mina, as the wife of the Nawab of Ranpur's eldest son, both abided by the law of Islam and kept themselves secluded and veiled, while Tanvir Singh had told her he was a monotheistic Sikh. And the colonel, whom Catriona assumed had at least been raised a Christian, seemed to profess no particular religion at all.

And Catriona felt it would have been disrespectful to ask. Any time she even mentioned the name of Tanvir Singh—told how they had ridden with the children out into the fruit orchards to the north of the city, or climbed into the hills, or related some observation he had made—Mina would pounce upon it like a playful but sharp-eyed cat.

"Do you not think Tanvir Singh most handsome, Catriona?" she had asked.

"Yes." Catriona was sure a blush had warmed her cheeks, but there was no reason not to speak the truth among her friends. "Yes, of course. He is a most handsome gentleman."

"Good. It is good that you should think so. I worry that he does not have admirers because he travels so much, back and forth and all across the world, from kingdom to kingdom. It is past time he settled down with a lover, if he cannot yet take a wife."

"Surely you don't mean—I am not Tanvir Singh's lover!" she protested as heat rushed up her neck. Mina's, and even the begum's, frankness in all things marital and carnal had not yet ceased to amaze Catriona. "Nor do I have any ambition to be."

"Do you not? Then why do you seek his company if you do not want to taste the delights of his body?" the wide-eyed beauty had asked. "You do not think just to tease and play with him?"

"Heavens, no." The heat was insinuating itself under her skin, curling lower into her belly. "I would never do such a thing. I like him very much. He is my friend." Catriona struggled to explain her wonderful, comfortable friendship with the tall trader even as her thoughts raised the less comfortable but strangely compelling feelings she had tried to stifle. "We both share a love of horses."

Mina had raised one perfectly arched brow, and pursed her lips skeptically. "And do you talk always of the horses?"

"No, we talk of many things. But certainly not of being lovers."

"And why not? I have seen the way he looks at you. And this is not the look of a friend." Mina had sat back on her cushions with a knowing laugh. "I have shocked you with my frank talk, but my brother has been alone for far too long. And you are the first woman of any race or creed that he has ever introduced me to."

"Am I? Surely he has many friends?" The whole world seemed to be Tanvir Singh's friend.

"Of course. He is a man of the world. Everyone between Kabul and Calcutta knows the name of Tanvir Singh. He does have many friends, but very few that he would invite into my father's home. And certainly none before you that he has asked to introduce to my esteemed mother."

Catriona had felt all the responsibility of the honor. "My dear princess, you cannot know how greatly I esteem your friendship. And you, Nashaba Nissa Begum." Catriona had turned to include the dignified lady in her appeal. "I hope you do not think I am unworthy to be a friend to Tanvir Singh."

"No, no," Mina had cried. "Never unworthy, for you are as generous and truly good-hearted a person as can be. But you are *unprepared* for the ways of the world. If you value my friendship, then you must value my advice. Especially my advice about Tanvir Singh."

"You are alone in the world," the begum agreed. "Without a mother to teach you and take care of you."

Clearly the two women had been talking about her. "My aunt has been very kind."

The begum shook her head. "But does she teach you the arts of being a woman? Does she get you a husband?"

"Well, not exactly." Catriona had no desire to discuss the messy situation with Aunt Lettice and Lieutenant Birkstead, and Lord Summers—how Lord Summers kept practically throwing her at the lieutenant—with the inhabitants of the *zenana,* even though they probably already knew. Though they were closed off from the world, it seemed the world and his wife, as the saying went, came to them. "Let us just say that their efforts have unfortunately come to naught."

"Then we must do what we can to help you," the begum asserted.

"We must," Mina decreed. "We will make you beautiful. For only when you feel beautiful, and feel the strength and power of your unique pale British beauty, will your eyes be opened. As will his. And you will understand how it is, and how it is meant to be between you two."

"I'm not sure—" She hadn't been sure. But she had been aware. And Mina could tell.

"Look at him when next you see him," Mina urged, "and think on my words, dear sister. Look at the strength of his hands and the breadth of his shoulders, and ask yourself if it is only friendship that you seek. Ask yourself if it is friendship that makes your breath come fast beneath your breasts, and makes your body feel new underneath your skin. Ask yourself."

And Catriona had.

It had taken only that gentle urging to give way to the thoughts and feelings that had lain dormant within her. To the enticing heat that curled deep in her belly when she looked at him. So she had asked. And she had seen.

And she was seduced by the possibilities Mina had so cleverly suggested. Seduced by the idea of being beautiful and enticing and powerful. Seduced into submitting to the sensual pampering of the *zenana*. She was massaged and brushed and threaded and anointed until she glowed. Until she felt beautiful and new beneath her skin.

And Tanvir Singh had most definitely noticed.

Thomas leaned his forearm against the stout barrier of the door to Cat's chamber. He could hear her on the other side of the panel, hear her shallow breathing. And he knew that she remembered.

"You looked beautiful," he said as he crouched down on his haunches so his low voice would carry under the door. "I'll never forget how you looked that day. Did you know that Mina had invited me to come and sit with you, and listen to music? And I came at the appointed time, only to find you were not sitting in the pavilion listening to music. You were dancing."

The image that arose before Thomas's eyes was shocking because it was so familiar—revisited night after night—and still so vivid. The sight that had greeted his eyes that afternoon had been straight out of his waking dreams—secret thoughts and images he had conjured for himself out of fantasy and lust.

Mina and her attendants were teaching Catriona Rowan to dance in the flowing northern style. And in order to set Miss Rowan free to comport her body into the sinuous twists and turns of the Rajasthani dance, they had persuaded her out of her tight-buttoned English clothes and long, concealing sleeves. Out of the confines of her stiff whalebone stays.

"You were dressed in a long, full-skirted version of *salwar kameez* in dark, lustrous sapphire silk so blue and so fine that it rustled and whispered secrets as you moved." Thomas put words to the memory. "And your flame-colored hair was unbound, and fell in a plait like a bolt of apricot silk straight down the middle of your back. Do you remember? Mina had adorned you with a cascade of her heavy Mughal jewels that shimmered around your face like a waterfall of color whenever you moved."

And how she had moved. Though the whirling rhythmic steps of the dance must have been new to her, she had taken to them with a natural grace, a cleanness of line, and a lightness of step and heart that brought joy and easy expression to every movement of her body, from her bare, hennaed feet, to the long, white line of her arms as she raised them above her head in a movement that made her body arch so that her sweet breasts pressed tantalizingly against the straining fabric.

He was struck as dumb and immovable as a fakir as he watched from the doorway, set aflame with lust, incinerated with the need that pounded through his veins with every beat of the tabla drum.

And then he heard her laugh. "You were laughing. And there was nothing delicate or light or coy about your laughter—it was open and wholehearted and it bubbled out of you, full of joy. As if you had just that moment learned what it was to be happy."

Mina had been laughing, too, and calling direction and encouragement to her pupil as Catriona copied the movements of the other dancer, and stretched her body into the stylized poses.

And the sight of his goddess dancing loosened something within him. Something he could not call back under harness again. Ever again. It had broken free and it had risen through him with all the fury of a dust storm.

And his only thought was a ferocious accusation—how had she who seemed so innocent, so untainted by the sordid needs of the world, become so full of such physical knowledge? Such an awareness of her body? Such pride in the erotic tension of her flesh?

While his mind detailed the changes in her supple mobility, his body had gone rigid with shock, or dismay, or more properly—oh, yes, that was what it had been—seething jealousy, even as he knew that no other man had put such animal awareness beneath her skin.

And he knew in that moment, that he would do anything to be the man to do so.

The thought calmed him somewhat. Which was good, because at that moment one of the Begum's ladies espied him in the dark of the archway and set up a high-pitched, giggling fuss.

And in less than a moment, the sapphire temptress was gone. "You blushed scarlet when you saw me." He went on with his story, hoping she was listening on the other side of the door. "Though you pressed your hands together as Mina did, and bid me welcome, you seemed to find great interest in your bare feet."

He had not taken pity on her. He had not let her escape. "I asked if you were quite well, because you were so flushed and quiet at seeing me. But Mina saved you from having to speak. 'She is very well, as you can see, Tanvir. Have you not noticed the differences? No doubt you will be full of disapproval, with all your Sikh beliefs, but I think she looks lovely. So much more refined, don't you think?'" Mina's own face had been wreathed in a smile of sly triumph.

Thomas closed his eyes to conjure up the image of what he had seen. "And I had to look again, to see that the delicate arch of your eyebrows had been enhanced by the threader's art. And I knew, Catriona, that there would be more displays of such art on your body. Much more. And much, much less. I knew that under the sapphire silk your skin would be completely bare."

Thomas had had to force himself to act like Tanvir Singh, to be passive and not react when all he could think of, when all he could envision in his mind's eye, was her pale, white, extraordinarily bare flesh. Lust stirred and rumbled, unbidden and uncontrolled, like gathering clouds within the landscape of his body. Most definitely Thomas's body—Tanvir Singh should have felt only disapproval, or at the very least disappointment at such a disturbance to Miss Rowan's godhead, for the Sikhs never cut their hair, nor shaved or threaded the hair from their bodies.

The pavilion, which up until that moment had been spacious and cooled by the sweet evening breeze flowing across the high ceilings, had began to narrow, until it held only the small patch of floor upon which she stood.

"And then you looked at me." Thomas continued to spin the memory out until he could once again feel the stunning sensations he had felt that day. "And I saw something—awareness? Or even perhaps desire warming your eyes. Because you let me look at you, with heat racing across your face and sweeping down your neck, drawing my eye across the delicate architecture of your collarbones and shoulders." And lower still. He had imagined following that warm flush down, down beneath the long skirts of the fitted dancing robe that would have no stays or petticoats, down the sweet scoop of her belly to her long, pale white legs. "Was I wrong?"

Behind the door, Cat did not answer. But no answer was response enough. She did not deny his claim.

Then he had been right, that night in the Begum's *zenana*. She *had* looked at him the way a woman looks at a man. A man she wants. He had known it then, and that knowledge had been all the fuel the raging fire of his imagination had needed to conjure up an image of exactly what Catriona Rowan would look like when she was naked beneath him, her body spread before him like a pale pagan offering.

When, he had thought unequivocally. Not *if.*

Oh, Mina could be proud of her work that day. She had aroused and discomfited them all to a nicety. Just as she had surely hoped and planned. But Mina had known enough to say nothing to him. She had only smiled in her contented way, and turned away to conveniently busy herself with some other task.

But he had not turned away. As if he had no will of his own, as if his hands were not at his mind's command, the tip of one finger had reached out to trace along the delicate line of her brow.

"I fear you do not approve, *huzoor.*" Her voice had held a whisper of something like pride, or defiance, that pleased him. He could not bear for her to feel anything like shame.

To his own shame, it had taken an effort to speak as Tanvir Singh. "It is not for me to approve or disapprove. Thy body is thine own, to do with as thou likest. Thy body is thine to adorn or not, as thou wouldst please, and not any other."

But it had pleased him. Immensely. Beneath his *sawar*'s Sikh robe and turban he was simply a man. An Englishman very far from the home he had forgotten, and a man who found the imagined landscape of Miss Catriona Rowan's pale, smooth, naked body unbearably erotic.

And Mina had known it. She had continued to offer him temptation beyond his power to resist. "Do you like my gift, Tanvir? Does our Catriona not look beautiful and as a woman should?"

"Yes," was all he had allowed himself to say.

And he had allowed himself to recline on a divan, and watch as Catriona Rowan was persuaded to dance and stretch and move with the grace of the surest cat. His Cat.

Mina was nearly purring with pleasure. With her, his discomfiture slanted toward anger. "Careful, Mina," he had said in a voice low enough for her ears only. "She is not a doll or a toy for you to play with. And neither am I."

Mina was unchastened and unbowed. "But how can I resist when you look at her so? When your eyes come alive the way they do when you behold a beautiful horse. You have never shown such interest in a woman before. Not a woman of your own kind."

Thomas had been startled by the acuity of the soft, spoiled sister of his heart. As far as Thomas knew, only the colonel and the begum knew of his true identity— Mina had been a child of no more than two or three when they had concocted their plan to create Tanvir Singh. "Be careful of your words, sister."

"Rest easy, my brother," she had assured him. "She is beautiful, even though she is *angrezi,* and you are alone."

"And I must stay alone. A horse trader does not take a wife unless he wishes to stop trading horses. And I have no wish to stop trading horses."

"Ah. It is as I thought. You look at Miss Rowan and already you think of taking a wife."

"Mina," he had admonished in his sternest voice.

But she had laughed at him, pleased with herself, and he would get nowhere arguing with her and protesting what she had already confirmed. So he could only join in her teasing. "I think of a great many *other* things to do with Miss Rowan besides take her to wife. Just as you intended, and so cunningly arranged that I should."

The Princess of Ranpur did not bat an eye. "I must have all the cunning because your Miss Rowan has none."

"Oh, don't underestimate her. She has enough."

"Aha. You have what—touched her? Kissed her? Have you had a taste of her yet? Once you have a taste, she will be inside you and will never go away."

And Mina had been right. The thought of taking Catriona Rowan to wife had set up camp within his head. And it did not go away.

It was still there in the dim afternoon of a gray English day. And Catriona Rowan was still on the other side of the door.

But at least she was no longer on the other side of the world.

She was here now, and if she was not exactly talking, she was at least listening.

"Do you remember the day you went swimming?" He settled down to sit with his back against the wall, so he could turn his head and speak to the crack between the door and the jamb. "I was not at the palace to greet you. I had spent too long trying to convince a Rajput breeder to part with a stallion of Arab blood. And by the time I found my way to Colonel Balfour's the heat of the day was upon us."

Her quiet voice carried to him through the panel. "The sun had baked the scent of curry into the air, until the afternoon was drenched in a deluge of spice."

Yes. That was what the day had been like. That had been the magic swirling in the air. "I thought the ladies of the *zenana* would be dozing upon their cushioned divans with sleepy servants pulling the punkahs to fan the household. I thought perhaps I might be able to get you alone."

Thomas had followed the liquid sounds of laughter and water along the high screened passageway overlooking the begum's garden, until the happy shouts and splashing lured him farther, around to the deepest, most private part of the palace. There, at the very heart of the property, a stream that wound its slow way down from the hills had been artfully diverted and dammed to make a deeper, non-ornamental swimming pool.

Most of the ladies and children luxuriated around the shallows at the sides in various states of undress, so he stopped and would have turned back, intent upon not intruding upon their privacy.

But there she was, his red-gold goddess, slowly stroking her easy way through the green water on her back, like a naiad or some bright, misplaced Celtic water sprite. Her spun-ginger hair streamed and floated out around her like a living bloom, as did the white cotton of the long chemise she wore to preserve her modesty.

And under the clear green water, her bare limbs had flashed, long and sinuous and luminously white. Her long legs scissored with slow rhythm as her arms stroked through the water, pale and gleaming.

He had held himself entirely still. Well, perhaps not entirely still. The one part of himself he could not discipline into stillness had grown appreciative and hard at the very sight of her.

She dove down smoothly, stroking toward the bottom, and he was treated to the lure of her curved, cotton-clad bottom before she disappeared beneath the surface. In another moment, she surfaced and drew in a deep lungful of air, and then eased onto her back to float.

And his mouth went dry.

Now he understood Mina's casual invitation for the challenge it was. For as Catriona floated on her back, and closed her eyes to the bright press of the sun, and abandoned herself to the water, his eyes were open wide. He could see through the wet cotton fabric that now clung to her body with glorious transparency. And he could *see* that she was entirely and gloriously naked—he no longer had to imagine what Mina's talk of threaded eyebrows and beauty had meant. The evidence was now before his eyes. The ladies of the zenana had indeed adorned and pampered Catriona like a princess in accordance with Hind's standards of beauty. And they had threaded every last tuft of red-gold hair from her body, leaving her mons naked and bare, and through the wet, transparent fabric, unshielded from his eyes.

Lust—deep, unbridled, and uncivilized by any attempt at thought—coiled through him like a snake, steady and potent. If he had wanted her before, he was now stunned by the savage ferocity of his need.

It wasn't as if he had not seen women similarly groomed before—it was the custom for women to remove the hair from their bodies. But it had never affected him so before. This was not merely the casual appetite for the carnal. This was need, a need that had only to do with her. This white, white Scottish girl, gleaming like the rarest pearl in the sunlight. But unlike the dark-haired beauties he had seen similarly groomed, she did not just look nude. She looked naked.

His mind had chanted the word: naked, naked, naked. Incantation or curse as he watched stupefied with need that was perilously close to yearning. Naked, naked, naked.

And mine. Mine to take. Mine to hold. Mine to keep. Now.

The only thought that had kept him from going to her

then had been that he was in Augustus Balfour's home, in the begum's palace. Thomas's peculiar sense of honor, and years of self-discipline and privation, kept him in place, even when his naked red-gold goddess made her way to the shallows and began to climb out.

He had turned his back to further spare himself the sight of her long, lithe body as she took up the napped cotton cloth a servant handed her to dry herself, and closed his eyes and leaned his head back against the cool of the wall.

But there was no escape. He had burned for her.

He still did.

Chapter Thirteen

From that moment on, he had stopped thinking. The years of service, his duty to the company, his allegiance to Colonel Balfour—all fell away before the need that was an ache that grew unbridled, until he was sure it would rend him in two.

But he had waited calmly, even patiently, by the palace gate to escort her back to the residency, until she came into sight. Somehow, even in the aftermath of his clandestine violation of her privacy, it was even more erotic to see her in her own constricting, buttoned-up European clothes. To know that beneath all those concealing layers of cotton, behind those stiff whalebone stays, underneath those yards of dull gray fabric, her luminous skin lay hidden, like a pearl beneath the callused, rough shell of the clam.

He helped her mount Puithar, and the burgeoning feeling of possessiveness grew stronger when he had her under his hands. His palms lingered at the smooth curve of her waist. His fingers slid over the strong architecture of her booted ankle to arrange her stirrup just so. Any excuse to touch her. Any excuse to stay close enough to inhale the lush scent of jasmine and lemons that clung to her like joy. Any excuse to merge reality with his dreams.

They walked their mounts out of the gates, and through the waning day slowly, letting the children ride ahead,

drawing out every possible minute of the quiet dusk by
some unspoken agreement. Evening was falling upon the
land, and the sky was lit with a hundred delicate colors of
pink and orange and purple like a signpost of God's quiet
extravagance.

Side by side they rode on, and he was aware only of her.
Conscious only of the yard of space separating them, attuned only to the small movements of her hands and feet
as she brought the mare fractionally closer. And closer
still. He checked himself, making sure that it was she who
was inexorably and purposely closing the gap, and not he.
He watched, drunk with anticipation and need, heady with
hope, praying to every god he had ever loved to make it
real, and let him not be imagining the blissful fact that his
goddess was drawing ever closer.

And then her knee was whispering against him, her
thigh nearly touching his thigh.

She did not look at him. She kept her gaze steadfastly
forward, and so he reached very carefully between
them—he could no longer resist the compulsion to let his
fingers caress a fold of her long riding skirt. Just the once,
before he made his fingers fall away from her. But though
she would not look, he would, and he saw her eyes blaze
shut like a falling star, an omen of benediction.

When they neared the cantonment the dusk had deepened, and so he let the children draw ahead through the
gate before he steered Catriona away, down along the long
line of deep, shaded shadow against the enclave's tall,
bricked wall. He lifted her from the saddle, and she braced
her hands against his shoulders as he set her down, sliding
them slowly down his arms, as if she were as loath to stop
touching him as he was to release her.

"Tanvir Singh." She said his name, and he wanted nothing more in that moment than to tell her the truth, and ask
her to call him Thomas. Just that once. Just so he might
hear his own name on her lips when he kissed her for the
first time.

"It's all so very strange. I feel—I want . . ." Her voice

was a whisper of confused hope that trailed off into silence, unable to articulate the need that crackled between them like the frisson of heat from a lightning storm.

But he knew what she wanted from him, even if she did not.

"Yes." That much he managed to say before the drunken mixture of lust—confined only by furious amounts of self-restraint—and relief had spilled into his blood like the spring rains swelling a river.

Because she looked up at him with the entirety of her open soul shining in her eyes like the pale gray moon, and he knew nothing was going to keep him from kissing her.

But she was young, and too trusting, and he had to be sure.

"Mem," he began. And then he gave himself the gratification of saying her name—the pleasure of having the pomegranate taste of it on his lips. "Catriona. I am thy friend. So I will tell thee the truth, which is that I very, very much would like to kiss thee. And more, much, much more. But thou art . . . confused in thy feelings. And thou art forbidden to me."

She did not try to deny that truth. "Why?" she asked instead, her voice soft with the first faint bruising of hurt. "You said all men and women are equal in God's eyes. Why may we not be equal enough to even kiss?"

Because once he started kissing her, he might not be able to stop. "Because God does not make all the rules. Men do."

But he did not believe in the rules—he had spent the greater part of his life as Tanvir Singh flouting them. So he gave lie to everything he had just said, and bent his head and touched his lips to hers with a swift surety that made her breath come fluttering out of her mouth in surprise.

She watched with open, wondering eyes as his mouth took sure possession of hers. Her lips were soft—so deeply, deeply soft—and pliant, and moved ever so slightly, so tentatively, against his. He did nothing more to touch her, only kept his lips against hers, tasting slowly, taking little sips of her, never drinking too deeply. It was she who put her hands on him, she who grasped his sleeves, holding him still before her, so he would not move away, so he would not leave before she could think better of this kissing in the gathering dark.

But she did not think better of it. She kissed him back, learning how to appease the low thrum of pleasure he knew he was evoking within her. When her eyes fell shut with the effort to contain all the sensations, and the butterfly ends of her eyelashes swept against his cheek, he was done in.

His hands rose to touch her, to find the delicate solidity of her arms within the voluminous folds of her sleeves, and gather her against his chest. Encouraging her to follow her desire. Asking her to trust him with her pleasure.

She warmed to the physical passion slowly, unbending by degrees, learning her way by delicate increments. And he led her on, with longer kisses, moving from the pliant softness of her lips to the long slide of skin along the side of her neck, teasing his mouth down the tendons, letting his fingers delineate the edge of her high neckline. Discovering the arrow-straight line of her collarbone beneath the sturdy cotton of her collar. Pressing the heat of his desire against the fabric, nipping gently through the layers to find the skin beneath.

And her head was tipping back, giving him permission, acquiescing to the intoxication of pleasure. He ran his hands up the side of her neck and into her hair, cradling the fragile strength of her skull, angling her face just so, stroking his thumbs along her cheeks until she opened to him.

He tasted her carefully, savoring the tart pomegranate tang of her lips, and easing his way within the softness of her mouth. He breathed in her sweetness and her goodness as if they would save him from himself. As if the fragile scent that arose from behind her ear could hold his baser instincts in check. But when she brought her hands to his waist, and pressed herself into him, he could feel his control slipping away, degree by degree, until his hands had stolen around her back and he had gathered her to him, kissing her over and over, bending her back over his arms and holding on to her as if she alone could tether him to this world. As though she alone could save him.

From what, he did not know.

He only knew that she felt perfect in his arms. She felt right.

As if she were the rightest thing he had ever done in his life. As if the press of her lips against his had changed him in some basic, profound way.

She had felt it, too. She had opened her eyes and looked at him, running the soft pads of her fingers across his features with inquisitive wonder, as if she would memorize each and every line and curve of his face. As if he had been something new and unknown she had chanced to discover for the very first time.

"Tanvir Singh," she whispered. But she had looked at him with such wonder and trust, the weary heart he had never thought capable of deeper sentiment turned over in his chest and began to throb with something perilously close to gratitude.

And then she lit his gratitude and sentiment on fire when she smiled, and threw back her head and gasped and laughed with such wicked, slippery delight that he wanted to show her just how much more wicked he could be. How much more delight he was prepared to give her. So much delight she would laugh and gasp for hours and days. She would laugh and gasp with pleasure until they were old and gray.

He bent his head to take the lobe of her ear between his teeth. He bit down gently, delicately, and a shivering shudder ran down through her body, and Thomas knew there was an answering echo in his.

He maneuvered her back against the wall so he could lean into her, and ease himself with the weight of his body bearing into her. She answered not with passivity, but with a renewed energy. She wrapped her arms around him and held him tight to her, as if she wanted nothing more in the world than to be as close to him as possible.

She was assertive in her recklessness, exploring the taste and texture of his skin. Stroking the backs of her fingers across his beard, placing one curious thumb above the heavy pulse at the hollow of his throat, curling her hands around the back of his neck, holding on to him with a pliant strength that drew him harder against her.

They had kissed and kissed, and he had fallen so deeply under her spell, he could not remember who he was, or who he was supposed to be, as if he had drunk too deeply of her intoxicating allure.

It wasn't until he curved his palm over the top of her breast that she drew back, startled and even a little afraid of what she wanted. She stared at him, fear and desire pushing and pulling at her with almost equal force. But fear, or awareness, or some other scruple cleared the haze of pleasure from her brain, because she grew pale in the twilight.

She opened her mouth as if she would speak, and then either changed her mind, or simply could not think of the right words.

"Thank you," he offered to stem the silence, "for the gift of yourself and your beauty." And he stroked his thumb over her lower lip, both to reassure her of his sincerity, and to satisfy his unassuaged compulsion to touch her. He threaded his fingers through hers—a gesture of intimacy and trust. A gesture of companionship, and of complicity. "You must know I dream of showing you what I know of love," he told her. "How I dream of you doing the same. I dream of you baring your body, and I arranging you on scented pillows for my pleasure. For our pleasure."

She had retreated from him at that, frowning at his words, until he realized he had spoken as Thomas Jellicoe, and not Tanvir Singh. That he had instinctively spoken as his true self.

But the inconsistency was enough to make her retreat from her fearlessness. She turned away. "I know nothing of love."

He drew her back by cupping her face in his hands. "Catriona. Thou mayest know little of this kind of love, of touching and intimacies shared in the quiet dark, but thou knowest a different sort of love—the love of living with an open heart."

She looked up at him, her pale, oval face painted shimmering silver by the purple light of the evening sky. "Tanvir. Is this madness to hope we can share our hearts?"

"No, this is my only bulwark against insanity. This is real, all else is madness."

And it still was.

He still burned for her.

"Cat." At Wimbourne Thomas felt as gray and flat as the afternoon light falling on the stoic wood of her bedchamber door, and just as stripped bare. "Was I so easy to forget?"

Catriona did him the honor of giving him the truth, though her answer was so low he could barely hear her through the stout panel. "No."

Thank God. "I've never forgotten you. Never. Every day you are the first thing on my mind when I wake in the morning, and every night, the last."

Her sigh was so deep it was audible. "You seem to have forgotten *some* things. You seem to have forgotten that you abandoned me." Her voice gained fragile strength, as if she were steeling herself for the uncomfortable task at hand. "You said you loved me—or maybe you didn't. Maybe I just imagined that you said you loved me. But you never meant it, or else you would have waited for me. But you didn't mean it then, so you can't mean it now. You're only saying it so you can get me to go back. To make it easy for you."

There was too much, too many different accusations to answer. "I didn't leave you that last night." Of this he was sure. The night she spoke of—the final night they had been together, only a day after their first kiss along the cantonment wall—was indelibly etched in his memory. "You're the one who left. You're the one who never came back."

"I came back, Tanvir—" She stopped herself from saying his name, and he felt all the weight of her confusion and disappointment. "I came and you were gone. All of your camp along the flaming river—every tent and cushion, every last horse. Everything. Even the dung had already been scavenged."

"No." He was on his feet now, and rattling at the door. "No. I came for you. I came. I followed you. The moment I let you leave my tent that bloody last night. I knew it—I knew it was a mistake, so I followed. I was practically upon your heels when you got to the residency. I called to you. I tried to stop you."

"No. I never saw you there." Her voice was just as sure. "And you weren't at Colonel Balfour's, either."

"Balfour's?" His voice rose until he was sure half the house could hear him. He didn't care. "But you went to the residency. I saw you running into the bloody *residency*. Everyone else, all the servants, and even some of the people from the cantonment who had come, were running the other way, abandoning the place, but you—you went *in*."

Flames had been coming out of the windows on the upper floor by the time Thomas got there—their orange glow could be seen from across the city. Thomas closed his eyes and he could instantly see the nightmare scene before him. He could still smell the sulfuric stink of desperation. "My God. The place was a holocaust. Of course I was there, Cat. Did you honestly think I didn't come to help you? To find you?"

He should never have let her go that last evening, the last time he had seen her. Never let her leave him. He should have heeded his instincts and kept her by his side. He should have held her and protected her and loved her until she had no more thoughts of the residency or the people there. He should have.

But he had not. He had kissed her and let her go, and let her walk out of his tent and into the enveloping dark until she was lost from his sight.

Her departure had filled him with a gnawing emptiness—with suspicions and doubts about her ability to return to him—that he could not explain and could not exercise. He tried to allay his sudden misgivings with action by calling his *sa'is,* and ordering his caravan to break their camp by the river, and be gone as soon as possible. He wanted his men gone long before dawn, headed northwest for the Punjab and the passes through the Hindu Kush. He had wanted no trace of Tanvir Singh left in Saharanpur.

Because somehow, some way, he was going to take her with him, and a Punjabi *sawar* did not ride slowly into the mountains with the much beloved kinswoman of his Excellency the Resident Commissioner, Lord Summers. Not if he wanted to keep his head attached to his shoulders.

But he had wanted her more than he had wanted his head. He had been more than willing to take the risk. She would be worth any price. So he would disappear. They would disappear together.

Yet, he hadn't been just a Punjabi horse trader—he had been a spy. And the spy Tanvir Singh had no business taking Catriona Rowan, a pale British girl, with him upon the road, roaming across mountains and deserts in search of secrets. What if the privations of his rough, nomadic life wore her down and eroded her steely sweetness? What if the hardships that would surely befall them washed her desire for him away like the lashing winds that poured through the mountains?

No. He had pushed such misgivings aside. She was not some soft, cosseted girl. She would take to his life, to his horses and his freedoms, as if she were made for it. Made for him. He felt the truth of it deep in his gut.

And perhaps he didn't have to run away with her in the dawn. Perhaps now that she had chosen him, now that he was sure of her, he could also be Thomas Jellicoe, if he chose to. Perhaps he could regain the other half of his life. Perhaps he should. He should make plans and think of the future—a different future, in a different land. They could go anywhere. He could even take her back to England, to Downpark. He could save her from the harsh winds of fate, and give her a life of comfortable ease. He could give her the life of a princess.

"Huzoor, huzoor!" The whisper had roused Thomas out of his fantasy.

A stable boy from the residency—the stable boy to whom Thomas had passed a steady supply of rupees to keep Tanvir Singh informed of the Memsahib Rowan's comings and goings, and the second servant to come from the residency that night—stood at the corner of his tent, beckoning urgently and pointing to the south. *"Huzoor,* thou shouldst know. All is in an uproar!"

Thomas had turned from his tent, and followed the direction of the boy's arm, up and away into the distance. To the south, and the direction of the cantonment, where an immense column of smoke roiled like a huge chimney into the purple evening sky. Where some distant building was outlined against the black of the night sky by fire.

The residency. Where Cat had gone.

Thomas was already running, shouting orders as he went for his horse, trying to think of possibilities and plans, contingencies and stratagems, but there had been nothing but a cold blade of dread and fear shredding his chest and clouding his brain. Every fiber of his being, every muscle and bone and sinew strained to get to her. To stop her. To save her from the danger boiling like molten death into the dark sky.

And as he jumped on his horse, racing toward the smoke that curled through the sky, filling it with inky soot and the acrid scent of ash and destruction, the first tongues of orange flame licked the darkening sky.

The top floor at the rear of the building was almost entirely engaged by the time Thomas tore through the cantonment gate past the wildly shouting porter.

But he was too late.

He spotted her instantly—her long, lithe silhouette stood out starkly against the bright orange light of the conflagration. He had almost caught her. Almost.

At that point she had been on foot and even running full out, she was not nearly as fast as he, mounted on horseback. But she kept on running. She did not so much as pause at the sight of the building burning down before her, but rushed in headlong. Her stupid, wide, gray English skirts brushed against smoldering door frames, a walking rag waiting to catch fire.

But in she went.

He vaulted to the ground and tore after her, but people were streaming out of the building in her wake, running against him like a tide. The deputy resident, Fielding, was trying to stop the servants from fleeing, and organize some sort of bucket chain for water, but he was shouting the wrong words.

"You there!" Fielding's hand clawed at his arm. The deputy resident was white with fear and pink cheeked in consternation. "Make these fellows listen. We've got to get the furniture out of the reception rooms if possible. And keep the devils from stealing everything they can carry."

Thomas slowed only to roar a few words at Lord Summers's *sircar,* threatening him with eight kinds of invective to perform his bloody job, but by the time he had reached the reception room there was no sign of her. No sign on the long, circular stairwell. No sign in the other rooms of the ground floor or the rear courtyard.

More servants were coming out of the house, and he pushed them toward the doors to the veranda, asking in both Hindi and Urdu after Memsahib Rowan, until he saw the eldest Summers boy, Arthur, who was moving across the lawn gripping his young sister Charlotte. Behind them was a young amah with the youngest boy, George.

"Where is Catriona?" he shouted to them as the crackle and chatter of the greedy flames grew louder.

"She went for Alice," the boy croaked out, gesturing hopelessly in the direction they had come.

"Where?"

"Above. I don't know. She led us down and went back. She said she'd be right back." Arthur doubled over with his hands on his knees, hacking out the smoke fumes. Charlotte had begun to sob, her tears leaving a trail through the soot clinging to her cheeks, so Thomas picked her up, and steered Arthur farther away, onto the lawn where small crowds were beginning to gather—servant women huddling in clumps, clutching each other, and people from the cantonment looking on in passive dismay. On the far south side of the building, servants were still hauling out furniture onto the lawn—working under the direction of company men who used all their energies to save the priceless antiques instead of to ensure that women and children were safe.

Jackasses. Bastards. Useless parasites. Thomas cursed them into his beard.

Thomas turned back to enter the house the same way he had exited, but the veranda roof collapsed down in front of him in a shower of splintering timber and sparks. He shielded his face with his arm in front of him, but he circled toward the back of the house, looking for another entrance, another way to get in and get to her. There had to be a way.

He ran along the edge of the formal garden just in time to see a dark silhouette of a man stumble out of the building in a cloud of smoke and fall tumbling onto the lawn.

"Cat." Even as he ran toward the figure he knew it could not be she.

And he was right. It was Lieutenant Birkstead, his coat gone and his sleeve smeared in soot and blood. Enough blood to mean he'd been shot.

In a fire?

Thomas hauled the man to his feet by what was left of his shirtfront. "Who else is still in there? Did you see Miss Rowan? Or Alice? She went for the child." If Birkstead had made his way out, perhaps she could, too.

Birkstead wrenched away from him as if Thomas were the one who had shot him. "Get your hands off me. I don't know what you're talking about."

Thomas let Birkstead go, but pressed him for an answer. "I'm talking about Miss Rowan and Alice."

"No," Birkstead answered, but something lit in his eyes—some spark of understanding or realization. The bastard was lying. Thomas was sure of it. Everything about Birkstead's defensive posture—his good arm was out in front of him as if he would ward Thomas off—was wrong. And he had a bullet hole in his other arm.

A bullet hole Cat might have put there. She'd had that bloody gun with her when she'd left the encampment.

"Where is she?" The words wound out of Thomas's chest in a deep, animalistic growl, full of threat and the promise of savagery.

"I don't know. I swear." Birkstead was scrambling backward, his boots slipping in the grass, kicking up debris, trying to escape into the darkness of the garden behind. "Jesus. If I had I would have—"

Thomas went after him. He had no time for patience. He had no time for logic and sanity. He had no time for anything but brutal, direct, punishing force. He didn't even reach for his weapons.

He sent Birkstead reeling to the ground with one savage blow, making good on his promise to himself to rearrange the lieutenant's face. But despite the fresh blood gushing from his broken nose, Birkstead tried to scrabble to his feet, fighting to get away with a wild, feral strength. Thomas closed his mind to everything but finding the man's weaknesses—the lieutenant had already lost blood, seeping out of the wound on his arm and soaking into his sleeve, and he had a lung full of smoke, and no matter his desperation, he wasn't going to last long.

And Thomas had learned to fight dirty. There was no sense in wasting anything like honor or fair play on a jackal like Birkstead. He had the lieutenant jerked up by his hair and in a choke hold without breathing heavily. "What have you done with her?"

Even as Birkstead's hands clawed at the forearm Thomas had wrapped around his neck, Thomas felt nothing for him. Nothing. He wrenched Birkstead's wounded arm back brutally. "Where?" he roared into the man's ear. "Where?"

Birkstead's only response was a howl of pain, but desperation and fear had made something less than human out of Thomas, and he had nothing of pity or patience left. Viciousness coiled through him like a snake, pure and uncivilized. He rammed his elbow with brutal force into Birkstead's bullet wound.

And the bastard didn't even get a full cry out of his mouth before he collapsed, slumping to the ground unconscious.

There was no time to regret his rash stupidity in giving way so easily to violence, so Thomas dropped Birkstead to the ground, and immediately returned to searching the outline of the building, scanning the windows above for any sign of movement, any sign of life—some clue as to where to search for her—before he plunged inside.

The narrow hallway was choked with smoke, but he crouched low and pushed on, trying to reckon which way Birkstead had come. "Above," Arthur Summers had said, so Thomas searched for a stairwell, for any way to get him to the upper stories.

Stupid, stupid to have let his fear goad him into knocking Birkstead out. Infinitely, moronically male of him to be so driven by rank, riotous jealousy. Ruinous of him to waste his best hope of finding her.

He should have dragged the bleeding bastard back in with him, forced him to show him the way where thick plumes of smoke were curling down from the ceiling, searing into his lungs, obscuring his sight and burning his eyes.

Thomas unwrapped his turban to cover his mouth, and felt his way to the foot of the servants' stairs at the back of the house. But the upper floors appeared to be nearly engulfed in fire. Everywhere he looked was nothing but heat and smoke and red-orange flame that drove him back step by step, until he was stumbling down the stairs, propelled out by the fury of the fire, until he was at the outer steps again.

Birkstead was gone—crawled back into whatever bolt-hole he had come out of—so there was no one Thomas could ask, no one on whom he could unleash his impotent fury.

Then, the very top edge of the outer walls of the building began to waver as the interior supporting structure was fully consumed. Thomas watched in stunned disbelief, numbed by his inability to do anything but stand as the walls slowly crumpled, collapsing in upon themselves with a moaning roar.

In the wake of the strange, suspended numbness, a wave of heat pushed him backward even as his feet were moving forward, not accepting the evidence before his eyes. He had to get in, so he could get Catriona out. But there was nothing but flame and seething embers. Nothing left to enter into.

The residency was gone. And so was she.

No. He fought back the pain tearing at his chest. She couldn't be gone. He would have known. He would have felt the loss of her if she were truly taken by the fire. He would have felt the irreversible rending of his very soul.

But he still felt hope—a swift, though defensive and delusional, surety that she must have survived. She *must*. She was too determined, too alive. Too young. He would not allow fate to be so very cruel.

So he who had defied fate for the entirety of his adult life had stayed, walking around the edge of the burning hulk of the building, doing what he did best, questioning every single servant he could find, in at least a dozen languages. What had they seen? Where had they been? Who had they spoken to?

"Burned," some people said. The whole family was assumed by many to have perished in the fire.

"No," he had insisted stupidly. "Arthur and Charlotte and George got out. They were all out on the lawn. I *saw* them. I spoke to the boy, Arthur, who said Miss Rowan had gone back for Alice, but said she would bring her right out. Someone must have seen them."

No one had. Servants shook their heads and looked fearful, and the company people closed ranks, shutting him out with cold shoulders and haughty looks that asked what business was it of an itinerant horse trader to be asking questions of their resident's family?

He left them to their willful ignorance. If they wouldn't help him, he would help himself. He would find the information he needed on his own. He always had. But hours he had spent, combing through the wreckage, trying to find the amah he had seen with the children, pushing hope against foolish hope, until there was nothing more to be done. Until he had to face the truth. Until all he could do was hold off the bottomless black well of despair that threatened to overtake him.

The damage was done. His heart had been pulled apart not in one swift, painful rending, but slowly, through the long night. The chill of loss had crept upon him by slow, aching degrees like a killing frost, withering everything in its path.

And so he had found his horse, and mounted, and turned its head to the north, and rode out of the Doab Valley and into the night trying desperately to outrace the voracious pain of oblivion before it could catch him and consume him whole.

Chapter Fourteen

But his instincts had been right. She had been alive, somewhere, hiding. She was alive now, still hiding, and if not
exactly well or happy, she was at least separated from him
only by a single door.

Which he could break down if he bloody well had to.
But he didn't want to. He wanted her to open it.

"I came, Cat," he insisted. "I was there." It was the one
thing he was still sure of. He had stayed until all hope had
been lost. Until there had been nothing to see but dying
embers. "You were the one who disappeared as if you had
ceased to exist."

"Yes," she finally agreed on another deep, drawn-out
breath, as if she were gathering her fragile strength. "Our
plan rather worked too well."

"Your plan?" Had she *planned* from the start to disappear? To leave him? He couldn't—wouldn't—believe it.
She had seemed so sincere. Thomas pressed his forehead
against the panel, trying to hold himself still, hoping and
waiting for the words he was longing—had been longing
for years—to hear. For some explanation that would keep
his hope alive.

Instead, she said only, "I can't tell you how much it
means to me to know you came back. And I thank you for
your kindness."

Thomas strangled back a vile oath. "I don't want your thanks. I didn't do it from *kindness*." How he had come to hate that word. "You must know. You must know I did it for you. And I will do anything else I have to—scour the earth, take bullets out on the lawn. Anything, Cat." He sounded frustrated and maybe even a little desperate, but he had to convince her. He *had* to. "I will take care of you—I can protect you. And we can start anew, and begin to trust each other again, if you'll only give me the chance."

"We can't start anew, Mr. Jellicoe." Her tone was just as determined, still trying to keep him at a distance, but her voice was weighted down with weary resignation, as if she were trying to convince herself as much as him. "I know I said I was the same person, but I'm not. I've changed. I've *had* to change."

"I don't believe that. I can see you past your wall of prim composure, Cat—behind your lavender and starch. I can see the girl you once were."

"It's not just composure and lavender and starch, Mr. Jellicoe. It's . . . too much has happened. There's too much that has already happened. And too much still to come."

He couldn't think of what was still to come. He could only think of here and now. Of Cat. Of making her believe him. Of showing her she could trust him. Everything else would follow in its time. "If you think you can't be Catriona Rowan, then I will love Miss Anne Cates." He raised his hand to thump the pad of his clenched fist against the door, as if he could push his sincerity, his resolution through the panel and into her. Hammering away at the wall of her defenses, brick by brick. "I don't care. You're the one who just said it's only a name—that you are still the same person underneath. I love you no matter who you think you are."

"Mr. Jellicoe." Her weary fatalism chilled him. "You can't love a lie in me any more than I could love the lie in you."

But he could hear her voice begin to come apart—the edges of her composure fraying under the strain of the day—and he knew he had to press his advantage. "Then we will start anew now that we both know the truth. We will face what is past and what is to come together. I will protect you, *kaur*," Thomas insisted. "I called you that then—my princess—and I will make you my princess now. Just trust me, Cat, please. Just please open the door."

Thomas felt the portal flex slightly beneath his hands and forehead, and for a moment he felt a sliver of hope slide through the widening cracks in his façade of control. But she must have only turned to face the door, because he could hear her more clearly even though her voice was nearly shaking with the effort to retain her own composure.

"You mean to be kind, but you don't understand. It's best this way." He heard another sigh, and he could almost feel the small, wry smile in her voice, when she added, "I was right, you know. Son of the Earl Sanderson. You really were a hidden prince all along. But you can't make a princess out of a Scottish sow's ear. Men like you aren't meant to help the Miss Anne Cates of this world."

"For God's sake, Cat. You ought to know me well enough to know I care nothing for what I am *meant* to do. I care only about you." He took a deep breath, but the words came easily, smoothly, without hesitation, as if they had been merely biding their time in the back of his mind, waiting for their chance to get out. "It's not best. And I don't mean to only *help* you. I mean to marry you. I meant to marry you in Saharanpur." He pushed aside the looming regret, and kept his mind concentrated on the present and future. "But we can do so now, as soon as possible, and make a new life together."

"A life?" She pronounced the word as if it were as strange and foreign and faraway as a Tibetan monastery. "You can't mean it. What about your family? What about Saharanpur? And the fire? And people saying that I did it, that I was the one who killed them all? Do you mean to forget all that?"

"It is already forgotten."

"No." Her exhale was less forlorn, but no less weary. "Mr. Jellicoe. Not even the son of an earl, nor even an earl himself, can make a charge of arson and murder be forgotten."

"But I did. My God, Cat! Did no one ever tell you? Did you not know? There is no charge. I went to them. I went to the judiciary committee the company set up to investigate the fire and the allegations against you. I told them you were with me."

The ache inside had grown so intense Catriona thought it might consume her. It was loneliness and heartbreak and every unmet need she had ever had. It was dark and needy and deeply, deeply selfish. It was a gaping gulf that had grown too wide to ever cross, and too strong for her to disobey.

And now he was telling her that she had been wrong. Astonishment was a tepid word for the hot jolt of disbelief that cracked through her like a bolt from a summer storm. Every nerve and fiber in her body trembled and vibrated with icy heat.

Catriona found her voice somewhere at the back of her throat, and when she did, it was as thin and threadbare as her heartbeat. "Say that again."

"I went to the judiciary committee." He spoke firmly and clearly so she might hear him through the wood of the door. As if he knew she had curled her ear to the panel to better listen. "I told them that you could not possibly have done any of the things of which you were accused, because at the time the fire started, you were with me."

Catriona couldn't move. She was too shocked. Her skin prickled everywhere on her body, and she felt cold and hot all at the same time—unbalanced as if the floor were tilting beneath her. As if the whole of the earth had fallen over sideways.

All this time. All this time she had lived with the fear. All this time she had lived with the burden of knowing other people thought the worst of her, and wished the very worst upon her. But Thomas Jellicoe had not.

She wanted to see him. She wanted to see the evidence of the truth on his once familiar face—his once beloved face—and hear the words again. She needed to be sure his reprieve was real and true.

Catriona's hands sprang for the doorknob, spinning it open with cold, clumsy fingers.

And there he was, on the floor on the other side of the door, rounding to one knee in front of her. He looked wretched and exhausted, worn out as if he had run all the way from Kabul to Wimbourne. His hair was nearly standing on end in disarray, and inky dark circles surrounded his deep green eyes. But at that moment, he was perilously beautiful.

"Do you swear it?"

He didn't hesitate. He nodded, emphatic and sure. "I do. I swore it to them then, and I swear it to you now. I spoke for you. I told them we were secretly betrothed."

"When?" She could not possibly keep all the aching regret, the years and years of breath-stealing loss and longing and loneliness from her voice. She was breathless, as if she, too, had run all the way from Saharanpur to Wimbourne. And she had, in a way.

"When did I tell them? Six months or so later. When I came south again from Kabul and Lahore." There was something that sounded very close to regret in his voice, too. Or perhaps it was shame. He reached to take her cold hand in his, much as he had the first day she had met him, his large hand enveloping hers. "That was the first that I was told—by Balfour—that you'd been accused and presumed guilty, but no charges had been pursued since you had been assumed dead. But while the judiciary committee were still pondering what to do with the information, word came from England that the children were in fact alive, and safe, and had somehow, rather miraculously, made their way home to England with no one the wiser. For myself, I was shocked"—his deep voice cracked and splintered like dry wood—"and elated—my God, you have no idea how elated—to realize that you must have escaped the fire. It was the begum who told me that you were alive, because you had come to her. Clever girl, to think of her." His big, calloused hand squeezed hers lightly, a tender, tentative encouragement. "Not even Balfour, her husband, knew for sure that you still lived."

No. Colonel Balfour would not have known. It was the begum and her *zenana* of surprisingly well connected ladies who had been a wonder of clandestine contrivance. For a woman who never left the confines of her house, the begum had a network of contacts that would have put the company men to shame had they even conceived that such a thing existed. It was the begum who first heard the insidious rumors that spread from the cantonment that Catriona had been to blame. It was she who had helped Catriona, she who had hidden Cat and the children behind the high walls of the *zenana*. She who had made swift, sure, deviously effective decisions. The begum had seen to it that Catriona and the children had already been spirited well away by the time the company men had thought to look for her at the old palace. "Did they believe you?"

"I made them believe me. I *made* them listen." With each statement he shook her hand a little with emphasis. "Though I did have to have Colonel Balfour with me to vouch for my character. And my identity."

"Your identity?" Catriona still could not get her breath.

"As the Honorable Thomas Jellicoe." His half-smile was as careful as it was wry. "Up to that moment my real identity was known only to Colonel Balfour, and to a file at the bottom of a dusty locked drawer in some company office—fortunately not all of the cantonment's files had been destroyed in the fire. But that's when I gave up being Tanvir Singh."

"For me?" She still couldn't breathe, but now she didn't need to. Relief was making her giddy. All this time. All this time she had let the fear conquer her. All this time she had worked relentlessly, in the long days and nights in the loneliness of her exile, to push all thoughts of him aside, to convince herself that he had cared nothing for her. That he had thought better of loving someone like her.

But he hadn't. He *had* loved her.

He still did.

The thought was as wonderful as it was terrifying.

Relief made her more than giddy. Heat kindled behind her eyes, brimming over to spill wet, warm salt down her cold cheeks. She was too full—too full of trembling, weak, unfamiliar joy. She took her hand from his to pull out a handkerchief. "Just like that?"

"Just like that." He gifted her with one of his slow, encouraging smiles, and carefully thumbed the warm wetness from her cheeks. "The moment I realized what I had to do, I took up my knife and cut my hair. Just like that."

Catriona could see it as if she had been there—the dark sweep of the long ebony locks, the quick, decisive flash of the talisman of a knife that had always ridden in his waistband. His beautiful long hair—the emblem of his faith and covenant with his God. Forsaken in a moment. Just like that. "Such a sacrifice."

He shook his head. "No sacrifice at all if it could bring you back."

But it hadn't brought her back. Not for two long years, while they both suffered, it seemed. Her heart was so full of relief and gratitude it hurt to speak. Her throat felt as raw and aching as if she had been crying for hours and hours on end. Who would have thought that joy would prove to be as cataclysmically painful as despair?

But relief shouldn't make her long for the feel of the warmth and weight of his hand on her skin again. Gratitude shouldn't make her lean in closer so she might inhale the very English essence of him once more. Joy shouldn't make her ache to comfort him for everything he had lost as well. He had endured as much as she, but somehow, he had managed to survive with his love and faith intact. To be steadfast and whole, where she had been inconstant and untrue, even to herself.

She had been more than inconstant. She had doubted him. She had even hated him for failing her. For not being everything she had set him up to be—her champion and her savior. But alone at night, facing the inevitable truth that came in the dark quiet of her rooms, when there was nothing, no children, no lessons, no saving activity to take her mind off the loneliness, she had wrapped her arms around her middle under the soft blankets, trying to hold the fear at bay, and consoled herself with the memory of his tender friendship and his careful, sure, evocative touch.

She ached to feel that touch again. She wanted to lay down the burden of her cares into his safekeeping, if only for a moment. And fear had worn her down—she was not strong enough to resist his wordless appeal. She turned her cheek and leaned the weight of her cares into his palm, and allowed herself to rest for just a moment. Just a moment.

Even if the relief, the ease, lasted no longer than a moment, it would be enough. Enough to bolster her onward. Onward to the next inevitably hard decision she would have to make. The next painfully hard thing she would have to do.

But not now. Now she could close her eyes, and lean her cheek into the cradle of his big hand, and rest. At last.

Catriona felt his other hand skim along the line of her jaw to caress her cheek, cupping her face before his lips brushed tenderly against hers. Just once. Then his arms came around her, steadfast and sure, and that was all that mattered. He was holding her, murmuring her name over and over, until she was enveloped by the comfort of his heat. By the surety of his strength. By the promise of his passion.

"Tanvir—" But he did not look like Tanvir with his English face and English haircut. She reached to finger the blunt ends of his hair, and he closed his eyes again, as if it were an agony of experience when she touched him. He looked vulnerable, shaved and shorn like Samson. But she was no Delilah wanting to tame him, and take away his powers. She wanted the sum of everything he was—the innate command of the son of an earl, the wiles of the sly Punjabi *sawar,* and the skill of her exotic lover. "It's so strange and hard. I don't even know what to call you."

"Thomas." His voice was rough, and almost strained, though his tone was sure. Emphatic even. "Thomas, please."

"Thomas." The word felt as foreign and exotic upon her lips as "Tanvir" had once been.

He closed his eyes as if he needed to hold whatever he was feeling—his own relief or gratitude—deep inside. "Again," he murmured as he drew ever closer.

"Thomas."

Like an incantation, his name worked unseen magic. He smiled, that dazzling white smile that had enchanted her so. And he was smiling at her, and threading his hands into her hair as he whispered, "You don't know how long I've waited for you to say my name."

This she understood. She understood what it was like to live as a stranger in one's own clothes, within one's own skin. To never have the luxury of being oneself.

"Thomas." It was easy now, so easy and so wonderful to give him the small gift of his name, though it was scant recompense for his suffering. So she stuffed her damp handkerchief back into her pocket, and she took his dear, different, familiar face in her hands, and leaned toward him, offering herself.

He lowered his lips to hers slowly, with much of the same care and deliberation as before, but once he tasted her, he began to kiss her with firm, unyielding intent. He took her mouth completely, with hungry lips and possessive tongue, overwhelming her, bending her head back with the force of his desire.

She could only be thankful for his strength—the strength that had endured the years of separation, that had spanned the gulf of time and loss that had kept them apart.

His kisses pressed upon her, over and over, buffeting her like wave after wave on a shore, his tongue and taut lips snaring all her attention, engaging all her senses. Yes. She did not want care and tenderness. She did not want anything of the past. She wanted to feel the press of his passion upon her now. She wanted to forget everything of regret and loss and longing, and for once be sated.

And he was sating her. "Cat," he murmured again and again as his kisses filled up the desperate, deep well of her longing.

He kissed down the side of her neck, nipping at the sensitive skin, overwhelming her with each sensation. But then he pulled back for a moment, his big hand cradling her skull, holding her so she could read the truth of his words in his piercing green eyes. "You said I didn't tell you the truth—that I wasn't myself with you in Saharanpur. But I am the same man. I loved you. I adored you. I made love to you with the same hands, the same mouth, the same body."

She remembered it all as if it were yesterday—the care and adoration. And she wanted it again. "Make love to me now."

He needed no other encouragement. He was there, swinging her into his arms, shouldering the door closed behind him without taking his eyes from hers, without breaking the fragile enchantment of the moment that separated them from everything that had gone before, and everything that was yet to come.

She kept her eyes open as well. She wanted to see everything. Wanted to feel everything—the beginning of whiskers along his jaw, the rough strength of his careful hands, the reassuring heat from the furnace of his chest. The heat that reached into the cold, empty center of her chilly existence.

He kissed her with heat and force, and a possessiveness so raw and open and full of lust and longing she had no defense against it. She wanted none. She was empty of everything but hope and searing need. Hope that had flickered in the dark hidden recesses of her soul, refusing to be extinguished. Need that grew with every stroke of his tongue, every taste of his taut, smooth lips.

He kissed her with everything he was and had ever been—every ounce of care and need, every iota of skill and finesse—drawing her out of herself until her body began to feel light and liquid and alive under the surface of her skin. As if the weight of fear had at least temporarily been lifted.

Her breath began flying in and out of her chest as he

trailed hot kisses down the side of her neck, nipping at the sensitive tendon, finding the secret place at the turn of her nape that made her shiver. Catriona angled her head away, giving him greater access, appeasing the low hum of want that built like ripples across the surface of a pond, reechoing and growing stronger in every place he touched. His lips rounded to the hollow of her throat, and she could feel the rising cadence of her heart where it beat against his lips.

She needed to touch him, too. She needed to taste the warm salt of his skin, needed to run her hands through his silken hair, and tumble the short, unruly locks through her palms.

She kissed his face, letting her lips skate across the smooth warmth of his upper cheeks, along the pliancy of his mouth, taking little sips of him, as if too much at once might intoxicate her. But she had already drunk too deep, because he was loosening the buttons at her collar, and her head was falling back, arcing away to let him kiss across the delicate, sensitive skin along the top of her chest.

Beneath the layers of chemise and stays and gown, her breasts grew full and tight with longing, and she couldn't contain the gasp of needy entreaty that wound out of her mouth as sensation flooded under her skin.

He came back to answer her unspoken question, kissing her silent with his lips and his tongue. Filling her senses until every thought and feeling began and ended with his kiss.

And she was falling again, or coming back. That was it. Coming back to him. To herself. To the rightness that had always been between them. But she *was* falling as well, her head cradled safely in the palm of his hand, until she was lying on the floor, secured there by the glorious weight of his body atop hers, and she could luxuriate in the press of his warmth, and the safety of his embrace.

Catriona felt heat build in her throat and behind her eyes, but she didn't realize that she was crying until he stilled, and then kissed away the salt of her tears. Which only made her cry more. All those years, she had never shed a tear. All those miles, and she had not once crumbled.

"It's stupid." She sniffled, and tried to reach back into her pocket to retrieve the damp handkerchief.

But he did not object, or tease. He turned his head, and laid his head against her chest, and held her tight, as if all he wanted in the world was to simply be with her. As if he understood that once opened, the floodgates could not easily be closed.

They stayed like that, sprawled on the rug much as they had been on the lawn, his long-muscled legs twining with hers, pinning her skirts to the ground. But this time she welcomed his weight and his comfort while she tried to gather her thoughts—to figure out what came next, what else she needed to have the courage to tell him.

But what came next was that as her quiet gasps and hiccups subsided, Thomas began a slow exploration, idly reacquainting himself with the varied topography of her body. Though the rest of him remained perfectly still, his hand was quietly making its way down the length of her upper arm, tracing the span and curve of her waist, and delineating the seam of her stays beneath her ribs. Up and down, his clever fingers stroked, back and forth, bringing her senses back beneath the heated surface of her skin. Winding her higher and higher, until she was straining toward his hand, silently urging her breast into the weight of his palm.

And then not so silently. "Thomas. Please."

He answered by curling his hand firmly around her breast, and kissing through the sturdy cotton of her gown, wetting and nipping through the layers of fabric until he found her nipple. The sensitive peak instantly contracted into a tight bud as need spiked through her, hot and nearly painful in its bliss.

"How long has it been, Catriona? How long has it been since anyone touched you? How long has it been since you let yourself feel pleasure?"

"Forever."

He bit down gently through the material, teasing and abrading with his teeth and tongue, until she arced up off the floor, into the weighted pleasure of his hand, taut as a drawn bow, ready to fly loose at the slightest pressure. But he did not set her loose. He rolled the lean weight of his hips onto hers, fitting his body intimately with hers, and then took the same pains with her other breast, kneading and abrading the nipple into an exquisite peak with his hands and mouth.

Need—want and lust and desire—grew and grew until it was a physical thing, an insistent feeling of sharply pleasurable pain driving her on. Pushing her toward the irresistible lure of the pleasure he loosed within her. And she wanted more. "Thomas, please."

More of him. More of the potent forgetfulness. More of the sensations that pushed her out of the narrow confines of Miss Anne Cates's small existence. Away from distrust and fear. Away from hopelessness. Toward him. Toward Thomas Jellicoe who had never stopped loving her.

He gave her more, kneading her breast and toying with the sensitized peak with one hand while he used his clever wiles on the row of buttons marching like sentinels down the front of her gown. He spread the edges wide, and worked his nimble way loosening the ties, insinuating his long, agile fingers beneath the edge of her practical, front-lacing stays, and under the thin layer of her threadbare cotton shift to tweak the tight-nipped bud, and send streaks of jagged sensation stretching deep into her belly.

"So prim and practical," he murmured with his lips against her skin. "You have no idea how erotic your practical, plain cotton underthings are to me. How I have fantasized about you and your prim, translucent English shift."

Catriona wanted nothing more of primness and practical restraint. She wanted to reach up and rend her plain cotton shift in two, and boldly bare her breasts to him for her own erotic pleasure. She wanted to bare him as well. "Please." Her voice was high, strained and eager, full of the turmoil of her need.

His answer was a muttered oath, more Punjabi than English, that vibrated and echoed through her into her bones, feeding her restlessness, making her shift and surge beneath him until his fingers closed around her nipple, tweaking it possessively before he took the peak fully into his mouth and sucked hard.

She gasped and squeezed her eyes closed, so there was nothing but his hands and his mouth and his possession of her body. But even as he laved and teased her with his lips and tongue, his other hand began to furl up the long length of her full skirts, gathering the hem of her dress and petticoats into his fists, sliding the heavy material up her legs, over her knees and sturdy stockings, across her thighs until she felt the cool air on the skin at the tops of her practical, unadorned garters.

But there was nothing sensible or practical left about her when his clever, clever hand found the warm entrance to her body with swift, devastating precision.

Her gasp echoed off the ceiling, and her thighs clenched around him in convulsive shock and helpless, keening want.

He levered himself off her, coming to kneel between her legs with his knees pressing against the inside of her thighs, pushing the rest of her skirts higher to give him unimpeded access to her body. And then he looked down and he stilled, one hand within her, and one resting on the scoop of her belly.

"My God, Cat," he whispered above her. "I knew how it would be. I knew how your body would look."

She opened her eyes to see him staring at her body, uncovered and naked from the waist down, and she wondered if she ought to be abashed at the earthy, impetuous force of her need. In Saharanpur, she had planned and prepared and groomed her body for him—had taken her own erotic excitement in doing so—had gone to him under the clandestine cover of the dark, not in the revealing, flat, gray light of a rainy English afternoon. Not on the floor of her employers' house.

She would have twisted her thighs together to cover the primitive nakedness of her body, or pushed her skirts down to hide the shock of red hair covering her sex, but he splayed his rough hands across the tops of her thighs and up across the scoop of her belly, raking through the ginger curls, as he exclaimed with a sort of stunned wonder, "I always knew you were made of flame."

And then he lowered his head to kiss her there. There, where the pulse of her flesh beat as strongly as the heart within her body. Where she ached to be rejoined with him. Where his clever fingers and tongue claimed her with the same sure possessiveness with which he had kissed her mouth. With the same skill he had taught her in the warm, perfumed dark of his India.

He angled his head to stroke her, pushing and pulling her back from useless thoughts of the past. Back into the present, back into the pleasure and passion of the moment— the time and place where nothing existed but the two of them and the obliterating pleasure he could give her body.

He set up a rhythm, slow and steady at first, and then escalating, stronger and stronger and higher and higher, until every part of her—her lungs and the palms of her hands and the muscles on the inside of her thighs—seemed to fill with pulsating heat.

He stroked her again with the tip of his tongue, and she was left gasping for air and grasping onto the rug for purchase, for something to tether her down, holding on for dear life so she would not fly into a hundred sparks of light and desire.

"Thomas." His name was like a prayer on her lips, and then repeated over and over in the silence of her mind. Thomas, Thomas, Thomas. Higher and higher, tighter and tighter she climbed. Tauter and tauter he drew her. Onward and upward, until she was bucking and bowing, reaching out to scratch her fingers against the bare wood of the floor, pressing herself toward him. Toward the need and the heat and the pleasure that flew just beyond, hovering just out of her reach.

And then he turned his hand just so, and white heat

burst within her, from under her skin. And she was gone. Grasping the brass ring of heat and smoldering bliss tightly within her grasp.

For a long, long moment the only sound was the heaving of their breath and the pounding of her uneven heart in her ears. She was so dizzy with release that she could have fallen over had she not already been sprawled in inelegant abandon across the floor. She felt upended, as topsy-turvy as if she had been tipped over the edge of Wimbourne's ancient battlements.

"Thomas. My God." Her lungs felt buoyant, as if she would take breath and float up to the ceiling if his hand across her belly had not been holding her down to the earth. She reached for him. "Oh, how I missed you."

He kissed her again, and whispered against her neck, "I've missed you as well. But no more." He was peeling off his coat, flinging it behind him and setting his hands to the buttons at the fall of his breeches.

And she spread her arms wide, welcoming him to her body. To her love.

He braced himself above her with one arm, as he kissed her mouth and settled his weight between her legs and—

"Thomas?" The door behind her head rattled. Viscount Jeffrey's voice came again. "Thomas, is that you?"

Chapter Fifteen

Thomas shot his hand out over Cat's head to brace the door firmly closed against his brother's untimely interruption. For a long, nearly excruciating moment the only sound in the room was the heavy throttle of his heart in his ears and the huff of his labored breathing, but then the sounds of the house—of children's voices and running feet, the gossipy chatter of rain against the windowpane, and the everyday clatter and noise of the busy house—reasserted themselves.

Bloody, bloody, bloody hell. Damn his brother to the far corners of the Himalaya. And damn himself. Because he had not done so much as wash the dirt of the road, or the grass of the lawn from his face before he had gone after Cat like a starving man.

"Thomas?" A heavy rap shook the panel. "Miss Cates?"

"One moment, please, sir." Cat's voice was unsteady, but she had already pushed her skirts down and scrambled up from the floor—good God, the floor. He had been about to take her on the bloody floor—and had hurried across to the other side of the small room to her washstand.

What must she think of him? Nothing to what he thought of himself at this moment. He had meant to woo her. He had meant to convince her that he could be relied upon. He had *not* meant to fall upon her like the jackal he had named Birkstead, devoid of all semblance of self-restraint.

And now he was shoving in his shirttails, and buttoning up his bloody breeches while the lord of the manor, his brother, made increasingly ominous noises on the other side of the door.

"Miss Cates, are you quite all right? Thomas, I know you're in there. I can hear you seething."

A glance at Cat showed her hiding a face gone scarlet with mortification. But Thomas refused to be embarrassed. And he refused to let her be mortified. "Not to worry. I'll see to James," he said, and ducked through the door.

He shut the portal behind him firmly, but before Thomas could even raise his hands to forestall the lecture that he could feel coming, his brother was upon him.

"What the hell is the matter with you, Thomas? Are you ill?" Thomas let James grab his arm and pull him half the distance across the room, well away from Cat's door. "What have you been doing up here with Miss Cates? My wife is already telling me that I need to cast you out of the house, and I haven't the faintest idea what I am to tell her when I find you closeting yourself up with my servants." Just as he had earlier, James kept a hold of Thomas's arm, as if he really did fear that Thomas might be in the throes of a jungle fever.

Lady Jeffrey, who was hard on her husband's heels, was not so nice. She was still delicately fuming at her new brother-in-law and profoundly concerned for her governess. "What have you done with her?"

"She's right here, safely locked behind her bedchamber door, as she has been for the past three quarters of an hour."

"But you were in here with her, and you locked Cassandra out." James's brow was as deeply furrowed as the dark clouds piling up in the sky outside.

"I'm sorry," Thomas said, even though he was entirely uncontrite. "But it was necessary I speak to your Miss Cates alone so I might put forward my proposal."

Cassandra's face cleared only a little at that news—she

was still obviously put out at her brother-in-law's high-handed ways—and she needled him with the cold tip of her lavender stare. "Thomas, do not think you can fob me off with . . . folderol." She waved away his explanation. "I very much doubt Miss Cates was interested in whatever it was you proposed to her. Did she—did I—not make it very clear that you were to abide by my rules, and Miss Cates's rules, which preclude closeting yourself alone with either young ladies, or members of my staff, and especially young ladies who are both? What are we to think? Have you lost your mind?"

"No, ma'am," he replied as sincerely as possible.

Some of the inquietude left her voice, and she said more gently, but no less vehemently, "You are our guest, Thomas, but this is her *home*. Do you have any idea what a position you've put that poor girl in? Do you have any idea what it's like to be beholden to other people for the very roof over your head and the food you put in your mouth? I won't have her made to do anything she doesn't want to do. I won't have you after her like a dog in a manger because you once thought you knew her well enough to make unfounded assumptions about her. I don't care about what might have happened in the past—everyone makes mistakes—but I won't have you propositioning her in our house." The crystalline violet eyes leveled at him, leaving Thomas feeling like a naughty undergraduate caught out by the porter.

"My dear Cassandra. I may have been a pagan and a spy, but I'm not a cad. I haven't been propositioning. I've been proposing, if you must know."

"Well done, Thomas." James looked, if not exactly ecstatic, then at least relieved at this evidence that his younger brother's morals had not drifted too far afield in pagan parts.

But Cassandra was not giving Thomas any benefit of the doubt. "Proposing what, exactly?"

"Marriage. What other sort of proposal is there?"

"Well!" She drew back in perfect imitation of a well-polished, ornamental poker. "If you need *me* to tell you that, then you're certainly not the man of the world that James has taken you for."

Over Lady Jeffrey's tiny, delicate head, her far less delicate husband gave Thomas the kind of satisfied don't-underestimate-my-wife look that only an older brother can give at the punishment of a younger sibling. And he was right—at this point in his life, Thomas should have learned to recognize the kind of woman who had steel running down her delicate spine.

"I do beg your pardon, ma'am." Thomas attempted a more sincere tone of contrition. "But I assure you, my intentions are entirely honest, and mindful of the proprieties."

"It's more than just the proprieties of the situation, Thomas." Cassandra reached out to touch his sleeve, in wordless appeal. "Miss Cates is more than a servant. She is vitally important to us. You know the children adore her, and that she is teaching them more than we had ever expected. And Mariah . . ." She turned away for a moment, and her husband took her hand in his, steadying and supporting her. "She has been giving Mariah back to us, Thomas, bit by bit. Returning her to us. Surely you can see that, and just as surely you can't be so selfish, or so lust crazed that you would put Mariah's future in jeopardy."

It was affecting, this display of emotion and loyalty. It spoke well of both his sister-in-law and of the woman who inspired such loyalty and devotion. Catriona deserved not to be taken for granted. She deserved people who weren't going to let her down. But he wasn't going to let her down. Quite the opposite.

"Cassandra, I have loved this woman from the first moment I saw her. I have lost her. I have thought her dead. I have looked half the world over for her, and now that I have found her again, I am not going to let her go. Not for you, and not even for your children, who are my family and mean the world to me. I am going to take your Miss Cates from you one way or another, and frankly, I'm beginning not to care how I do it."

"Steady on, Thomas," James cautioned. "No need to get

all hot and ardent. I should be the first to wish you happy, but there are a few things that need to be sorted out first. What about the charges you spoke of? Arson and murder, you said? How do you plan to defend her from those?"

"He already has."

The moment Catriona spoke, Thomas came instantly to her side, tucking her hand into his, and offering her the strength and protection of his arm as she faced her employers with as much of her normal calm and composure as possible. Lord and Lady Jeffrey had been everything supportive on her behalf—she had heard them chastising Thomas while she put herself to rights—but it would be another thing entirely for them to support a marriage between their governess and their brother. Especially when their governess had lied to them about both her name and her rather inglorious past.

But Lady Jeffrey surprised her. "Dare I hope, dear Miss Cates," she asked with a tremulous smile, "that this means your answer was yes?"

Catriona had made no real answer before, and she made none now. And she had no desire to speak with the kind of openness that a truthful response required—the kind of honest answer Thomas *deserved*—in front of the viscount and viscountess. "My lady. Please don't think—"

Thomas broke in. "I know I'm not perfect, Cat. God knows I'm not." She didn't know whether he spoke to simply keep her from speaking, or to spare her from having to address so private and still unsettled a topic in front of his family. Whichever it was, he did her a kindness for which she was grateful. "I've made mistakes. I made grave mistakes with you. Mistakes for which I'd like to atone."

It was heart wearying, the way fate had conspired to keep them apart. But fate was not done with them yet, still hard at work with her pry bar. Catriona still had to honor the devil's bargain she had made with Lord Summers's mother, the dowager duchess. Alice still had to be protected. And now Birkstead had to be stopped.

"Thomas, please." His willingness to be so open and forthcoming with his thoughts and feelings still astonished her. "Spilt milk cannot be put back into the pail. The past is gone, as finite and ephemeral as a dream." And she was awake now, and there was no going back to sleep.

"An admirable philosophy, to be sure." Lord Jeffrey was still frowning at them. "But the charges?"

Thomas responded much as he had when they had been alone. "I testified to the company's judiciary committee on her behalf. I told them Miss Cates"—he shot her a glance of apology—"that is, Miss Rowan, had been with me at the time. Which was the truth. I also told them she was my betrothed, and that she had the full and unquestioned support of my family, as well as me." His gaze shifted to linger in some sort of unspoken communication with his brother, before it returned to Catriona. "And so she was cleared of the charges. But unfortunately, she did not know of this development until today, and has been, until this point, in some fear for her life."

"And still is, if what you say about those wild shots on the lawn is true." Lady Jeffrey's anger was transforming itself back into deep concern. "Oh, my dear girl. How frightened you must have been!"

"Yes, your ladyship," Catriona said carefully. "Very frightened. I hope you will be able to forgive me."

"There is nothing to forgive. There are reasons enough to pretend to have a different name, I should think." She made an elegant gesture to encompass the circumstances. "What I don't understand is how anyone who knows you, and knows your caring ways, knows the way you are with children, could have ever thought you had done something so terrible." Lady Jeffrey was generous to a fault—another person, it seemed, who was prepared to think the best of her.

As Catriona knew exactly how—another fact that would not be to her credit—it was Thomas who responded. "I imagine someone—the real murderer—was trying to shift the blame, and Catriona made a convenient target. Everyone believed her dead, so she made the perfect scapegoat."

Oh, he was clever and smart, her Thomas Jellicoe, and saw things that other people didn't. But he didn't see everything. He couldn't even begin to guess it all.

"Dead? Yes, but who would believe such a thing of Miss Cates—Miss Rowan?" Cassandra was insistent in her belief in her Miss Cates's goodness. "A person cannot truly change who they are, the way a cat cannot change its stripes. Anyone who knew her would know she was good."

Such willful kindness on the part of her mistress was a loving charity that Cat felt she couldn't possibly deserve. The truth was that the residents of the British cantonment did not know her at all—Catriona had taken pains that it be so. She had avoided those people who she thought would have stood in judgment of her—and anyone who she thought might be under the influence of her aunt Lettice—in favor of her friends at the old palace. She had held herself apart from the cantonment long before they had ever rejected her.

And when powerful and influential voices had spoken out against her, naturally, people would have accepted their accusations without needing any proof. It was simply the way with power—those who had it usually made sure they could keep it, no matter the cost.

Thomas hesitated for another moment, but then he said, "It was said that Catriona was her uncle-in-law Lord Summers's lover, and that his wife—her aunt—found out about the affair."

Oh, Lord. Yes, the lying, scheming jackal knew just how to twist the knife—how to take a single grain of the truth and screw it round to his advantage. Too smooth and plausible by half. It only wanted that—that she be labeled an adulterer as well as an arsonist and a murderer. Her past was like a stone she simply couldn't swallow.

Thank God she had listened to her fear, and to the begum, and run when she did. The company men would have seen her hanged from the flagpole in front of the Saharanpur barracks at dawn without so much as a word of protest if she had not fled from their rough justice.

"That couldn't be true," her mistress insisted, though her hand had risen to her mouth in shock. Lady Jeffrey turned wide eyes on Catriona, silently begging for her to refute the charge. "Who would say such a thing?"

"Lieutenant Birkstead." Thomas all but spat the name out. "Who else?"

There was no one else. The jackal had warned her of the risks of defying him. He had screamed his vile, mortal threats through the empty, burning halls of the residency. He had sworn he would find the only person who had fully witnessed the depth of his depravity. And she had let him think that person was she.

It was exactly as the begum had told her within hours of the fire. The quiet begum—whom no one else in the company community had ever seen, and thus had never thought of—had kept her finger on the pulse of all of Saharanpur, and her ears open to all the talk, from the pious murmurings over prayer in the Jamid Masjid, to the petty complaints and accusations of the cantonment. The begum had known which way the wind was blowing, even as the ashes of the residency were still floating down upon the city. And without any prompting from Catriona, the begum and all the women of the *zenana* had predicted how it would be— powerful voices, male voices, would speak against Catriona, and there would be little she could say or produce in her defense. It would be her word against the lieutenant's. And the children would suffer. Alice most of all.

Alice, at whom he had screamed his filthy threats. Alice, who had been the only one to see it all.

But Thomas, for all his spying wiles, could know none of that. He could only know that the bastard Birkstead had had a bullet in him that would have needed explanation.

"What else did the *Badmash* Sahib say?" It was best they knew all of it.

Thomas nodded. "*Badmash*, indeed. Colonel Balfour told me the lieutenant reportedly staggered out of the garden of the residency with a ball in his arm, and swore in front of the surgeon and the assistant commissioner, Mr. Fielding, that you had put it there. That you had shot him because he had come to propose, and found you in a tryst with your uncle, the lord commissioner. And that you had shot them all, and set the place on fire to cover it all up."

She had always known the lieutenant's capacity for lying was nearly infinite. So, too, was his invention. And his ruthlessness. Catriona felt the return of fear prickling under her skin.

"Did no one think to question this lieutenant?" Lord Jeffrey asked. "Did no one take the time to gather other testimony to corroborate this accusation?"

Lord Jeffrey was a man who believed in the sovereignty of the law. He could not conceive of the way India had been governed, by a company so intent upon their profits they would sacrifice all else, especially the spirit of fairness and impartial justice, before it.

Thomas, who probably knew even better than she what the long reach of the company had been like, just shook his head. "No one, apparently. Until I came. But as soon as I made my statement to the committee, and the records of my identity were checked and verified, Birkstead was conveniently invalided out. Left to come back to England to recover from his wounds."

This was news to Catriona. "Six months after the fact? He must have been hurt more badly than I realized."

"Yes." This time his look was grim, and perhaps even guilty. He looked away and frowned. "I don't think he was ever able to return to active duty."

There was something he was not telling her. "What happened, Thomas?"

Thomas was not to be swayed from his purpose. "I was about to ask the same of you. I saw you go into that fire, but I never saw you come out. And Birkstead swore he hadn't seen you, but I know he lied."

"That night?" So Thomas must have found the lieutenant while she had burned the soles of her feet escaping across what was left of the roof. "How funny that he should have told you the truth. No, he didn't actually see me."

"What happened, Cat? How did you do it? How did you get out?" he asked. "For the life of me I could not find out. I asked every peddler and beggar from one side of the city to another. I ran Mina to ground in Ranpur, only to be told that I was an undeserving jackal, but that she knew nothing of you, as she had been sent by her mother to return to Ranpur to the house of her husband."

It had been a diversion, a brilliant conceit of the begum's that Mina and her grand retinue of bearers and palanquins, painted elephants and their shaded howdahs, would leave first thing in the morning. Amidst all the stir of Mina's preparations, Catriona and the children had slipped quietly out of the Balfours' compound in a nondescript, closed oxcart, bound in the opposite direction, to the southwest for the begum's sister in Rajasthan. "Surely that wasn't all Mina said?"

"She also said that I had been a fool, and that I didn't deserve you. I told her she was wrong."

Oh, yes, Mina was wrong. It was Catriona who did not deserve steadfast Thomas Jellicoe. "She told me I was a damned fool as well."

"Yes, she would." He smiled, but the warmth didn't reach all the way up to his eyes. The steady probe of that green gaze told her there would be no more evasion. And perhaps it was time.

"What happened, Cat?"

It was past time for the truth. "What happened was that I fell in love with you. And the lieutenant did not like it."

The lieutenant, in the long run, had only liked himself. He had not especially cared for Lettice, he had openly disliked Cat, and he had certainly hated Tanvir Singh. But the lieutenant had not let anything so insubstantial as his personal feelings stand in the way of his ambition. He was ambitious for power and control. And he meant to get both by marrying the resident commissioner's well-dowered niece, Catriona Rowan.

He had used every means at his disposal—underhanded and overt—to try to cozen her into favoring his suit. He asked to sit next to her at dinners though she refused to speak to him. He sent flowers though she fed them to the goats. He smiled charmingly, always publicly solicitous for Miss Rowan's health and comfort, though he said filthy, unrepeatable things under his breath that only she could hear.

She had taken savage delight in thwarting him.

But when his patience wore as thin as his alleged charm, when she had continued to ignore his increasingly blunt propositions, the lieutenant had resorted to intimidation.

The night before the fire, the night she had first kissed Tanvir Singh, it had been the lieutenant, and not the wily spy, who had stood in the dark and listened. It had been the lieutenant who gathered secrets about her.

She had been cocooned in a bubble of happiness that night, as she walked the mare back through the cantonment's iron gates. She had felt protected by her secret, buoyant with the thrill of her first kiss, and the excitement of something deeper and more important than infatuation.

And suddenly there he was, Lieutenant Birkstead, waiting for her on the path in all his handsome, blond glory, idly smoking on a cheroot. "Well, well. Our adventurous young Miss Rowan finds her way home at last." He took a deep draw of his smoke and stepped in front of her, casually barring her way with his scarlet, uniformed body. "Out in the world gathering experience, were you, my dear? Consorting with the natives?"

His voice had been snide and dark, and veering toward aggressive, and Catriona knew a threat when she heard it. She backed away into her horse's neck. She had absolutely no desire to speak to the man, and less to be trapped into an encounter with him. But she had also learned that he liked nothing more than when she ran away from him—he liked the excitement of the chase, the thrill of the hunt and capture.

So she had stood her ground. The mare was protection enough—the animal grew fractious and haughty in the lieutenant's presence, tossing her head and showing her teeth, and nickering ominously. The lieutenant stopped well clear of Puithar's reach.

The horse's good sense and protective instincts gave Catriona courage. "It is common knowledge that I visit with the Princess of Ranpur and her mother the Begum. And that I do so with my uncle's permission. So it is no concern of yours, Lieutenant."

"Is is not? Because speaking of your uncle, Lord Summers, you'll find that he considers me an excellent prospect as a son-in-law. Most excellent. Told me so just today. So you'll want to watch yourself, my dear. I'm a tolerant man, but not particularly partial to other men's leavings."

Catriona had felt the first thrust of the jackal's verbal assault, but she wasn't about to concede any ground—if he smelled blood, he would only chase her harder. "Aren't you? I would have thought you particularly adept at such a scenario." She turned and let her gaze rest meaningfully on the part of the residency where her aunt's rooms lay.

Birkstead barely had the grace to flush—a wash of higher color appeared momentarily on his gilded cheek, before his arrogance chased it away. "Careful, little mouse. Don't involve yourself in business you know nothing about, when you've got so much trouble of your own. I doubt your uncle would like to hear of how you just spent the past half hour, pushed up against the outer wall with your skirts rucked up to your ears by a native *boxwallah* of dubious character."

The threat struck her like a sharp, well-aimed dart, sure and lethal. But she kept still, kept quiet, and kept her distance, letting him spew his dirty insinuations into the night while she wondered what it was that he wanted this time. A kiss? A grope the likes of which he thought he'd just seen? She had refused him all before and managed to keep her distance. But he was clearly becoming impatient.

Catriona let out more of the rein between her clenched fingers to surreptitiously give Puithar her head.

Birkstead did move back half a pace when the mare tossed her head in his direction, but he held his ground as well. "I've rather liked your little game of superiority and unavailability." He slid her one of his condescending smiles. "It made you seem unattainable, a prize worth having. When now I find you're rather *too* easily attainable. That your protests and virginal posturing are all for show. You know, my dear, it won't do for you to be secretly panting after the natives. You'll need to curb that deplorable tendency after we wed."

"Just as you need to curb your deplorable tendency to pant after other men's wives?"

He laughed and tilted up his chin to blow a careless stream of smoke into the night around her head. "You've got some spark and fire, I'll give you that. You're not quite the pale little dishrag of a girl you like to let people think, are you?"

It was everything she could do not to strike him then—a ringing slap against the broad flat of his cheek that would leave a livid swath of red skin like a warning flag of temper flying across his face. A mark that would proclaim, to any and all who came near, *This man is a worthless bastard*.

But she didn't strike him. He was too full of suppressed violence for such an action to be met without retaliation. So she clenched the palm that still itched to hit him as hard as his words had hit her, into a fist so tight it tingled, and tried to stare him down. "You must want money rather badly, Lieutenant, to go to all this trouble for a girl you don't even like. Gambling debts, is it? Or is keeping other men's wives expensive?"

He flashed her that all-too-charming, golden-boy grin. "Surprisingly economical, really. As is bribing servants to keep track of people who are important to me."

"You're disgusting." She wanted to spit the invective at him.

"If I am, you'd better get used to it."

"Never."

"Never is a very long time, mousie," he said with mock severity. "And I *know* things. Things you don't want anyone else to know."

His words stole over her like a killing frost, riming the inside of her lungs. It was suddenly painful to draw breath, the same as when she'd contracted the pleurisy years ago in Scotland.

"Ah. That got your attention, didn't it? Very good. You're almost quivering with your curiosity."

It wasn't curiosity. It was dread. Mortal dread.

But Birkstead had smiled at her discomfiture. He took one last draw on his cheroot and exhaled a plume of self-satisfaction into the night, before he ground out the stub with the toe of his boot. "It will be quite the catfight, getting you into bed." And he laughed at her, his darkly blue eyes glinting with predatory delight. "I'm quite looking forward to it. Just be sure not to give it away beforehand like a slut."

His casual cruelty made her lash out. "Like you?" Or her aunt Lettice. There seemed to be more than enough sluts to go around.

He laughed still. "Jealous of Lettice, are you?"

"No. What I am is disgusted." And afraid. She scrambled up into the saddle, so she might have the advantage of Puithar's height to give her some distance from the vile man. "Don't speak to me again. Don't even act as if you know me."

But he hadn't listened. He had laughed. "I'll speak as I like. You're mine, mousie. And the sooner you understand that, the better off you'll be. Don't make me do something you'll regret. Because you know I will do whatever is necessary to bring you to the altar."

He had turned and ambled off into the dark, leaving his threat lingering in the air like the stench of his cigar.

And he had continued to do just as he pleased. He had gone on doing it until he had ruined everything. Until he had destroyed her more effectively than if she had let him hit her.

It was what they all did—men—they did as they pleased. And she'd had enough of it.

Chapter Sixteen

Catriona had decided to do something about Lieutenant Birkstead at the next available opportunity in Saharanpur, but that had not worked out at all well. It had, in fact, ended in murder.

And it had been her fault, if not her hand that did the deed.

It was she who had stirred the hornet's nest. It was she who had been insistent and adamant and convinced of what was right. So damnably sure. And so utterly wrong.

It had seemed such a straightforward sort of thing to do, to go to her uncle immediately, and simply tell him that she was not interested in the lieutenant's less than attractive offers. She had already tried begging off all social engagements that were most likely to bring her into contact with the lieutenant—with no protest at all from her aunt. But the damn man had a way of insinuating himself into the residency. That night had not been the first time he had taken her unawares on the pathways, or the stairs and corridors. It unnerved her, his easy, unrestrained access to her life. It unnerved her that despite her antipathy, he still seemed to take her eventual capitulation for granted.

And so she had resolved to put an end to it as soon as possible, before she had time to think and change her mind or become intimidated. She found Lord Summers in his library, where he often smoked a cigar and enjoyed a brandy before he and aunt Lettice embarked upon their social rounds.

She had not even hesitated on the threshold. "Good evening, sir."

"Catriona." He had welcomed her with a kind smile. "Come and sit with me."

She returned his smile, and crossed to the cane-backed armchairs where he reclined. "You seem to be in a rather expansive mood this evening, my lord." He would be in less of one when he heard what she had to say, but there was no avoiding it.

"Indeed, I am, my dear. And so will you be. Come and sit with me for a moment."

When she had seated herself in the chair across from him, Lord Summers took up her hand. "I cannot tell you what a pleasure it has been to have you as part of the household. What a help you've been to Lady Summers, and a wonderful influence with the children. I don't know when we've had a happier time."

His words were a welcome balm to her soul. And she agreed with him—she had never had a happier or lovelier time. With the exception of Lieutenant Birkstead's attention, her time in Saharanpur had been a delight. And there were so many other pleasures to outweigh the lieutenant. Pleasures that she would be free to pursue once she put Lord Summers straight. "Thank you, sir. It has been a joy to know my cousins."

"And I know they feel the same. Arthur has told me you're more accomplished than any *three* riding instructors he's ever had. Quite a compliment from a young lad, I might add."

It was thoughtful of her young cousin to give credit to her rather than Tanvir Singh, who had always been kind enough to speak with the boy and give Arthur the benefit of his instruction and advice. "Arthur has become a very good rider. Very good, steady hands." Arthur would grow to be an exceptional man someday—Catriona firmly believed a man's character was revealed in the way he treated both his servants and his animals.

Her uncle-in-law pinked with pride, but was not deterred from his original point. "And as loath as I am to part with you—"

"Then you shall not." Catriona spoke quickly to stop Lord Summers from following his intended path, but he was in too genial a mood to take heed of any warning in her tone.

"But I cannot be so selfish." He smiled and patted her hand. "And it is a comfort to know you will not go far. Perhaps we will even manage to keep you with us at the residency."

"I will go nowhere, Uncle," she insisted. "Truly. I have no wish to leave. For any reason." She firmed her voice even more, and looked him in the eye to make sure he understood her intent. Her life with her cousins was perfect, just as it was.

But Lord Summers was blind to any other possibility but the one he had already envisioned. He could not be so easily dissuaded from his own intent. "Not even when you find out that a certain fellow has made his intentions known to me? Not even when you find that you are to be the happiest of women?"

She would get nowhere with Lord Summers by being subtle. "I hope, Uncle, you do not refer to Lieutenant Birkstead."

"Aha! But I do." And then Lord Summers finally read her distress in her expression. "But what do you mean? Do you mean you do not welcome his suit?" Surprise made his face florid. "He is the most sought-after officer in the entire residency."

Then the entire residency was blind. As blind as poor Lord Summers. But she could not become one of them. She would not join them in their willful self-deception.

"I have no doubt of that, sir." Catriona measured out her worlds in an effort to be as kind and as politic as possible. "But I fear we should not suit."

He sat back in his chair, as if her antipathy to Birkstead were unfathomable, and he could not think of any reason to believe her. Then his face cleared when he hit upon his answer. "Ah. You think that you are not good enough for him. My dear child, let me assure you—"

"No, sir." She could not let him go on in this vein. Not good enough? Her new uncle was a generous, jovial man, but he knew her so little, really. He could not be any more mistaken in his conjecture of her opinions. If only her uncle could see past class and caste and titles. "Please understand. There is no circumstance, of birth or fortune, his or mine, that would change my mind. Please believe me when I tell you, we are entirely unsuited."

"No, no. Not at all. You will suit, for he is handsome and talented, and you are rich."

"My lord?"

Lord Summers laughed and patted the hand he still held captive within his own. "It is done, Catriona, for I have spent the day settling a fortune of your own upon you. You must know you are like a daughter to me. And all the more precious because you are not. No one could have done more for your cousins. No one could have loved them better."

"My Lord Summers." His extraordinary kindness made heat build in her throat. "You make too much of it. I love them for themselves, and not because I expect recompense for it."

"You shall have it, nonetheless. I can do no less."

Catriona could not refuse such generosity. She did not want to refuse. Such money would give her independence at the very least, and let her marry where she chose—far, far away from the hidebound, narrow cantonment, and the Lieutenant Birksteads of the world. Into a whole other world, perhaps. Money of her own would be a godsend.

Gratitude tightened her throat, and made it hard to speak. "You are truly generous, and I thank you from the bottom of my heart. But I also know, and hope you will believe me when I tell you, that Lieutenant Birkstead and I will not suit. We will *never* suit."

He sat back to consider her. "Have you given this serious consideration?"

"I have, sir. I have." She had to make him understand. She had to. "I have tried to consider his suit, but he is not a man I can either love or respect." Her heart was thudding at the hollow of her throat, pushing the words she didn't want to say upward toward her mouth. It took everything she had, every ounce of self-restraint and tact, to make her uncle understand, and at the same time not reveal too much.

But he would not allow her the luxury of easy evasion. He frowned at her, as if he was afraid she had taken leave of her senses, or was suffering from some missish over-abundance of modesty. "Will you not at least tell me why you feel you should not suit?"

She tried to choose her words carefully, but every piece of truth was a potential disaster. "He has a reputation as . . . a rake, a ladies' man, only not with ladi—"

"My dear." Lord Summers interrupted her with another easy, unconcerned smile. "It is only natural that he should be something of a swain. He is, after all, a handsome man, and he is charming. You should not put too much stead into rumors."

She did not know how else to make him understand. "I would hope that you would know me better than to think that I would believe idle rumor, sir. What I know of the lieutenant, I have observed firsthand, without resort to rumor or innuendo." She took a breath and forged ahead. "I have seen him with married ladies of this cantonment."

"The lieutenant is a great favorite of all the ladies, of course."

Catriona wanted to be kind and circumspect. But her frustration, and her anger for her uncle, made her imprudent. "Sir, I have seen him kissing married ladies of this cantonment with carnal intent, and I have heard him making assignations with married ladies."

"Have you really?"

"Yes. He is neither discreet nor prudent. If I, who do not care much for socializing, have seen evidence of his dalliances, it is highly likely that others have gained knowledge of his indiscretions as easily as I have." Catriona wasn't sure if he was truly astonished, or he simply didn't believe her. But she could not reveal the whole truth without making a complete and utter hash of it. "Please. Don't make me say any more. Please believe me, and let the matter rest."

Lord Summers's eyebrows rode high across his face for a long moment before he spoke. "If it is as you say, and perhaps he had not always behaved so well as he ought in the past, we must assume that he is a changed man. He has declared himself smitten with you. Smitten, my dear. He declares he will have no other, and I believe him."

"Why? Why do you believe him?"

"Why should I not? The lieutenant is an intelligent, hardworking young man. An excellent officer. He looks after the cares of this cantonment as if they were his own."

Of course he did, the jackal. There was profit in such vigilance. And the bloody man had clearly spent more time making up to Lord Summers than he had to her. And with much better effect, for Lord Summers believed Birkstead, where she did not. "The lieutenant has never spoken of his finer feelings to *me,* sir, if indeed he has *finer* feelings. For my part, I am sure such effusions are contrived, for Lieutenant Birkstead can be in no doubt of my low opinion of him."

"You have spoken to him?"

"On almost every occasion when we have met. Lieutenant Birkstead is well aware of my feelings toward him, sir. He can be in no doubt."

"But he spoke to me of his wishes this very afternoon. He was effusive in his hopes."

It ought to be heartening, that her uncle was such a trusting, well-intentioned man, but his obtuseness regarding the lieutenant was more than wearying. "And may I ask, sir, if the lieutenant is aware of the amount of money you had planned to settle upon me?"

"Of course, for why would I not tell him? I encouraged his suit. You know I have worked to throw you together."

"I thank you for your efforts, sir. Truly I do. No father could have done more. But do you not see that his persistence in the face of rejection might be fueled more by ambition for your money, than by any love or affection or even respect for me?"

Lord Summers's blank face showed that he had indeed *not* thought such a thing, at all. And that he was perhaps put out at Catriona for suggesting it. Indeed he was displeased—every inch of his face was growing taut and hard. "You have quite made up your mind, have you not?"

"I'm afraid I have, sir. I thank you for your care and generosity. I just don't think Lieutenant Birkstead is as worthy of your generosity as you have thought him."

"Yes, perhaps. Perhaps not." Her uncle-in-law was pensive and unhappy with her—his brow was still beetled with concern and his mouth was turned down in an unhappy moue. He stabbed out his cigar. "Just promise me you will think more on it before you dismiss him out of hand. Promise me that you will give him a chance to prove himself worthy of you."

There was no chance. There had not been since the moment she had seen the dratted man in Aunt Lettice's greedy arms. But she had pained her uncle enough for one evening. It was enough that she had spoken. It would take time for Lord Summers to come around to her way of thinking. She had to trust that he would, in time, observe Birkstead, and see for himself.

But it seemed prudent, at that moment, to give in. "I promise, sir."

It would not be her last lie. In fact, it proved to be the first of many, many more.

The next lie flew out of her mouth not more than a few minutes later.

Because he must have been there, Birkstead, outside on the veranda, listening to her conversation with her uncle. And he did have a servant at the residency who was in his pay, because within minutes of her conversation with her uncle, the lieutenant was back at her, full of well-honed threat.

She had gone into the central courtyard at the back half of the house, where there was a tiny garden, to settle herself. To think for the first time about the future, about what she *did* want, and if, after she had disappointed him, her uncle-in-law would prove true about the settlement, how she might use that money to further her goals. She had no desire to go back to Scotland, but she knew she would have to make a home of her own somehow, somewhere. Perhaps here in India, or farther north, in the kingdom of the Punjab or Kashmir, beyond British influence or reach. Tanvir Singh would advise her on where she might go.

And then the jackal was suddenly there, jarring her out of her thoughts of travels, and caravans, and horse traders, materializing out of the dark like a phantom, silent and menacing.

"And there she is." Birkstead stepped across her path again, smiling at her in the focused, self-possessed way of a snake hunting its prey. "My elegant, contained little betrothed."

Catriona stopped short of running into him, and fought to keep her composure over the inelegant, uncontained pounding of her pulse in her throat. She should have anticipated him. She should have remembered his talk of casually bribing servants.

She let her resentment push her toward anger but she kept her voice low, conscious of being overheard. "I am not your betrothed, Lieutenant. Nor will I ever agree to be. You know that."

He smiled, and shook his head as if it were she who were particularly obtuse, before he leaned in closer to whisper his threat. "It's funny the things one knows. About you, for example."

She would not take his lethal bait. "You know I don't like you."

"True. Very true. And at this moment, I *don't* especially

like you. But your new fortune, on the other hand, remains most endearing."

His offhand, open contempt steeled her spine. "Ah. Sarcasm. So refreshing. I'm sure my uncle will be interested to hear of it." She would have turned, and gone back the way she had come, but she didn't like to turn her back on him—he still had that glint of predatory pleasure shining from the dark depths of his eyes—so she backed toward the stairs leading out of the courtyard.

"Perhaps. But I rather think your uncle won't hear of our little exchange of sarcasm. In fact, I'm sure of it."

And he was very sure. He was almost smug with certainty. Catriona swallowed the acid tang of apprehension rising in her throat and waited.

He didn't keep her in suspense—he was too happy, too smug to keep his peace for long. "Yes, you will be surprised by all I know about you. You left Scotland rather precipitously, did you not?"

The tight knot in her throat moved lower into her chest where it sat like a hot coal, burning away the last traces of her confidence. She had to wet her dry lips and throat to speak. "I left when my parents died, and I had no remaining family." The growing heat within scorched her voice.

His smile slid up one side of his face. He really was a jackal of a man. "But that's not exactly true, is it?"

"No," she countered with desperate determination. "It is *exactly* true." Her throat was so dry it was a wonder her voice had not cracked in two.

He smiled with the amoral satisfaction of a hunter who knows it has trapped its prey. "That's not what they're whispering around Glasgow."

The hot, choking heat seared throughout her chest, and out into her arms before it burned its way down into her belly. An image rose unbidden to the surface of her mind— her father at his end, quietly and coldly dead in the damp green grass, his eyes looking up at the empty heavens as the fading echo of the pistol shot moaned through the hills above the Avon water.

But Birkstead was not done toying with her. "I have a report, you know. A report that I instigated, on Lord Summers's behalf." There was the predatory, lupine smile again. "You didn't think that an unknown girl could just show up, from out of the blue, and impose herself upon the resident commissioner without any notice, did you?" He shook his head at her inferred foolishness. "Oh, no. I decided to find out what I could. And I found out something very interesting."

She backed away from him. She couldn't help herself. The animal instinct to run reasserted itself with a blind fury. Birkstead was a living, breathing, lethal threat, and no matter how she told herself that he could not possibly know what had happened in Scotland, her courage could not withstand the assault without moving a prudent few feet backward.

She tried to steel her spine. "There is nothing interesting to find. My family died of typhus." That at least was partially true. Her mother and brother and sister had all been gone within the span of a fortnight. As had others—cousins and strangers alike. "Half of Glasgow died that fall. At least, half the people in the poorer neighborhoods did. You may accuse me of being low, of taking advantage. It is true, I *am* poor and obscure. I have only one relation in the world who is not either of those things, and he is my uncle-in-law. And all this I told him myself when I arrived in Saharanpur."

Lieutenant Birkstead was not at all moved by her recitation of her sad facts, only amused as he strolled nearer. "So modest. So effacing. But I know better. I know what you're *really* like." He drew close enough to whisper, "And I know what you did, little mouse. I know."

The burning heat in her lungs chilled to ice, even as she steadfastly denied it.

He could not know for sure. He could not. No one knew. No one had seen. No one had been there.

She forced the words upon her lips. "And what is it you know?"

"That your father was a traitor, a United Ulsterman, and was on the run when he died before he could be taken for the noose."

The chill was spreading through her body, turning her as cold and numb as she had that night in the woods outside of Glasgow. The night she had sat with her father's body until it had grown cold and stiff. Until there was nothing she could do, but pile his body carefully with rocks to form a cairn, so it could not be scavenged by the wolves that still roamed the woods. So they could find him, and perhaps take his body to a priest.

"Some said he killed himself, like a coward, rather than be taken. Some said he simply died from a fall he took in his escape, just as he ought."

The numbness was spreading to her feet, for she could not run. She could only stand there, frozen in horror, while he chipped away at her, like an axe splintering apart the ice.

"But do you know what I say, mousie? I say no one who kills himself, or dies alone in the woods, makes his own cairn."

The cold within brought a savage, biting pain. The pain that she had carried with her like a grave marker across all those leagues of dark deep sea. Across all the miles of hot dust-whipped roads. The pain that had never gone away, but could no longer be pushed aside, an ache to nurse in some other, less dire time. The time of reckoning had come.

"Nothing to say? Cat got your tongue, my little mouse? Good. Let's keep it that way, shall we? You keep quiet to Lord Summers about your *objections* and *won't suits,* and I may be persuaded do the same, and keep your little scandalous—and conveniently felonious—deed quiet. I won't tell your uncle what I know of you, and your father in Scotland, and you won't tell him anything more about me. That way we both get what we want."

"And what is it exactly that you want, Lieutenant?" The words were nothing but the ghost of her breath in her mouth.

"Why, you, little mouse." He ran his hand across her

hair carefully, testing her acceptance of his possession, as if he thought her as fractious as her mare, and was being careful not to get bit. "You and all your lovely mousy money. And influence as a part of the resident commissioner's family. I'm ambitious for us, you see, little mouse. Nearly as ambitious as *you*." He kept touching her, and while she was still, and made no move to stop him, or break his hold, he reached out and traced a finger down her nose, and tugged in cruel mockery of playfulness at her chin. "I thought I was going to have to wait for years, until little Alice dear grew up. But then you showed up, my ambitious little mousie, like a gift from fate. Yes. I think we will treat together very well. Very well."

Though she was cold and shaking with the effort, she drew slowly and carefully out from under his hand. "And what does my aunt think of your ambitions, Lieutenant?"

His answer was the slyest smile of them all, curving around one side of his mouth like the jackal he was, sliding silently through the long grass. "Let me worry about dear Lettice, mousie. You just keep your little mousy head down, and keep your little mousy mouth shut tight."

It was already shut tight. An ache crawled along her jaw from the pressure of her teeth clamped down to hold in her disgust and fright. She backed away from him as carefully and steadily as if he were an unpredictable, wild animal, until the sight of him was lost to her in the dark pressing silence.

She kept her mouth shut, and her head down all the way to her chamber, trying in vain to stop the voice in her head telling her to run. Now. Before he could talk.

But where would she go? She had already run halfway around the world. Was she prepared to tackle the other half?

Perhaps, her brain whispered. Perhaps with Tanvir Singh.

He would help her. With Tanvir Singh she could roam across mountains and down valleys. Over frontiers. To Punjab and Kashmir, and beyond. Perhaps even to Tibet. She could leave the cantonment and all questions of caste and color and cuckolding behind. She could be done with dark ambition.

She could become the new person Mina and the begum, and even Tanvir Singh himself, had been encouraging her to be. She could be his lover. He had said he wanted more from her. He had said he wanted to do more than kiss against dark walls. Surely he wanted her enough to take her with him?

And to whom else could she turn? The colonel, and Mina and the begum? The old palace would be the first place Lord Summers looked, and she had no other friends. Only Tanvir Singh had the means necessary to spirit her away and out of British-controlled India.

Yes. Going to Tanvir Singh would answer for everything.

She would not let her fear return her to the cold, shivering, frightened girl she had been that autumn day in the hills above Avon water. She was not that girl. Something fundamental had changed, and she was no longer just the pale, mousy girl the Jonathan Birksteads of this world thought they could intimidate into doing their bidding. She refused to be.

She would choose differently.

Chapter Seventeen

That last night in India, Catriona had quickly shoved as much of her clothing as she could into the practical Scots knapsack that was all the baggage she had brought with her from Scotland. She hated that she would have to leave so much behind again, and take only what she could carry. The elegant pieces of clothing, the beautiful, fairy-dust evening gowns that had been gifted to her would have to remain. Alice could have them, when she was a bit older— Catriona would not need such luxuries if she were to live the life of a horse trader. She would be clothed differently from now on, in plain *salwar kameez,* but in the meantime, she would take only sturdy, practical clothes suitable to the cool of the hills, and a few small personal items.

And her father's gun.

Catriona drew the ancient pistol out from under the stack of shawls where she had hidden it in the bottom of her chest of drawers. She had not touched the weapon in months—since the day of her first ride with Tanvir Singh. She had not felt the need. But she ought not leave it behind for Birkstead to find and postulate over, and she certainly might need it were she confronted by the jackal again as she made her surreptitious escape.

The thought brought a quiver shivering its way along

the surface of her skin. What had her father said? *I've lived by the gun. I'm prepared to die by the gun, too.*

Catriona was not so prepared, and her hands shook as she made the careful movements of measuring out shot and powder.

But at last it was done, and there was nothing left to do but hope for the best—that she would never be called upon to use it—and go away from the residency as quickly and silently as possible.

She hesitated for a long moment, torn between her desire to say good-bye to the children—to kiss the little ones, Charlotte and George, as they lay sleeping. To tell Arthur he was the best of lads, and to hug sweet Alice and tell her she loved her—and her instinct to run as far and as fast as her feet and her mare could carry her, away from Lieutenant Jonathan Birkstead and his malevolent knowledge of her past.

Instinct won out, but the delay cost her. She made her silent way out of the residency—away from Birkstead and his twisted version of marital bliss, away from the house of spies and lies—via the dark of the walled garden, before she turned toward the unguarded stable gate at the side of the garden. All the time, she was searching with new eyes for Birkstead's paid accomplices, seeing in every shadow a potential enemy.

She had never felt so hunted. So exposed. It had been one thing in Scotland to think that she might be followed—to think that someone, anyone, might know what she had done to escape and survive—but it was another thing entirely to *know* that her every movement was being noted and reported.

And who would do such a thing? The elderly gate porter who always waved and smiled? The grooms who stood back so respectfully when she took out Puithar, or the houseboys who had seemed happy to run errands or take messages to Mina at the old palace? And what about Namita, the *ayah* who had been assigned to look after Catriona as if she were her shadow?

It was Namita who followed Catriona through the garden, and who chased her through the gate. The *ayah* pleaded and admonished in turn. "Oh, mem! What do you do? Thou shouldst not go out alone at this time of the night," she wailed. "There are more than one kind of jackal in the streets. Nothing good can come of it."

There was more than one kind of jackal loose in the house, and nothing good was going to come of that, either.

"Go back inside the house, Namita. Nothing bad is going to happen." The lie slipped easily off her tongue. "I only want to walk for a while, alone. I know my way around the garden well enough to go blindfolded."

Namita did not believe the lie. "And where wilt thou go blindfolded, and with thy baggages in the dark?" The *ayah* clung to Catriona's arm like a limpet. "What will I tell the lord sahib when he finds that I have let thee go alone into the night?"

"And is it only Lord Summers that you will tell, Namita? Who else has been paying for your loyalty?"

Namita looked conscious—though she shook her head in denial she could not meet Catriona's eyes. "Please, mem," she begged. "The *Badmash* Sahib, he . . ."

"Yes, I know." Catriona wanted to be angry, but she knew that whatever pennies Birkstead was bribing Namita with were undoubtedly a welcome increase in her probably pitiable wages. But still the knowledge that her own servants, who had helped her dress and knew all the intimate details of Catriona's daily life, had betrayed her to Birkstead—the thought of what Namita might have been made to reveal to Birkstead sat like a cold knot in Cat's stomach. "I wish I could offer you more, to buy your silence, but I can't." Catriona hadn't a penny of her own to her name. "So tell him I've gone into the night. Tell him I've gone to Tanvir Singh, and see if he dares to follow me."

Namita's face turned ashen with fear, and she clutched at Cat's sleeve. "Oh, no, mem. Do not do it, I beg thee. Nothing good can come of it. Nothing. Thou wilt be killed in the night."

"I will not be killed." She would do Birkstead absolutely no good dead, and she had all the protection she thought she might need, deep in the pocket sewn into her riding habit. Catriona pulled herself from Namita's grasp. "And I *will* go."

Her resolve carried her into the stable where she slipped Puithar out of her stall with only a bridle—her saddle was stored too high for her to retrieve without much noisy trouble; another sin of interference to lay at Birkstead's head?—before she slipped away into the night.

As she hurried along in the shadows under the trees toward the encampment along the other side of the river, a different sort of feeling gave way to the suspicions Catriona carried out of the residency. She had no trouble upon the dusty roads at the fringes of the city—she rode Puithar at too great a speed for anyone to accost her—the showy mare identified her to every nodding beggar and smiling fakir along the way as the *angrezi* girl who was the friend of Tanvir Singh, as someone under his protection.

It was madness, surely, the heady, intoxicating feeling pounding up from her heart—this understanding that there was no turning back. She had slipped the traces of polite, respectable expatriate life, and there would be no fitting her back to the harness. No matter what Tanvir Singh said—if he accepted her or not—she could not go back. It was a nerve-racking gamble to trust that Tanvir Singh meant what he had whispered to her in the close confessional of the cantonment wall—*This is real. All else is madness.*

But it would have been a greater madness to stay and let herself be manipulated by Birkstead, to take the scraps of life he surely meant to feed her. If she accepted the marriage Birkstead and her uncle offered, she would live the rest of her days in fear and abject misery. Nothing—no privilege, no reputation, and no family—was worth such a sacrifice.

And then there was no more time for second thoughts and regrets—she was there at the edge of the encampment along the shaded banks of the river. Catriona knew her

way through the bright tapestry of colored tents and pavilions that made up his caravan, though she had never been
there at night, and never before come alone. She halted and
waited for the hard beating of her pulse to slow and her
breath to lengthen enough so she might draw a deep,
steadying lungful of the evening air before she dismounted.

In the middle of the encampment, bright fires leaped
from torches and braziers, and lanterns turned the tents into
beautiful glowing cubes of color. Catriona had envisioned
Tanvir Singh's world being comprised solely of men—a
nomadic, almost monastic existence—and she had never
seen females during her daytime visits with the children.
But at night, women seemed to be everywhere—servants
moved about the tents among the horsemen, married women
tended to their husbands, and in the distance she could
hear the tabla drums, sitar, and jangling bells of dancing.

If anyone paid her more than a passing glance as she
wound her mare through the tents, she did not notice, so
consumed was she by the sights and smells and sounds, and
the curiously pleasant flight of butterflies battering about
her belly in anticipation. But she had not passed unnoticed.
A tall *sa'is* appeared suddenly, and bowed and gestured
with a sweep of his arm that she should follow him.

He took her reins and conducted her through the make-
shift lanes toward the center of the camp, to a sumptuous
tent where the two brightly clad young women danced by
the light of a fire in the flowing northern style of dance
Mina had taught her.

The audience was arrayed on low, cushioned divans
behind the dancers, so the fire cast them in silhouette. And
there he was—reclining against a bolster pillow with the
same animal grace that had first drawn her eye.

The insistent rhythm of the tabla and sitar insinuated
itself into her blood, pushing her forward, until she drew
close enough so she could say his name. "Tanvir Singh."

It was enough. It was all that was necessary to sharpen
his gaze upon her, and bring whatever business or pleasure
he was conducting to an immediate end. Tanvir Singh

came swiftly to his feet, and said something she did not understand in Punjabi. The rest of the people—servants, *sa'is,* and dancers alike, dispersed and melted away into the gathering darkness, until there was no one but the two of them.

"My friend. Where is thy servant?" He took in both her attire and the bag clutched in her hand before he looked behind her, as if searching for such a retainer, or perhaps someone from the residency who would have accompanied her.

His deep voice was graven with concern, and Catriona tugged the hood of her cloak to shield her face. "There is no one," she assured him. "I came alone."

His keen gaze cut back to hers. "Thou shouldst not be here alone."

"I had to come." She could feel the weight of every unseen gaze in the place touch upon her and identify her despite the cloak. No doubt the gossip would reach the bazaar within the hour. "I need your help. Please."

He heard the note of uneasy uncertainty creeping into her voice, and gestured to the open flap of his tent. "Come, where we can talk and be private."

He took her hand, but held himself away from her, and led her with ceremonious politeness under the canopy of the tent, where they were sheltered from the majority of the caravan's curious eyes. Or perhaps they were not curious, and *angrezi* women often visited Tanvir Singh on their own, without escort. Perhaps she was not as unique as she wanted to believe, and had made a mistake in coming there.

But she had only to look across the camp to the dark ribbon of the river, and then downstream toward the cantonment and residency, where she would be trapped for the rest of her life if she turned back now.

No. It was not a mistake. She knew him better. She knew herself better.

"How can I help thee, *kaur*?"

She turned to him, to Tanvir Singh, to the steady trustworthiness that lived in his warm, green eyes. To the careful, respectful way he held her hand within his. To the ease with which she trusted herself with this man.

Tanvir Singh did not grab at her and try to intimidate her. Tanvir Singh did not murmur threats, and sleep with her aunt.

But it was one thing to decide to cast her lot to fate, and another thing entirely to actually do it. She looked at the tented room behind the gauzy curtain separating the porch from his sleeping area, where a rich carpet covered the ground and the low mounding of a cotton mattress was covered by soft cushions and cocooned in a silence so deep and profound it captured all the brave words, all the eloquent arguments and forthright pleas she had prepared at the back of her tongue. "I . . ."

He took some pity on her, or else he saw the wisdom in making their conversation less public still. He spoke another low word in Punjabi, and a manservant appeared to put out the lanterns, before he, too, faded back into the dark.

"Tell me what it is that troubles thee."

All the speeches, all the reasons and explanations she had rehearsed in her mind fell away. She could only tell him the bare truth. "I came to be with you."

He did not mistake her. Nor did he look away. But he gazed at her for such a long moment, his green eyes poring over her, that she thought he meant to refuse her. But he didn't.

He crossed the thick wool carpet that made up the floor of the tent and held back the curtain that led to the glowing interior. Inviting her in. "Come, then."

Catriona entered into his small, private world—his portable realm of dark, richly patterned carpets, soft, white cotton mattresses, bright pillows, and swaying canvas walls. Though it was only a tent, no formal mansion or tiered, carved stone palace was ever as enchanting.

Because it was his. It was his home, where she had never gone before. Her gaze scanned the room, taking it all in, looking for clues about the private man who was

Tanvir Singh. But Tanvir followed her in, and passed by with only the slightest touch to her arm, before he snuffed out the light of the lamps and plunged them into the velvet darkness.

"The lamps cast shadows upon the walls," he said by way of explanation, and the butterflies that had been fluttering about her insides took wing all at once, flinging themselves against her heart with giddy, fraught abandon.

If she took this step, it would be irrevocable.

And Tanvir Singh understood that. "I am only a man, Catriona Rowan." He reached out to caress the air below her jaw. "A man who wants to breathe the scent of jasmine from the soft skin at the side of thy neck. Who wants to take down thy hair the color of apricot fruit, and spread it through my fingers. A man who wants . . . thee," he finished simply. "Do not offer what thou dost not mean to freely give."

In the cocooning dark, his words warmed her and the low timbre of his voice insinuated itself deep below the surface of her skin. Something that had to be joy broke loose and went tumbling deep into her belly.

"I do mean to offer." She had nothing else of value, except herself. She could offer him the only gift she had. "I do mean to freely give."

And she began to do just that—she set down her satchel, pushed back the hood of her cloak, and pulled the pins from her hair, one by one, gathering them carefully into the palm of her hand, as if their neat alignment could keep the rest of her circumstances from flying out of her control.

But nothing was really within her control. Not Birkstead, and certainly not Tanvir Singh. She did not hear him move, but she felt the solid warmth of his body as he came up behind her and brushed his hand through her loose hair, raking his fingers through the length of it, and lifting it aside to bare her nape. Catriona turned her head aside, curving the length of her neck away from him, closing her eyes to give herself over to him, waiting for his touch.

It came at last, the merest, merest glance from the back of his fingers—an impression of warmth and sensuality. He slid his hand slowly upward, carefully delineating the curve of her neck before he turned and swept the pads of his fingers down along the tendon and out across the bridge of her collarbone to her shoulder. Her skin came alive beneath the cover of the layers of her English gown and the confines of her shift and stays. Every part of her, every inch of skin leaped with awareness and anticipation. With one brief moment of contact, he had filled her with longing for his touch.

He pulled her back against him then, gently settling her back against his chest, letting her rest against him. "We have begun, my *kaur*," he murmured into her ear. "And already thy body calls out to mine. Already thy skin heats to my touch. But it is not yet too late. It is not yet wrong for thee to think better of thy offer." He wound his fingers into her hair and tugged gently, holding her still so his lips could find the exact spot where her collar met her flesh. "You must understand." He held himself entirely still, as if they stood together on some great precipice, and one further movement would tumble them headlong into an abyss. "You must understand that if you offer yourself to me, I will most assuredly have you. I will have you bared to my touch. I will have you naked and spread for me in all your pale, luminous glory. And I will worship your body with my hands and my tongue and my body. I will teach you everything I know of pleasure and delight. Bare and naked," he whispered, "with nothing between us but passion."

Her chest was already rising and falling in rapid agreement, and her skin was tingling with anticipation of his touch. It had grown exquisitely sensitive and she felt the deep tug of something that must be want flaring strongly within. "Nothing between us."

She raised her hand to show him she meant it, to put words into action, and began to work loose the tight line of buttons at her wrist.

He rounded his hands around her shoulders, and then trailed them lightly down the length of her sleeves. "Let me, my *kaur*. I want to undress you."

His arms enclosed her and held her steady against him, leaning back into his strength as his clever fingers plucked the buttons loose one by one, and his lips played along the line of her neck, and his teeth glanced along the sensitive tendon.

When the buttons at her wrists were free, she turned within the circle of his arms and brought her mouth to his to kiss him with the same fierce tenderness he had been lavishing upon her. To press her lips to his and worry at the taut line of his smooth flesh with tiny nips, the way he had taught her.

It was slow and measured—a promenade toward seduction, a courtly walk instead of a headlong rush. He took his time with her, drawing out each sensation, lingering and waiting for the yearning to work its way through her, to let the pleasure seep down into her bones until she wanted each next thing, each stronger touch, each possessive caress, each show of passion that pushed her ever higher toward a goal she did not understand but could sense was waiting. Waiting for her. Beyond. Hovering just out of reach.

He was everything of patience, when she had none. He was everything of caution when she wanted done with it. He tasted her slowly, carefully, as if every single moment mattered. As if she were spun glass, and if he lifted her too high she might shatter from the pressure. But she was made of sterner, stronger stuff. She was not a fragile tea-cup of a woman to be sipped at delicately. She was strong like Scots whisky—hot and volatile, ready to combust. Ready to make him combust. She wanted him to drink her down until his head was spinning and the world was turning around the place where their flesh met.

But his care could not but affect her. And the moment after she wanted him to rely upon her strength she was glad that he did not. How long had she waited to depend upon someone else? How long had it been since she could trust someone else to carry the burdens that needed to be borne?

"Please," she said, unsure of what exactly she was asking for, but sure that he would understand and give it to her. She could trust him to do what needed to be done. "Make me naked. Quickly."

"Oh, there is no need to rush. We have all the night. And all of the day. And the following day. And the day after that. And the night. Every night."

But he had not been idle. While they kissed, his fingers had worked assiduously at the buttons down the front of her jacket. "So tight and closed up. All those buttons marching up and down your stiff bodices, enclosing the soft woman behind. So erotic. You have no idea how your buttons have tempted me."

In far less time than it had taken to button herself into the habit, the fasteners were slipped loose, and she was becoming more undone by the second. With each incursion of his mouth upon hers. With each kiss that grew bolder and bolder still, until she did not know where she was or what the state of her undress might be, only that his kiss had insinuated itself with hers until it seemed as if she could think and feel of nothing else but the sinuous rapture of his tongue within her mouth, and the feeling like morning that awoke and stretched within.

And then he pulled back to push the loosened jacket off her shoulders. And she was helping, pulling away the tight lower sleeves, working first at the hooks of her chemisette, and then at the hooks at her waist, but he placed his hands over her hands to still her. She looked up at him, but he was looking at her throat, at her body as it was revealed.

"So beautiful. So pale and exotic," he whispered, though she did not think he could see her—the velvet darkness pressed close. A single fingertip traced along the loosened collar of her chemisette, and she could feel herself leaning into him, seeking out even the slight pressure of that long, clever finger.

Beneath his eyes, beneath the linen chemisette and shift, behind the confines of her stays, her nipples contracted to tight needy peaks. Her breath came shallower still, her breasts pushed higher over the top of her stays by her rising excitement.

He leaned his head down and placed a single kiss right in the hollow of her throat, and for the first time in her life, Catriona thought she might swoon. Her eyes swept shut, and her knees felt weak, and she clutched at him for balance, for sanity, for more of the heat and overwhelming pleasure that swept across her skin like a hot wind.

She was clutching at him, holding on for dear life, and she could feel the sinuous line of his shoulders, lean and hard from the years of riding and travel in the hills, and she let her hands search across the smooth muscles of his back and down the long strong column of his spine.

But he was moving away, his mouth no longer on her skin, and he was kneeling in front of her, a supplicant almost, reverent as he continued to undress her. His hands were back at the hooks at her waist, and in another moment he was helping her to step out of the pool of fabric at her feet.

But she had told him she was no idol to be adored. She had told him she was as human and flawed as any other woman upon the face of the earth—probably more so.

She came down on her knees as well, to be his equal. And she was impatient to touch him, to kiss him, to feel the hard strength of his shoulders beneath her hands. His hands were at the last fastenings of her chemisette, pushing the fabric wide to glance over the warmed skin above her stays and shift.

"So many, many layers. A gift to be unwrapped." And then she felt his hand run down the length of her thigh until it came to the weight of her gun. "Oh, my dangerous girl, my *dacoity* bandit queen." His low chuckle vibrated through her, as his fingers searched to find the deep slit in the side of her petticoat, and into the long, pistol-shaped pocket beneath. His hand closed over both pocket and gun and pressed the weight of the pistol between her thighs. "So dangerous. So brave, my northern goddess of flame. I shall have to divest you of all your weapons, my *kaur,* save one."

"And what is that?" Her voice was low and breathless—it was a wonder she could speak at all over the pounding of her heart.

"Your smile."

She practically launched herself at him, throwing her arms about his neck, and kissing him with everything she had within her, every ounce of gratitude, and wonder and love. And they were falling, tumbling down onto the low mattress, rolling in each other's arms, giddy with happiness and the rush of pleasure that came from knowing that at last they were together.

And somehow she was free of her petticoats, and her legs were wrapping themselves around him, and they were kissing, kissing until she was laughing out loud from happiness.

"This is not good to laugh at a man as he is making love to you, *kaur.*"

"Tanvir. Tanvir, Tanvir, Tanvir. If I laugh, it is because I have never been so happy. I have been solemn for far too long."

"I will make you happier yet, my Cat. Just wait and see." His clever fingers were making short work of the lacing on the front of her stays.

She wanted to undress him as well, to unwrap him for herself, to peel off the long tunic to find the beautiful warm caramel of his skin. To give him the same kind of pleasure that he was evoking within her.

And then her stays were free, and his hand covered the roundness of her breast and he was kissing the hard peaks through her shift, wetting the fabric, making it cool and damp against her skin. And she was arching into him, giving herself to him, abandoning herself to the exquisite pleasure that blossomed deep as the pull of his lips created a tight needy heat between her legs.

He peeled the shift off her and the night air caressed her bare skin.

"Naked," he said, his voice turning rough. "Nothing to shield you from my eyes. So very, very naked." The low cadence of his voice was as heavy as a touch, pressing into her.

A glance of want stabbed into her belly.

"A naked gift to me." He looked up at her with his warm green eyes glinting in the darkness. Those eyes that watched and saw everything, every blush and stammer, every change that she had let Mina's servants make to her body.

Every sensation was new and fresh and magnified a hundred times over. The cool evening air on her shoulders, the warm waft of his breath against her navel. The heat of her skin along the inside of her thigh as he slowly, slowly rolled her stockings down.

And then she was nude, lying before him as he knelt above her, poised on the brink of something powerful and new.

"Naked," he said. "Bare to me. Completely bare."

And he touched her. One single finger. One point of contact with her skin. The tip of his index finger brushed a spot on her belly exactly halfway between her navel and her bare, smooth mons. He drew the tip of his finger across her sensitized skin in a minute circle, slowly tantalizing her. Nothing more than his finger riding lightly on the surface of her skin but she felt it all the way through her, deep inside, a tight constriction of pleasure that spread through her, drenching her in need.

"So gloriously, beautifully naked for me."

"Only for you." She had never felt so vulnerable. Or so completely powerful. "And you are not."

"No. Not yet." He stood and he reached up and began to unwind the long skein of his scarlet turban. When the last stand of fabric pulled away, he shook his head and the long dark, uneven hair fell in elegant disorder over his shoulders.

She was spellbound. He looked young and wild, an elemental force made man. But in freeing his hair, he seemed to have freed something within himself, some last vestige of gentlemanly restraint. He fell to removing his belt and dagger with a tense efficiency, tossing it aside and stripping off the jerkin covering his tunic, dropping it where he stood.

Yes. That was what she wanted. Forgetfulness. Carelessness. Need. Need. Need. Nothing but yawning, hungry need.

And oh, she needed him. She needed him to appease the long ache of unkindness, and doubt, and sacrifice and longing, longing, longing for something that had for so, so long seemed just out of reach, always beyond her tenacious grasp.

She let it rise within her, the willful forgetfulness, the reckless disregard for the past and the future and anything else that wasn't now. That wasn't him or her or pleasure and need so strong it burned under her skin like a fire that could not be contained by anything but more recklessness.

The moon rose outside the curtain of gauze and began to bathe the canvas walls in silver light that shone enough to turn his skin a shining, dark silver as he stood over her.

He moved aside so the wash of moonlight fell across her skin, tinting her a shimmering, pale pink. "I want to look at you."

She wanted him to look. Though the weeks in the *zenana* had changed her, her body looked foreign to her, a pale shimmering carnal offering, and she could not stop herself from sliding her hands down across the plane of her belly and glorying in the sensuality of the feel of her own skin beneath her fingers.

"Yes," he encouraged her. "You are beautiful. Because you are yourself."

She didn't feel like herself. She felt new and daring and free all at the same time. A sound as elemental and raw as the wail of the winds through the trees wound its way out of her mouth.

"Shhh." He closed her mouth with a kiss, and came down next to her, his long, sleek body filling up the space next to her. She turned into him, wrapping herself around him, pulling herself into him. Into his scent and his very being. The exotic scent of patchouli clung to his hair and perfumed the air around her, and she was lost in the haze of him.

Chapter Eighteen

Catriona watched him through eyes stretched wide in the sheltering dark, fascinated by the sight of him looking at her breasts, at her body. Held before him by her need, made still by his hot gaze as he followed her down, leaning in to kiss her mouth once more before he whispered, "Open to me."

Her body was stretching, arching within his hands, and she was aroused by the exquisite feeling of his dark, masculine hands stroking her pale, white breasts. She closed her eyes and gave herself over to him, to the white-hot pleasure that burned under her skin as his hands drew down the length of her body, from her collarbone, down across her aching breasts, along her belly and down the long run of her legs. Again and again, until she was moving beneath him, arching and twisting in anticipation, opening to him as the soft rush of sensation broke over her.

He stirred the backs of his fingers along the inside of her thighs, and she felt her body draw taut and ready. Ready for the pleasure he fed her like a sweetmeat. And then his hands were on her, parting the folds of her flesh. Her skin prickled in anticipation as his work-roughened hands teased at the tight heat at the junction of her thighs.

And she couldn't draw breath, couldn't think, couldn't do anything but wait. Until the moment when the tip of his tongue slid into her and she could hear the harsh, hungry sound she made as she gasped air back into her lungs.

He answered her with a murmur of his own that vibrated into her core and echoed throughout her body like a shout. The warmth of his mouth filled her, heating and lulling her, both arousing and soothing, as she floated higher and higher, buoyed on the rising tide of pleasure. Adrift on the warm passion he lavished upon her.

Until he drew away for the briefest moment, and then with one deftly precise touch, he licked her once more. In a way or in a place that made the edges of her body unravel and melt away, loosening and tightening the tangled skein of heat within.

She let out a breathless sound, as if she could no longer find air. As if she didn't need air and was happy to go under, drowning in her pleasure.

Tanvir touched her with his tongue again, his touch swirling through her, sending ripples spreading out under her skin until she felt the waves reach the palms of her hands, and there was nothing but him and his mouth and bliss pouring into her.

Until there was more, and she felt him slip his finger inside her, touching her deeply, stroking gently and strongly all at the same time, until a pleasure so sweet and intense it was almost pain galloped in.

Her hands closed in fists in his long, soft hair, and she knew she was nothing but desperate yearning and need that he brought out of her. Another sound, a gasp of frustrated want, poured out of her, and he heard her and understood, because in the next moment another finger followed the first and she began to feel full, as if he only could fill the frustrated well of her longing.

With his hand in her, his tongue swirled over her one last time, and she cast herself loose, out into the soft night, out into the enveloping oblivion, floating away on the bliss.

She let it carry her downstream, drifting along on the rushing torrent of her breath rising and falling as if she had drowned and could only pull air back into her lungs.

She felt dazed, and lazy and so happy she could not think. "Tanvir," was all that she could say, a breathless whisper of heat and wonder.

"Kaur." His voice came closer, and the mattress shifted as he moved over her to lean down and kiss first one, and then the other of her closed eyelids. And then the pad of his thumb brushed against her lower lip, a gentle proposal of a kiss. His mouth followed his hand with a deeper kiss, and she opened her mouth to him, to the heat and friction of his tongue. To the yearning hunger that reasserted itself inside her at the taste of him.

And he was kissing her with the same sort of hunger, as if he were as desperate as she. As if he had at last exhausted his share of patience and prudence and caution. As if he, too, had a need that only she could fill.

The weight of his body pressed her deep into the soft mattress and her senses were filled with him, with the taut texture of his mouth, with the exotic scent of patchouli, with the soft fall of his hair as it brushed against her breasts, with the sharp rasp of his teeth as he kissed his rough way along the line of her jaw.

Her head fell back, and he kissed lower, touching his tongue to the hollow at her throat, and moving on until his lips and tongue were at her breasts, teasing and nipping, tugging at the seams that bound her. And she was arching up to him, giving herself, offering him the entirety of herself if only he kept giving her the pleasure, the fierce bliss that was as potent and addictive as opium.

She wrapped her arms around his neck, holding him against her and raking her fingers through his long, wild hair. Holding herself just as tight. She clenched her leg muscles together and was shocked at the stabbing rush of pleasure that rose so easily.

He levered himself away, and she felt the loss of him, of his heat and his weight holding her down, keeping her from floating away. Before she could pull him back, he found her hands, and interlaced his fingers with hers, holding her surely as he placed their hands over her head.

And then he was kneeling between her legs, kneeing her thighs apart, and she was open and vulnerable, stretched past the limits of experience and imagination, and she felt the blunt velvet probe of his body as he settled his weight into her hips. And he was pushing into her, stretching and filling her, slowly making his way into her body until he was sheathed fully within.

"Cat." He said her name like a prayer, like an incantation to an unknown God who might bless them with nothing but heavenly bliss.

She felt heat and pressure, and pleasure and pain all spilling together, tumbling her like a wave. And then he was moving, too, advancing and retreating like the tide, slowly gathering strength like a wave, until the current rose in him as well.

He made a sound that was both anguish and awe, as if he were drowning in it, too. As if he could no longer hold the deluge back. He leaned his weight into his hands where they were joined with hers above her head and she felt her body bow up toward him, and his body came against hers more fully, and when he surged into her again, she felt him all the way to her core. And then farther, because he leaned down and took her breasts between his lips and teeth, closing around her sensitized nipple, sucking and sending a burst of blissful heat radiating through her body.

And still her body pressed upward toward him, wanting more of him, wanting more of the friction of his taut belly against her. More of his strength. More.

And then he let go of her hand, and her hand rose to cradle his head, to hold him to her breast, to keep him there lavishing her with pleasure. But his hand was not idle, and skimmed down, sliding across the flat of her belly, and lower, grazing across the bare flesh of her mons. He stroked across that naked, naked skin before he parted her flesh and brushed a feather-light touch across the place where his tongue had been before. Sensation burst from her again and she was loose, rushing over the edge.

And he was with her, clutching her, swept away with

her, falling, falling over the edge, floating down into the tranquil pool below.

She stayed there, buoyed along by the afterglow, as her heart eventually slowed its pace and her breathing returned to normal. It seemed like hours before she felt herself equal to even opening her eyes. Tanvir lay on his side next to her, stroking her fine, flyaway hair away from her temple. He leaned over to kiss her there. "Stay with me."

"Yes." She was lingering at the last edge of ecstasy, wanting the languorous feeling of satiation, of rightness, to last as long as possible before the world intruded with its concerns and cares.

"No." Tanvir rose up on one elbow to look down at her, and his voice was low and rough with something more urgent than drowsy satiation—it was the need to explain. "Be with me. Always. Come away with me. Now. Tonight."

Relief and joy poured into her lungs until she thought she might drown of happiness. Catriona had not thought she could feel any happier, any more complete than she had up until that moment, but she had been wrong. The feeling of finally, at last, achieving her heart's desire filled her with a giddy delight that left her breathless with laughter.

She rolled onto his chest to look into the depths of his warm green eyes, to be sure that she understood him, and he understood her. "Do you mean it, truly?" she asked. But then she didn't bother to wait for the answer. "Yes. I'll go with you wherever you want."

His answering smile was a gift. "Wherever *we* want."

"Yes." She said it again and laughed out loud, because she was so deliriously, monstrously happy, and it felt good to say it again. "Yes. Yes." She wrapped her arms around his neck and punctuated her assents with kisses along his collarbone to the hollow at the base of his throat where she could feel his heart beating steadily under her lips.

"Thank God." His relief was audible. "You don't know what I was prepared to do if you said no."

She had never before remembered hearing him speak

so informally, so colloquially, using the familiar form of address. But if the intimacy they had just shared was not grounds for some greater informality, Catriona did not know what would be. "You don't know what *I* was prepared to do if you had not asked." It was remarkable—providential even—that they should be in such accord.

He was frowning over his smile, unsure if she was teasing him. "Were you?"

"Yes. I have brought my little bag, you see."

"I see. And I am glad of your forethought. Because now we may be gone from Saharanpur as soon as we rise."

"But we do not yet have to rise."

"No, we don't."

She kissed him again, a slow, leisurely exploration of his taut lips, too full of love and gratitude and happiness to speak. In another moment she was swept up in the heady pleasure of his mouth upon hers, until she could think of nothing but the tide of want riding within her.

"Catriona." He said her name on a sigh of such satisfied sweetness, as if she were a holy place he had chanced upon in a storm. "You have no idea the pleasure your name gives me. The pleasure I take in being able to say it freely. I don't think I will ever tire of saying it."

"You can say it all the way into the mountains."

"I will. And beyond. And I will tell you other things as well."

"Let us go then." She pushed herself off his chest. "Let us get away before someone tries to stop us. Before one of the household spies tells on me—everyone, you know, seems to be in someone else's employ for the purpose of spilling secrets."

Tanvir's dark head came up sharply at that, and she felt the weight of his gaze press upon her through the moonlit dark. And for the first time, it made her nervous.

"I mean no disrespect," she tried to explain. "I just imagine I was simply too naive to see that it is the way of the world before."

"Yes," he said easily enough. "It is the way of this

world. Hind is rife with opportunities to earn baksheesh. And you are right to want us to get away before we have to spend any more."

And like a warning omen from her reawakened fate, a low voice came from the other side of the canvas walls. *"Huzoor."*

Tanvir went to the door flap, and he answered in a language Catriona did not understand. Then he frowned at her. "Your servant is here and insists on seeing you."

"Namita?" Oh, Lord. Catriona felt the first faint stirring of unease. She had no idea that her *ayah* would brave the terrors of the night to come find her unless she had been sent. "I never thought she'd come after me."

"How did she know where to find you?" Tanvir's tone was careful.

"I told her." Catriona was suddenly regretting her bravado. "But I thought she would be too frightened of the dark to follow me." And Catriona had also hoped Birkstead was too afraid of Tanvir Singh to interfere.

She began to hastily retrieve her clothes from the floor, fumbling with her petticoats, twisting them around her waist to tie them up, so she didn't completely understand the long moment of livid silence that was punctured by a vile-sounding Punjabi oath. "We will have to take her with us. Who else knows you are here?"

"I don't know." She was lying—or at least thinking very wishfully. She tried to step closer, to see him and read his expression in the dark. So she could see him and gauge how much he understood. "Lieutenant Birkstead has spies in the house who have been reporting to him about every ride and every swim."

"Swim? The jackal has spies in the old palace, as well?" He bit off another oath. "Why did you not tell me this before?"

"I don't know." Catriona suddenly felt more than foolish or naïve. She felt genuine fear. "I didn't realize it before. I meant to tell you—it—he—was one of the reasons I came here tonight—Birkstead. I'm sorry I forgot."

"Mem!" Namita had heard Catriona's voice, and called from directly outside the tent. "You must come at once."

"I'll send her away," she said to Tanvir. "I don't care about Birkstead, or Lord Summers. I've made my choice. I'll send her away, and we can go, just as you said." Catriona finished buttoning her bodice, and pushed through the gauzy curtain separating the interior from the tent's porch. "You should not have come." She kept her voice low, and pulled Namita aside, away from the *sa'is* who eyed them speculatively. "What on earth is the matter?"

"Thou must come home, mem. The house is all aroar."

"It's impossible, Namita. I told you. Who sent you?"

"Arthur, mem. Thou must come."

"Arthur?" Of all people, Catriona had not expected Namita to mention her quiet cousin. It must be a trick, some ploy of Birkstead's to bring her back. She wanted to give the persistent old woman a hard shake and send her on her way. "I don't believe you."

"I told him, mem, but this is the truth of it, I swear to you. The lord sahib has found the *Badmash* in the house, and it is all terrible—such shouting and breaking of things. Thou must come."

Oh, sweet Saint Margaret. She had done this. She had told Lord Summers too much, and put the proverbial cat among the pigeons. Or more accurately she had set a jackal against the pigeons. And now everyone would suffer.

Tanvir Singh stepped through the tent flap with a lantern that illuminated the tight set of his handsome face. His hair was still loose and unbound, rippling over his lean shoulders. His tawny, honey-toned skin all but glowed in the lamplight. He looked sleek and animalistic. He looked dark and dangerous. Catriona had never, ever seen a man so perilously beautiful.

And she had to leave him. She had to go and make it right even though she wanted to be with him. And she did not want to go back. "I have to go back to the residency."

Namita was pulling at her arm in agreement. "Yes, yes. Make haste, mem. Make haste."

"I have to go," Catriona said again. "But I'll be back, I promise. I'll find you here at dawn." Her voice sounded small and inadequate, but he was looking at her through the dark fall of his hair, with something very like pain in his green eyes, as if he were no longer sure of her. As if he thought she was lying. As if everything they had just said and been to each other had never happened.

She had to make him believe her. "I'll be back. I swear it. I promise. And you promise me you'll be here, waiting for me. Promise it."

"I swear." His voice was low and quiet, but no more reassuring.

"I swear it as well." Her voice grew tight with heat. "I swear on my family's grave I'll come back. I will." Her throat ached with the effort not to cry. "Tell me you believe me."

He didn't answer. Instead, he kissed her—a hard, hungry stamp of his possession and need—before he let her go. "Go if you must. But make haste, my *kaur*. Make haste."

"I will, I promise."

Catriona cast one last look at the man she loved, and let Namita pull her along to where the *sa'is* held Puithar. "It is terrible, mem, terrible. Such fighting."

"You never should have told them I'd gone, Namita, then they couldn't fight over me."

"No, no, mem. It is not thee that they fight about. It is the lord sahib and the lady memsahib. And the *Badmash* Sahib. Such screeching and fighting. Such anger. The children are afraid and crying."

The tight heat in her throat hardened into fear. "About Birkstead and my aunt?"

"Yes, yes. I knew nothing good could come of thee going away." Namita was nearly panting in the effort to keep up as Cat vaulted up onto the horse's back. "Such shouting and noises. Talk of honor and death. Arthur Sahib bid me find thee, and bring thee back right away. Oh, I knew how it would be."

Oh, why, oh, why had she not kept her mouth shut? Why

had she voiced her suspicions to her uncle-in-law? Why could she not leave well enough alone?

Namita shook her head, in both confirmation and denial. "It is bad, bad, mem. I knew that there would be murder in this night. I told thee." She tugged on Catriona's skirt and pointed across the river. "I told thee. Look. The air is already thick with it."

Catriona followed the *ayah*'s gaze to the southern horizon, where a dark plume seemed to be congregating into a darker thunderhead. Smoke. And below, the first faint traces of flames began to lick the night sky. "Oh, Holy Saint Margaret." The children.

Catriona abandoned Namita to the care of the *sa'is* and rode for everything she was worth, leaving the *ayah* and the grooms, and Tanvir Singh far behind while the world began to burn down around her.

Chapter Nineteen

But Catriona had kept her promise. In the end she had gone back to him—fled from the damaging rumors and evil innuendo that had crept across the dark lawn as she and Alice had stumbled out of the burning house. She had gone to him with the firm and unshakable belief that he would help her.

She had taken the children in her arms and taken the sandy path along the river. She had hidden them in the dark shadows and kept them all from harm. And she had waited in the deserted encampment for what seemed like hours, fearful of moving and revealing herself, until it was clear he was the one who was not going to fulfill his promise.

It was only then, in the middle of that dark, sleepless night, that she had thought of going to the begum. And the begum had saved her. Saved them all.

And now Thomas Jellicoe told her that he would have helped her. That he had in fact gone to help her. And that fate alone had kept them apart.

But she was tired of letting fate have the upper hand.

Catriona straightened her spine and faced the Jellicoes assembled before her, in the nursery sitting room, waiting patiently—or in Thomas's case, impatiently—for her answers. "It all comes down to Birkstead."

"I knew it had to be him. I knew it." Thomas looked at her, and she could see the conviction, the relief of being proved right in the set line of his mouth. "I knew it in Saharanpur when the bastard stumbled out of the residency, and I knew it again when the bloody jackal was so conveniently invalided out of India as soon as I revealed myself to the judicial committee as an Englishman and the son of the Earl Sanderson."

"Thomas," Viscount Jeffrey cautioned. "We need to listen to all of Miss Cates's story before we draw any conclusions."

Thomas looked to her. "Am I right?"

"Yes." There was no point in denying it. "You are right."

"Birkstead." Thomas ground the man's name between his teeth, as if he were learning to like the bitter taste of it. As if he'd disliked the man for years, but was finally glad of a reason to hate him.

"Yes." Now that she had committed herself, the words came tumbling out of Catriona's mouth as if she couldn't spit them out fast enough. "It must be him. I can't imagine who else it might be who would want to shoot at us. I can't imagine that both of you should have found me purely by chance. He must have followed you."

Thomas's face narrowed. This was a possibility he clearly didn't like to admit—that he might have brought the steaming plots and heated intrigues of Hind chasing after him across the cold, dark sea. "Has he never tried to—" He hesitated for the barest of moments, peering into the depth of her eyes to prepare her for what was to come. "Has he tried to kill you before?"

But she was no longer shocked. "No. Not here, in England." Of this she was sure. She had waited and watched for Birkstead, worried and fearful that sooner or later, one way or another, he would not be able to resist playing the law's mortal messenger.

But she had wanted it that way. She had wanted Birkstead to focus his attention—his hate and anger and fear of retribution—on her. She had promised to do so.

James seconded her assertion. "We've never had so much as a cross word directed against Miss Cates. That is,

Miss Rowan. I do hate to think so, Thomas, but it did seem to start with your arrival."

Thomas nodded at his brother grimly. "Agreed."

"So what do you suggest we do now?"

"Now? We sit tight, and protect this family, while I find him, and I kill him." He was adamant. The veneer of civilization given to him by his buttoned-up English clothes could no longer contain the savagery she had never seen in him in India. "No inquiries. No committees. No bringing to justice. Only retribution."

"No." Catriona could hear her horror ringing in her own voice. "You can't mean that. You can't mean to be just like him."

Thomas would not relent. "I don't mean to be just like him, Cat. I mean to see that justice is done. He has killed before, hasn't he? You saw it in Saharanpur, otherwise he'd never still be after you."

"No," she said again, shaking her head. Indeed, her whole body was trembling. She wrapped her arms around her middle, as if the knowledge that she had tried to keep to herself—the knowledge she was still trying to deny—was shaking her apart. "I didn't really see anything. It wasn't me."

Thomas took her in his arms. "But you did see something? You must have. Perhaps it's something you don't know you saw, but Birkstead thinks you did."

"No." She took a deep breath and let it out, firmer in her decision. "That's not it at all. It's that I promised. I swore an oath that I would never tell."

"You promised Birkstead? Why in hell would you do that?"

"No." She shook her head.

She had kept her long, silent bargain for so many years. Too many. Because now other children had been threatened. And Catriona could no longer reconcile sacrificing Mariah, or any of the Jellicoe children, to keep a promise made so long ago.

"Who did you promise, Cat?" His voice was insistent, uncompromising.

"Whom," she corrected automatically. "To whom did I promise." But the time for promises was over. Birkstead was already here, lurking somewhere just out of reach beyond the manor walls, watching and waiting, and she knew better than anyone what he was capable of. The depth to which he would so easily and instantly sink for no other reason than to salvage his savage pride. "I promised the dowager Duchess of Westing."

"That scolding old sow?" Viscount Jeffrey pulled a rude face.

"James!" his viscountess chided. "That is not helpful."

"My point is that *I* shouldn't like to cross the dowager duchess," the viscount clarified. "She's an imperious, first-rate warship of the old school. Always makes me feel as though I've just been caught out doing something terribly ghastly. And I'm a grown man with children of my own to scold, so I see why Miss Cates—Miss Rowan—shouldn't like to defy her."

Thomas was still there, still insistent. "Duchess or no, you need to tell us what happened, Cat."

He was right. It had gone on too long. Too many secrets. Too much sacrificed for others. "She said she didn't want any more trouble for her grandchildren—my cousins, Arthur, Alice, Charlotte, and George, the children of Lord and Lady Summers."

Catriona remembered the dowager's exact words. *I don't want my son's or my grandchildren's names dragged through the mud. I don't want them so much as mentioned in a broadsheet. They have suffered enough.*

They *had* suffered enough. And so had she.

"You took the four Summers children to the dowager after you escaped from India?" Thomas again, with his sharp intellect, figuring it all out. Adding it all up.

"Yes." She took a deep breath. "But I'm getting ahead of myself."

"Yes," Thomas agreed. "I need you to go back to the beginning. What happened at the residency, Cat? Start with the fire. That was the last time I saw you. You running into that godawful fire."

"It wasn't all the way on fire, the residency, only the upper floors, at the back of the house. But the children's rooms were on the top floor, although in a different wing from the fire. But they were my main concern, so I went there."

Catriona closed her eyes, but she could see it now as if she were still in the residency—the long dark floorboards of the corridor, the tight, narrow confines of the stairwell, the high white ceilings filling with smoke.

She didn't quite know where to begin. Every memory brought fresh pain, and the return of the helplessness, the feeling that she had absolutely no control. "I had gone up the service stairs."

She had bypassed by the huge central stairwell with its massive drafts of air that would feed the fire she could hear beginning to roar from above, and headed to the north side of the house, to the children's wing, where the narrower servants' stairwell had doors and segregated landings that might keep the draft of fresh air from fueling the spread of the fire into that part of the house.

"By the time I got upstairs, Arthur had Charlotte and George, and a young amah—the nursery maid—at the door of the nursery." She would never forget the look of Arthur's face—ashen, ravaged by doubt and fear, and by a horrible knowledge that had made him look older by years instead of hours. "I showed them the way to go. Led them down the same stair I had just come up, and then across the back landing at the first floor, to the upper veranda."

"Yes." Thomas was nodding. "I saw them on the lawn, when they came out."

"But Alice wasn't with them. Arthur said they heard my aunt and uncle arguing. The whole house heard, I should think, since it woke the younger children up. That was probably when Arthur sent Namita for me," she said as an aside to Thomas. "But later, when Arthur smelled the smoke, he immediately went to get his brother and sisters—oh, thank God he did. Thank God he was such a brave, calm, and courageous lad. I hate to think of what might have happened if he had not. But Alice wasn't there with Charlotte and George. He thought she must have gone to see her mama."

"But you *did* get them, Miss Cates," the viscountess assured her gently, as Lord Jeffrey corrected, "Miss Rowan," behind her. Lady Jeffrey nodded, but continued. "You were calm and courageous as well, and made sure they escaped."

"Yes. Thank you." The thought was only the smallest comfort. Though the children were alive and well, they were as lost to her as if she had not found them. But that was a small price to pay to keep them safe.

Cat had left them at the exterior doorway, and plunged back up the stairs two at a time to the first floor, where she had headed toward the back of the house, to her aunt's suite of rooms overlooking the gardens.

"It had gotten hotter, and harder to see. Smoke was filtering into the air, sliding along the ceiling above my head, roiling down the corridors like inky thunderclouds." She had crouched down, instinctively trying to stay away from the smoke, putting her sleeve over her mouth, and trying to hold the terror that sped her heart, and made her pant for breath, at bay. She had to find Alice.

She had acted on instinct, guessing that Alice would have crept down the back service corridor to her mother's dressing room, just as she had often done to watch Lady Summers dress her hair, and put on her jewels in the evenings. Alice had often come back to the nursery with fingers scented from the perfume from her mother's precious bottles of attar of roses and gardenia scent.

"I could hear a low sort of crying. It was hard to tell, because of the fire. But it wasn't just the fire." It had been the terror, for Alice, and for herself.

Catriona's stomach cramped into a tight fist at the memory. "I felt my way down the dark tiles of the servants' passage behind my aunt's dressing room, only to find the slatted door locked. So I climbed through the passage's outer window, out onto the veranda, to get some air and to try and go in from the other way. That's when I saw that one of the heavy slatted shutters on the window of the dressing room was ajar. And I thought perhaps Alice might have crept in over the windowsill."

She had been right. Catriona had pushed the heavy, louvered shutter open, and after a moment of letting her eyes adjust to the dim, smoky interior, she could see Alice, crouched on the floor with her eyes wide and dark with fright, peering in fascinated horror through the thin ribbon of light coming from the room next door.

"I heard noises coming from the bedchamber next door—Lieutenant Birkstead was there, in the other room. 'Christ, Lettice,' I heard him say. His voice was tight and tamped down with pain and disbelief." Even Birkstead had sounded shocked.

"I spoke to Alice quietly, so Birkstead wouldn't hear me."

Catriona had whispered, "Alice dear" as she laid her hand on the child's shoulder. But at Catriona's touch, a high, thin keening sound startled out of Alice, who turned to her with eyes dark and a face blanched white with terror. "I put my hand over her mouth, so he wouldn't hear us, but when I pulled her away, without her holding it closed, the heavy, teak double door began to slowly swing open."

The line of light widened gradually, and Catriona scrambled backward, pulling the child in her lap into the narrow, shadowed stairwell that led up to the perch reserved for the punkah wallah, the servant who would have sat in the tiny balcony alcove above, pulling the string to keep the long banner of the hinged fan moving to cool her aunt's rooms.

"Birkstead must have seen the door slowly opening. Because he said, 'Who's there?' and then I heard his footfalls on the floor."

"I dragged Alice backward, but she was clinging to me, almost too heavy in my arms, stiff and awkward in her complete terror."

"How old was she?" Lady Jeffrey asked gently.

Catriona was grateful for the respite. "Eight years old, my lady." Too young to have been exposed to such horror.

But Thomas was impatient for her testimony—her evidence of Jonathan Birkstead's guilt. "So you were on a staircase?"

"Yes." Catriona drew her mind back to the narration. "The little narrow staircase at the back of the dressing room, that led to the small clerestory balcony where a servant would have sat to pull the ceiling fans."

"So you were between the first floor and the second?" Thomas asked. "Higher up?"

"Yes. Up there, it had already begun filling up with smoke rolling down from the ceiling." Catriona had scrambled backward up the stair, into the clerestory space filled with obscuring smoke, as below, she could hear Birkstead push his way into the dressing room.

"And because I couldn't carry her and keep my hand over her mouth, Alice said, 'He killed her. He killed Mama.' I couldn't stop her. And he heard her. Because he said again, 'Who's there? I can hear you.'"

Catriona could still hear the shocked disbelief in Birkstead's voice, and feel the answering rise of hysteria in herself.

"He came nearer, down below, somewhere near the bottom of the stairs, while we were choking on the smoke, but trying not to make any noise.

Catriona had kept pushing backward, as far away from him as possible, until she hit a wall at her back. The smoke grew thick, curling down at them like ghosts from hell. She had dragged her skirt up over her mouth, and put her face down next to Alice's to cover her mouth, as well. In her arms, Alice was shaking with shock and terror, holding herself in a tight little ball. The child had her eyes scrunched, shut tight, as if she could stop the events from happening just by closing her eyes. If she didn't see it it couldn't be. But she did speak.

"That was when Alice said, 'It was Mama who shot

Papa. Mama did it. To be with the *Badmash*. She said she would go away with him, and leave us. And that's when he shot her. And then he started the fire.' "

And Cat knew that even with her eyes shut and sealed as tight as a tomb, the girl would see nothing behind her eyelids but the image of her father, and then her mother, being shot before her eyes. No matter if she blocked her ears, she would hear nothing but the sharp belch of the gun. No matter that Cat was holding her tight, she would feel nothing but cold, hatred, and fear.

"I was feeling my way along the wall, trying to find the window—there were these ornamental lotus-shaped stained-glass windows in the transoms over the doors, and up in the clerestories, too. And I could hear him below, throwing furniture about, overturning tables to find her. 'It will be your word against mine, Alice darling,' Birkstead said. 'And who do you think they'll believe? Just come out and I can help you.' "

Catriona had shut her eyes against the stinging soot the way Alice had, as if she, too, might shut out the sound of the jackal's lies. "And that was when I found the latch on the window, and I was trying to push it open with one hand—it was on a central pivot." She made a rolling motion with her hands by way of explanation. "And I was trying to keep my skirt over Alice's mouth with the other, and there was another sound below—of furniture being jostled or crashed about. But mostly all I could hear was the awful, greedy whistle and hiss of the smoke and flames. And then, just when I got the window open far enough to push Alice through, this huge concussion knocked us flat, and we both almost jumped out of our skin from the shock."

"The report of a gun?" Thomas's voice again, quiet next to her ear.

Catriona kept her eyes clenched closed. "Yes. The report of a gun," she echoed, "fired near the bottom of the stairs. I suppose it was the vibrating concussion of the shot that echoed up the stairwell. I remember it hitting my face like a hard slap. And then another blast roared out." Another crack of death and destruction. But at that point it hadn't even shocked her. It had sounded inevitable. It sounded right, as if she had been waiting to hear the inevitable knell of destruction.

"I folded myself, my body, around Alice. I held her tight against my chest, covering her ears, and pressing her into me so she wouldn't hear it."

Its meaning was unmistakable—Birkstead was trying to kill Alice, just as he had her parents, who lay dead on the smoldering carpets.

"And despite everything I did to muffle the sound, Alice knew. The poor child let out a sound that was a piercing cry of savage pain. High. Raw. Anguished. And terrified. I thought she had been hit. And Birkstead heard it, too. He said, 'Alice? Alice, is that you? Where are you? Show me where you are.' I could hear him at the bottom of the stairs. So I shoveled Alice out the window onto the flat part of the roof that covered the first-floor veranda, pushing her away hard to make room. And she was sobbing, and my heart was just pounding in my ears and in my chest, and I was crawling through, scraping against the edges of the window frame because I was so much bigger, scrambling to try and squeeze through. And I could hear him behind me, his boots on the steps, coming up the stair."

"'Alice,' he said. 'How long have you been there spying? Alice?' And he said, 'You can't hide from me. I'll find you.' And I could hear him better, so I knew he was nearly there, and I whispered, 'Go,' to Alice. 'Go!' And because the latch to the window was on the inside, I jammed my foot against the bottom of the window, so he couldn't swing it out. And I had to hope that the smoke would fill up the clerestory again, and that he wouldn't be able to see me through the colored glass of the window. And the window did rattle against my foot, just once, and then I heard him yell, 'Do you hear me? You're going to burn to death in here, Alice. You're going to burn.'

"He may have said something more, but the roof was growing hotter, and Alice hadn't gone. She was still balled up in a little heap. So I left the window, just hoping that Birkstead couldn't fit through, or didn't have another gun to shoot at us, but we had to go. The roof felt so hot I thought . . ." Catriona couldn't really remember what she had *thought*. She had been overwhelmed by the simple animal instinct to run, to move as fast as she could. "I dragged Alice up, and hauled her down the length of the balcony. No. Actually, I think we were on the roof of Lettice's veranda. The tiles felt hot through the soles of my shoes. And I thought I just had to concentrate hard, and will myself to keep walking, like those fakirs who walk over coals without being burned. And—" Catriona took a deep breath. "I don't remember exactly how we got down. We went from one roof to another, moving downward, and I was pulling and pushing and carrying Alice. God, poor Alice. And then we were out on the north lawn, where some of the servants gathered in clusters, gazing back at the building as the flames gathered strength and broke through the upper-story walls. And we found Arthur. And Charlotte and George."

She had been numb with relief, and frightened still, too. Unsure of where Birkstead might be. If he was still looking for them.

"More people came, their dark silhouettes dancing in front of the orange glow. Troops from the barracks. Servants, and people from the cantonment." But they left them alone and did not intrude upon their silence as the children clustered around her. She couldn't remember how long they had stood there, a tiny island of orphans.

And that was when it had hit her—now all of them were orphans. She was the only family they had left.

And then she had heard it. The whisperings. The denunciation.

"People started talking. I heard them say, 'I saw him myself. They found him in the garden. Miss Rowan, he said. Shot him. Shot them all, is what he said. He said Miss Rowan shot him.' And I did not wait to hear any more."

Nor did she speak. It would not matter what she said, or how she defended herself. Birkstead's words were only a start. She had seen the living malice in his eyes enough times to understand the nature of his character, and the words he had shouted at Alice still echoed in her ears.

He was as clever and ruthless as a jackal. He had told her himself. She would need friends. And she had only one. She turned to look at Thomas Jellicoe, at the promise in his level green gaze. "So I went to you. Only you weren't there. It seems logical now, that you weren't, but then, I could barely breathe, let alone think." She let the thought trail away. She wanted to be done with regret.

"No," Thomas said. "I was there, at the fire, looking for you. Beating Birkstead into a pulp."

"Did you? Thank you."

"No. Don't thank me. I should never have done it. If I hadn't, he might have talked. He might have told me where you were, and I might have—"

"You might have died looking," she finished for him. "If you had gone back in then, I doubt you would have made it out. We barely did." Her lungs had ached for a month, and she had not been able to draw breath for days without raspy pain scratching down her throat. She had barely been able to speak. None of them had. Catriona had never heard Alice speak again.

Lady Jeffrey drew Catriona into a brief embrace. "My dear Miss Cates—Miss Rowan, I should say. But the name is no matter—what matters is that you did the right thing. You got the children out, and made sure that they were safe, and now you are safe here with us. You may be assured of that."

Lord Jeffrey was not so easy. "The child, this Alice, can corroborate everything you have said?"

"Yes. But the duchess—Lord Summers's mother, the Duchess of Westing—said she would never let that happen."

Not that the imperious old woman hadn't been pleased by Catriona.

"I thank you for returning my grandchildren," the duchess had said. "We are most appreciative. And we are prepared to reward you suitably. And handsomely. On one condition."

"Anything, Your Grace." Catriona had been ready to do anything—anything for those children who were her only family.

"That you never, ever divulge what you have just told me to another living soul. Not to anyone. Not even to the authorities. Ever. I will help you. I will help you disappear, and become a new person. I will give you money. But I will not let this sordid story come out. And if it does, I will know where it came from, Miss Rowan. I will know whom to blame. And blame I will. I will give credence to their accusations. I will say that you confessed your crimes to me. I will feed you to the wolves. Or I will help you. If you keep quiet."

It had been so painful a blow Catriona felt as though she, too, had been shot. And the searing pain was still there, buried deep beneath layers of Miss Anne Cates's calm, caring control. An ache that grew the longer she tried to push it aside.

But she had said she would do anything for them, and so she had kept quiet. She had disappeared. But Thomas Jellicoe, who was also Tanvir Singh, had found her. And not only he, but Birkstead as well.

"My dear Miss Rowan," Lady Jeffrey chastised carefully. "Not even a duchess can be above the law."

"I hope you will forgive me, my lady, but that is not my experience of the world. The dowager Duchess of Westing is a cousin to the king, and with abundant money and power, may do as she pleases. And *I* must do only as she pleases."

Thomas seemed to understand. "And it pleased the dowager to let the world believe that a crazed, nobody of a relation of her son's wife killed Lord Summers, rather than face the cold truth that Lady Summers killed her husband, and that her lover then killed her?"

Catriona nodded, but something that had to be relief—

the relief of finally being understood, of finally, finally admitting the truth—spread like warmth through her. "Yes. And she was right. Because as long as that story is told, Alice is safe."

Lord Jeffrey drew back in indignation. "This is a country of law, and no one, not even her grace of Westing, may put herself above it, nor require others to do so."

Thomas was slightly more to the point. "Catriona, did she ask you to formally take the blame? Did you sign anything?"

"No. I just agreed to maintain the assumption."

"And she required you to do that how?"

"To keep quiet. Never repeat my story. Never ask Alice to repeat her story. Not try to clear my name. Her grace was the one who suggested I take another identity. She said a new name would serve me well. Even better than the last." The idea had appealed to Catriona at the time. She had still harbored some faint faith in the power of starting anew. "The duchess gave me money and a new name. And references. She was the one who recommended me to Lady Grimoy in Paris."

"Paris?" Thomas's deep green eyes lit up in revelation. "Of course. The letters. When you were at school there."

"Letters?" Catriona didn't realize he had known she had been at school in Paris—but then anyone who had been at Colonel Balfour's party that night might have heard—and she had never spoken of the letters. But he was canny, this Thomas Jellicoe. He had stolen secrets across one half of the Punjab and down the other side of Hind, and he was looking at her now with those penetrating green eyes as if he had secrets yet to tell.

"I kept them, your letters. The ones you left behind in your satchel when you ran off to save the day, or rather the night. And you did save them that night, Cat. You did. And you made your way to Paris, to your convent school, to take shelter there. Clever girl. Very clever." Something that might be admiration was warming his voice, and he was smiling at her the way he used to in India, that smile that crinkled up the corners of his green eyes, and curved that wide, sly scimitar of a smile across his handsome face.

She had been clever. She had aimed at Paris and the sanctuary of that convent from the moment she had understood that she was on her own—on her own, and in charge of four orphaned, grieving children.

She had thought about Paris, about the tree-lined streets and the shady parks, as she sat huddled in the curtained oxcart trundling through the night toward the western desert. She had diverted her cousins with stories of the sights, of Les Invalides and the beautiful soaring architecture— triumphal arches and elegant homes. She had medicated them with the promise of a return of ease and grace while they had crossed the wide, empty Thar Desert, following the caravans moving to the west, toward Persia and Arabia, across mountains and plains. She had enchanted them with descriptions of the delicate fashions—the silly sleeves and the ridiculous bonnets—as they made their way across the Arabian Sea. She had conjured the smells of coffee and bread arising out of the bleakest of eastern dawns.

She had shut her mind to the pungent earthy aromas of marigolds and curry. She had banished all thought of bright silks and jeweled saris. She had closed her mind to everything of India, and set her sights resolutely west.

"I was to stay in France, taking governessing positions from families traveling or living there. But Lady Grimoy was adamant that I come back to England with them, and help see her daughter Augusta Grimoy out. And then I came to you." She turned to Lady Jeffrey. "It seemed as if it would not matter where I was, or who I was, as long as I should not have any contact with my cousins."

"She cut you off from them, just like that? After all you had done?"

"Yes. I will admit it was a wrench." God, it had been more than a wrench. Months and months of traveling together, often in disguise, learning to lie to fend off attention, carefully counting out the money the begum, had given her, never knowing if anyone was on their tail. Remembering over and over again what had happened.

Alice had had terrible nightmares. Terrible.

And then that day, in Paris, when she had met with the dowager duchess for so long in the cool quiet of the cloister, she had come back to her room to find they were gone— just gone. The children had been removed to the duchess's hotel, and forbidden to her.

Catriona had been numb with the pain.

It was for the best, her grace had said. Best for the children and their safety. Best for Catriona to start her new life. And indeed, Lady Grimoy had sent for her within the hour. So Catriona went. She was too devastated to do otherwise.

"Her grace said if I ever spoke up about what had happened, then she would tell them the opposite—that I had confessed to her, and thrown myself upon her mercy, which she had granted for the children's sake, since I had done her the service of bringing them to her."

"She can't do that, Miss Rowan." Lord Jeffrey was firm in his conviction. "Or at least she ought not to. But if she's stubborn enough to perjure herself in a court of law, then so be it. A decent prosecutor—and we will find an excellent prosecutor, Miss Rowan. Most excellent. Superior. A decent prosecutor will have the truth out of this Alice— she is how old now, Miss Rowan?"

"No, no," she protested. "She will be only ten years old. But please, I promised. She's been through too much."

"Catriona." Thomas took her hands. "Birkstead has done murder. And has attempted to murder you here. He has to be stopped. For Alice's sake as well as yours."

"But he doesn't know about her. Not for sure. He suspected, but that was why I was willing to take the blame, so he wouldn't know about her."

"Catriona." Thomas shook his head. He wouldn't be convinced. "The thing that matters is that he has to be stopped."

"But how? He's out there somewhere, waiting, taking his potshots as he wills."

"My dear, darling girl." He pressed a kiss to her forehead. "It's very simple, really. I'm going to go after him, and track him down, and kill him."

Chapter Twenty

Thomas felt a sort of calmness, a swift surety, a confirmation that his convictions were correct. With that calm came the knowledge that he wanted nothing more than to do what Lieutenant Birkstead had once accused him of—slit the bastard's throat from ear to ear. But he was no longer Tanvir Singh, carrying a lethal curved blade and a long, horseman's pistol in his belt. And while he had once been a *sawar* and a spy, he had never been an assassin.

But he was both Tanvir Singh and the Honorable Thomas Jellicoe, son of the Earl Sanderson. He would have to be as careful and cunning as a panther to take on the jackal. But make no mistake—he was going to avenge this very great wrong to the woman he loved in the most basic and most elemental way possible.

Cat was just as vehement in her insistence. "No. No more killing."

"Yes, Thomas. Surely there has been enough." Cassandra's hand rose to her mouth to cover her shock at the chilling bluntness of his assertion. "We must trust the law will do its work."

Catriona looked at his sister-in-law the viscountess with eyes that were a hundred years old. Eyes that were full of a kind of desperate envy and pity, all at the same time. "Unfortunately, my lady, the law works most efficiently to help those in power, not right wrongs, or help the oppressed."

"I refuse to believe that, Miss Rowan," James stated flatly. "I am the magistrate in this district. I am the law, and *I* am determined to help you."

"Yes," Cassandra agreed. "You may rest your trust in Lord Jeffrey. He will not let you suffer. Nor your cousin Alice. Especially Alice. But oh, I cannot help but wish you had faced these outrageous accusations in India. Then it might never have come to this. I am sure you might have trusted Thomas to help you."

Catriona shook her head. "Thomas was not there, my lady," was all she said. "And Alice . . . was not well. She was entirely transfixed with terror. She couldn't sleep and she wouldn't be alone—she clung to me as if she were in constant fear of being taken back—and I didn't think she should have to face him. I knew how it would be if it came to a trial. If I put Alice up on a stand as a witness with Birkstead looking at her like the slavering, sinister jackal he was. He would have intimidated her. It would have been his word against hers, if indeed she could even speak. And my word against his. And so I ran. We all ran. I could not leave Alice to be worked over by the likes of Birkstead or his un-judicial committee."

"The begum helped you?" Thomas prompted. He wanted every piece of missing information. He wanted to make sure he understood each and every moment that she had spent between that awful night and now.

"Yes," Cat said, though it was evident from the pale exhaustion in her face that she was growing weary with the telling. "We left that night—or maybe it was morning by then. I don't remember. But we were gone within what seemed like a short time of our darkening the begum's door. We bundled into an old, nondescript, closed oxcart and went west toward Jaisalmer, while the begum had Mina pack up her entire retinue to return east to the king-dom of Ranpur, where the company held no sway."

"A diversion." Thomas approved of the begum's tactics. "And it worked beautifully. No one, not even Colonel Balfour, suspected. You went to the begum's sister, I collect, at the fort at Jaisalmer? And from there across the desert?"

"Yes." She wrapped her arms around her middle again, as if to hold herself together. "And he's out there somewhere, watching us, coming and going as he pleases, waiting with his gun."

"I'll take care of him." Thomas spoke with all the quiet conviction he felt. "You can trust this to me, Catriona. Birkstead will not be allowed to prey upon you a moment longer."

He would have kissed Cat, then and there, because she was finally looking at him with something approaching admiration. And because he wanted to. A quick hard kiss that spoke of possession and promises yet to keep. Because the truth was, *he* had not fully trusted her in India—he had never trusted her with the truth about his identity. A truth that had eventually led to him being able to clear her name, but which might have saved them all endless heartache, as well as the enormous distress of their current predicament, if he had only shared it then, before she had needed it.

But the past could not be bought back, except by an investment in the future. A future he would be damned if he would concede to Birkstead.

And the sooner he proved to her that she could trust him, and rely upon him, the sooner she could learn to be happy again. "James," he addressed his brother. "What have your men come up with?"

The lord of the manor seemed cautiously happy for the change of subject. "My groundskeeper found fresh hoofprints on the west side of the outer wall, leading south to the gate, but no farther. And he's asked around the village, and at all the coaching inns hereabout, and from what he can tell, the only noticeable stranger who seems to have come along fits a description of you." James cocked up his mouth in a wry smile. "They were especially concerned that they had given *you* our direction in Sixpenny Handley. The publican there apologized most profusely to Peters."

Thomas didn't miss a beat. "With a family as large as yours there's bound to be the odd black sheep."

Neither did James. " 'Odd' being the operative word."

"Yes, I think we've firmly established my character, or lack thereof, James." But it felt good to settle into the easy rhythm of friendly sibling bickering as an antidote to the seriousness of the situation—a sort of momentary relief to the sheer intensity of the story Cat had just told them. But it wasn't a story—it was real. And it had happened to her. Whatever he had imagined his sufferings to be, they were nothing in comparison to hers. She had done everything she could to save her family, only to have them taken from her. He had lost her, but she had lost everything.

"Well." James recalled him to his duty. "You were the one who said he had experience in these matters—what do you suggest?"

"Someone has to have seen something." Thomas ran his hand through his strange short hair. "A man doesn't just ride up to the wall of an estate like Wimbourne, practically stuck in the middle of the village, at ten o'clock in the morning on a summer day when all the world and his dog is up and about on his business. Someone knows. They just don't know what they've seen."

"I've sent men out, asking up and down the length of the village and beyond, if they saw something unusual."

"Ah. There's your trouble."

"I beg your pardon?"

"It won't have been something unusual, then. It will have been something normal, something they didn't think to remark upon. Our malefactor won't have a large sign hanging over his head saying, 'I'm unusual, pay attention to me.' "

"Well, if you're so very much better than all my men, then by all means, have a go at the villagers."

"Thank you. I believe I will. But we need to look for

one person. He's bound to be conspicuous—he's the sort who can't stand not to be."

"And that sort is?"

"Unmitigated bastard."

"What's a bastard?" piped one of the younger children who were suddenly spilling around Cat's skirts, fresh and rosy faced from their baths. Christopher, he decided, the youngest boy—his voice was still as soft as the girls'.

Thomas looked down to find a mirror of his younger self looking back at him. The little boy was gazing up at his uncle with the same forthright equanimity Thomas had once possessed when dealing with horses five times his size, and Thomas felt a kindred spirit kindle within. How nice it was to learn it would take more than his rangy, looming presence to discomfit his nephew. "A bad man. But I'm going to take care of that."

And then they were all there, her charges, filling up the nursery until it was crowded with their robust, boundless energy. Questions came from every side, talking nineteen to the dozen.

"We aren't meant to go outside again, until it's safe." Amelia, he judged, skeptical and prudent. "Papa told us we couldn't."

"You almost missed tea." That was the twin who was slightly taller—Gemma. Always counting, and keeping track in James's letters, was young Lady Gemma.

And indeed the nursery maids were just now streaming in with trays laden with pots of steaming tea, boiled eggs, and toast soldiers.

"My apologies." Cat immediately met the battery of their appearance with easy, calm reassurance. "It has been rather a topsy-turvy day, hasn't it? Why don't you all come to the table, and we'll have our tea now."

"Yes. That is a very good idea," Lady Jeffrey agreed. "And you can all see that Miss Cates is quite well, and you needn't have any worries for her."

Yet the wobble in the lady's voice said otherwise, so Cat was swift in her reassurances. "Oh, absolutely. But I should very much like a nice cup of tea, and some jam to set me to rights. Don't you all? I'll see to everything, my lady."

But Thomas was not about to miss this opportunity to meet his nieces and nephews properly, and neither was he prepared to let Cat out of his sight. "I'm sure we are all in need of fortification after our trying day. I know I am." He followed the children to the table, but seeing that the chairs were all quickly taken—no hangers-back in the Jellicoe family—he simply picked little Mariah up and set her upon his lap. The child accepted his presence just as serenely as he accepted hers, even when her eggy fingers reached up to touch and stroke his face. He merely kissed her fingertips as if it were a normal occurrence for him to take food off a child's hands. As if he did it every day. "Is that raspberry jam?" He pointed his chin at a pot on the table.

"Yes." Gemma looked at him with something of a scowl, as if she thought her uncle a bit dim not to recognize raspberry jam when he saw it.

Her somewhat precocious tone didn't affect him in the least. "I ask because we used to have the most marvelous raspberry jam at Downpark, when I was growing up. I haven't had any in years."

Pippa immediately passed him the jam pot. "But this *is* Downpark jam. Granny sends it for us."

"Well, Mrs. Downpark Cook sends it, really," Gemma clarified. Always one to have the last word—punctual, correct Gemma. "Because *she* makes it, but Granny is the one who has her send it to us when Mrs. Downpark Cook puts it up."

Thomas was not prepared for the strange shift within—the minor earthquake that was the restless refitting of the edges of his soul. He sat dumbfounded—he who had kept his head while spying on maharajahs and shahs—for a long moment while Mariah smeared more egg on his chin. "Granny?" he finally asked. "You call your grandmother—my mother, the Countess Sanderson—Granny?"

"What else would we call her?" Amelia asked.

Thomas felt entirely at sea, as he had the moment he

had first arrived—as if he had only just stepped off the ship and the land was still behaving badly underfoot. He was bewildered. Almost bereft. Because he was just now understanding all the changes the years apart from his family had wrought. Just now taking account of the loss. "Grandmama, I suppose," he finally sputtered. "Granny just sounds so . . . cozy."

"Well, she *is* cozy." Little Christopher piped into the conversation. "And she smells lovely."

"Mr. Jellicoe? Thomas?"

Cat was looking at him with concern, a careful pity warming those cool gray eyes. She who knew what it was to lose family.

"Yes." He made himself smile at her to show her he had recovered. "She always did smell of roses, as I recall. So very English. I prefer jasmine. And lemons. There are lemons and jasmine in India."

Just like that, Cat's pale, composed face went up in flame.

Oh, yes. He could still conjure Tanvir Singh from behind the confines of his rumpled English clothes. He still had the ability to discompose her defenses in a room full of strangers. Even in a room full to the brim with children.

"Tell us about India, Uncle Thomas." For the first time the oldest boy, Jack, who had been holding back while the other children chattered, asserted himself into the conversation.

It was astonishing looking at the boy—he was James in miniature, a vision from Thomas's own youth. James was eleven years older than Thomas, and his most lasting impressions of his older brother had been of a tall, strong young man, who looked so very much like this boy before him, who carried himself with some of the same solemn gravitas—the weight of being the heir. Just like James, this boy would be Earl Sanderson someday.

"I worked for the British East India Company. And I was a spy." It felt good to speak it so plainly. But though he said it out loud to the children, he was looking at Cat, who had gone still and quiet. Listening. "It was not much of a job for a gentleman, I grant you, but it was the job I was given, and I was very good at it."

"Very good." The words slipped out under Cat's breath. "No one would have known. No one did." She was trying to preserve her Miss Anne Cates persona, all buttoned up, full of prim starch, her spine precisely aligned in a straight unbending line. But he had made her bend before. He would do it again.

"Did you know Uncle Thomas in India, Miss Cates?" Jack asked. "I didn't know you'd been there."

"I did." Gemma was full of a younger sister's one-upmanship. "Pippa and I knew."

Catriona turned a stern, questioning eyebrow upon the girls, but Jack was ignoring his sister's provocation, and already asking another question. "I'd like to be a spy. How did you get the job?"

"I studied very hard, for a very long time, at home at Downpark to learn almost every language under the sun—or so it seemed at the time. Arabic, Persian, Urdu, Hindi, and Punjabi to name the few that became the most important."

Jack looked properly impressed. "I know French and German, and Dr. Tallmadge comes from the vicarage to help with my Greek and Latin. But those . . . Arabic and Urdu." He pronounced the words carefully, as if they contained some volatile magic. "Will you teach me?"

"You'd have to ask your father, lad. My brother may have other plans for your education that are more attuned to your place as the future viscount."

Jack pulled a put-upon face. "I don't want to be a viscount, and count sheep and corn and keep tenants happy. I want to be a spy and ride horses across the desert."

"How do you know about riding horses across the desert?"

Jack had to think about that for a long moment before he shrugged. "Miss Cates tells the most marvelous stories in the evenings. Not like fairy tales and princesses, but proper yarns with ships and adventures. She told one about a caravan of horses and camels crossing the wide western desert."

"Did she now? Proper yarns?" He looked back at Cat. "I begin to see."

Until this afternoon, what Thomas had truly known about Catriona Rowan would have filled a teaspoon. He had thought her experience in India had been limited to her journey upcountry from Calcutta, and the area around Saharanpur. But the trek across the desert of western Rajasthan was one of the ancient overland trade routes linking Hind with the kingdoms of Persia and Arabia, and beyond that the near east of the Ottomans and the Levant. He had crossed that wide arid expanse himself only twice in his travels.

But he would never in a thousand and one years have thought that Catriona Rowan, alone and frightened, would have been able to navigate such an arduous route. And neither had the company officials who had sought to apprehend her. "You went across the Thar Desert."

She did not answer him, and kept her face as calm and expressionless as the Buddha as she sipped her tea. "I tell stories about Paris, and Nova Scotia, and Siam as well."

"But I like the Persian ones best," said Jack. "With the dromedaries."

"I like the one with the elephants all painted with dots of colors, and the beautiful crimson howdah with the princess," added Pippa.

Gemma let out an audible sigh of happy accord. "I like the story where the elephants fell in love."

Thomas regarded his princess, his newly revealed Scheherazade, over the top of Mariah's head. "Elephants falling in love, Miss Cates?"

She didn't even blink, or miss so much as a beat. "A most tragic story. They were entirely unsuited."

"Ah. I see," he murmured as the children objected to such a characterization of what was obviously a lovely little tale. "I'd like to hear it sometime."

"The elephant story is fine for *children*," Jack said, trying to regain control of the conversation. "I want to know more about being a spy. Who did you spy on?"

"Upon whom did you spy?" Catriona corrected in her Miss Cates mode.

Though he looked at Jack, Thomas noticed that Catriona's eyes were all for him. So he answered her. "Everyone. But mostly on the Maharajah Ranjiit Singh's kingdom of the Punjab." He let the words flow off his tongue in the vernacular, giving them spice and flavor for the children's enchantment. "A powerful, most dangerous man, the maharajah, and an enemy of the East India Company. Though I hardly thought so. Privately, I admired him."

"And did you have to slink around, and hide in dark alleyways and palace halls to listen to people?"

"No. The best way to be a spy is first, not to look conspicuous and as if you are watching other people, and second, not to hide. It's best just to blend in. To hide in plain sight." Thomas leaned back in his chair, and while still balancing Mariah carefully on his knee, he reached back to take up a beautiful shawl someone—presumably Lady Jeffrey, or with luck, his Cat—had left over a chair. Within a moment he had twisted and wrapped the fabric into a turban, just as he had morning after morning, for so many years.

"Ooh," breathed Pippa when he had finished. "Oh, my."

"You look just like the man in Miss Cates's drawings," said Gemma. "The one—"

"Genevieve," Catriona interrupted in her most starched, repressive, chiding tone.

But Thomas's dear niece Gemma was made of sterner, or at least less obedient, stuff. "But he does," the girl insisted without batting an eye. "You must see that it is so. The one in your sketchbook."

Thomas was beginning to harbor high hopes for Gemma. "I should very much like to see such a sketchbook," he said, rising from the table in anticipation of his darling and daring niece doing just as she ought not.

Gemma was up, and had bolted across the nursery and into Miss Cates's bedchamber before Catriona could voice any further objection. She emerged clutching a red, leather-covered book with a swiftness that spoke of much stealthy practice. Oh, yes. This one was certainly *his* niece.

"Genevieve," Catriona said again with quiet authority. "It is rude to intrude upon anyone's privacy in such a way. I did not give you leave to make free with my personal possessions."

"Yes, but you showed them to us that time—" Gemma stopped a foot short of the table with the book wrapped protectively against her middle.

Catriona did not need to raise her voice or rail at her charges—her steady gaze and equally steady, grave tone were enough. "I do not give you leave to make free with my personal possessions," she repeated quietly.

Thomas was impressed. Her words held none of the understated rebellion of her verbal engagements with her aunt in Saharanpur, but the same steel, undercut with soft generosity, ran through both. Her kind honesty—the sort of kindness she had so praised in him, and which he had all but disdained—was so devastating because it was so sincere.

Under such pressure, Gemma folded like a house of cards. Or at least she folded politicly—her voice was hardly contrite. "I'm sorry, miss. We're sorry for going into your things, Miss Cates. Aren't we, Pippa?"

Pippa, to her credit, stood by her sister, who was clearly the inciting malefactor of the duo. "Very sorry, miss," she echoed loyally. "But the drawings are *so* beautiful. The ones with the watercolors especially."

Thomas could not withstand such a lure. And he was not kind. So he stood, and by virtue of his height, simply reached out and plucked the book from Gemma's hapless hands before Catriona could retrieve it.

"No—" Cat tried to stop him, rising precipitously out of her chair, but he forestalled her by the simple expediency of handing Mariah off to her, so that she had no choice but to take the little girl.

It gave him the few seconds to move back to his seat at the table and flip open the sketchbook.

"Mr. Jellicoe." Catriona unsheathed the full force of her breathlessly sharp steel on him. "That is a private book. It is not meant for others to look at."

Ah, but he was impervious. "So I see." About half of the book had been used, filled with pencil drawings and the occasional vivid watercolor sketch. "I was a spy, Miss Cates. Surely you knew enough of me in India to know I don't mind bending a rule or two, and prying into other people's private lives."

The scowl she sent him—one emphatically raised eyebrow, and the rest all tight, pursed lips—was masterful in its efficiency. "Then I pray, Mr. Jellicoe, that you will prove me wrong and do the right thing."

"No such luck." His fingers stopped riffling through the pages when the sketchbook fell open to a page with a pressed flower, and a note of the species and the date. Next there was a pretty watercolor of golden-pink honeysuckle. A green tree-lined avenue of a European-looking city. A beautiful charcoal sketch of Mariah's seraphic face.

Around him, the children crowded his elbows, leaning over the table.

"There's the elephant." Amelia pointed a jam-sticky finger at the next page. "That's the lady elephant."

In a delicate wash of color, a pink-speckled Asian elephant with brightly painted markings looked soulfully out of the page, her crimson bedecked howdah and parasol wavering upon her back.

"Very true to life." She must have done it from memory. She could hardly have snatched the sketchbook from the fire. Almost everything else of theirs had been consumed in the blaze. And there were no telltale smoke or smudgy ash marks.

Gemma reached over her siblings' shoulders, and turned a few more sheets to the correct page. "There."

And there he was. Mounted upon his horse, with one leg thrown casually across the pommel, leaning forward to smile at an unseen person, one hand propped upon his hip and the other lightly holding a mango. It was labeled *Sawar*.

Gemma turned the page to another. A charcoal sketch of his head, swathed in a turban, and his eyes looking out from the page as if they were looking through the viewer. *Huzoor*. The night of the party at Colonel Balfour's.

And another pencil drawing. This one of just his face, with his hair unbound, falling in loose arabesques around stark cheekbones and piercing eyes, tinted green with the only dash of color. The only time she had seen him thus, the night she had come to him. The night he had lost her.

This was how she saw him. From memory.

Thomas felt the air around him stand still. Even the children were struck dumb with some sort of reverence.

Catriona looked at the picture, and not at him. "Yes," she said quietly. "That is your uncle. We were well acquainted."

She remembered everything. And what she might not remember—those things that had mercifully slipped from her mind in order to forget the pain—he would give to her slowly and gently. A gift of memory, like the taste of almonds, and the scent of night-blooming jasmine.

It *was* love, deep and abiding, and growing still, despite everything. Despite the lies and loss. Nothing else could explain the absolute fullness of his heart, thumping like a loud drum in his chest.

Catriona felt it, too; though she said nothing, and turned away from the sketchbook, the flush of apricot color across her cheeks remained.

But he willed her to look at him, willed her to believe in him with the same unerring ferocity with which he believed in her. Willed her to trust him with her heart. With her life. "I've told you, your secrets are safe with me, Miss Cates. I'll take them to my grave."

Chapter Twenty-one

To his grave.

The words echoed endlessly in Catriona's head. Over and over, as if she might wear them down to something more manageable, like a pebble smoothed down upon a shore.

It was no wonder she slept badly. She tried to rest, to close her eyes, but all she could do was stare at the ceiling while the rain outside continued to pour down, chattering relentlessly against the windowpane and chiding her for hiding under her safe, soft covers, and worry about what might happen. Worry about losing him all over again.

She ought to be doing . . . *something.* But what? Even Thomas had finally been persuaded that there was nothing to be done at night, and in the rain. But what about the morrow? What would come of his plan to track Birkstead down? Nothing good, of that she was sure.

The only solution she could think of was the one she had thought of first. The one that had never failed her—to run. As far and fast as she could.

All she had to do was convince Thomas.

Thomas. The Honorable Thomas Jellicoe was Tanvir Singh, and he was him. But whichever name would prove to fit him better, she missed him. She wanted his reassuring strength warming her lonely bed. She wanted his arms around her, holding her tight and making her forget all her worries for tomorrow.

But Lady Jeffrey had seen to it that Thomas was given a room far from the nursery, on the opposite side of the house, nearer to his family. With whom he had been compelled to spend the rest of the evening. Just as he ought.

Without the comfort of sleep, Catriona rose from her bed to wash and dress just as the first faint purple light of dawn colored the sky over Wimbourne. Outside the windows the heavy clouds of the storm appeared to be lifting and clearing, promising a fairer day. Which meant that Thomas would start his search for Birkstead.

For her part, she was anxious to see Thomas, and determined to speak to him and tell him all the things she had not yet—the whole of the uncomfortable truth. Willing herself to be brave. Knowing she might lose him all over again, before she had ever really had him.

No. She could not let herself think that way. Thomas Jellicoe had been steadfast—he would be still. He had said he loved her. He had said he wanted to marry her.

But she was going to have to put his love and steadfastness and offers of marriage to the test.

Outside the window, another long, shimmering ray of sunshine lanced through the clouds. If only their deadly problem with Birkstead—at large and with a gun, shooting at them from inconvenient distances, endangering everyone at Wimbourne with his potshots—would resolve itself as nicely and neatly as the weather. But there was no such chance.

Lord Jeffrey had arrayed his men to range over the estate to make sure no interloper could penetrate the grounds again. The gamekeepers' men walked like sentries at the gate to the lane, their rifles tall and glinting dully in the overcast morning light. But Wimbourne was set right against the heart of the village, and was a working farm as well as a manor. People were already coming across the lane in front of the church that rose at the edge of the manor's grounds—the girls who worked in the kitchens, as well as lads bound for the stable block, leading horses back from pasture or out for some duty on the home farm. The ground looked damp beneath their feet, shimmering green with heavy dew in the intermittent shafts of sunlight, dampening their boots and shoes, and muffling their steps. To the south a patch or two of blue sky was threatening to break through the last of the storm clouds—the kind of early-summer day that lured people out of doors. And made for clear shooting.

Catriona tried to shake off the feeling of rising goose-flesh through action. She was about to open her door, so she might be out and about and doing *something,* anything useful, rather that stew in solitude another minute, when from four stories below, came the percussive slap of leather boot soles upon the slate stone pathways next to the house, and then the crunch of footfalls upon the gravel lane leading to the stable yard.

Something, some instinct or premonition made her return to the window, and peer down, waiting for the person to come into view. And in another moment, Thomas's broad shoulders, clad in an oilcloth redingote, hove into view and then disappeared into the stable.

He was going now. He was going after Birkstead. And he was going to be killed.

She had to stop him. Catriona immediately snatched up a shawl from the shelf in her wardrobe, and would have left to follow him immediately, but the sight of her traveling case gave her pause. And for no reason that she could discern, she took up her father's small pistol from where she had left it at the top of her traveling case. It dropped like a heavy pebble into her pocket, and she smoothed down her skirts by force of habit, before she rushed out, clattering down the back stairs and out a little-used side door into the morning's damp without pause for breath or decorum.

She hurried down the silent paths toward the stable until the chilling sense of urgency within prompted her to break into a run.

"Thomas? Thomas!" She wheeled to a stop in the stable

doorway to catch her breath, and peer into the dim interior. Her senses filled with the pungent, low, pervasive smell of earthy animal and hay. The warm aroma was like a touchstone for her soul—it was the smell of home, peaceful and calming. That homey, damp, earthy scent gave her strength. And purpose. "Thomas!"

"Not an especially good day for a long walk, Cat. It's coming on again to rain."

Thomas Jellicoe waltzed out from between the stalls as if he had nothing better to do than prowl about in the darkness of the dawn. As if he were quite at home doing so, scouring stables and bazaars alike. Even the old-style redingote of his English riding clothes flared and swirled around him like his eastern *sawar*'s robes.

Thomas Jellicoe had passed the night with better result than she. His transformation was nothing short of remarkable. His coat was brushed, and his boots were polished, and his dark wavy hair was shining in the early-morning sun. And even though his face was freshly shaved of the dark whiskers that were all that was left of his beard, she could see the resemblance to Tanvir Singh in his bearing and demeanor. That easy masculine grace that made everything around him too delicate, or too effete, or too clumsy.

He was perfection. And he was smiling at her. Just as he had among the stalls of the Rani Bazaar.

She had to work to remember that she wanted to speak to him about something important. "It is not," she said for lack of anything more pertinent to say to deflect his aura of dashing charm. "Coming on to rain. It's clearing."

"So much the better." The long coat made him look disreputable and handsome all at the same time. "Well. Here you are," he said, and reached out to take her hand. "I suppose it was too much to hope that you would stay tucked up and out of harm's way. So I won't ask nicely." His voice rumbled out of him, steeped in a sort of jaunty, gallows-humor weariness. "Go back inside, Cat. It's not safe for you to be out here."

"And it is safe for you?" she countered. "Did it never

occur to you that Birkstead shot at you, too, Thomas? That he could want you dead just as much as he wants me?" Her voice began to rise in proportion to her growing fright.

"Yes," he answered simply. "It occurred to me last night, as I was sitting through a very stern tongue-lashing about the proper decorum for all things having to do with a wedding from James and his Cassandra—mostly from Cassandra. No stammering bride anymore, she. That Birkstead does have plenty of reasons to hate me. After all, you jilted him for me, did you not?"

The very idea brought her chin up sharpish. "I never jilted him. I rejected him out of hand."

"Good to know." He smiled at her. That smile that promised to reward her for her discernment. The blasted smile that was designed to take her mind from guns and assassins and every other thing that didn't involve the dazzle of his mouth mere inches from hers. "You have very good taste."

"You can't charm me into doing your bidding, Thomas. Did you mean to just leave here without me—or anyone else—being the wiser?"

"Yes, actually. That was my plan. It still is. I would like to start my hunt without anyone the wiser, as you said, without raising any large red flag that says, 'Look at me. I'm riding forth.' Stealth is my objective here, Cat—much can be accomplished by stealth." He put his hands on her shoulders and leaned in to place a kiss on her forehead. "But I can see I also have to stop you from doing some kind of a runner. Though I will have to admit," he added with more of that roguish charm, "you are rather good at it."

Doing a runner. She'd only ever thought of it as staying alive. But she couldn't tell if he was being droll, in an effort to be charming and amusing, or to intimidate her into doing his bidding.

Either way, there was no point in evasion—the advantage was all to him, with his piercing green gaze and his intelligent, devious spy's mind. "I've had experience. And if I go—as, I told Lady Jeffrey from the beginning, I ought—then he will follow. If I fly my red flag that says, 'Look at me, I'm doing a *runner*,' then Birkstead will follow. And the danger will be removed from Wimbourne."

His eyes narrowed, and his brow creased, as if he were seriously considering the feasibility of such a plan. Her breath lightened for the barest fraction of a moment, before he dashed her hopes. "No." He shook his head again, stubborn and determined, and thoroughly convinced he had the right of it. "I won't use you as bait. And it's best to have him on our territory, where we have men and materiel, and can have contingency plans."

She closed her eyes to the sight of him—long and lean and earnest. So bloody, bloody earnest. "And what is your contingency plan if you are killed?"

"I won't be. It will take a lot more than an invalid of a former lieutenant with bad aim to do away with me."

She wanted to stamp her feet, or punch him in the chest to make him understand how dire the situation was. How easy it was for someone as amoral as Birkstead to kill. "Don't underestimate him, Thomas. All he needs is one lucky shot."

"A man makes his own luck, and he hasn't been lucky so far." He shook his head again, unconvinced. "You still don't trust me to take care of you, to protect you. To protect them all." He shot a glance to encompass the house. "But I will. I swear to you, I will."

It would have been easier if he hadn't started to be so kind. The heat which had started behind her eyes began to seep down into her bones, making her ache with the longing.

"Oh, Thomas. Is that why you're doing this? To prove your love to me? I would much rather you didn't. You and they"—she threw an arm in the direction of the house, too—"are all I have left, all I have of family, or love, in this world. How can I let either of you be jeopardized? How can you expect me to?" It hurt to speak—the heat of unshed tears closed up her throat—but she had to say it. She had to try. "If you loved me, you would come away with me. Now. Before another shot is fired in anger."

Even in the face of such a plea, he did not hesitate. "Cat. That won't stop the reckoning—it will only postpone it. And I will not let *you,* or my brother's family, or my father's family, be jeopardized. It took me over two years of looking before I found you again, Cat, and I mean what I said. I mean not to let you go. Never to let you run, or be forced to run. I won't let you be forced to disappear on me again."

She turned away from his perceptive gaze, afraid he would see beyond the surface fear. Afraid he would ask her why, why it was *easier* for her to run than to stay. Because he kept getting nearer and nearer to the heart of the matter.

"You can't just run away from the past, or from your troubles. Believe me, Cat, I have tried. Everywhere you go, the same thoughts will be there in your head, reminding you of what—and who—you've left behind. If we face these troubles now, together, there is no need for you to leave."

Oh, Lord, yes. That was why there was *every* need. "You don't understand." Not in the least. Those thoughts he dismissed too easily, those *reminders,* were all that she had, and she'd learned to live with them fairly peaceably. But the point was, she was alive and free and able to remember, if she chose. She wasn't running away from the past so much as she was running away from the present, from the threat that was all too real.

"I mean to end this, Cat. One way or another."

"But the *other!* What if he kills you? What if he kills more people in an effort to get to me? Why do you persist in this need for a confrontation, for a fight, when what would be best for everyone—for you and your brother and his family—is for me to go, and to let Birkstead know that I've gone? Why not at least draw him away from here first, so that Wimbourne is safe?"

"They will be protected. You will be protected. Here." It was a simple statement—an ultimatum.

Catriona's hand insinuated itself into his lapels, holding him tight, determined not to let him go. Determined to try everything within her power. "Do listen to yourself, Thomas. Please. You're the one who said I was rather good at doing a runner. You said I was clever. I did manage to make it all the way across the globe by myself. Twice."

He looked wryly displeased to be reminded. "You said the begum helped you."

"Helped. But it was not as if she left the *zenana* to escort me out of India, was it? I did manage that part all by myself. I assure you, I can take care of myself."

"One experience does not make you prepared to face what is out there, Cat. You have no idea—"

"I have every idea. I listened to him threaten me, and threaten to kill Alice, Thomas. I survived him coming after us. And I have seen worse still. I didn't spring into being like some goddess from the head of Zeus, or rise out of the sea on a clamshell, the moment you decided to notice me in India, Thomas. My experience of the world is broader than you might think. I can take care of myself." If nothing else was true, this was.

"Still carrying that stick around, are you?"

She felt the weight of the gun in the pocket she'd sewn into her quilted petticoat. "Yes, but I wish to God I weren't. I wish there were no need. And if I left, there would be no need for anyone to be walking around Wimbourne with a gun at every gate."

"There is a need," he disagreed firmly, "as long as Birkstead is on the loose. Do you think he's not going to come back here and finish what he started, no matter where you are? You are protected now, with people who love you and who believe you. He knows that. He knows you will have told us your tale. That's why I want you to go back inside and—"

"No. You're not listening to me. If I leave, he will think that I didn't tell you. I never have before. I—"

"Cat." He laid his finger across her lips. "You can't change my mind."

"What if I tell you I won't marry you if you go through

with this? That if you want me, you'll have to come with me."

She had whispered the words, but she might as well have shouted them. It seemed as if everything around her stopped and stood still, waiting and listening for his answer. Her own heart was pounding in her ears.

He was still, too, almost holding his breath as he weighed her words. And she would have spoken, would have said something more to tip the precarious scales in her favor, but he whispered, "Hush." And she felt the brush of his determined sigh. "Cat—"

"Please, Thomas. Please." She didn't care if she had to beg. Nothing mattered but that he, and his family—the family she had come to love as well and as deeply as any she had ever had—were safe. "If you love me, and you want to marry me, you will come back into the house with me, and you will help me plan how best to leave."

He took her face in his hands, and rested his forehead against hers. "And to think I admired the steel in your spine. I think you'd rather I had dragged you across the Hindu Kush as a browned horse trader." His tone was exasperated, but not angry, as if she amused him even as she infuriated him. "Is that it?" he murmured. "Now that I'm a proper Englishman, and not dark, forbidden fruit, you're not so interested in doing my bidding? And forgive me if I point out," he added in a lower voice, "that you were interested enough in my bidding yesterday, when you let me lick—"

"Thomas!" Catriona could feel her face flame to the roots of her hair. "You're being purposely obtuse. Your Englishness has nothing to do with it."

He was smiling again, kissing the corner of her eyes. "Am I? I suppose it's nice to know you're rejecting me for myself, and not because of my regrettable lineage."

His kisses were bittersweet joy—a pleasure she could not allow herself. "Your lineage, Thomas, was never, *ever* in question. Not as yourself, and not as Tanvir Singh. I loved you for *yourself*!" Her voice was growing thin, throttled down to nothing by the heat in her throat.

"Ah." Everything about him grew quiet, as if her words had drawn all the teasing bedevilment out of his tone. "Good to know."

And then, very carefully, he brushed his thumb across her lips. Slowly, carefully. And then he kissed her. Very, very carefully.

His lips were taut, and tasted bittersweet like summer hay, and everything, everything she had longed for and dreamed of and thought she had lost forever. And she was drawn back into him, as if he were the bright star at the center of her universe. As if he were life itself.

"Ahem." There was an overloud clearing of throats, and then someone said, "Miss? Thought I heard voices out here. Are you needing some assistance, miss? Is this fellow bothering you?"

"No," Thomas Jellicoe said, and tried to keep kissing her.

But she was extricating herself from his arms, and hoping the fresh morning breeze would help cool her flaming cheeks. "Thank you, Mr. Farrell." She chanced a glance at Wimbourne's stable master. "I appreciate your concern. But there's no need. This is Mr. Jell—"

"By God in all the heavens." The largest man Cat had ever seen stepped forward out of the murk behind the stable master. "Is that you, Master Thomas?"

"Broad Ham? My God, Broad Ham." Thomas's answer was all for the huge coachman stepping out from the middle of the aisle of stalls. "Ham. How've you been keeping?" Thomas gripped the man's meaty paw, and was enveloped in an enormous, back-pounding embrace. "My God, man, you haven't aged a day."

"That's clean living, that is," the man called Broad Ham answered equably. "They said you was back from the other end of the world at last, but all I had to vouch for it was that by-God mare that they said you'd brought—"

"Mare?" A burst of something painful and potentially destructive—like hope—cartwheeled through her chest. Her voice struggled out of her mouth. "What mare?"

Thomas gave her Tanvir Singh's smile—that white, roguish slash of teeth that curved up one side of his face like a scimitar. "In the midst of everything else, I'd forgotten I've a present for you. Just along there." He pointed into the shadows beyond, behind the large man planted like an oak tree in her way. "Have a look."

Her feet were already moving, dodging around the men—the grooms and lads who shrank back, out of her way—running, her boots echoing on the cobbles. Looking back and forth, first left, then right. A gray. Another gray. A bay carriage horse. A midnight black—

There she was. But the vision was blurred by the fresh heat burning her eyes. She dashed the weakness away. "Puithar. Puithar."

The mare had her head out over the door, waiting. Waiting patiently for Catriona to come and throw herself against the majestic animal's neck. Accepting Catriona's teary tribute as her due.

Catriona couldn't draw breath. She was fighting for each particle of air, fighting to breathe in and out around the shallow hiccups and sighs that she couldn't control. She had to close her eyes against the hot sting of tears, and she pressed herself into the warm comfort of her animal's neck. "I thought you were gone. I thought I'd never—"

Puithar nickered, low and understanding, and rubbed her nose against Cat's hair, as if she, too, needed a moment to confirm the identity of her own true love. As if she, too, were as deeply affected by the arrival of the person who meant so much to her.

But of course, it was nothing but foolishness, to think of the mare as hers. The mare was Tanvir Singh's. She always had been. And now that Tanvir Singh had become Mr. Thomas Jellicoe, she belonged to him, and not to Catriona.

She would have pulled back, and stepped away, but a

hand came to rest against her back, holding her in place, keeping her gently supported against the bottom half of the split stall door.

"She's missed you, too, you know. Treats me as if I'm second best, no matter how many Kashmiri apples I feed her."

She let Thomas talk nonsense, while she once again fought to put herself to rights. Damn him for acting so kind. Of course he had kept her. Of course. "She likes the Gaelic."

"Yes, I imagine she does. I'd like to hear it sometime as well," he added in a low tone meant for her ears alone.

"Then don't leave me," she returned in the same whisper.

He heard her, because his hand flexed against the small of her back. But because he could not give her the answer she wanted, he gave her silence instead.

Which she exhausted on the mare. "Puithar," Catriona crooned as she pulled back to stroke down the velvet muzzle. "You gorgeous creature. You're too thin."

"She didn't like sailing. And for that matter," Thomas murmured, "neither did I. And I have plans for my recuperation."

"Damnedest-looking mare I ever did see," the man called Broad Ham said from somewhere behind Catriona, saving her from having to make an answer. "But you always had an eye for the horses, Master Thomas. How's your driving?"

"You'll be disappointed, Ham." Thomas spoke over his shoulder, but he did not leave her side. "Haven't touched the ribbons in nigh on fifteen years. But I did breed some superior horses while I was on the other side of the world, and this mare here is going to be the start of my stud. Out of the same great-great-great-great-grandsire as the Darley Arabian. Went to Arabia myself to pick stock, I'll have you know. I've a notion to breed her to a racing Thoroughbred here and see what I can make of it."

"Always good with the horses, you were. Good to see you've kept it up."

"I have." With one last intimacy of pressure against

Catriona's upper back, Thomas returned to the conversation. "Thought about it for years and years, starting a stud. The whole time I was in India. And I also thought about asking you to come, and take your chances with me as well, if you were still alive when I got back." Thomas's tone turned wry and familiar. "You must be getting too old to be driving my father's carriages, out all times of the night, in all weather."

The coachman was philosophical in the face of his master's son's friendly impudence. "Pays me well, the earl. Not many men can say they've been coachman to the Earl Sanderson. His grays have been famous, year in and year out."

"I'm hoping it's year out, and you'll fancy your chances with me, Ham." It was educational to see Thomas Jellicoe's convincing charm working upon another. It made it easier to picture Tanvir Singh charming secrets out of horse-buying generals from Delhi to Lahore and Kabul. "A farm somewhere in the country around Downpark, I was thinking, or north a bit, closer to Epsom or Ascot. I've made my fortune in the east, Broad Ham—I'll pay you in rubies, if you like. Not even the earl can pay you in rubies."

"Now, what'd I do with rubies?" The big man shook his big head, but he was grinning. "And I don't like to leave your father. Don't like the look of some of these lads we've been getting nowadays. Veterans, they say they be, and your father, he's too kind. He don't like to turn a man who's served the king away, but they're not fit, them lads, like they need to be. Not fit."

"You could be in charge of hiring our lads, Broad Ham. Manager of the stud, you'd be, like a gentleman. I'll even deed you a farmhouse if I have to."

"Don't care about titles." The big coachman raised his eyebrows, and turned down the ends of his mouth in an expression of consideration. "But a snug little farmhouse, now, that's something I just might like to see."

"I'll see to it straightaway." Thomas's enthusiasm was a palpable thing.

A palpable, disconcerting thing. It was strange to hear

him talk so openly about his future. A future he seemed to have been thinking about for years. The whole time he had been in India with her, perhaps, pretending to be Tanvir Singh. Knowing he would come back to this—to being the Earl Sanderson's son—to start his future.

Had he always meant for her to be a part of it?

But it was not a question worth answering, because the bare truth of the matter was that, any moment now, he was going to put that future in jeopardy by chasing blindly after Birkstead.

"Well, almost straightaway." Thomas turned to indicate Catriona, with an openly proprietary smile, as if he hadn't another care in the world. As if he weren't determined to go hunting men. "I've a thing or two to do first, Ham, but you mark my word—a stud in West Sussex or Berkshire. It's all but a done thing. Promise me you'll think about it." He was nothing but sure, breezy confidence.

Broad Ham made another considering face. "I'll have to talk to your father the earl first."

"Yes, of course." Thomas laughed and clapped the big man on the back. "I suppose I ought to do the same as well."

"Ha-ha. Always were an independent one, you were." Broad Ham reached out to shake Thomas's hand. "Good to have you back, Master Thomas, good to have you back."

"Thank you, Ham. It's good to be back, at last. It's been a very long time."

"That it has."

Daylight was fully up now, and Catriona could hear the rest of the stable workers, the grooms and lads, moving in their loft above. And the animals were getting restless for their morning feeding. The day was beginning to go on without them.

If only. Catriona glanced back at the house, wondering if she might be able to enlist Lord Jeffrey to help her convince Thomas not to go out alone.

"Brilliant to see you again, Broad Ham," Thomas was

saying as he took note of the direction of her gaze. "Brilliant. I know my brother and I can count on you to keep a sharp eye out for our shooter. I've a mind he's a blond man, about twelve stone or so. Military bearing. Very spit-and-polish. I'm headed out to check if there is anything left of his tracks after that rain we had last night, but first, if you don't mind, I'm just going to take my bride here—" He caught Catriona's hand and tugged her closer.

Oh, that was doing it a bit too brown. "I am not your bride, Thomas," she insisted. "Not unless you are prepared to change your mind in the matter of Lieutenant—"

"I need to make sure my *bride-to-be*," he clarified more loudly to the two fellows who smiled in return as if he were the most amusing chap in the world, "makes it back to the safety of the house."

The big man called Broad Ham looked Catriona over as if *she* were a fractious filly who might need a firm hand. "We'll just leave you to that then, young sir."

And Mr. Farrell touched his hat brim, and said, "I'll just be getting the mare for you, sir."

Catriona put up her chin. "I can take care of myself, Thomas."

"I know that now. But I will ask you, for me, if you will please do me the honor of returning to the house? Mind you, if you don't agree I am just as prepared to pick you up bodily and tie you to the bedpost in my chamber—which will also serve to give me a rather extraordinary incentive to return quickly and in one piece—to keep you there. But I will take your promise instead. And don't bother lying. I can always tell when you're not telling the truth." He smiled, that wide slash of white teeth that was all rogue, and he gathered her close again.

And with her hands clutched around his neck, she found that he smelled of rain and soap, and she had the strongest urge to put her lips against the skin of his neck where his pulse beat. The longing was a physical pang, ringing through her like a church bell.

She had to make herself think, make herself impervious to his charm and his promises and the intense knowledge of what they had shared between them that flared from his eyes.

She had to think of Alice.

"All right. I will return. But only—"

"No buts. Please. I'm not stupid or reckless, Cat. I know what I'm doing. Let me get the lay of the land, and then I promise you I will be back, and we can discuss then, with my brother and his men, what's best to be done at that point."

Mr. Farrell brought out Puithar, and before she could voice another objection, Thomas swung himself into the saddle.

Catriona didn't think she had ever seen anyone so right, so completely relaxed and alert and at one with his animal, despite the wickedly long horseman's pistol that he drew out of his saddlebag to bristle out of his belt in place of his missing knife.

"No dagger?" She tried for wit, but failed when her voice wobbled miserably.

He smiled and patted his waistband. "Oh, I've a knife, don't you worry."

"But I do worry." Good Lord. That was almost all she did, had done for years—worry. It was too ingrained a habit to give up now. "Because there is plenty to be worried about. Birkstead is out there somewhere, no doubt lying in wait, just longing to get another shot at you."

"Better me than you," he affirmed instantly. "Let him wait. I assure you, Cat, I do know what I'm doing. I spent years and years traversing the land, with my head down and my eyes wide open. I know how to find him."

"As long as he doesn't find you first. This isn't the Punjab, Thomas. Things are different here."

"Things are different here," he acknowledged. "But people are not. From one country, one landscape to the next, people are essentially, invariably the same. They have the same wants, the same needs, the same iniquities and virtues, the same pride and conceits that make them act in predictable ways. Trust me. Birkstead is clever, and had the advantage of surprise, but he's lost it now."

"Promise me you will be careful."

"I promise you, on my life."

Chapter Twenty-two

At the end of that remarkable speech, he leaned over and wrapped his hand around the back of her neck, and kissed her with the same firm, overt possessiveness out in the open space of the stable yard as he had in the privacy of her bedchamber. He tasted clean and strong like water and hope and patience, and Catriona didn't think she was ever going to be able to fill the well of longing for the very essence that was him.

And then he let her go.

Catriona felt her lips tingle and her cheeks blaze with heat, but there was no one but a few disinterested stablehands to see. The stable master and the coachman Broad Ham seemed to have left them to their privacy so she could attempt to keep from crying in peace. All she had left to do was pray for Thomas to come back in one piece.

It seemed rather a lot to trust to a God who had already proved his disinterest.

"Be careful," was all she could say.

"I always am." And with one last kiss, he let her go, and was off, wheeling Puithar to set off down the drive in a spray and clatter of gravel.

Catriona watched until he disappeared out of sight behind the corner of the gatehouse, before she turned back for the house, where she would no doubt worry and fret, and think of vile, loving names to call him if he didn't come back to her in one—

Her way was blocked by a Downpark groom. At first, she registered only the distinctive buff and blue-trimmed livery of the footmen and groomsmen who had come from Downpark to serve the Earl Sanderson and his countess.

"Begging your pardon, miss," he said in a tone laced with exaggerated, ironic politeness.

His nearly rude tone made her take a step back, to go around him, but he moved again in front of her, and reached to take her by the wrist, as if she were weak and might fall, or had lost her way.

That was when she raised her glance higher, and found herself staring into the malevolent blue eyes of none other than Jonathan Birkstead.

No. Please God, no.

She reared back away from him, toward Thomas disappearing down the lane. And she opened her mouth to let loose the scream that was clawing its way out of her throat, but the jackal grabbed her face in a hard pinch that covered her mouth before anything more than a garbled sound of surprise could make it past her lips. He had her backed around the corner, with her head twisted and furled silent and tight against his chest, before she could do anything else.

"You weren't expecting me now, were you, mousie?"

Catriona felt a chill crawl across her skin at his use of the detestable nickname, and she tried to scream anyway, though the raw sound only vibrated out of her muffled mouth, and drew no attention to them as he began to drag her down the shadowed little alleyway between the stable and the orchard wall.

She clawed at his hands, trying to find purchase, trying to catch hold of anything that might stall their progress as he continued to drag her backward, into the dank alley behind the carriage house. His hand across her mouth smelled of horse and muck, and manual work with brass and leather—no longer the begloved, refined limbs of a privileged officer. But he was real. She had not conjured this particular devil out of her vision of hell. And the panic pounding in her veins was as real as it had been the last time she had seen his face, straining to identify her through the thick smoke and flames of the residency.

But he looked so different from the man she remembered. From the corner of her searching eyes, she could see that his seraph's golden looks had been marred by an ugly broken nose, and his elegantly tousled locks had given way to the rough, sheared crop of a man who was accustomed to wearing wigs.

A servant.

Despite the disbelief and panic stealing her wits and chilling her breath, she tried to make sense of it all—Birkstead, with rough hands and rougher looks, a servant in Downpark livery at Wimbourne.

Was he really a servant at the Earl Sanderson's estate? He could have come to Wimbourne several days ago with the Sanderson coach bearing the visitors from the Earl Sanderson's estate at Downpark—as a footman or groomsman or outrider. Not to find her, but trying to find Thomas—the Honorable Thomas Jellicoe, the third son of the Earl Sanderson. It would have been a relatively easy thing for him to find out about Thomas's family—their estate at Downpark in neighboring Hampshire was well-known.

He might have had no idea that the governess Miss Anne Cates was Catriona Rowan—if he had even heard of the lowly governess at all. But he would have heard in the stable that the master's brother had come home, and he would have seen the highly recognizable mare for himself. And he must have come looking for Thomas, but he had found her as well—another wretched, unhappy accident of fate.

But it didn't matter if he had sought Thomas—she was the one he had now.

He had dragged her, flailing and fighting, down the stable alley, past the steaming piles of sawdust and manure, and into the walled orchard beyond, muffled with thick, deep green grass and swathed in obscuring, blossoming trees.

Catriona fought and kicked and twisted with every step, clawing at the hand across her throat, doing everything she could to impede their progress away from the crowded stable.

Birkstead grunted a filthy curse when her boot found his shin, but he was as strong as he was diabolical. He wrestled her to the ground easily, and put his boot across her windpipe, so he could pull a double-barreled carriage pistol from beneath his coat and press it down hard between her eyes. "Maybe this will help you decide to keep still." Catriona felt the hammer cock back with sickening metallic efficiency. "And keep your mouth shut." His fetid breath poured over her. "Not a word, mousie. Not if you'd like to live beyond the next five seconds."

She did want to live well beyond the next five seconds. She wanted to live well beyond the next five years.

But she couldn't manage to agree with him, not with his boot crushing her windpipe, so she closed her eyes to blot out the glint of the metal barrel in front of her eyes, and obliterate the sight of him standing over her, full of malicious triumph.

But she couldn't keep them closed for long. She had to look. She had to reconcile the stunning man she had known with the strangeness of this diminished ghost. He looked so ordinary in his livery—there was no leering smile. No brutally handsome face. No scarlet officer's coat to make him stand out. No helpful sign that proclaimed one of the most dangerous, murderous men in all her world had found his way amongst them.

Up close to him in the shadowed sun of an English summer day, she could see—and smell—the ravages the years had wrought. The good looks that had given him the face of a fallen angel had faded since she had last seen him in Saharanpur. His face was worn, hollowed out and coarsened, perhaps by pain. His left arm now hung limp and useless by his side. The strong scent of toilet water that had clung to his spotless uniforms had now been replaced by the reeking odor of fried onions and stale sweat.

He looked as if the depravity that had always lived within him had finally worked its way up to the surface, as if the darkness within now colored his once fair skin.

Her thoughts must have been apparent in her face, because he smiled and shook his head chidingly. "Come now, and just behave yourself. I'm not a monster, mousie."

Oh, but he was a monster. She knew it better than she knew anything else. Just being near enough to hear his voice had her pulse slamming against her skin, and her belly wrenching into a panicked knot. Every contrary instinct in her body was screaming at her to run.

The comments the coachman, Broad Ham, had made in the stables blazed into her brain. "Veterans," he had said, but, "Not what they need to be." He'd been talking about Birkstead. It must be difficult, if not nigh on impossible, to be a one-armed groomsman. No wonder Birkstead looked ground down. Good.

If she were to survive, she would have to take advantage of that. It would be impossible for him to hold on to her and a gun at the same time. It would have to be one or the other.

The thought calmed her somewhat—"somewhat" being a relative term when a man was pressing that same gun into one's forehead—by giving her something to concentrate on. She dragged her hands through the grass, searching vainly for anything she might use as a weapon—a stick, or a stout rock. Anything.

Nothing came to hand.

And then the pressure of the barrel against her skull eased, but he was already hauling her up by her hair. Sharp, stabbing pain seared across her scalp, and then was gone, replaced just as quickly with the return of the pistol barrel digging and cutting into the soft skin under her chin from the weight of his jagged rage.

His voice panted into her ear as he pulled her back against his chest. "Move it along, now, shall we? Nice and quiet as a mouse." He flicked his head in the direction of the hedgerow to the east. "Quickly. Before I'm tempted to take my revenge prematurely."

Revenge. As if *she* had done him a wrong. As if he really thought she were the one who had ruined his hopes and dreams in Saharanpur, and not the other way round. As if *he* had nothing to do with the deaths of Lord and Lady Summers.

With her head tipped back from the relentless force of the gun, it was hard to see much, but she could tell he was moving her slowly, step by quiet step, out of the orchard and through the tall lines of hedges, taking her farther and farther from the sanctuary of the manor house.

The world became only the swath of blank gray sky above her head, the pain of the sharp end of the barrel cutting into her skin, the sound of his breathing—or was it hers?—labored and tight, and the smell of his coat against her, stale with tobacco smoke and horse and sweat.

But Birkstead's employment at Downpark begged another question—had Birkstead known all along who Tanvir Singh had been underneath his turban and beard? Had the lieutenant been playing with them all the while, through banquets and rides and charged, intimidating encounters? Had he out-spied the spy?

"Have you figured it all out yet, my little gray mouse?" His breathing was labored and tight from their exertions, but she could hear the sneaky triumph in his voice. "I'll be disappointed if you haven't."

Catriona swallowed around the pressure against her neck. "You've been waiting for him at Downpark."

"Very good. Sharp as always, our intelligent, ambitious Miss Rowan." He let out a tight, panting bark of a laugh. "Imagine my surprise and delight"—he huffed the words in her ear—"when I was rewarded for my troubles, in the bloody trip to Wimbourne, on the back of that bloody carriage, only to find next day that peculiarly distinctive mare of yours being brought into the stable. Imagine that." He paused for a moment, looking around the hedge with sharp, jerky movements, before compelling her to move on.

"You're much cleverer than I. I never knew . . . he was . . ." She let the sentence trail off, out of breath from trying to breathe against the incessant pressure across her windpipe.

"Didn't you?" He made a grunt of derision. "He made it sound as if you'd known all along, in Saharanpur, when he gave his evidence."

"Did he?" She echoed his question, to buy herself time, to keep him talking. "Hummed us all, didn't he?" Catriona had no idea what she hoped to accomplish, other than to keep herself calm and distracted from the insistent hammering of her heart in her throat. And to keep Birkstead busy talking, so he was too busy to shoot her. To give her more time.

"And I knew my luck had turned." Birkstead ground out another harsh laugh. "And sure enough, not only do I finally find Thomas bloody Jellicoe—speak of the devil and up he pops—but I find him in the middle of his reunion with the long-lost Catriona Rowan. I always did have all the luck."

"Not that lucky," she gritted out. "You missed."

His indignation leached out of his chest in a thin growl. "Unfortunate that. But now I've got another shot, haven't I? And this one's already too close to miss."

The rising pleasure in his voice, the malicious calm with which he stated it, chilled her until she began to lose feeling—began to lose track of her fingers and toes. Parts of her were going numb—with shock or fear, she wasn't sure. She wasn't sure of anything except Birkstead's virulent malice, as potent as it had ever been in Saharanpur.

And even one-handed, he was just as strong. He manhandled her around to the back side of the churchyard, and she had a ghastly thought that he meant to kill her there, and bury her there in the deep shade beneath the towering yews.

But Birkstead apparently had other plans. He pushed

her up against the cool stone of the church, and then he shouldered open the small side door and hauled her into the dim interior.

Wimbourne's parish church was dedicated to Saints Mary and Bartholomew—and how those two had ever gotten together was a mystery known only to the early church builders—and served as the parish church for the village of Wimbourne, even though it was situated within the manor grounds. Last Sunday the service had been packed with parishioners craning their necks to look at the latest arrivals of the viscount's family, especially the Earl Sanderson and his elegant, Belgian-lace-clad countess. Now it was as empty as a grave.

It took a few long moments for her eyes to adjust to the dimness of the church after looking up into the morning sunlight outside, but she had a fairly good view of the empty vestry as he pulled her inexorably backward, down the long line of tidy pews, and past the baptismal font where baby Annabel was to be christened after the Sunday service later in the morning, toward the small door that separated the vestibule from the bell tower.

Something about the cramped, hunchbacked little door, and the scaffolding of the stairs beyond, leading steeply upward, panicked her anew, and as Birkstead made to shove her through before him, she abandoned her hold on the pistol levered into her jaw.

Catriona shot her left arm out, and kicked out her opposite leg to jam straight against the door frame. She could feel the panic edging in—her heart was slamming against the wall of her chest and her breath was coming in audibly shallow gasps. She tried to breathe through her nose, tried to think. "Where are we going?"

She sounded weak and breathless. Desperate. Mousy.

"We're going up." His voice was a heavy hiss at her ear, as he tried to exert pressure against her braced arm—long enough and hard enough for her to feel a searing ache in her elbow joint as he tried to force her to break. And then just a bit longer, until her arm began to tremble under the strain.

Catriona felt her teeth sink into her lips as she gritted her jaw, and willed herself to endure. As long as she possibly could. She had to be stronger somehow than Birkstead. She had to find a way to prevail. She had to be smarter—she had survived fire, and desert and desertion. She couldn't crumble now.

But Birkstead was as strong as he was clever, and even meaner than he was clever. Just when she thought she could almost endure no more, he suddenly relented and jerked back from the door, enough so that she lost purchase against the door frame. And as he reared back, he shifted violently sideways, and cracked the side of her head against the stout oaken planks of the door.

Pain cleaved through her like a scythe. Everything went round-shaped and curious and darkly strange for a long moment, and all she could register was a ringing silence so deep and profound it deafened her for a stunning moment before everything—every individual sense in her body— came roaring back with a viciousness so overwhelming, it consumed her whole.

And when the volcanic spurt of pain relented enough for her to regain a portion of her wits, she heard the heavy fall of a metal bolt—the sound of the door being locked behind them—and she was being once more dragged by the neck up the narrow maze of the rickety wooden staircase toward the belfry.

The hard, hot heat of panic ripped open her chest—it was something of a wonder that she wasn't leaking blood onto the stone floor below. She could taste the salty metallic tang of blood in her mouth where she had bitten through her cheek.

She immediately resumed fighting, wrestling with the arm against her throat, kicking and stomping with her legs and feet, trying anything and everything to impede their progress above. Because absolutely nothing good could come to her above. Because it was a long, long way down from the top of Wimbourne Church's bell tower.

Birkstead grunted and hissed as the blows found some

small purchase. "It won't make any difference, mousie. You're going over the edge. You're going to hang yourself in shame."

Something was desperately wrong. Thomas could feel it in the air. He could practically smell the sulfurous stink of hidden evil wafting across the fields.

Thomas drew the mare to a halt in the middle of the peaceful lane. He had sent himself on a fool's errand. The tracks that he was following—the same tracks that the groundskeeper and his men had laboriously tracked yesterday—were Thomas's own. It was he who had ridden the mare, with her small hooves and distinctive horseshoes, down this lane from Sixpenny Handley, and paused just there, to look at the manor house he had read of in James's letters, but never seen before. It was he who had stood and admired the view of the tall, crenellated manor house while the meadows had whispered their strange green welcome around him.

This morning the hedgerows were silent, as if beast and birds were hiding—as if the land itself were withholding something, some knowledge that he could not yet discern.

But Birkstead was here somewhere, close by. Thomas could feel it as if it were a hand at his neck.

What was he missing? He stared up the track heading back to the lone inn at Sixpenny Handley, mentally retracing his steps, forcing himself to consider James's theory—that Birkstead had followed him to Wimbourne. Because Miss Anne Cates *had* been living quietly within the neighborhood for almost a year before Thomas had arrived. And the shooting had occurred immediately after his arrival. Maybe his brother was right. Maybe *he was* the bad penny.

But he would find no evidence between the hedgerows—last night's rain had obliterated most of the tracks. So Thomas set the mare back toward the east, where the village sheltered against Wimbourne Manor's flank. It was a small village—one main thoroughfare, with smaller lanes branching off it, and only one small public house. Thomas rode slowly, up the main street, in the same way Tanvir Singh had been used to riding by palaces and *havelis* alike—watching carefully, but with an outer ease and nonchalance that belied the alertness with which he scanned the fence line and the rooftops of the outbuildings, and with which he listened intently for every sound or footfall.

But nothing seemed out of place. Nothing was off.

And something was pulling him back to Wimbourne Manor—the intense quiet, perhaps. His ears had been attuning themselves to the strange sounds of the English countryside—the hum of bees and dragonflies, the lyrical racket of sparrows in flight above the fields, the industrious thrum of the working village. But there was no cheerful racket, no sound but the eerie sweep of the rising breeze through the tops of the trees.

It was Sunday—early, before services that would come later in the morning. That could account for some of the lack of activity, but there was more—a fraught watchfulness in both the village and the manor.

Or it could just be his overactive imagination that saw perfidy everywhere. It could be the years of ingrained suspicion that had him chasing ghosts when there were none.

He looped through the village and headed back onto the manor grounds, where he found Broad Ham prowling like an overlarge bear toward the paddocks.

"Ham?"

Broad Ham caught the edge in Thomas's tone without any further elaboration. "Sommat's amiss. The animals are as jumpy as flies."

"Yes." It was only a partial relief to know he wasn't the only one who felt it. "He's here, close, our shooter. Blond man, about so tall"—Thomas held up his hand in measurement—"twelve to thirteen-odd stone. Handsome fellow, once, with yellow curls. Broken nose now. And maybe worse."

"I got lots with broken noses—but worse, you say, like mebbe useless arm?"

"Where?" was all Thomas could ask.

"Stable. One of the lads I was telling you about. Veteran. Barrington, that'd be. But buggered off he has, and good riddance. Useless piece of loose baggage."

Thomas let off a pungent Punjabi oath and followed that with a rather more Anglo-Saxon one for good measure, which made Broad Ham's bushy eyebrows fly up toward his hairline.

"Fuck *all*." Thomas's eyes instantly shifted toward the stables, and he damned himself for a blind, single-minded fool. He had been so sure that he knew better than anyone else. He thought he alone had eyes and ears that saw what needed to be seen. He could have saved himself—and all of them—immeasurable injury if he had only listened to James and sought out the wisdom of his men. But no. He had been too preoccupied with thoughts of Cat to think of checking with Broad Ham or Stable Master Farrell. He should have bloody well known better. "How long's he been gone?"

"Didn't come back after his turn at night patrol this morning. I had my lads on guard with your brother the viscount's men. Good with their pistols, my men are. Trained to be. And your fellow Barrington had army training as well. Veteran, like I said, though he's only the one good arm."

Birkstead, too, seemed to have learned well the efficacy of hiding in plain sight, and obscuring his past by taking a new name. "Damn him to hell. He's armed then. He's the one, Broad Ham."

"The shooter?" Broad Ham scoffed. "Out on the lawn? Oh, I don't know 'bout that, young sir. Not likely, really. The man's good enough with a carriage pistol, but that's near all he can handle. He's only got the one good arm. Charity to keep such a man in a stable when he can't even shovel shite. But a marksman with a long gun? Not likely. Couldn't even hold it, could he?"

But that would explain why the shots seemed to come from the hedge itself. Birkstead would have had to brace the barrel of any rifle on a limb of some sort. But the reload time was problematic. More likely he had two guns, and took the second shot at them with a carriage pistol, designed to be lethal at close range, but much less effective at a longer distance. Which would also explain why, out on the length of the lawn, the shots went wide. "Which arm, Ham?"

"His left is the one as hangs down limp at his side. Took a ball he said, in the army. Broke the bone, it did."

It had been Thomas who had broken the bone, that night in the garden. Good. For the briefest of moments, Thomas was glad it was he who had maimed the bastard, if it had kept Birkstead from being able to kill Cat. But a useless arm was another reason for Birkstead to have nursed his grudge into hatred, and turned his thoughts toward this sort of violent revenge. Another reason Thomas should have done things differently that night.

But the past couldn't be changed—only the future.

"But where in the bloody the hell is he now?"

And that was when the church bell began to clang.

Chapter Twenty-three

Thomas wasn't going to find her in time. He had left, and she was entirely on her own, just as she had always been. She would have to find a way to stop Birkstead by herself. The thought did little to calm her terror, but it did steel her resolve.

"How will they know? How will they know I've hanged myself in shame? They already know I didn't do it—kill Lord and Lady Summers in Saharanpur. Mr. Jellicoe told them so. They'll never believe you."

"Never say never, mousie." He laughed at the repetition of the adage, but she heard something else—a familiar inflection, a rolling *r* and a roundness to the *o*. There was a faint Scots ring to his accent she'd never heard before. Was he doing it on purpose, to make fun of her? To remind her of his threat?

"They'll believe me when the only one to say otherwise dies as well. They'll know you both lied."

Thomas, he meant. He meant to kill Thomas after he had killed her.

Catriona scrambled to try and come up with something else to stall for time—something else to delay what Birkstead wanted to make inevitable. "Hadn't I better confess, then? Hadn't I better leave a proper suicide note, expressing my shame and regret?"

"Oh, no. You're not distracting me like that, mousie. And who'd believe an ambitious little thing like *you* had anythin' of shame?"

There it was again, the Scots brogue, sliding into his voice every time he said "mousie."

"Then at least tell me how you did it." She grasped at the shortest of straws. "If I'm to have your sins on my soul for all eternity, at least tell me what happened."

He stilled slightly, and she felt him turn his head toward her. "Don't be coy now, mousie."

"No. I wasn't there. You know that."

"Of course you were. Someone was. I heard you," he insisted.

Alice. But she would rather die than have him know that. So what she said was, "Maybe you did hear me. I was looking for my aunt, but I never found her. And I never so much as saw you that night. I have no idea how you even knew I was there."

It was a garble of lies, but it did the trick. The arm lashed across her neck relaxed a fraction.

"Your lover." The gloat floated back into his tone, but at least he was talking. And while he was talking, he wasn't trying to wrench her off the railing, or throw her down the height of the bell tower. "Tanvir Singh put the idea in my head, didn't he? That's what you'd call ironic, isn't it? He came lookin' for you—touchin', that, your heathen, native lover being so devoted—askin' if I'd seen you. And then he turns out not to be a heathen native at all, but the Earl Sanderson's get—his bloody third son—and everyone defers to his opinion. But he was the one who told me you were inside. And when everyone thought you'd died in the bloody fire as you ought, it was simple, really, to turn the blame upon you. You made it so easy with your clandestine ways—sneakin' around to see yer dark-skinned lover. But I would have had you anyway, you know. It would have worked, and we would have been happy together."

His malice was exceeded only by his self-delusion. But

Catriona made a noncommittal sound of sympathy. Anything to keep the man talking. Anything to keep him listening to the sound of his own voice resonating up the tower walls instead of thinking about killing her. "But?" she prompted.

"But Lettice ruined it all. She was the jealous one. She was the one who didn't want to let me marry you."

Poor, doomed Lettice. "She was in love with you."

"Love." Birkstead spat out his contempt. "No reason to ruin everything."

"Yes." Catriona sighed out the lie. "I couldn't agree more."

"I'm sure you do, mousie. Think you'll bag an earl's son, now. Or did you know then? You must have with yer ambitious, high nose-in-the-air ways."

Catriona didn't disabuse him of this notion. "You're Scots," she said instead, letting the old inflection slide into her voice. "You had the nerve to call me a dirty, ambitious savage when you were no better yourself."

"Aye, I'm better. I'm better, because I made myself better. I earned everythin' I ever got. Not like you, with your rich relations, and your lord for protection."

She had no response that would suffice, nothing to contradict the truth that she had quite purposely allied herself with her rich relations. "Not much protection now they're dead." She had no idea what prompted that particular piece of idiocy, only she felt she needed to say something, anything, to keep him occupied and allay his antagonism.

But as a conversational sally, the mention of death was an abject failure.

"So now you know why, mousie. So we'll move right along to the how."

"It's all so stupid. You're so stupid. I never even saw you that night. I never saw anything. So killing me will do nothing but add another murder to your soul."

But her words were falling on deafened ears. She could feel him behind her, gathering his strength again. She stopped fighting Birkstead and grappled one arm, and then her legs, around the post of the stair railing, while she kept tight hold of the gun at her throat.

Birkstead gave a sharp tug against the gun, and when she didn't budge, he snarled, "Let go, or I'll kick your head in."

"Go ahead," she muttered. If she didn't let go, he couldn't kick her head in without letting go of the gun himself. They were at a stalemate. Except that Birkstead was mostly bigger, and mostly stronger, and certainly meaner. Or at least more willing to impose pain. But she was through with appeasement. "Kill me, and bring him running. He won't rest until he's brought you to justice. Thomas Jellicoe has tracked you this far, and won't rest until he's sent you straight back to hell."

"I'm already in hell," he ground out. "Crippled and workin' like a bloody servant. And Thomas Jellicoe? I have plans for him. I've had plans for him for quite some time. *I'm* the one that found him, that tracked *him*. He was easy enough to find."

"Did it ever occur to you, you filthy jackal, that he wanted to be found? That he came here to find you? That he wanted the opportunity to punish you for wrecking his happiness as much as you wanted to punish him?" It didn't matter if her statement were true. It only mattered that the thought might wedge itself in that devious, whirling brain of his, and foul up the gears for even a moment. All she needed was a moment.

And there it was a foot away—the slack cord of the bell rope hanging like an afterthought down the middle of the tower.

She cast her fate to the winds and let go of the railing, throwing out her arm, reaching blindly for the rope as Birkstead reacted, instinctively wrenching her back toward him as her weight pulled him toward the void. But she had just enough momentum to grasp the rough hempen fiber and hold on while Birkstead pulled her back with enough force so they both crashed into the stone wall of the stairwell, as the bell clanged out its alarm above.

Pain cleaved through her skull, but she didn't care. If there were any justice left in this world, pain should be slicing along Birkstead's jaw like the sharp end of a razor, and his mouth would be filling with the briny tang of blood from the collision with the jagged-faced stone.

Let him feel one eighth of her pain. Let him.

Her own head was on fire with the punishing heat of the blow. But it felt good. It felt *real*. At last, they were no longer fencing.

And the bell had sounded—the clapper had clanged dully against the bell at least once. But it was enough. It had to be enough.

But for the moment, nothing changed. Except that her legs were no longer clutched around the post railing, and Birkstead was refilled with deadly ire. Birkstead was as fast as he was slippery, and he gave in to his basest instinct and kicked at her knee with enough force to hobble her before he resumed dragging her upward by the simple expediency of ramming the barrels of his gun up into the soft skin under her chin.

The pressure tipped her back, off balance, and forced her head up again, so that she couldn't see anything but the blindingly bright sun streaming into her eyes through the deep arches of the belfry. But she held on to the rope with one hand as she groped instinctively against the pressure of the gun with the other. She clawed at his wrist, and her right hand blindly and stupidly grappled into the volatile, hairpin firing mechanism of the gun.

Against her fingers, the flintlock fell, crashing toward the firing pan.

Catriona flinched away from the imminent concussion and shock that she was sure would blow her jaw off. But one second lengthened into two, and two into three. And nothing happened—Birkstead held firm against her pull, and the point of the barrel still ground into her flesh. She was still alive and whole. Her breath was still sawing in and out of her chest as if she had run all the way across Wimbourne's fields.

She had not set the gun off with her clumsy grappling. The gun had not fired. Or rather, it had misfired. One of the two flintlocks—the left barrel—was pressing down upon her fingers, the sharp edge of the flint cutting into her knuckles, which were jammed between the hammer and the frisson. Her fingers, it seemed, had prevented the flint from striking.

And because Birkstead had only his one hand with which to hold the full weight of the pistol, he hadn't been able or hadn't thought to cock both barrels. From what she could feel with the tips of her fingers, the hammer on the right barrel remained at half cock.

She made an involuntary sound of relief and fear and frustration. She had no idea what to do. No plan for how to take advantage of the situation.

And then Thomas's deep voice echoed up the stairwell. "Let her go, Birkstead, and there's no harm done."

"Son of a bitch," Birkstead snarled in her ear. "How in all hell did he get—"

"He was a spy, for God's sake, man. He picks locks. He has any number of insidious talents you can't even imagine."

Catriona still couldn't see Thomas, but neither could Birkstead, because he was tense and twisting for a vantage point from which to locate his nemesis. But Birkstead did have his response at the ready. He raised his voice to carry down the length of the bell tower.

"I have a vivid imagination. And at the moment it's occupied with all the ideas about how I'm going to kill you both. But it must be gratifying, mousie," Birkstead continued in an overloud aside. "All that show of devotion. And does he know what he's so devoted to? Does Singh, or Jellicoe, or whoever the bloody hell he is, know that all this time he's been pantin' after a criminal? At least I knew what you really were, and was smart enough to only be in it for the money."

"You're the criminal, Birkstead." Thomas's voice gained strength, sounding nearer as it echoed off the stone walls. "You're a murderer. All the evidence is against you."

"Really, it's quite touchin', your naïveté," Birkstead said evenly, as he twisted her around, back and forth, looking for Thomas, as if he might be behind him. "We used to think it was the little mousie, here, who was naïve—that's what Lettice thought. But the Scots chit is the one who's played everyone for fools. Haven't you, mousie? She's more conniving and ruthless and ambitious than even poor Lettice. You really ought to know. Show yourself and I'll tell you."

There came back no response. No sound but the creaking of the stair beneath their feet as Birkstead edged upward with his back pressed firmly to the solid stone walls, and his gun wedged ruthlessly into Catriona's flesh. "Tell him, mousie," His shout echoed down the tower. "Or shall I?"

She tried to be brave. She tried to think and be clever. "If I tell him," she said in a voice choked and cracked with fear, "then he won't give a good goddamn about me, or what you do to me. He'll just shoot us both where we stand." She craned her head against the pressure and pain of the gun at her throat, and imagined Thomas, standing like a highwayman across the stair, with his hands full of metal. "He's bound to have at least three guns."

"Four." Thomas's voice came from nowhere and everywhere all at once. "And I aim to empty all of them."

"Plus he's got two good hands." She was shaking now, barely in control of herself. But she kept on. "And his guns are fitted with percussion caps. Much more reliable than flintlock. So." She slid her gaze as far as she could into the corners of her eyes to measure Birkstead's expression. "I rather think it's best we just stay mum on that topic if we hope to survive, don't you?"

The nonsensical nature of her stream of conversation momentarily put Birkstead off just enough—the pressure of the gun under her chin eased slightly. Enough. Enough so she could move her head to see from the corner of her eye Birkstead lick his dry lips.

"There is no 'we,' mousie. I'm going to kill you both."

Birkstead must not have had a decent governess, for he

hadn't done the maths—two beings to shoot, and only one gun, with two shots in all. One of which *she* had already kept from firing. And the other wasn't yet cocked. Unless he had another gun she hadn't seen, or felt pressing into her back—

Oh, God, she hadn't thought of that.

So there they were. Thomas somewhere below with his long, lethal-looking horseman's pistol, and Birkstead nestling his double-barreled carriage gun in the soft underside of Catriona's chin. And Catriona with one hand on the bell rope and the other wrapped around Birkstead's gunlock.

And then she slipped on the step, and jerked downward for just a moment. But a moment was all it took.

The roar that enveloped her was so massive, both she and Birkstead were slammed back into the wall. For a sickening moment, Catriona felt a distant, numbing sort of pain, as if she'd been kicked in the chest by a horse. And she could smell the sulfuric stench of black powder wafting through the air.

And then Birkstead let out an animal hiss of deep, mortal pain.

But he didn't let go of her. He clung to her, pulling her closer instead of pushing her away, using her as a shield. She could feel the warm sludge of his life's blood soaking into the back of her gown.

"If you shoot again, I'll make sure you hit her." Birkstead's voice was raw with the ragged edge of tight pain.

From somewhere below, Thomas made no answer, while Catriona and Birkstead were stuck ten feet from the top of the bell tower. Thomas lurked below, and Birkstead was hit and seemed unable to move higher. There was nowhere else to go.

The time was now. Now. Before Birkstead said anything else, or thought of his next move, or Thomas acted on his.

Catriona sent up a hasty prayer—although why a God to whom she had long since given up praying should pay her any attention at this point was beyond her—and spoke. "Thomas."

His answer came back instantly, low and sure, and somehow, exactly what she needed to hear. "I know."

And she stopped thinking. She trusted.

Catriona tightened her grip upon both the rope and the barrel of the gun, and said to Birkstead, "I misfired your gun."

Birkstead reacted with an audible hiss that steamed filthy invective into her ear. And then his hand tensed hard under her grip as he pulled back the trigger.

When nothing happened, not even the click of the mechanism moving, he stupidly, vainly tried again, and again yanking back the trigger until he lost his hold upon her.

It was enough to give her room. Room to jump.

Catriona pushed away from him, and dove over the rail, clinging to the rope like a macaque in a tree, swinging across the space until she crashed hard against the edge of the stairway opposite.

Behind the railing, Birkstead was cursing her with a vile Anglo-Saxon epithet. He jerked the gun away, as if he would fling it out of his hand. But he didn't.

And she was stupid, so stupid. Because she had taken the chance that he would forgot about the other barrel of the double-barreled pistol. She had gambled her life on the chance that he wouldn't be able to recock the gun, and shoot her. Or worse, Thomas.

Birkstead steadied himself on the railing. "I'm sending you to hell, mousie."

But the light was going out of him—his eyes were growing glassy and dark. Thomas's ball had found its mark in Birkstead's upper chest, just below his shoulder, and the jackal had too little left of strength.

And it came to her—a moment of perfect, almost serene clarity and calm.

She didn't have to do anything. Thomas was there. Thomas would protect her. She wasn't alone.

She wrapped her feet around the rope, loosened her hands, and followed her heart. And let gravity pull her downward.

And she was falling. Suspended in the air for one sickening moment with Birkstead's livid, horrified face only yards above hers. The deafening report of a gun exploded into the air. And she closed her eyes and consigned herself to the void.

It was the tangle of her skirts that saved her.

As she was falling down the length of the bell rope, her palms blistering with the ropey friction, the air turned thick and heavy and liquid, and she felt almost as if she were buoyed up, swimming through space like the acrobats in the park in Paris, catching up a trapeze. The full length of her skirts and petticoats had ridden up and tangled themselves around the rope, slowing her descent.

And then the air thinned, and everything sped up. The rope pitched her sideways, and she went sailing toward the cross-rail, which knocked the breath out of her lungs. Everything went red and dark—she could only see the color of blood behind her eyes.

She let go, and gave in to the numbing pain engulfing her chest. And then her lungs expanded and she was choking, because the neck of her gown—her plain, sturdy, durable day dress—was pulled tight against her throat.

But that was because someone was gripping the back of her dress—fisting the fabric tight to haul her over the railing and into his arms.

Thomas.

He was clutching her against his chest, one fist twisted in the fabric at her back, and the other cradling her head tight against his throat. He collapsed backward, slumping into the wall before the two of them slid into an ungainly heap upon the wooden stair.

Catriona was still all topsy-turvy. Every bone and sinew in her body was nursing some private, individual ache, and her ears were ringing as if she were on the inside of the church bell. All she could feel was a distant wave of weary pain—but she was fine. She was alive.

It was over.

Something too unsteady to be relief landed heavy in her gut, and Catriona closed her eyes and concentrated upon breathing.

Voices rose and reverberated up the stone stairwell— more than she would have expected. Viscount Jeffrey, giving orders in a cold voice, and Mr. Peters, the steward, giving calm, practical advice. The coachman, Broad Ham, and other men from the stable talking about getting a door off its hinges for the purpose of moving the body.

The body. Birkstead.

But no one came near them. Thank God.

She opened her eyes to the sight of two long legs encased in soft, travel-worn but beautifully polished boots twisted in her skirts. Braided together, the two of them were. For better or for worse.

He eased his grip on her, and peered down at her through the veil of her fallen hair. "Are you hurt?"

"No. Yes." Catriona shook her head, but couldn't bring herself to look at him. "But I think I might be sick."

He tipped her scarf so her head was between her knees. "Are you hit?"

"No," she managed to gasp out. A momentary inventory of her aches revealed nothing more substantial. "No."

"Good. Just breathe." He didn't say anything more. But she could hear his heavy, controlled breathing, and then he pushed her hair that had come out of its bun—what with being dragged across the manor and having a gun shoved into her face and all—out of the way, and rubbed the back of her neck a bit, which seemed sweet and kind. And very much like him, like Tanvir Singh. Or at least like the Tanvir Singh she had fallen in love with.

But they were one and the same. One man. The man who had come to help her, just as she had hoped he would.

Her belly slowly began to unclench. Relief sagged through her, taking the last of her strength. Her bones felt as if they had turned to pudding. But they were all safe. Thomas must have shot Birkstead. He had done what he was supposed to do. And she had done what she was supposed to do. It was over.

But it wasn't, really. There was more still to be done. "I need to tell you something."

"Birkstead is dead, Cat. He can't hurt you anymore. Whatever you have to say isn't important anymore." His hand gently probed along the underside of her jaw, as if he needed to assure himself that she was indeed whole.

"Birkstead might be dead, but he certainly still has the power to hurt. You heard him." Her mind was too full of blame for any kind of denial. Full of the hard, unforgiving shame, the cold stone of guilt that had wedged itself deep into the cracks in her soul. The ugly truth she had spent years and years trying to outrun.

She had always known it would catch up with her one day.

And today was that day.

But not here, with the smell of gunpowder and death, and the cold stone walls closing in on her. "I need to get outside. I need air."

He granted her wish by the simple expediency of picking her up, and carrying her down the steep stairs and out of the church until they were in the quiet of the garden, where he found a bench to simply sit, with her in his lap.

She made an uncertain start of it. "Some time ago—in Saharanpur—Birkstead said he had discovered something that was not to my credit in Scotland." Catriona shut her eyes. "And he said if I didn't marry him, he'd put it about that I was wanted for murder in Scotland."

"Hush, Cat." Thomas tucked her more tightly against his chest. "He was an out-and-out bastard. He certainly had murder on his own mind. If you think I would believe anything that came from his twisted brain . . . He would have said anything to malign you, and spread lies—"

"No." She did not look at him—she couldn't yet bring herself to—but she could picture him above her, next to her, shoving his hand through his hair in that endearing gesture of rumpled frustration. He was being kind. He had almost always been so kind.

"They are not lies." She could barely hear herself speak—her voice was as thin and dry as the endless western desert. Nothing would ever slake it again.

Because when she steeled herself, and screwed down her courage to raise her eyes, the look Thomas gave her was something past incredulous. Past betrayal. Past despair, into some other place—a circle of hell, perhaps, reserved for people like her who so recklessly threw away such a love as he had offered her.

He looked away from her, into the bright sunlight breaking through the clouds, squinting his eyes against the glare as if even that pain were preferable to looking at her.

But she did not look away. She could only stare at him, now that she had the freedom to do so, now that no other eyes were watching, and his own demanding gaze was turned away. He was so strange and so familiar all at once, this handsome Englishman who looked and laughed and kissed like Tanvir Singh.

She nearly closed her eyes against the devastating power of the moment—the moment when he would finally see her for what she really was. But she didn't. She kept her eyes open to take his palpable hit. Because she deserved it. And because she had to finally admit it. "It's true. I am a murderer. I killed my father."

Chapter Twenty-four

Cat started to shake, either from the shock of Birkstead's death—although Thomas's own shot had hit its mark, it was her action that sent the man to his death—or from the weight of what she had just confessed, Thomas couldn't tell.

He took off his coat and wrapped it around her shoulders, and pulled her to him. "It's all right, Cat. He can't hurt you now. He's dead."

She shifted under his hands, as if she wouldn't allow herself even that small comfort. "It's not all right. He's dead."

Thomas didn't know what to say to refute that particular piece of illogic, but he continued to hold her anyway, his big, horseman's hand ranging over her small, tense back, trying to rub some warmth into her arms, waiting patiently for the terror to subside. "You'll be all right, Cat. You will."

"No." She pushed out of his embrace, and tried to draw a deeper breath, but she looked done in, as pale and off balance as she had when he had dragged her through the hedge. When she raised her gaze and looked at him fully, her soft eyes had gone hard and dark with something beyond fright. Something he recognized as self-loathing.

God help them. If she was going to confess to murder, she was going to need a drink. Hell, *he* needed a drink.

"Broad Ham?" He called back to the orchard gate to the huge coachman, who, he noticed, had kindly taken a stance across the entrance, blocking others' ability to venture any closer with his massive back. "Miss Rowan is in dire need of a bit of a wet."

Within a few moments, a flask of unknown content was silently proffered.

"Here." Thomas uncorked the stopper, and held it out to Catriona. "Take this. You need a drink of this."

She took the flask with white, trembling hands, and gulped down a healthy swallow, only to come up gasping. "Oh, sweet Saint Margaret!" She breathed out a waft of pungent fumes. "That's Scotch whisky."

"Is it?" Thomas took a swig himself, and tried not to gasp as the fiery liquid burned like a smoky peat fire down his throat. "It's my first taste of whisky," he wheezed, "so I'll have to defer to your superior knowledge."

She did not respond as he'd hoped with either a smile or a laugh, but she did say, "Thank you," before she blew out a long shaky breath, and straightened her spine as if she were preparing herself to tell him something else he didn't want to hear.

He took her hand, because despite the fact that she was sitting down, she was still none too steady, and because he could not shake his own compulsion to touch her, to assure himself that she was all right, and alive and near, and not lying on the floor of the bell tower in broken bits. "Do you want to tell me what happened?"

She shook herself slightly, as if she were a stack of papers she could tidy by shaking them all together. But her eyes, those clear gray eyes that were incapable of subterfuge, met his steadily. "No. But I will anyway. I had to leave Scotland, much the same as I had to leave India. Because I had killed my father."

She said it again, and still he could not believe her. Of all the things he had thought and learned about her and her family, this he never suspected. He had read each and every one of her letters—the letters he had found in her satchel, the letters she had received from her absent family—and each and every one of them had spoken of a close and loving family. Each one had been full of love and laughter and close affection for one another. Her parents—and there had been letters from both her mother and her father, but most especially her father—had spoken warmly and openly of how deeply missed Catriona was while she was at school.

"How?" was all he could think to ask, even though he was dreading the answer.

"With a gun. His gun." She made a hiccup of sound—half groan and half wail—as she drew the piece from the depths of her pocket. "Oh, Lord help me. I had it all along. I had it in my pocket, and I could have used it to—"

She made a small, fleeting gesture of overwhelming revulsion that told him she never could have used the weapon. And then she put her head down, took another deep breath, and made herself continue. "My father gave me this gun for the express purpose of killing him."

The bone-chilling implication of such a thing had her shaking again. Thomas kept hold of her small, cold hands, and hunkered down in front of her, so he could see her downturned face. "Tell me."

"That he had been dying—halfway to dead by then—ought to make a difference. But it doesn't, really. It feels the same." She closed her eyes and took a deep breath, her face a pale oval against the dark green of the grass and trees behind her. "If I had been found out I'm sure they would have charged me not for the killing—although I'm sure they would," she contradicted herself. "But for depriving the crown of the opportunity of finishing the job they had started, and stretching his neck."

Thomas's mind was scrambling to understand. He started with what little he did know. "Your father was a wanted man?"

"He was." She took another deep breath and let it out, as if she had to remind herself to breathe. "He had been a newspaperman of some repute, fame even, in some circles. United Irishmen's circles. He had owned a newspaper in

Belfast, and published in support of the United Ulstermen." In the telling her voice had lost her governess's polished tones, and returned to the Scots cadence of her youth, the lilting brogue full of color and intonation that he had loved in India. "And when the authorities there began to crack down, he emigrated to Glasgow, as did many others of his political sympathies. I was a baby then, but there was always political talk at our house, growing up. To me it just seemed normal, not seditious, or treasonous. But I suppose it was. That's why they sent me away to school, to Paris, when I was older. My mother was related to the old Duke of Hamilton, and when things grew uncomfortably dangerous at home, somehow money and a place at a good school were found for me. But I didn't understand that then. I just thought I had got lucky, although I missed my family terribly."

She would have done. He imagined she had been much like she was in India, deeply appreciative of her surroundings, but just as deeply aware of what she owed her family in making the sacrifice. "How long were you there?"

"Years. Long enough so that I was blinded to their real situation at home. How far in poverty they were descending. And then the typhus took root in Glasgow, and they succumbed, one by one—my mother and my brother and my sister. I came home against their wishes, as quickly as I could, but it was too late to do anything to save them. They all died but Da. One by one. And I was supposed to be thankful that I was spared."

He could not tell her he was glad—glad beyond thankfulness that she had been spared. Deeply thankful that she had not arrived at the height of the contagion only to succumb herself. "I'm sorry," was what he said instead, though it was little enough in the enormity of her loss.

"Me, too." Her voice was small and tight. "Grief swallowed my da whole. It made him rash, and reckless. And treasonous. He printed pamphlets and broadsheets publicly blaming the epidemic on all the inequities of the government, and the crown, and most especially on the new Duke of Hamilton, the old duke's nephew, who had closed his door to us poor relations when my mother had gone to him for help, asking him to take my brother and sister in, to keep them safe from the epidemic. He did nothing for them, and nothing for the people."

James had come into the garden to stand quietly a little ways away, and listen, and Thomas was suddenly conscious and glad of the strange blessing of his own family, there to help and support him.

"And he would not cease, my father," Catriona continued, "saying and printing more and more incendiary things, until the magistrates put out a warrant for his arrest for sedition and treason. And they almost got him. My God, they almost did. But he got away, through some damp alleyway or fetid gutter the magistrates knew nothing about. He took me up into the hills. I thought we were going to walk away from it all. Make our way to Edinburgh or Dumfries. That's what he talked of anyway. Until he didn't."

There wasn't much he could say of comfort, though the raw pain in her voice tore at him.

"He had taken a bullet that I wasn't aware of. I . . . I should have realized." She was shaking her head, and swallowing, trying to speak though her voice was cracked with strain. "But . . ."

"You were young, Cat." He held on to her clenched hand.

"Not that young." She wouldn't take any comfort, though the effort to tell him her story was clearly taking its toll. "I was nearly nineteen. A woman grown. I should have seen. But I was angry at him for the chaos and the poverty in our life. Angry that things . . . had deteriorated. And I was too full of my own discomforts that day, walking out into the wild. I didn't understand that he was so badly hurt until we were well away from any shelter, out in the hills above Avon water."

She pressed her lips between her teeth. "When he couldn't go any farther he lay down. And then he handed me his gun. And asked me to do it. To kill him, so he couldn't be hanged."

The shock that gripped his gut was grief for her. All this time she had had this pressing on her soul, weighing her down. And he had never seen it. Oh, he had known there were untapped depths in her, he had admired the steely strength in her spine, but he had never thought about the forces that might have created those depths. Or how deep they really went. Or what they might have cost her.

He took another look at her then, without the prism of Tanvir Singh's lonely admiration to make her into something fresh and naïve. He had certainly wondered about her—wondered what made her different from the other memsahibs, what made her seem like a living bloom in a vase full of wilted hothouse flowers. But he had never imagined this—the horror she must have endured. "And you did it, of course. You would do whatever was asked of you by your family."

She closed her eyes. "Yes."

Her quiet admission tore him apart, but his anger was all for her father, who had professed to love her, for asking such a thing. "He should have had the resolve to do it himself. To send you away, and finish himself off."

"He didn't want to be a suicide. He didn't want the sin of it on his soul."

"So he put it on yours?" His voice was full of his pain for her, mingled with shock and disbelief.

A solitary tear broke loose from the corner of her eye and fell freely down the pale slide of her cheek. "He said I'd have time to be forgiven, and be shriven of my sins."

"And do you feel forgiven? Have you been shriven of your sin?" He did not wait for her answer. "You will have to forgive me if I think your father a selfish bastard."

Catriona let out a weary sigh, and closed her eyes to let the tremulous tears streak down her face. "Perhaps. Perhaps he was. But what's done is done, and can't be undone. So, as I was saying to the Viscountess Jeffrey last evening, I'll have to be leaving you. I have no want for you, or Wimbourne, or your family to be tainted by the accusation that you harbored a murderer."

His love for her was an ache—a physical pang that radiated from within his chest. "Catriona." He took her arms in his hands so she would look at him, and understand what he was saying. "What you did that day in the hills does not make you a murderer any more than what I did today makes me. I—we did what we had to do to stop Birkstead. And you did what you had to do. You say the past is past, and cannot be undone—so be it. As far as I'm concerned, you belong with me. If you need protection from some ancient charge, I will protect you. My family will protect you."

"Don't you see? I can't ask them to do that. I can't—"

"I can," he said before she could get her next argument marshaled. "I will. And Catriona, I went to Glasgow. I looked for you there. I asked after you. I was a spy—I know how to find things out. I heard the whispers, just like in India. And I don't care."

"All this time you knew, and you never said anything?"

"No. Because it didn't matter to me. It *doesn't* matter to me." He tried to swallow down the heat that was crawling up the back of his throat, but he had to tell her. "We're neither of us saints, Catriona."

This was the thing. This was that indescribable feeling, the connection, that had called to him from the very first moment he saw her—his soul had recognized its other half.

All along, she had been as morally compromised as he—a remorseful angel, he had thought her. This was what he had seen in her—this unselfish willingness to damage her soul if it meant she could save others.

He could finally see what that resolve, the steely spine he had always admired, had cost her. Her control was in proportion to her fear. If her calm exterior appeared formidable it was because her fear was just as great.

"No one else in the whole of the world knows as much about me as you do. Not Colonel Balfour, nor the Begum, nor any of my family. Only you know. So I can't—I won't—just let you go, and leave to try and find another family somewhere, and do what you've done here. Not just teaching, but binding yourself to them. I can't let you try and find another child like Mariah, to whom you can become entirely indispensable. A child who you know will always need you, need someone to care for her. And you want to be that person, so you never have to leave. So you never have to give her up."

She tried to close her eyes, to shut him out, but he had already seen through her. He had already divined the most secret yearnings of her closed heart. He could see it all now.

"You want a family to belong to, the way you belonged with those children in Saharanpur. You must have loved them extraordinarily to do what you did for them. You gave up your life as Catriona Rowan for theirs. Just as you did for your father. And the deceased you never spoke of, in Scotland, your mother and brothers and sisters. God only knows how you sacrificed for them through the years."

Not enough. Not enough to save them. Catriona's failures with her own family haunted her, coloring every decision she had ever made. Urging her now to do what was right, and not what felt pleasing or easy.

Thomas drew back to look at her anew. "Family is the *only* thing that ever really mattered to you." He said it with a sort of wonder that he had not noticed this telling detail before.

And it wasn't strictly true. He had mattered to her. They had mattered to each other. But she had to do what was right for everyone, not just the two of them, so she said only, "Yes."

"Cat." His voice was full of a kind of bewildered pity. "Don't you want children of your own?"

It was the question she tried not to ask herself in the quiet, dark moments in the middle of the night when the past could not be kept at bay. It was the question she would not answer, because if she did, the withered stone of her heart would crack even wider under the pressure of hopelessness.

But, oh, how she wanted. Every fiber of her being ached

with the need to hold her own child in her arms. To be able to love without restrictions, without waiting for the children to be sent to her, and without watching them run to others when her time with them was up. To know that nothing and no one could separate them.

But there were no assurances, no absolutes. Her own mother had seen two children die in her arms before she herself had succumbed, brought down by her broken heart as much as by the disease that had ravaged them all.

Cat was nearly overwhelmed by the loneliness that hollowed her out. She felt empty, missing. Without whatever it was that gave Lady Jeffrey her purpose and strength.

And now Thomas was here, reminding her of the dreams that still came to her nightly. Reminding her of how long she had been lonely.

"But don't you understand?" He was holding her face and thumbing the salty tears from her cheeks. "That's what I am offering you—what I want to give you. Your own family. With me."

"But what about *your* family? What you owe them?" She tried to keep the plea, that small insistent seed of hope, from her voice.

He kissed her—a solemn benediction. A pledge. "I have given them fifteen years of my duty. I owe them nothing but my love. And my happiness."

"But they will always be looking at me, knowing. I could never stay here now. Even if by some small chance Lord and Lady Jeffrey did not object, there would always be this cloud, shading their perception of me. And I couldn't bear to see you. Or see your family. And think of you every day. It would be worse than before. Much, much worse."

"Only if you allow it to be." His hands firmed on her arms. "But all right, if you insist—if you have to leave, then we'll leave together. We'll go to America, or wherever you want. Wherever we can raise horses and a family together."

She took his hands and set them away from her, until his hand fell back to his side. And then she held her trembling hand out to shake.

He looked at it as if it were as dangerous as a snake. As if he could not divine what on earth such a gesture could mean. But he withdrew a step to stand, and he bowed—a gentleman's gesture, those manners she had once thought as fine and polished as a maharajah's jewels. But she could no longer see him, because the heat and the need were building up behind her eyes, blurring her vision.

"Please, Cat." His voice was low and as threadbare as a fakir's beard. "No kiss before you break my heart?"

"No." This time she spat in her palm when she held it out to him. So he would understand. "I was hoping for something better."

Thomas spat in his palm and pressed it to hers. "Anything."

"Love me. Love me and marry me, and make me happy."

Thomas did not stop to ask polite questions as to whether she meant love in a physical or a more metaphorical and emotional sense. To him his love for her was one and the same—abiding, persistent, and strong.

He was made to love her and only her. He did not let go of her hand in his, but used it to pull her toward him, into his chest, so he could wrap his arm around her neck and kiss her.

Her mouth was soft and firm and sweet and bitter and everything, everything he had been longing for. And she was kissing him back, opening herself to him with all the sweetness and generosity he had remembered, and all the heat he had forgotten.

He kissed her to tell her everything he had tried and failed to say. He kissed her to convince her that she was the only one for him, and he for her. He used every ounce of finesse and skill and passion he could use in so public a place.

And his fierce, strong, fragile girl was kissing him back, wrapping her arms around his neck and clinging to him as if he were the only thing keeping her upright. Thomas left her lips to skim across the unspeakably soft skin beneath the line of her jaw, where that foul bastard had pressed his gun. He kissed away the hurt, kissed away the pain. He let his hand flow into the fine silk of her hair, as he kissed and nipped and kissed and nipped some more on his way down the long delicious slide of her neck. He was inundated with the scent of lemons this time, not lavender, but still starch. Still prim and crisp. How strange that such a homey, ordinary smell should become so erotic? But it was.

He tried to be careful and slow. She was in a state of shock. He tried to have some restraint. He did try. But he couldn't seem to help himself. He could not be next to her and not breathe her scent. He could not be within ten feet of her and not want to touch her.

His hand had risen to her face, and the tip of his finger was smoothing along the line of her eyebrow. Her lovely arched, erotic eyebrows. It was fuller, and a bit darker now, from whatever she had said she put in her hair to darken it. Part of her camouflage, like a bird that wears dull winter plumage to blend in with its surroundings.

But her eyelids were fluttering against the pad of his thumb, keeping time with the accelerating pulse along her temple. And she was not moving away. She was leaning toward him, as susceptible to his nearness as he was to hers.

"They've grown back a bit. But I can still see the girl underneath, if I try hard enough. She's under there somewhere."

For a very long moment she looked at his face, searching it in much the same way that he searched hers, as if he were one of those old Mughal palace ruins they had once visited, with only the barest outline of the walls still visible to make it recognizable. "Am I so hard to find?"

No," he answered. "No. I can see you plainly. All of you. Every lovely inch."

She turned her face so that her cheek rested in the palm of his hand, like a wild animal tamed to his touch. "You've always been so kind."

"There you are again with 'kind.'" Kind was not what he wanted her to think when she looked at him. Kind was not a characteristic that made solemn young ladies toss up their skirts and kick over the traces. Kind was not going to win her over. "I'd rather be something else. Something ardent and persistent. Something more than a lover. Marry me, Catriona Rowan. Please." He didn't let her answer. "I'll wear you down. I'll keep at it until you say yes."

"Thomas—"

His name on her lips was like a prayer—a benediction—and she could not know how long he had waited to hear her say it. "Say it again."

"Thomas."

"Again."

"Thomas, Thomas, Thomas." She smiled at him through her tears. "Yes. Oh, sweet Saint Margaret, yes, I suppose I will."

As if it were that easy. As if it were the simplest thing in the world and she had not made him wait these years and years.

He thought joy, or at the very least relief, would ring through him like a bell, but the warm, almost mellow feeling that spread through his lungs was quieter, but no less fierce. It was gratitude, and love and lust. Lord, yes, lust. He couldn't get enough of her, and so he tugged her across his chest so she slid into his lap and he could kiss her over and over.

"Say it again."

"Thomas." And then she smiled at him. That breathless, openmouthed smile that she had given him when she had been spread out on the soft cushions beneath him, repeating his name over and over as he had rocked into the soft acceptance of her body.

He smiled back, his happiness writ large across his face. "I meant 'yes.'"

"Yes, Thomas."

He kissed the sweet, soft corner of her mouth. "Today. As soon as possible."

"Is such a thing possible?"

"I'm a prince, remember. The son of the Earl Sanderson. For me, anything is possible."

"Thomas." Her voice was mildly chiding and mildly amused. But he didn't want anything mild from her.

"I'll get a special license. My father or James can arrange it, and make all the trouble of having influential relations worthwhile."

"Certainly." James's voice drifted to them on a gust of laughter.

"Can you do that, really?"

"Yes." Thomas was sure. Entirely, wholeheartedly sure. "And they had better hurry, because I refuse to be parted with you for even so long as a night. Since the day I landed in England, I've thought of nothing but you. All this time, I've waited. And I won't wait any longer. I refuse to deny myself the pleasure and privilege of waking up next to you in the morning light."

She nodded, and then shook her head, and made an unpleasant face, squeezing her solemn gray eyes shut even as she smiled, and he realized that she was still crying.

In all the time they had been together, in all the time they had been friends in India, he had never seen her cry like this. "You can't cry now. Not when we're to be happy."

"Of course I can. I can cry now because I'm happy. Happy enough to cry."

Epilogue

They were married in the Church of Saint Margaret and Saint Bartholomew, in the parish of Wimbourne, in the presence of God, and themselves.

Just the two of them.

And of course the rector. And Lord and Lady Jeffrey. And the children. And all the other servants from Wimbourne, who felt it their sovereign right to come and cry their tears of joy over their Miss Cates, as was.

But Catriona did not cry. She was done with tears. She was done with spleen and disappointment. She was marrying the Honorable Thomas Jellicoe. She was a new woman.

And she was trying to get married in the most unobtrusive manner possible. But it was impossible. It appeared she was too well loved.

The countess had insisted on gifting her with a lovely sea-blue carriage dress of silk gazar, and an endless row of buttons—Thomas would like that—as well as a long length of delicate lace to adorn her new summer bonnet that the housekeeper and housemaids had all contrived to give her.

Gemma and Pippa had conspired with the gardeners to create a sweet-scented posy for her to carry. "It's ivy for endurance, because you've endured, Miss Cates," Pippa said with starry-eyed fervor.

"Miss Rowan," Gemma corrected, always in the right.

"And lily of the valley for returning to happiness, and primrose, of course, for eternal love."

"Aunt Catriona, very soon," Pippa amended. "I shall like that ever so much more, having you as our aunt."

"I shall like it, too," Catriona said. And despite her pledge to the contrary, Catriona did feel tears welling at that. She had wanted a family—she had always wanted a family—but she had not realized that her heart's desire would be achieved so quickly. But it was. In a matter of minutes, she would become part of the Jellicoe family, and the bonds of dedication and devotion that she had worked so hard to create would be made permanent.

Blood wasn't thicker than gratitude. The Viscount and Viscountess Jeffrey insisted on standing as her family. The viscount himself gave her away, folding her arm over his elbow, and looking at his brother with as grave and fierce a scowl as any father ever could.

And there was Thomas, waiting for her, looking as tall and dark and as handsome as any storybook prince ever had.

And Catriona knew, if she lived to be a hundred years old, she would never forget this moment, this feeling of indescribable happiness. When she was old and gray, she would remember the words and the look on his face, and smile, and think of everything else that had passed as a dream.

And then they were walking together down the long stone aisle, while all of Wimbourne cried and clapped and sighed around them, out into the sunshine of a cloudless blue English summer day.

"Are you ready?" her prince asked her.

"Oh, I sincerely hope so," she said. "But I'm already married to you, so you'll just have to take me, ready or not, as I come."

"My darling Mrs. Jellicoe. Ready or not, I should like nothing better."

"[An] Essex romance has it all: nonstop action, witty repartee, and deft plotting. From the bow to the mast, from battles to ballrooms, [with each] reckless bride . . . Essex delivers another read to remember."
—*RT Book Reviews*

Don't miss these other *scandalously* delightful novels in the Reckless Brides series
by **Elizabeth Essex**

ALMOST A SCANDAL
BREATH OF SCANDAL
SCANDAL IN THE NIGHT

From St. Martin's Paperbacks